Praise for Sarah Shankman's

SHE WALKS IN BEAUTY

"IF MURPHY BROWN DECIDED TO GIVE UP THE BRIGHT LIGHTS OF TELEVISION TO BECOME A NEWSPAPER REPORTER, THIS COULD BE HER STORY. . . . Sam is something special. Acerbic, irreverent and unintimidated by anything or anybody—her personality adds a touch of wry to the distaff roster of the mystery genre. . . . Shankman also employs a trenchant, slightly off-the-wall wit to flesh out the narrative and the secondary characters, some of whom are so memorable and well-drawn that they could spin off into their own books. . . . You can't help but like good ol' Sam, although she'd probably call you a soft-hearted wimp because you do."

—*The Sunday Press-Enterprise* (Riverside, CA)

"As Sam divides her time between investigating and her visiting New Orleans beau, constant commotion reigns. An amusing romp."

—*Library Journal*

"Shankman's witty heroine again evinces a winning combination of grit and finesse."

—*Publishers Weekly*

A Mystery Guild Dual Main Selection
A Literary Guild Alternate Selection
A Doubleday Book Club Alternate Selection

"THE WRITING IS SMOOTH, THE STORY'S SETTING IS FASCINATING, AND THE CHARACTERS ARE STRONG AND REALISTIC. . . ."

—*Rave Reviews*

"An unending parade of picaresques . . . cool rap with a southern accent . . . rambunctious, overstuffed . . . but FUN ALL THE WAY."

—*Kirkus Reviews*

"Read *SHE WALKS IN BEAUTY* and you'll find out how good a sleuth Samantha really is."

—*Orange County Magazine*

"*SHE WALKS IN BEAUTY* is peopled with some of the funniest characters since the Keystone Kops met Miss Beautiful. . . . What a background is the Miss America Pageant. . . . It's all just too funny. . . . *SHE WALKS IN BEAUTY* SEEMS TO BRING THE GENRE TO A NEW HIGH . . . with a laugh a page. The cross-purposes and coincidences keep this book moving with people that you grow to care about . . . very highly recommended."

—*Mystery News*

"Amusing . . . Shankman's a bundle of fun on such fascinating pageant lore as bugle beads and rhinoplasty. . . ."

—*The New York Times Book Review*

"SARAH SHANKMAN IS A VERY TALENTED WRITER."

—*Atlanta Journal Constitution*

Books by Sarah Shankman

Impersonal Attractions
Keeping Secrets
Now Let's Talk of Graves
She Walks in Beauty

as Alice Storey

First Kill All the Lawyers
Then Hang All the Liars

SHE WALKS IN BEAUTY

A SAMANTHA ADAMS MYSTERY

SARAH SHANKMAN

POCKET BOOKS
New York London Toronto Sydney Tokyo Singapore

For William Jack Sibley,
my all-time favorite cowboy

This book is a work of fiction. Names, characters, places and incidents are either the product of my [the author's] imagination or are used fictitiously. Although there are references to the Miss America Pageant and to real people who have been involved with the pageant, this story is not based on any real events associated with the pageant or with real activities of pageant participants. This book is not authorized by or connected with the Miss America Pageant or its sponsors.

POCKET BOOKS, a division of Simon & Schuster Inc.
1230 Avenue of the Americas, New York, NY 10020

ISBN: 0-671-73658-2

First Pocket Books paperback printing October 1992

10 9 8 7 6 5 4 3 2 1

Cover art by John Howard

Printed in the U.S.A.

With special thanks to:

The Miss America Pageant and staff in Atlantic City and the former Miss Americas and contestants who shared their experiences.

Gary Bradley, for the technical assistance and many other kindnesses. Sandra Scoppettone, for generously reading. Dr. Robert Albo, for the magic. Ellen Danna, Nathalie Dupree, and Barbara and Jeff Malm, for opening their homes. Cheryl Sullivan, for the Atlantic City tour. Chris Wiltz, for putting me on to the loup-garou.

Frank Deford's *There She Is* was an invaluable source, as were John McPhee on the Pine Barrens and Ginie Polo Sayles's *How to Win Pageants.*

Thanks to Meg Parsont and all the others at Pocket Books who shepherd my work along, and to Johanna Tani for her eagle eye.

And as always, thank you, Jane. Love you, Harvey.

She walks in beauty, like the night
Of cloudless climes and starry skies;
And all that's best of dark and bright
Meet in her aspect and her eyes:
Thus mellowed to that tender light
Which heaven to gaudy day denies.

—George Gordon, Lord Byron

Life is a beauty pageant.

—Thierry Mugler,
fashion designer

God don't like ugly.

—Southernism

...Prologue

How to spend the Labor Day weekend? Sam could come up with a hundred ways. Covering the Miss America Pageant wasn't one of them.

A tall, pretty woman with short, curly dark hair, Samantha Adams had just turned forty. And with that anniversary she had begun to believe that a wolf whistle now and then wasn't the worst thing that could happen to a thinking woman. But Miss America? Bubble-headed young flesh bouncing down a runway? Surely, Hoke had to be joking.

She stood in the office of the managing editor of the Atlanta *Constitution* with her hands on her hips. "I know you call the shots here, Hoke, but in case you've forgotten, life-style, entertainment, and froufrou aren't my regular beat. Remember me? The reporter who specializes in blood, gore, bad guys shooting up the little girl behind the counter in the fried chicken joint because she ran out of dark and crispy, didn't get their change back fast enough?"

Hoke wasn't listening. "It'll be a nice break for you. Get you to the beach, out of this heat, away from ringing phones. You can kick back for a week, do your race-walking on the Boardwalk."

"A *week!* The thing's one Saturday night! Besides, I'm taking a couple of extra days. Harry and I've rented a place on Martha's Vineyard."

"Sorry about that, Sammy. And, FYI, the pageant spans *two weeks,* actually, start to finish. The girls are taking a train, just like the old days, the *Miss America Special,* Philadelphia to Atlantic City. There's a week of rehearsals before they begin interviews on Sunday before Labor Day—"

"My God," Sam interrupted. "They let you judge that, what was it, Miss Liberty Bell down in Valdosta last spring, and now you've become a beauty pageant junkie. Oh, Hoke. What does Lois think about this?" Hoke's wife already spent half her time shooing off the never-ending parade of pretty young secretaries the guys in the city room called Hoke's Cuties.

Hoke shot her an indignant look, but the pose didn't fly with the lollipop poking out of the corner of his mouth. His internist had said, Give up smoking or living, take your pick.

"How many contests *have* you judged?"

Hoke leaned back, scanned the ceiling. "Four," he finally admitted. Then he lurched forward. "Now, this Miss Dogwood Festival, Rae Ann Bridges, is the loveliest girl you've ever seen—"

"Yes, Hoke. She won Miss Georgia."

Hoke leaned across his desk. The overhead fluorescent light bounced off his skull beneath his crew cut, accentuating the hound-dog bags beneath his eyes. "She's going to take the Big One. The title. Rae Ann's a shoo-in for Miss America, no doubt about it. You'll want to interview her before you go."

"I'm ecstatic for you and Rae Ann, Hoke. And I think you ought to fly to Atlantic City and cover the story yourself. Shoot a little craps. Have a little fun. I'd leave Lois behind, though. Tell her you've checked into a mental institution for a couple of weeks to have a few shock treatments. Recover your equilibrium."

"*Very* funny, Sammy. There's nothing more I'd love to do than go up there, but—" He extended a hand, the responsibility for the whole shooting match, morning and evening papers both, lay heavy upon it. "I can't tear away from here. And Burton"—Burton Edwards, the features editor, would be the logical choice, if there *were* any logic to the *Constitution*'s sending someone to Atlantic City—"Burton is the most cynical so-and-so south of New York City. He'd savage the pageant."

"So will I! Count on it! You think I won't, when you're stealing my weekend? Sending me to watch bimbos twitching their butts down runways? Mink eyelashes and falsies—"

"They *don't* wear falsies."

"Oh, Hoke. Honey. What you don't know—"

"Well, Rae Ann doesn't."

"You don't want me to do this. Really. Sentence me to real estate, obit, anything—after I'm back from the Vineyard."

"Once you get there, Sammy, and you see how smart these girls are, how sincere, how wonderful the pageant system is, teaching them poise, giving them all that scholarship money—"

"Hoke, no. Pretty please. I'm begging you."

"Just sleep on it, Sammy. Besides"—he took his scarlet sucker out of his mouth and inspected it carefully—"you're already scheduled to go."

Sam slammed in a tape and belted out "Sweet Dreams" along with poor old dead Patsy Cline. Patsy always made her feel better. She was driving too fast down Peachtree toward her weekly lunch with Charlie, plainclothes, Atlanta PD. They always met at Mary Mac's, an Atlanta institution, for chicken and dumplings, three vegetables, gossip, and iced tea. Miss America, indeed! Boy, Charlie was going to love that one. He'd never stop teasing her. And Hoke would run it on page one, no doubt, along with the football scores.

No wonder she was thinking of leaving the paper, though

she'd been there (and back in Atlanta) only a couple of years after a twenty-year sojourn in San Francisco. Despite a raft of good people still on staff, the *Constitution* wasn't what it was when they'd enticed her away from the *Chronicle.* Its slant had suddenly shifted from a flirtation with serious journalism back to pop reporting with large pretty pictures done up in four color—rather like television.

Sam was confused. On the one hand there was her job, on the other her sweetheart Harry. Both were problematic. Both brought her mixed joys. Were they mutually exclusive was the real question.

She'd met the handsome (and much younger) Harry Zack in the spring when she was in the Crescent City. Harry, a gray-eyed, broad-shouldered songwriting insurance investigator, had gotten in her way at first. Had gotten under her skin later. Had said a lot of things she'd prefer a man didn't say.

He'd been talking a lot about love lately, had even used the M word.

Sam wasn't sure she was ready for love again, much less marriage. All the men she'd ever truly loved seemed to have a way of disappearing, deserting, or dying.

Besides, she'd said to Harry last night on the phone, you'd better give some serious thought to hooking up with a woman ten years your elder, especially one who had skipped the line where they were handing out the mommy genes.

He'd said it made him no nevermind. Harry, who'd grown up Uptown among the blue bloods of New Orleans, had a real Downtown way of talking.

Just you wait, she'd continued. You'll be strolling by a playground one morning, little kiddies screeching Daddy, Daddy, you'll change your mind. The old lady on your arm'll already have gone through *her* change. I'm not gonna be studying babies, Harry.

You're just saying that 'cause you think I want you to move over to New Orleans.

Don't you?

Of course I do. Ain't nothing to eat over there in Hotlanta

except yuppie food and collard greens. No music to speak of. One of us has got to do it. The choice between Atlanta and New Orleans—no contest.

What's wrong with the way we are? I hop on that plane almost every Friday evening at six o'clock, cross that time zone, and it's still six when I get there. Even time to relax a little before we go out to dinner.

Talking trash, Sammy.

What are you talking, son? Relocation and *up*heaval.

Son's talking commitment.

Oh, Jesus.

On the other hand, maybe she ought to give it some thought. *Half* a commitment's worth, maybe. She'd tell Hoke to take his silly assignment and shove it. Miss America, indeed! Hand him the job while she was at it. It wasn't like she needed the money, thank you kindly, Jesus. Independence was what her inheritance was for. Maybe she could take a little house *near* New Orleans over on the north side of Lake Pontchartrain, get away from urban rot altogether, in a place like Mandeville. No, Covington. She'd work on the true crime book she'd been wanting to do for a long time.

Covington. Yes, that'd do it. She'd settle into a nice old house with a center hall and a veranda and oaks draped with Spanish moss and write her book while the ghost of Walker Percy, who'd lived near the village until his death, prowled around the neighborhood. She'd have oyster po'boys for lunch with the St. Tammany Parish courthouse gang in that old café where Harry had once taken her—where time had stopped in about 1950, and they talked about the Longs, Huey and Uncle Earl, as if they'd dropped by yesterday. Now, *that* ought to furnish her with some material.

Harry could come visit on weekends.

But wasn't that what he was complaining about now—weekends? And wait until she told him about Hoke putting the kibosh on their plans for Labor Day.

Well, she couldn't think about that anymore right now. She had to concentrate on changing lanes if she was ever going to make the turn in the here and now onto Ponce de Leon. She signaled, tried to pull out, got cut off, honked at, and flipped off. Hey, maybe it *was* time to move to a little town out in the middle of nowhere. The traffic in Atlanta was growing more snarly by the day, the influence, no doubt, of all those carpetbagging Yankees.

Now Miss Patsy had finished singing about her sweet dreams, and Sam, sitting at a red light one block away from Mary Mac's, popped in one of Harry's tapes. Strumming his guitar, he was singing the first song he'd written for her. *I thought I knew how angels flew till you stepped off the plane.*

Oh, Harry. The boy had a sweet baritone—and lots of other sweet things. What to do? What to do? Sam sighed and answered her car phone.

It was Charlie. Something had come up. Something he thought she ought to know about. Yeah. Uh-huh. Charlie always managed a doozie when he was late—which was almost every time they had a date. She listened to him with one ear.

Then she heard what he was saying. Skeeter Bosarge had escaped.

"What?"

"He's been on the run about eight hours. Now, we don't know where he's headed. No reason to think it's this way."

"Great. No reason to think it's not, either, is there?"

No, there wasn't. And just in case, he didn't want to frighten her, but maybe she ought to swing back and pick him up at headquarters. They could have a little chat about precautionary measures.

Indeed. He didn't need to remind her that Skeeter was stark raving crazy. The rapist/murderer had killed three women in Atlanta before Sam's series on him in the paper pushed enough victims who had lived, but hadn't told the tale, to come forward. Like most madmen, Skeeter needed someone to blame. He'd picked Sam.

"I'll get you, you bitch!" he'd screamed at her as they dragged him out of the courtroom after his sentencing.

"Melodramatic, don't you think?" Sam had flapped her

lips at Charlie, hoping her nonchalance would hide their trembling.

"Serious as death," Charlie had said then. Now he asked, "You got your .38?"

Sam reached over and patted the glove compartment as if Charlie could see her.

He couldn't.

But Skeeter Bosarge could. Rising from the back seat behind her, he could see her clear as day.

"Let's go have us some fun, pretty lady," Skeeter whispered as he slipped one big rough hand around her neck.

Sam froze. She'd never forget his filthy voice as long as she lived—however long that was.

She'd already hung up the phone. Oh, Jesus. Charlie couldn't help her now. No one could. Not even her trusty friends Smith & Wesson, so near—just about twelve inches from her fingertips if she could only reach out and touch them—yet so far away.

"It's just you and me, baby." Skeeter ran his other hand down her chest. She could see the blue letters HATE tattooed between his fingers and thumb by someone who didn't have very good handwriting.

Her mind stepped off and looked back. Here she was thinking about some needle artist in stir who hadn't learned the Palmer Method when she ought to be concentrating on getting loose from this maniac.

Well, it was easier than thinking about the realities. The possibilities. Skeeter Bosarge's particular brand of savagery.

She didn't want to die chopped into little pieces in a puddle of blood. She was too young. Well, almost young. She'd been obsessing recently about the cellulite on her thighs, the little lines at the corners of her eyes. But hell, forty was looking perkier by the minute.

Now what she had to do was concentrate, stop her stomach from doing loop-de-loops, deter the blood from coagulating in her veins. Maybe she and Skeeter could talk about this.

She eased into it. "How you doing, Skeeter?"

His answering laugh was filled with slimy crawly things. It made you want to take a bath.

Then he pinched her breast between his right thumb and forefinger, his left hand still around her neck. She resisted the temptation to reach up and slap his face.

"You been dreaming about me?" he crooned.

Only in my nightmares, you ugly sucker. She didn't say that. But he was ugly, with dank, greasy hair, a lowering forehead, too-long arms, dim, dumb eyes. He shuffled. Just looking at Skeeter was enough to give you the creeps.

Then his right hand moved. Up, back, and she felt the cool, smooth blade against her throat. Oh, God. Oh, Jesus. She was almost deafened by her heart's pounding. She was scared witless.

Skeeter growled, "Just in case you get any funny ideas about running a red light, blowing a stop sign, you try anything, you die."

He was preaching to the choir. She was a believer. She'd seen his handiwork. Skeeter liked to cut and carve and maim. He'd started with an old girlfriend, raped her, then cut her heart out and ate it. He liked to tell reporters he'd developed a taste for blood right on the spot. Yeah, Skeeter was one hell of an interview.

"Now, what we're gonna do is we're gonna have a little drink, then you get over to Monroe Drive, take that down to I-20, head east." His hairy fingers poked an open pint of bourbon against her lips.

Sam shied at the smell, then smiled. No, thanks, Skeeter, trotting out her most polite party manners as if he'd offered her petits fours on a silver tray at a debutante tea.

He smashed the bottle into her teeth. Try it sometime if you're feeling like beating up on yourself. It hurts even more than you might think. Her blood tasted of salt and rust. She ran her tongue gingerly across her front teeth. So far so good. Four teenage years of orthodonture not shot yet.

"Drink!" he screamed.

She screamed back: "I don't drink!"

She didn't. Not for almost thirteen years. Before that, she'd drunk for a bad long time. Oh, she was a juicer, all right. The kind who threw her shoes out of the car while it was weaving from side to side on the freeway, hunting for a victim. Who thought she was having a high old time stripping down to her skivvies in the middle of dinner, dancing nude on the tabletops for dessert. Who was all too familiar with the snout of the pig who rooted her awake at four in the morning when her blood sugar dropped, the porker who wore a name tag that read Remorse, who dug out all her transgressions, every last disgusting one, and spread them before her like truffles to be gorged, regurgitated, and scarfed up again.

Skeeter laughed his nasty old laugh. "I know you don't, baby. I learned a lot about you, what with all the spare time I had down in Reidsville. Talking to a couple other guys you helped put away. We used to make up stories about what we'd like to do if we got hold of you." Three beats passed while she thought about that. "Now, ain't life funny?" he crooned.

Sure, sure. She was about to counter with something chatty about what a small world it is, when he peeled away an inch-wide strip of the soft white flesh of her throat just like he was peeling an onion.

It burned like hell. But she didn't scream. He was far too close to the jugular. She didn't know how much time she had before the smell of her fear shoved him over the edge into something she didn't even want to imagine.

"Now." He tapped her mouth with the pint again. "You wanta drink?"

She drank. Again, he insisted. Again. Again. Again. Until the bottle was almost empty. Then he was pushing pills into her mouth. Chew, he screamed. The last of the bourbon seared her empty gut along with the 'ludes. Then they all joined hands and do-si-doed around her brain, where a drumbeat of secret longing for sweet release had been poised a dozen dry years.

Sock it to me, Devil Daddy. Give it to me, Mr. Booze.

Ooooooh, Daddy. I been pining for you. Waiting to run to you. Hide with you. Shuck the straight life, give it up to you. I want to lap you up, suck you up, savor you.

The car lurched. Skeeter slapped her so hard her head snapped. "Open your eyes, you lush. You're gonna kill us."

So why didn't he think of that before? But she wouldn't do that, would she? Naaawh. It was too much fun drunk-driving this cute little car that handled just like a roller coaster.

They passed a few blocks east of Martin Luther King's Ebenezer Baptist Church, then close by Oakland Cemetery. Confederate General Hood had followed the Battle of Atlanta from the old graveyard's promontory. Margaret Mitchell rested there, as did Bobby Jones, the golfer. Sam's mother and father lay near them in a marble tomb. She would too, sooner or later.

Today it looked like sooner.

At that, her parents' faces zoomed into close focus, pretty people dead all too young, falling out of the sky when their airplane did bad rollovers near Paris. Tears tracked down her cheeks, almost thirty years later.

The pills and the booze had pushed her over into easy sentimentality, teetering on the edge of maudlin. She *hated* that.

"You like cemeteries?" Skeeter asked as if he were talking about the weather. "*I* can't stand 'em. Daddy made us go weed Mama's grave every Sunday. It was creepy."

Sam snuffled. Poor Skeeter. She knew just how he felt, losing his mama. She and Skeeter Bosarge, the rapist/murderer, had something in common. They could talk.

And, in fact, she knew just what to say to him. "Why don't you let me go, Skeeter? I'll make sure they cut you a deal."

The choice of words was unfortunate.

"Cut me *nothing!*" the madman screamed. "Cut *you*, bitch!" The silvery knife skittered against her neck.

Well, that certainly snapped her back. It was time to get the hell out of there. Cars zipped by them on the interstate. What was *with* these people? Were they so snug in their air-cooled wraparound sound they couldn't see a woman with a knife at her throat?

"Take the Panthersville Road exit and don't try anything cute."

They were *there* already? It hadn't taken long, fifteen minutes from the time he'd grabbed her. Now everywhere she looked there were thick stands of trees, remnants of the forests that had once covered these rolling hills. Dark, deep woods, where nobody could find her.

Houses grew few and far between. They drove through copses of oak, pine, sweet gum, sprinkled with wild dogwood and azalea. Would they find her corpse in the copse just about the time they crowned the new Miss Dogwood next spring?

Left, Skeeter barked. Left, then left again. The blade snicked her throat with each word. How much blood had she lost? The street sign at the last turn read Hanging Tree Lane.

"'D'jew see that?" he giggled.

Cute. Skeeter was always cute. One of his trademarks had been the little poems he'd left at the crime scenes. They had always rhymed, and they were always obscene. Moon, June, bloody bazooms. Nice, twice, tit slicer. Yep, Skeeter had a way with words all right.

"Out of the car," he barked, loosening his hold.

A commotion of motion. Her Big Chance. She'd fight him on the beaches. She'd fight him on the shores. Gasping for breath, she lurched for the glove compartment and the .38, didn't even get close. He smashed her seat forward, bashing her head—already pounding with a premature hangover. Now he was out of the car, dragging her with him through gravel and grass. Skeeter was huge, and two years of weight lifting in Reidsville hadn't hurt him a bit.

The woods were lovely, dark and deep on the way to Grandmother's house, and the Big Bad Wolf had very big teeth. He bared them at her now, then slugged her with his fist. Stars twinkled, and her nose scrinched. She'd never known anything could hurt like this.

And she rather liked her delicate, arrow-straight nose. Vanity, vanity. Where does it get you?

To Grandmother's house? Before them stood a little cabin in the woods. Was this a fairy tale? A figment of her drunken imagining?

If not, maybe Grandma was home. Maybe she had a telephone. Maybe she'd call for help.

No such luck. They danced around to the back of the tarpaper shanty, this peculiar couple. Her fanny to his crotch, his arm crooked in a choke hold, his legs kicking her along like a recalcitrant partner who just couldn't keep the beat.

"Ain't nobody here," he grunted, and shoved her toward a stand of pines that grew right up to the back door. "Belongs to my old man, still down at Reidsville. You know what an old man is, sweetheart?"

She did. His sugar daddy, his boyfriend—undoubtedly even bigger and meaner and uglier than Skeeter—who'd faced off other inmates, hit 'em with the dead eyes, said Back Off! In return for some sweet stuff.

"It's been a long time since I've had a woman, *Miss* Adams."

She'd seen the last woman he'd had. Or what was left of her. The little pieces. The broken places.

Now her nose was killing her. The whittled place on her neck burned. She felt weak in the knees. Saliva pooled in her mouth. It tasted bright yellow. She was going to throw up.

"Don't you dare!" He shook her, and something in her nose crunched. She retched again.

Skeeter screamed, "I said *no!* You bitch! Don't!" Then he got in close, his breath hot and nasty, and crooned, "I want your kisses *sweet.*"

Then he jerked her up, grabbed her by the scruff of her neck, and slammed her against a tree. A thick rough rope materialized from nowhere. A magician, that Skeeter Bosarge. And he could do rope tricks. Loop-de-loop-de-loop-de-loop. The rope twirled, and she was neatly trussed.

Her mind stepped off. This was *not* looking good. How

was she going to manage this thing now? How had she, the control freak, let it get so far away from her?

Then hopelessness and helplessness stepped up and joined hands in her mind, ready to do a little minuet. She was reeling, so sick and dizzy she couldn't even focus. Skeeter was fading in and out of her private picture show. Or was he just dancing forward and back, back and forward, practicing a little routine?

Nope. He was just trying to find the right distance for his *real* magic act.

You know the one, Sam. The one where the man throws knives at the pretty lady.

"They were having a sale at the store where I stopped in Macon." Skeeter grinned and held up a whole brace of blades. Two dozen. Three, maybe. Enough to make plenty of holes in her. Blood would flow like booze spilled on a bar by a drunk couldn't hold her liquor. Remember her?

"They're gonna think you got drunk, fell down on a porky-pine, there's enough of you left to ID." Then he stepped back once more, took aim, and grinned.

God, Skeeter had bad teeth—and a weak chin. Probably the result of years of inbreeding. Here she was, a lifetime member of the Piedmont Driving Club (though she never attended, a point of pride—not to mention reverse snobbism) about to be skewered by south Georgia white trash. My Lord, the ignominy, as the Atlanta ladies would say.

The first knife flew and *ka-chuncked* into the pine a half inch from her waist. She could hear the blade quiver. She could smell the fresh resin filling the tree's wound.

And then she shut down.

The world, very small and very contained, held only herself, Skeeter, and those knives. One, Sam. Two, Skeeter. Three, knives. Like fog through the Golden Gate, a calm drifted over her. She was soft green hills rolling beneath cool gray clouds.

"Whoops." Skeeter pursed his mouth. "Damn! Well, practice makes perfect. We've got a lot of time for practice, don't we, sugar? And after a while, we'll take us a little break. See how else you can pleasure old Skeeter."

Somewhere deep inside the drunken maelstrom that, at present, passed for her brain, she knew she ought to be trembling. But there was a gift she had—which came in very handy if you hung around the likes of Skeeter Bosarge. When the going got very, *very* rough, Sam hung tough and absolutely calm. She was placid and still as a high mountain lake that had a steady date with the bluebird of happiness.

The still place came from years of reciting the Serenity Prayer—a plea for the ability to accept the things she couldn't change, the courage to change the things she could. And this, *this* right in front of her was one of the former. She wasn't about to change Skeeter Bosarge. Not now. Not unless she turned into Superwoman, flung off these ropes, and whupped his ass. So she'd just have to turn it over. Put it on the shelf.

Whap! The second knife didn't miss. And it hurt like hell, it really did, when a knife pierced your arm just below your elbow.

Somewhere, someone was screaming.

Zingggg! That one found the fleshy part of her right thigh. The screaming was growing louder, keener.

Ka-whap! Wailing, that baby was blowing. She sounded like Billie Holiday on speed.

Or Sam Adams on Old Crow and 'ludes, which is who it was.

Sam was screaming her head off. And pleading—or as close to pleading as she ever got. The kind of pleading Margaret Thatcher would do if you got her really pissed.

"Stop it, Skeeter! Stop it this very instant!"

"Who you think you are, my second-grade teacher?" He flung another knife and missed, which *really* burned him.

"Stop it, you bastard!"

He liked that. He grinned, then clucked. "*Sunday*-school teacher talking like that? Oughta be ashamed of yourself."

Then he grabbed up six knives at once. He drew back, one in his right hand, the other five sinisterly poised. He'd let fly a barrage like the mojo Watusis chucking their spears. He'd show the bitch who'd put him away. She'd snaked two of his most precious years—years he could have been doing good, sending sluts like her to burn in hell.

Suddenly another sound, a roaring of hallelujahs filled the sky. It sounded like glory.

And Skeeter was diving for cover, flying high and wide.

"That's right!" shouted an old voice, rich and magnificent. It had to be the voice of God. Sam was sure of it. "Get away from her, you bastard!" Now she wasn't quite so sure, but still, she liked it.

Then from behind a pine tree arose the face of her savior. He was robed in khaki—pants, shirt, a long-billed hat.

Malachy Champion, who was pushing eighty, had been a hunter all his life. Once he'd started collecting social security, he figured he could get by with pretending to forget the dates of hunting season—about which he'd always been pretty casual anyway. Malachy was out stalking his supper, mourning dove or bobtail quail, whichever flushed first. He liked little birds. You cooked 'em up, made yourself some pan gravy with the scrapings left in the bottom of the skillet, that and a mess of greens, some leftover corn bread in a glass of buttermilk. Hell, eating like that, a man could live to be a hundred—in the little house his children bought him right over there on the edge of South River.

Except for the bastards. There were all brands and sizes of bastards, and they did various and sundry things to drive men crazy. There were bastards in the government. Bastards on the TV. Bastards throwing garbage in the Chattahoochee. And then there was this kind of bastard crouching over there behind that rusting jalopy.

All the while, his shotgun at the ready, Malachy was steadily sliding forward. Suzie, the redbone hound bitch he'd bought in Louisiana where those old boys knew something about hunting, hung close by his left side.

"Stay, girl," he commanded. He didn't want her getting too close to danger, especially since he didn't need her to flush this varmint.

Suzie whimpered. Whatever it was, she hadn't come this far to be left out.

"Stay," he repeated gruffly.

She stayed, and Malachy stepped closer to the old rusted-out Ford the bastard had jumped behind.

Then, *zing*, a knife flew past Malachy's right ear.

He's going to die, thought Sam. My hero's going to die. And then I'm going to die. She kept waiting for the picture show of her life to start flashing, the way people said it did. Well, look on the bright side. She'd never know serious illness. And it would be nice to see her mama and daddy again.

Zing. A second knife darted and missed, and still the old man kept advancing. Then a third flew.

"Keep back!" Skeeter screamed. You could almost see the panic, electric in his voice.

"Why?" the old man asked evenly, as if that were the most natural question in the world. "I ain't afraid of dying. I'm old. How 'bout you?"

A fourth knife soared past and thudded among pine needles. The old man stepped closer and closer, now turning his back toward Sam.

Then a fifth knife lifted off, and a sixth, and it was that last one that found a target in Suzie's leg. She screamed, and Skeeter's head popped up wearing a grin of triumph, and then flew off, or most of it did.

For a shotgun—which spreads its tiny BB-like shot and will pierce and kill, but leave a little bird intact, at thirty yards—will turn a man's face to hamburger when fired at five. It might also tear his head off.

When Malachy fired, he was three yards from his target.

The old man turned to Sam, and said, Don't look. But she already had. Her eyes rolled up, and she sagged against the rope.

Then Malachy Champion laid a so-sweet hand upon her cheek, took out his own knife to cut her bindings. "There now. Now, now." He gentled her like a frightened filly. "That oughta fix his wagon. Can't stand a man picks on a woman. 'Specially a pretty woman."

Sam managed a weak smile before her lights went out. She

tried, but couldn't manage the words, trying to say, Thank you, sir, for the compliment.

The way Malachy told it later, for the two hundredth time it seemed to him—to the police, the GBI, the TV people, then finally to Sam herself when she was sitting up again in bed in the house she shared with her uncle George—he'd been tracking, see. About to flush some quail when he heard this woman screaming. Got her in his sights, thought, My God, look at that pretty girl. Pretty enough to be Miss America. What's that crazy fool doing to her? It didn't seem to him you had to think about that more than half a second, the time it took to swing the barrels of his shotgun over toward the perpetrator of the screaming.

"Miss America, huh?" laughed Uncle George, who was sitting right there with old Malachy in her boudoir, the three of them having tea like it was an ordinary occasion, like the man hadn't saved her life. "Sam was going to cover the pageant for the paper this year. Of course, now—"

Sam pointed to her taped nose. "Guess this got me out of that. Now, listen, Mr. Champion—"

"You don't say?" said Malachy. "Lord, Lord, I've watched that show since they started showing it on TV. 1955. That's the year Lee Meriwether took it. Pretty girl. Brunette. Looks a lot like you, young'un."

Your flattery, old man, won't get *me* to Atlantic City, she thought, and then thanked him.

"You're a fan of the pageant? I've always been, too," said George.

Since when? Sam wondered. Since when had her elegant uncle been interested in beauty queens?

"Oh, yes," Malachy continued. "One of my hobbies. Remember 'em all. All the way back to the beginning, 1921. Margaret Gorman. Girl had a thirty-one-inch chest. Pretty as a picture, though. Guess I'm glad times have changed." He rolled his watery blue eyes down the front of Sam's pj's. "Myself, I like girls a little more developed in that category. If you know what I mean."

Sam, who'd been fairly well developed in that category since she was twelve, did indeed. But what she wanted to know was—

"All-time favorite was Yolande Betbeze, from a good family down in Mobile, Miss Alabama, Miss America 1951. Gorgeous creature, told 'em all to go to hell later, they wanted to mess in her business. Worked with CORE when the integration started." Malachy nodded. "She picketed, sat in at lunch counters at Woolworth's. I always liked girls with some backbone, some spunk."

"Me too," said Hoke Tolliver. Sam's editor poked his head around the edge of the door. "Knock, knock." He was carrying a massive bouquet of calla lilies in one hand.

"I'm not dead," said Sam, "if those are for me. Looks like you thought you were coming to my funeral."

"See what I mean about spunk?" Hoke replied. "It's that kind of attitude that goes right out there and gets the story."

"Forget it," said Sam, sliding back down under her white cotton sheets. "I'm disabled. I'm staying here for the duration of my recuperation. Eating gallons of chocolate ice cream." And getting over her terrible guilt, even though she'd been *forced* to drug and drink.

"Now, that's a shame, idn't it," said Malachy Champion. "To have to pass on an opportunity like that. My heart's desire has always been to go to Atlantic City to the pageant. To be right there."

"Hey, Hoke," said Sam. "You hear that? Mr. Champion here'd *love* to cover the pageant for you."

"And I'd love to send him." He smiled. "But it might be a little tough to get him the credentials. You're not a journalist, are you, Mr. Champion?"

"Don't insult the man," said Sam.

"Of course, if you went, you could take him along," George said to Sam.

"Wait a minute! Whose side are you on anyway?"

"Oh, I couldn't think of going," said Malachy. "Old man like me, I don't much take to traveling anymore. And what with Suzie still recovering."

The man who saved my life is throwing in his injured dog,

who was an accessory to the saving, thought Sam. It's getting pretty deep in here.

"But on the other hand, if you went, you could bring him back an autographed program, the autograph of Miss America, in fact—"

Sam didn't let Hoke finish. "You're so sure it's gonna be Rae Ann, we could just call her up and get one from her right now. Surely she's already signed something for you, Hoke? A T-shirt, your BVDs?"

"Sammy! What on earth do you mean?" Hoke's eyebrows almost met his crew cut.

"Oh, I forgot that Rae Ann's a certified member of the vestal virgin society."

"Well," Malachy Champion drawled, "I reckon that would be pretty nice, if you went. You *could* bring me back a souvenir, tell me all about it firsthand, if you got up real close to the girls, to that Phyllis George. Maybe even Mary Ann Mobley. I always was partial to those southern girls."

"Okay," said Sam. "Whose idea was this? Hoke just happens to drop by with posies. Joins the two of you in pressuring me like crazy."

"We just thought it might help you to get up and about—and it *would* be nice to have those autographs—" said Malachy, trailing off.

George spread his hands wide. He didn't say a word, but the message was clear. Was it too much to ask, to do a little favor for the man who'd rescued you from a hideous death?

"You're a terrible old man, do you know that, George?" She wanted to get out of bed and punch him, but she was still too sore. "A manipulating, scheming, conniving, four-flushing, double-dealing cheat. A *lawyer,* through and through!"

"Retired lawyer," he sniffed. "Who's always been a fan of the pageant. Samantha, sometimes I think you're positively un-American."

"I'm not well." Sam pouted. "The pageant's in two weeks. I couldn't possibly."

"You'll be fine," said George. "Especially if you take Harry along with you."

"Harry! What's Harry got to do with Miss America?"

"Well, you know, it's the damnedest thing," said George. "I was with him on the phone yesterday. He flew over the minute he heard about the—incident," George said by way of explanation to anyone who cared, "and had to get back to New Orleans pretty soon, but he calls at least three times a day to check on Samantha. Anyway, *he* said it was the funniest coincidence, but he'd just found out that the young woman who's Miss Louisiana this year, from New Orleans, her name's Lucinda Washington, and she's—"

"Oh, my God." Sam fell back onto her pillows. "Don't tell me. Is she tall?"

"Real tall," said Hoke, who made it a point to know everything about Rae Ann's competition.

"Is she black?"

"She is," said Hoke. "Isn't that a miracle, her being from Louisiana? Wonder when Georgia's gonna name a black—"

Sam cut him off. "And she's related to Lavert Washington, isn't she? Harry's friend?"

"That's what he said," said George. "Lavert's second cousin. Maybe second, once removed. But isn't that wonderful? I remember you're so fond of Lavert."

"That's right. I've always been crazy about chefs who also chauffeur for the mob." But the truth was, she *was* crazy about Lavert Washington. "So I guess that means Lavert's going to Atlantic City to cheer his cousin on, and Harry wanted to go, too? Thought it'd be one big party? That's why he put you all up to this?" Sam had gotten up quite a head of steam for a sick woman. But if there was anything in this world she hated, it was being manipulated.

The three southern gentlemen—Uncle George, Malachy, and Hoke—looked at her in astonishment.

"Put us up to what, Sammy?" Hoke said finally.

"Shut up, Hoke. I'm going to kill that boy. Kill Harry. *Kill* him! And you should be ashamed of yourself, Mr. Champion. Guilt-tripping me like this."

"Doing what?" Malachy cupped his ear like he didn't understand, but she could see the little grin slipping around the corner of his mouth.

"Forget it," she said. "Okay. You win. I'll do it. And then"—she hung on that last word for a long minute—"I'm *quitting,* Hoke. I swear to God. This is the last straw. I'll do your damned pageant, not for you, but for Malachy, and get him his Miss America autographs, and then it's over and out. Speaking of which, clear out of my bedroom, all of you." She reached for the phone as if it were loaded with live lead. "I've got a few choice words to say to someone in New Orleans."

But in the end, after she'd finished blowing off steam, she thought, What the heck? Atlantic City was on the water, right? And a long weekend with Harry was a long weekend with Harry.

"We're gonna have such a good time, pretty lady," he'd said in his sweet, husky voice when she stopped yelling at him.

Besides which, that day Skeeter Bosarge had risen up behind her like a bad dream, she'd thought she'd never live to see September. Every day after that one, even if she did something silly with it, was a gift.

...1

HOWEVER, LESS THAN TWELVE HOURS INTO IT, SAM TURNED TO Harry in their huge round bed and said, "I can't tell if it's the pageant or Atlantic City, but I feel like I'm on Mars. Tell me I haven't fallen off the wagon again, Harry."

"No way, sugarplum. Probably the pink satin. It's making me bilious."

And certainly there was a gracious plenty of *that* in their high-roller suite. On the walls, swagged up to the center of the ceiling, where it was pinned by an awful crystal chandelier that was probably left over from the Taj—Donald Trump let the Monopoly decorator have it cheap. There was even a pink satin dust rufflelike affair around each of three toilet seats and the two matching bidets.

"Why couldn't they just give us a nice little Holiday Inn-ish room, Harry? A room for normal people?"

"Hell, they thought they were doing us a favor. I personally think it's kind of fun." Harry reached over and punched the remote control that opened the heavy rose drapes. "Ta-*dah*. The Atlantic Ocean. Doesn't that make you happy? Look at Harpo, he loves it." Sam's little blond and white Shih Tzu wagged his tail at the mention of his name, then gave Harry a hard look. The man was in *his* bed.

Yes, Sam agreed, the Atlantic was very nice. It did what oceans were supposed to do. "I bet *none* of the rooms face the rot and decay," she countered with what was really bothering her.

"Sammy, my Sammy." Harry reached over and snuggled her to his nicely furred chest. "You're here to cover Rae Ann and the other pretty little girls. You are not here to write an exposé about the slums out the back doors of the casinos, the rotten politics, the rubble, the whole South Bronx thing. Besides, it's been done a jillion times. Every time some reporter trashes the Donald, they run that same shot of the Taj rising out of the garbage dump called AC."

"Doesn't it seem to you slightly incongruous that the pageant brings spanky-clean girls from Westwego and Tooterville and Appletown *here?*"

"It's tradition, love. You read me all about it from the press kit on the plane. The pageants began here—more than seventy years ago. Now, *you've* been here only long enough to see one hour of rehearsal for the Saturday night TV extravaganza—"

"Harry, the girls were identical except for the different flavors. Fifty Chatty Cathy clones. And the production number sucks. None of them can dance."

"—As I was saying, enough time to eat one bad meal in a hotel restaurant followed by a night of *magnificent* lovemaking."

"For which I thank you very much. But we could have done that anywhere, especially on the Vineyard."

"You've not even been to Convention Hall except to grab your badge and watch that snippet of rehearsal—and by the way, if you don't get your butt moving, you're going to be late for your press conference—yet already you want them to relocate the pageant. Anybody ever mention you're a control freak, m'lady?"

"Yes, you. About twelve times a day. And *besides,* the press conference isn't till one."

"I thought it was eleven."

"Well, you're wrong. So we have time for a leisurely breakfast in bed and a stroll along the Boardwalk."

"Sounds good." Harry reached for a room service menu. Sam reached for Harry.

"Did I ever tell you how much I *like* your ideas?" he said in the husky voice she adored. "How I *love* tagging along on your trips with you and Harpo?" He snuggled her closer and nibbled her right earlobe. He had a thing about ears.

"You're a good little boy toy, Harry. Now close those damned pink drapes."

Well, there was certainly nothing pink or romantic or even remotely attractive about Convention Hall to which Sam made her way just before one. The glamour of the pageant did not extend to this mammoth arena that covered one block from the Boardwalk to Pacific and two blocks between Mississippi and Florida avenues. So what if the Beatles had once performed on its stage, if it had the largest pipe organ in the world? It was a cold, brick barn of a place built in the twenties, replete with eagle-eyed droves of security guards, oceans of enclosed parking lots, miles of winding halls, towering ceilings, acres of stony floors. Her footsteps echoed on the terrazzo. Forget the high heels, which caught in the Boardwalk anyway.

Finally, after two false starts, she found her way to the second-floor pressroom. Outside in the hall a chattering mob brandished notebooks, tape recorders, and cameras. Her people. A few looked vaguely familiar.

She found a seat beside a young blonde whose press badge read *Philadelphia Inquirer.* She glanced at Sam's tag, did a classic double take. "I read your stuff in journalism school!"

"Really? How nice." The kid meant it as a compliment, right? Sam glanced around the room. Yes indeedy, this was a young crowd. No editor in his right mind would send a seasoned reporter to cover this nonsense—certainly not before Saturday night. No one except Hoke.

"What are you doing here?" asked the *Inquirer.*

"I'm being punished."

The *Inquirer* nodded. Anyone in the newspaper game would know exactly what Sam meant. "But you're gonna be surprised. I did this last year, and it was fun."

"Uh-huh. I bet."

"No, really. You'll get hooked."

"Don't count on it. I'm a lot older and wiser, not to mention more cynical, than I look, sweetheart."

The *Inquirer* reached in her huge black canvas bag, fished for her wallet, pulled out a hundred-dollar bill, and flashed it in Sam's face. "One Ben Franklin says you're wrong."

"Are you crazy?" A hundred? Young reporters, hell, *old* reporters, didn't make that kind of money. And the girl was sure to lose. Maybe this was what Atlantic City and the casinos did to you. It was in the water.

"Sucker bet," said the *Inquirer*.

"Ho ho ho. Define your terms."

"By the end of this week you'll be a bona fide Miss America enthusiast. You'll see that the pageant is not what you think, nor the girls."

"We're talking major redeeming values?"

The blonde nodded.

Sam shook her hand. "You're on, cookie. I hope you've got a sugar daddy tucked away who can afford your flights of fancy."

"Marks like you, I don't need him." The blonde grinned. Then, "Uh-oh. Get ready. Here she comes."

"Who?" The room had filled. Sam craned her neck.

Why, Miss America, that's who. And there she was, live and in color, the outgoing Miss A, Lynn Anderson, a very pretty young woman in a scarlet suit. She really was stunning. Sam hadn't expected that. Her complexion was gold-brown velvet. Her dark hair curled in a boyish bob. Her eyes were Hershey's chocolate with almonds. Well, maybe she was no brain surgeon, but she certainly was beautiful.

Miss A was introduced by Barbara Stein, a bubbly little redhead in a bright yellow dress who was the pageant's executive director. Barb explained that Lynn was going to talk for a few minutes about the judging procedures, and then they could ask questions of the preliminary judges themselves. On cue, the door opened, and the seven judges made their entrance. The tallest of the women, and she was *very* tall, waved at several members of the press, who called her name.

"Eloise Lemon, a Miss America from the sixties," the *Inquirer* whispered. Oh, yes. She was one of the last ones Sam remembered before she'd grown up and stopped watching the pageant.

Now Miss America stepped up front and in a beautifully modulated voice said: "The Miss America Pageant is not a beauty contest."

Oh, yeah? Sam stifled a snort. Beside her the *Inquirer* nodded along—a self-evident truth.

Then Miss A did it again: "I want to emphasize this point because it's really important. The Miss America Pageant is *not* a beauty contest."

The sentiment would have been a lot easier to swallow if it weren't coming from the lips of one who was not only gorgeous, but built like a brick shithouse.

"There are so many other qualities the judges are looking for." Miss A lowered her volume and raised the wattage of her smile. They'd probably taught her how to do that in one of those pageant schools Sam had read about. "There's so much more than a pretty face she's going to need to get her through this very exciting but very tough year."

Miss A paused, her own gorgeous dusky kisser a perfect dead pan. She really wasn't kidding.

"Now"—she turned to the judges—"I'm not saying you ought to choose a dog, no matter how bright she is."

They laughed. There was an awful lot of bonhomie in this room. If it was going to be like this all week, Sam was going to need some insulin.

"But it's grueling as well as wonderful. Miss America's reign begins with a press conference fifteen minutes after she's crowned, another one Sunday morning, and she's in the NBC studio in Manhattan at five-thirty A.M. Monday for her appearance on the *Today Show.*"

So give Miss A three points for preparedness. Sam made a note.

"She'll do the networks, radio, magazine interviews, the

fittings for her traveling wardrobe, then she hits the road. And she better hit it with her running shoes on. Sure, she'll have that sparkly crown and some beautiful gowns along with her, as well as her traveling companion, but none of that's going to save her when the first *gentleman*"—she leaned into the word, turning and smiling at the judge nearest her, who was handsome, Sam thought, if you liked the smarmy type—"asks her the Big Question in front of an auditorium jammed with people."

Sam scanned her press release. This *gentleman* was Kurt Roberts, New York fashion and celebrity photographer. Most of the other judges seemed to be old hands on the pageant circuit, but there was no mention of his prior duties in that area.

"What's the big question, Lynn?" Mimi Bregman, a large, jolly, white-haired judge who looked like Mrs. Santa Claus in a red tent dress, beat the press to the punch.

Miss America winked at Mimi, then aimed her million-dollar smile back at Kurt Roberts. "Do you believe in premarital sex?"

"And how do you answer?" The photographer drawled, exhaling smoke through his perfect nose. Make that perfect nose job. Tall, lanky, he was good-looking in a self-satisfied sort of way. With his slick dark-blond ponytail, pastel Armani tailoring over a black T-shirt, turquoise bracelet, he looked like he'd watched too many episodes of "Miami Vice."

"No, I asked *you* that question, Mr. Roberts," Miss America purred.

Everybody laughed, including Sam. Everybody except Roberts, who narrowed his pale eyes. Mean eyes, thought Sam. What was going on between him and Miss A? She made a note. You could never tell what might turn into a story, and God knows with this twaddle, she was going to need anything she could scrounge.

"What they ask *me* is how does it feel to be the first Black-Vietnamese Miss America, and I say, 'Just great, thank you,' and then try to steer them on to something more important—like my platform."

Give the girl two points for spunk.

But the moment passed, and Miss A was spieling off the short version of her "platform" speech. The pageant now required each contestant to champion a "socially relevant" cause.

"I've tried to tell young people that *they* have to assume responsibility for their lives. That they need to put down the drugs, get off their duffs, figure out what their business is, and get on with it. No excuses. None whatsoever that'll wash with *me,* the daughter of a black American soldier whose real name my mother didn't know when he left her, alone and pregnant, in Saigon. We were boat people, my mother and I, and if *I* can make it, *I* can graduate magna cum laude from Berkeley, *you* can make it." Miss A pointed a pretty finger at the judges, and they all, including Kurt Roberts, sat up straighter.

Not bad. Okay, a tad too much flag-waving, but Sam was at least interested. She'd always been a sucker for a good immigrant story.

"Now, here's how the system works." Barbara Stein picked up where Lynn left off. "Our blue ribbon panel of preliminary judges started the preliminary interviews Sunday, finishing up just about an hour ago. The scores they give the girls for interview will carry over to the final Saturday night judging—"

"By the A team," judge Mimi Bregman interjected.

"The celebrity panel." Barbara Stein, who was tougher to derail than an Amtrak express, corrected her. "The preliminary judges' scores on interview carry over for thirty percent of the total scoring Saturday night. And, of course, it's *they* who determine the ten finalists from whom the celebrity panel will select the four runners-up and Miss America."

The other preliminary judges included two old hands from state pageants, both named Bob, both from the Midwest. They were both soft, round, fortyish, and pale and looked as if they should have been left in the oven a little longer.

Julian Temple, a flamboyant peacock of an older man,

complete with cape and silver-headed cane, had directed the Miss Mississippi pageant for thirty-two years, by God.

Eloise Lemon, on Julian's right, a Miss America from South Carolina, the tallest winner ever at six foot one, was still quite beautiful, and funny. "We have been working *so* hard," she drawled. "And I, frankly, am sick of these other judges' faces. We've been locked up together for days. It's so nice to see *yours,"* she said to the press. "With those wickedly cynical grins. I know you just can't wait to ask us some horribly rude questions."

"Don't let Eloise make you think we've been at one another's throats." That was the last judge heard from, Cindy Lou Jacklin. About thirty, also quite tall, blond, green-eyed, and pretty in a glitzy, frosted sort of way, she was a former Miss Ohio.

"Cindy Lou made ten," said the *Inquirer.*

That meant, Sam was already beginning to pick up the lingo, Cindy Lou had been one of the ten finalists the year she'd tried for Miss A. Now, according to the release, she did the weather in Orlando. Probably still had her eye on the Big Time, newswise. Definitely had her eye on Kurt Roberts, unless Sam was misreading her body language. Cindy Lou couldn't seem to turn away from him.

"Now, at the risk of being called Miss Bossy, I want to remind you again how terribly important these interviews are," said Barb. "Once again, the interview scores count thirty percent of the total and are *carried over* into the scores Saturday night, so that they're *crucial* in determining the final winner." Finally she opened the floor to questions.

"Eloise, how do you think the pageant's changed since you became Miss America?" someone called from the back.

"The girls are better educated, more articulate, better read, just better informed, more well-rounded perhaps than we were."

"But still they're judged in swimsuits."

"The girls make an appearance in swimsuits, yes. But they're not photographed on the beach in them. And they no longer do that loooooong fanny shot on TV."

"Would you like to see them done away with completely?"

"Do away with their swimsuits? Then, honey, what would you *have* them wear? Their birthday suits?"

Everyone laughed. But the questioner persisted. "Seriously, Eloise, doesn't the swimsuit competition make you uncomfortable? Didn't it then?"

"Then? You mean back in the 'dark ages'?" Eloise paused for the laugh, which didn't come. "Seriously? No. But then, you're talking to someone who'd do anything, who had plastic surgery, to become Miss America."

The crowd murmured in surprise.

"Oh, yes. I was only five foot seven before. I had six inches grafted into my calves."

It took them a moment to realize Eloise was pulling *their* legs.

"Speaking of cosmetic surgery, do you ask them in the interview," another reporter asked, "about any reconstructive work they might have had?"

"Hardly," sniffed Julian Temple, who looked like he might have had a tuck or two himself. "There are much more interesting things we'd rather hear them talk about."

Like what? Sam wondered, then shouted the question over the general buzz. *Like what?*

Eloise Lemon answered. "'Do you think Miss America should embrace any social causes? And if you were Miss America, what would your cause be?'"

Oh, Lord, Sam thought. Give me a break. "And how have the young women answered that?"

"How would *you* answer that?" Eloise shot back.

"I'd champion a woman's right to control her destiny by controlling her body. But being pro-choice probably wouldn't win me Miss America."

"Don't be so sure. Besides, one answer doesn't make the difference. It's the whole interview process, how they handle themselves. In fact, why don't you come up here and we'll show you how it's done," Eloise challenged.

The press corps laughed, then urged Sam on. *Do it. Do it.*

"Me?" Was Eloise for real?

"Yes, you," said Eloise. "Come on up here and we'll show you how it feels to be in the hot seat. Right now! Hurry up! Don't keep the judges waiting, young lady."

. . . 2

BIG GLORIA, THE MONOPOLY HOTEL'S HEAD OF HOUSEKEEPING, was keeping an eye on Wayne Ward. The sucker thought he was something cute. She'd asked him what he was doing, going in and out of rooms after they'd already been cleaned. He knew that was against the rules. Assistant to Mr. Franken, he said. *Special* assistant to the Man What Am, owns this casino hotel, not to mention half of the United States. Shoooot.

Gloria strolled down the hall of eighteen to get a better look.

"Wayne, what are you doing? I thought you finished all that last week. Big deal security doo-flatchies, whirly-diddlies you installed in the pageant judges' rooms." As if they didn't already have enough security in this hotel to put the FBI to shame.

Everybody snooping. In the casinos, dealers watching the players. Floormen watching the dealers. Pit bosses watching the floormen. Shift managers staring at the pit bosses. Assistant casino manager, casino manager, vice president; it went on and on, made you afraid to pick your nose—somebody would be taking pictures, accusing you of snorting, cheating, or dealing.

Wayne Ward let his icy blue eyes drift over toward her like he hadn't seen her before. Like he was being cool.

The truth was, he wasn't bad-looking—for a white man. He was around six feet. She could look him square in his cool blues. Though she'd like to squirt some Windex on those aviator specs covered with fingerprints set on his pointy nose. He wore his wavy brown hair long, like a girl's.

Parted in the middle, it hung down in his bony face. He was too skinny for her taste, jeans just barely holding on. Gloria liked a man who weighed in at about two fifty, she didn't have to be afraid she was gonna break him in two.

"Whirly-diddlies." Wayne laughed, snorting at what Gloria had said. Hee-haw. "I like that. Like to whirly-diddle you, Gloria."

Gloria didn't like that kind of talk. Down and dirty was all behind her now. She was a churchgoing lady. "Get out of here," she said. "Get on with you."

"Can't do it. Gotta finish my special assignment."

Wayne always talked like that. Special assignment. Special assistant. She'd noticed that about him before—and the way he wore that little black hat that said *Monopoly Special Staff* on it cocked to one side like he was marching off to war.

If you asked her, the man was too old to be playing soldier. He must be thirty, thirty-five, old as her. Certainly too old to be pretending he was one of Mr. Franken's top assistants, that was for sure.

The men who were numero uno staff, Gloria had seen them, her girls cleaned their rooms when they flew in from Dallas. They all wore nice dark suits.

Not blue work shirts, jeans, tennis shoes. That was Wayne.

Wayne, who she bet was crazy. The way he snorted when he laughed, cold blue eyes wild like a spooked horse. He had to be crazy, or on drugs, which in Gloria's book was more or less the same thing. He talked a lot about magic mushrooms he ate in Mexico. He should have left them to the Mexicans, like jalapeños. They knew how to handle that stuff.

"Yep, Mr. F's gonna like this a lot. Gonna be real proud." Wayne grinned, patting the big tool case he'd been carrying with him everywhere the past week. Like he had something *humongous* in there, was gonna slip to Misses Louisiana, Georgia, New Jersey, Texas, and West Virginia stacked right under one another in 1705, 1605, 1505, 1405, 1205—all in suites done in pale blue.

Then Wayne stopped in front of 1801.

Gloria didn't have to look at her room chart. That was

that nice newspaperwoman from Atlanta, Miz Adams, Harpo, her cute little dog, and her cute young man. That Adams woman had herself some good taste. The fact was, Gloria had already walked Harpo once. Miz Adams said she'd 'preciate it if she did, paid her five dollars for each time, twenty-five in advance, just like she'd passed Go, right on the spot when they'd checked in yesterday and Gloria was working an extra shift. She'd said she and the young man might be too busy to do it sometime, she didn't want to have to worry about him. The dog, she'd laughed, not the young man. He's the one I'd be worried about, Gloria had allowed. Well, don't you go walking him, Miz Adams had popped back with her pretty grin. Gloria told those porters downstairs, Keep away from that animal. Those boys, always bucking for extra tips, didn't know diddle.

Just like her Junior. Boys got to be sixteen, in trouble all the time, smart-mouthy, thought they were men. They made you wanta shoot 'em. Junior was real bright, but he didn't know squat. Twice this month he'd got nabbed shoplifting at Ocean One Mall down the Boardwalk. It was a good thing both times security was somebody she knew. Last time they called her up and said, Gloria, come on down here and get this boy. Send us a check for the $88.95 he owes us for a T-shirt says nasty rap things on it, pair of them Reeboks, cushion your feet, you blow them up.

Gloria was gonna blow something up, all right. Gonna blow up Junior's head.

She was mumbling that very thing to herself earlier this morning when that cute young man of Miz Adams's, call him Harry he said after he'd said good morning, came ambling along the hall with the little dog. Said he'd walk him, he needed a breath of fresh air. Gloria was still muttering to herself about Junior. The next thing she knew, she and Harry are having a sitdown, talking about Louisiana.

She grew up there, in the north part of the state in a little town called Bastrop. It stank like the paper mill. Her father was a carpenter, plumber, electrician, you name it, he could build it or fix it. Mama stayed home, raised the kids, all seven of them. Gloria was the only girl and the youngest. Sometimes Gloria wished she was back, that she'd never run off to Atlantic City when she was a young thing. She'd thought it'd be so cool to live with her aunt Baby and all those Yankees by the ocean.

Harry said he'd been up there, North Louisiana. But he said it the way folks from South Louisiana did, like they were talking about a foreign country. And it was, to them. North Louisiana was full of Baptists, white bread, no fun.

That sure wuddn't New Orleans. New Orleans was where people really *had* themselves a good time, like people in Atlantic City only *imagined* they were. Big Gloria said New Orleans was where she should have moved to, gone to stay with her aunt Beautiful.

Harry said why didn't she. He said he didn't know how she could stand all this ugly, even if it was right on the water.

She said it really did get on her nerves. 'Specially since you get one block behind the casinos, you got nothing but real bad slums. But there she was. She had a job. She had a little house out toward the Inlet she'd papered and painted and fixed up. You get situated in a place, even one terrible as this, you know folks, work in your church, it's hard to leave. And then there was Junior, her boy, the one's driving her crazy.

Harry'd said, Give me a dollar, Gloria. I'm going to earn you a stake to get you outta here, back home.

Get on with you, she'd said.

You'll be sorry if you don't. I'm a mean motorscooter when it comes to blackjack.

Now, thinking about Harry, it was like she conjured him up. Here he came again, just seconds after crazy Wayne swiveled a hip, feinted, let himself with his master key into 1803, that Mr. Kurt Roberts's room, who was a pageant judge.

"Did we win?" Gloria hollered down the hall.

Harry raised a little white baseball cap he was wearing, said Miss America Pageant on it. He waved it in the air like a cowboy, leaned his head back, and laughed, showing lots of pretty white teeth. That cap looked a lot better on him than

Wayne's Special Staff hat did on that goon. But anything'd look good on Harry, above that handsome face, those pink cheeks. She even liked the way his left eyelid drooped, just a little. It was kind of sexy, what with those steel-gray eyes.

"Won us a little bundle at the blackjack table. Sure did," said Harry. "And I tell you what, Gloria. I'm going to give you half of it to hold on to for us. So there's no way I'll lose everything, if Lady Luck deserts us and I go berserk." He handed her two hundred eighty dollars. "That's half of what I won, and half of that's yours to keep for good."

"Are you nuts? Why do you want to do this?"

"'Cause you're homefolks," said Harry. "And I think what homefolks got to do is stick together when they're out in the cold and cruel like this. We keep going this way, we'll get you and your Junior back to God's country by the end of the week. And that's a promise."

Inside 1803, Wayne Ward was hard at work. He was sweating like a pig even with the air-conditioning. Rooms like this made him nervous. Fancy drapes, pillows, cushions, knickknacks, carved woodwork, patterns—it was too much. There were too many things you couldn't control.

Of course, it was perfect for hiding things, which was only one of Wayne's many talents.

He was very clever about hiding things. Tiny state-of-the-art cameras tucked into the china cabinet at one end, a lamp at the other, constantly surveyed the living room. They worked even in the dark. He'd tucked more cameras in the bedroom (in the chandelier, bed canopy) and the bathroom (behind a two-way mirrored panel). The cameras fed videotape recorders and also projected live onto monitors in Wayne's studio. A couple of them needed a little fine tuning, which was one of the things he had come to do.

The phone taps were easy. The reception on the recording devices was perfect.

But not until today had he finished with his pet project. He *loved* implanting subliminal messages. It was really cool, and it was a miracle the things you could get people to do!

Wayne knew the subliminal business up one side and

down the other, which came in *awfully* handy if you're in the casino business. You plugged in "Play, play, play. Stay, stay, stay." Those suckers *never* went to bed, stayed up gambling forty-eight hours straight.

Where he'd refined subliminals was with Mr. F's FrankFairs. What you did was mix the words right into the stores' music track: "I am an honest person. I do not steal." You could cut down shrinkage, which is to say stealing, by one hell of a lot. Using subliminals along with the closed-circuit TV monitors and the TellTags, you could bump down your shrinkage twenty percent. You could bump *up* your sales, too, if you weren't too uptight. All you had to do was feed 'em things like, "Great sale in housewares. Stock up now." It worked like a dream.

'Course, it worked too when you fooled around. "I gotta go to the bathroom bad. Now." Wayne was up there in the control room of a store in Philly laughing like crazy until they figured it out. Mr. F had seen the humor of it, too. He had a good laugh, but he then took off those little round glasses he wore along with his Stetson, wiped them, looked real serious, and said, Wayne, it's funny, but it's not cost effective.

Wayne saw his point. All those customers running stiff-legged, knocking each other down to get to the rest rooms, they used toilet paper, soap, water, paper towels, cleaning services. The list went on and on. It was amazing.

But then, that was the kind of thing that made Mr. Franken who he was: Not just your run-of-the-mill casino-hotel owner, but king of the discount stores in the whole United States too. The world, actually. The Japanese couldn't get enough of him, and first day they'd knocked a hole in that Berlin Wall, he'd hit those Commies so fast with FrankFairs it'd made their heads spin. The Wall of China was next.

Wayne truly loved Mr. F, who, though only ten years Wayne's senior, was his daddy and his mama and his teacher and the Baby Jesus all rolled into one. No one else had ever been as kind to him. Certainly not his daddy, who'd split months before he and his twin brother John popped out of the chute. John, beating him by forty-five minutes, would always be Mom's favorite. Wayne never would catch up. *Fraternal* twins, Mom was always careful to say, like Wayne didn't have any feelings.

Mr. F never said things like that. He always called Wayne his right-hand man—which meant a lot, considering that Mr. F *really* didn't have one, right hand or right arm, that is. He'd picked Wayne up when he was down, recognized his skills and his innate human worth. Mr. F was very big on that, people's innate human worth.

Though Wayne had been a little worried lately about what Mr. Franken thought Dougie was worth. Mr. F's nephew Dougie was one of those suit-wearing jerks. He drove a BMW and thought a brand-spanking-new MBA meant he owned the world. He was sucking up to Mr. F the minute he hit the scene, fresh from Wharton. Wharton School of *Business,* he said. It made Wayne nervous. Mr. F couldn't have *two* right-hand men. One would have to be left. And *left-hand* meant left behind. Hind tit. Wayne had had enough of that with brother John.

That was why he was so set on making *this* a good job. He'd show Mr. F. You wanted a big job done right, you sent Wayne Ward. No smarty-pants MBA didn't know his butt from East Jesus. Period. End of discussion.

Out in the hall, Harry had just finished telling Gloria how he'd won the five hundred and sixty dollars in no time flat at blackjack—starting with drawing a pair of aces and splitting them to bet two red chips on each—when Wayne came sidling out of 1803. Gloria watched him absentminded-like reach back and jiggle the knob of 1801, Harry and Miz Adams's room.

Then Gloria watched the smile on Harry's face fade. "Hey, buddy," he said. "What exactly do you think you're doing?"

Gloria kept waiting for Harpo, who must be inside the room, to bark. Wayne wouldn't know he weighed only twelve pounds. Maybe he'd think he was a German shepherd.

"Don't think nothing, *buddy.*" Wayne put a little English on the word just to show Harry. Then Wayne gave him a shoulder and pushed on by.

Exactly what Gloria thought: Wayne was stupid *and* rude.

"Now, wait a minute." That was Harry. Wayne had pissed him off, Gloria could tell. The color in Harry's cheeks was glowing bright red now. He followed Wayne down the hall.

"Excuse me, excuse me."

Those words came from behind Gloria. She turned and saw this short white woman with a real pretty face like a Kewpie doll, big turquoise eyes, pale lips outlined dark. She was wearing a leopard print jumpsuit that was holding on real tight to her healthy chest with its paws. Her all whicha-colored hair was pulled up in a little curly thing on top, swished over in a big wave at the front.

The woman said in a little-girl voice, "I wonder if you could help me?"

Gloria had heard rich white ladies—most of them who stayed in this hotel were, rich, that is—talk like that before. Like they were helpless. The truth was, most of them were about as helpless as Godzilla once they got their minds on something they wanted.

Now, what was this one studying?

On down the hall, Harry said, "Man, I'm warning you. I'm going to call security right this minute."

Gloria thought Harry had made the right decision. He didn't want to lay his hands on Wayne. Wayne didn't have it in him to fight fair. Gloria figured him to have a switchblade tucked somewhere. That seemed about his speed.

"I *am* security, bub," Wayne announced.

"And *I'm* the Jolly Green Giant."

Miss Kewpie Doll pointed at the door of 1805. *"I'm* supposed to be meeting Miss New Jersey here."

See? thought Gloria. Rich white woman knew exactly what she wanted, no matter that the two men were about to tear into each other like a pair of pit bulls.

Turning her head this way and that, Gloria had about all she could handle following the three of them like they were playing Ping-Pong. It was a good thing that the old man who'd been there earlier looking for Mr. Roberts was gone. She'd *really* have her hands full.

"But there's no answer," Kewpie went on. "I'm a pageant hostess. You know, we help the girls with whatever they need, run errands for the pageant officials, some of us work as chaperones. I need to leave her something. Do you think you could let me in?"

Gloria thought the woman must think she was a fool. She must be some new reporter who'd dolled herself up, trying to get the inside scoop. Those pageant hostesses, couple of hundred white lady volunteers from the AC area, Absecon, some from down to Avalon, Stone Harbor, ran a tighter ship than even hotel security. They'd have all the room numbers memorized and besides, they'd know no hotel staff, nobody else for that matter, was letting anybody *near* those girls.

"Which room did you say?" Gloria asked it real polite, putting her on, knowing the TV cameras right up there in what looked like the sprinklers were recording her on tape. Audio and video both.

"Room 1805." Now Miss Kewpie was looking kind of flustered—like *that* was going to cut some ice. She scrabbled through her purse. "I think I have the right number. Maybe it was 1803? Or 1802? I think it was 1802."

"What exactly do you want with Miss New Jersey, ma'am?" Gloria asked, thinking this was her day. Here Harry was earning her a grubstake, for no good reason except the Lord must have sent him, all her praying at the Community Baptist Church down at the Inlet. Now this silly white lady and that stupid Wayne were taking her mind off her troubles. Junior. Aunt Baby in the hospital. Car payment overdue.

At that, Miss Kewpie bolted. She got up a pretty good speed on her, too, considering those high-heeled sandals. She disappeared through the stair door marked Exit like the devil was on her tail.

Back in the other direction, Harry was yelling at Wayne. "I think you're a hotel burglar, that's what I think."

Nawh, Gloria was about to tell him. Wayne's lots of

things, but I don't think he's that, when Wayne hauled off and punched Harry right in the mouth.

Awwwwh, thought Big Gloria. Such a pretty mouth too.

Harry reeled back and put up his dukes, but before he could do any good, Wayne turned tail and ran right down to the other fire door and disappeared.

"You dirty rotten bastard!" Harry shouted.

He looked just like Junior when he was little, having a temper tantrum, thought Gloria.

Harry was cute as heck when he was mad.

That was a thought Sam had had more than once, though Gloria didn't know that. Gloria also didn't know that Harry was *really* mad with himself because it hurt his pride to get sandbagged like that. If there was one thing his friends like Lavert Washington had taught him when Harry was the Only White Boy at Grambling was how to handle himself in a tight spot.

Losing it, man, was what Harry thought. You turned thirty, fell in love, your reflexes turned to mush.

Oh, yeah, Harry thought. Miss Samantha had herself a couple of warriors, all right. A silly little dog who wouldn't bark if Attila the Hun were at the door. And a slow boyfriend with a busted lip.

It was a good thing there was nothing on their agenda heavier than hanging out and making love, lying on the beach, watching a bunch of young things twitch their fannies up and down a runway while Sam took a few notes—or so he thought.

...3

SAM WAS LOUNGING POOLSIDE ON THE ROOF OF THE MONOPOLY, waiting for Harry. Halfway through the afternoon of the first day of this nonsense, and already she needed a break. Following the press conference, she'd interviewed Rae Ann

Bridges—Miss Georgia, Hoke's flame, and the raison d'être for her being there in Wackoland. The intensity of these people was unbelievable. They were serious as death about this beauty business. It was pretty terrifying.

Take the press conference. She was still feeling like a fool, playing contestant before the entire press corps.

"Now you understand," Eloise Lemon, the former Miss America, had said after they'd whisked Sam out of the pressroom, brought her back, and watched her plunk herself down (she lost points right there) in a straight-backed chair facing the judges, "this would be a smaller space with thousands of TV lights and a passel of other people watching. Hello, Samantha."

"Hello." Sam had giggled. *Giggled!* She winced now at the memory. And then the barrage had begun.

If you had to balance the national budget today, how would you approach it?

Why do so few women run for high political office?

You're from a border state with thousands of illegal aliens crossing. What to do?

Solutions to the AIDS crisis?

The savings and loan scandal?

The press's responsibility to watchdog the president and Congress?

Participating in the Miss America Pageant, so frivolous in the face of the Middle East crisis?

The most interesting book you have read recently, and why?

Public education in shambles?

The single most important event in the history of man?

Would you rather interview George Burns or George Bush, and why?

And so on. Even for a reporter who kept up, this wasn't easy. As Sam had leapfrogged from one question to the next, she'd asked herself, How do those airheads *do* this? Then, "Time!" and it was over. Her peers had cheered and stomped their feet. Maybe she hadn't been a complete washout.

Just outside the door, Mimi Bregman, the judge in the red

tent dress, had patted her on the shoulder. "At least an eight."

"Eight? A nine!" Sam had protested. But that was bravado.

"Let me buy you a drink, *I'll* give you a ten." That had been Kurt Roberts, right in her face.

Mimi had looked down her nose at him. No love lost there. And there'd been that question Miss A had powered right at him. What gave?

"Mr. Roberts has his *own* agenda," Mimi answered.

Oh, really? Handsy with the girls? Pressing them for favors? Was there scandal in the wind?

"He's a little forward, that's all." Mimi had squeezed Sam's arm good-bye and escaped to join the other judges—they traveled in a pack—and Barbara Stein, who'd been giving Mimi the eye.

Poolside now, Sam thought about Kurt Roberts while she scanned the contestants' headshots in the Official Miss America Pageant Program. Which one was Roberts bird-dogging? The blondes all looked alike. How could he decide? Or maybe he didn't. Maybe he just hit them up scattershot, working the percentages.

Like Hoke. Sam had once heard him say to a young reporter on the sports desk, Don't bother with fancy lines. Just keep asking, You wanta do it? You'll get lucky, you give it enough time.

Sam looked down at the picture of Miss Georgia. Miss Rae Ann Bridges, she said to the blue-eyed blonde's big smile, is that what Hoke asked you when they voted you Miss Dogwood Festival? *Wanta do it?*

She doubted it. The young lady whom she'd interviewed for the first time immediately after the press conference was hardly the Wanta Do It type.

Rae Ann had waved at her from the bench on the Boardwalk where they'd agreed to meet. She was shaking hands and signing autographs for passersby. Even prettier than her picture, she had those Dresden-doll looks—peach and cream and baby-blue eyes—you found only in southern girls. Rae Ann never stopped smiling, and she *touched* each person.

"It's just all been one big whirl," she'd gushed. "Since I won Miss Dogwood Festival, I've made over two hundred personal appearances. It's been wonderful practice for coming here, meeting all those people, sharpening my speaking skills. I tried out different hairdos and makeup each time, and also it's been a chance for me to witness."

Witness what?

Rae Ann's face glowed even brighter. "So many people don't understand about the pageant system. They think it's just a beauty contest, but physical beauty is the least of it." Her chaperone, a pageant hostess decked out head to toe in navy and green sports togs, nodded.

Uh-huh. Sure. So what was this about makeup and hairdos?

"Now, physical beauty is *part* of it." Someone had coached away much of Rae Ann's Georgia accent, but she still, once she warmed up, underlined and raised the inflection at the end of her sentences. "Just like Queen Esther, in the *Bible,* rose from obscurity to hold the most *prominent* position a woman could in her land, based *in part* on what she looked like? She, and all the other girls, were bathed and perfumed and adorned and taught good manners, and then the king *chose* among them for his queen? But once this *Hebrew* girl got to be *queen,* she not only got jewels, and a crown, and fame, and a palace, but she had a *forum* to *speak* from, a way to *express* herself and *help* others? If her *own* ideas didn't conflict with title regulations."

Sam, scribbling all the while, couldn't believe the great material. Great, sure, but for what? She couldn't make fun of Miss Georgia in the *Constitution.* She'd be lynched. "And what do *you* want to talk about?"

"I am a *role model* for young American women who have terrible obstacles to overcome—and there are *so* many of them out there?" Rae Ann gestured behind her at the Atlantic Ocean. "The *whole* purpose of the pageant is to promote *professional* and *personal* development for American women, and if *I* haven't developed professionally and personally, I don't know who has?"

It was some story. Miss Georgia dug in, ignoring her hostess, who was tapping her watch. Rae Ann carefully crossed her legs at the ankle, locked her hands on her thighs to avoid unnecessary hand motions, and poured out her heart.

You see, Rae Ann had started out as a pretty little girl who loved pretty things. Her mother, who had been widowed when her father's helicopter went down in Vietnam, didn't have much, but she was good at making do, and she made all Rae Ann's clothes. By the time Rae Ann was six, she was sewing too, and designing her own little dresses. In the fourth grade she made herself six dotted swiss outfits in one year: pink, baby blue, yellow, red, green, and all white.

When she was ten, her mother got married again, to a violent alcoholic, and within six months Rae Ann began to suffer his physical abuse.

"I didn't know how to tell my mother, and she was so much in love with him, I didn't want to break her heart, so I used the only weapon I could."

A gun, thought Sam. You shot him and did time. Can a convicted felon be Miss America? Even with just cause?

No, it was fat. She ballooned, thinking if she were ugly, he'd leave her alone. But that didn't work. When she was up to two hundred fifty pounds at fifteen and he still cornered her and beat her every chance he got, she ran away from home. An aunt in Valdosta took her in.

What she did for the next three years was sit and stare at the TV and eat. "My life was nothing but fried fast food, gallons of Coca-Cola, crocheting afghans, painting-by-the-numbers, 'Donahue' and 'Geraldo.' It made me feel a little better sometimes to see people on TV whose lives I thought were as bad as mine. Except most of them were skinnier than I was. And not nearly as young.

"Then one day I was flipping the channels with the remote—I never stood up unless I had to—and there was Cheryl Prewitt Salem on the religious channel, talking right at me from Tulsa, Oklahoma. Talking about the Lord and how He'd saved her. Had given her the courage to try over and over in beauty pageants, overcoming physical disabilities, to become Miss America.

"She gave me the courage to get up off that sofa, lose the weight, find my pretty self again and make myself some pretty clothes, get my GED, go on to junior college and get a design degree. And she gave me the courage to speak to groups of girls all over the South about abuse and what it can do *to* you. About God and what He can do *for* you.

"It took me three tries to win a local pageant before I won Miss Dogwood Festival. Then I took six months to prepare myself, along with all the wonderful people who've helped me and believed in me, to become Miss Georgia. And now I'm determined to win Miss America, so that I can have *that* platform to help girls from."

Not to mention the two hundred thousand dollars in personal appearance fees Miss A could expect to earn during her reign. But to mention lucre in the midst of all this beatitude seemed rude.

"The glamour side of the pageant business is great, but my biggest goal is to help others like Cheryl and God helped me. I hope I can make a positive mark on America and on the world.

"And, like Cheryl Prewitt Salem, I want to give something back to the pageant system. I want to witness for pageants as well as for the Lord. So, I know that whether I become Miss America or not, what I'll eventually end up doing, as *part* of my work at least, is designing pageant dresses for girls. There are lots of people who do that already, but I know that I could do a wonderful job for them."

Rae Ann's smile was as bright as a Broadway marquee, and real tears danced in her eyes. Sam was dizzy. Were they all like this?

"Beauty, pretty dresses, sexual abuse, helping others, I would never limit myself to one area," Miss Georgia continued. "We are one hundred percent responsible for the outcome of our entire lives. We, and God, who's written the script. Now, we can do the best we possibly can by looking into our own hearts and souls to make that script a good one, or we can take a peek over God's shoulder at the master script He's written for us and follow that one.

"We need to triumph over circumstances. We need to learn to look *down* on those circumstances from above."

Naw. Poolside, Sam closed the program on Rae Ann's smile. *Wanta do it?* wasn't the way to go with this girl. Sam couldn't wait to hear her sing tonight. "Don't Cry Out Loud" was her big number. Cheryl Ann Prewitt had won Miss America with it in 1980. It had already proved lucky for Rae Ann in the Miss Dogwood Festival and Miss Georgia. She was counting on it one more time.

A shadow fell across Sam's deck chair. "Hi!"

She jumped. She'd been visualizing Rae Ann on that big stage just like Rae Ann herself did every night before she said her prayers and went to sleep. It was only Harry. But what was wrong with his lip?

Before she could ask, someone was hailing her from across the pool.

"Hello, there. Hello!" It was Kurt Roberts over at the outdoor bar. Wearing his perpetual tan and white swim trunks, Roberts looked like he spent years in the gym. He would. "Doing your homework?"

Sam nodded, with a pained smile. What a jerk. Harry, still standing with his injured lip curled into a tight little grin, glanced at Roberts, then back at her. He didn't look happy.

"Do you like my picture?" Roberts was *so* loud. "It's in the program."

Sam shook her head, rolled her eyes at Harry.

"Your new best friend?"

"A judge. A real turkey." She took his hand. "What the heck happened to your lip, sweetie?"

He flopped down in the chair beside her. "I ran into a door."

"Kurt! Kurt!" That was Cindy Lou Jacklin, his fellow

judge, waving from the entrance to the pool. She was a long drink of water in a baby-blue bikini beneath an open man's shirt, those Miss Ohio curves hanging in there like she was still a contender.

Kurt crooked a finger at Cindy from his barstool, patted the seat beside him. Cindy Lou jogged over, wriggling with gratitude.

Sam looked back to Harry. "Now, this story about your lip. Why do I not believe you?"

"Because you're a very suspicious woman. Hey, I talked with Lavert. He's coming in tonight in time for the show."

"You're changing the subject."

"You noticed. What do you think that means?"

"You're embarrassed that I let you out of my sight for a couple of hours and you got into a barroom brawl."

"God, you're so good. And perceptive."

"You're not going to tell me."

"And smart."

They grinned at each other, Harry wincing. His lip *hurt*. Then a man behind them yelled, "Hey! *You!* Jerkoff! If it's not too much trouble, could we get a little service over here?"

The young waiter stopped dead in his tracks. Fury stained his cheeks.

Harry licked his cut lip and knew just how he felt.

Sam recognized the speaker's voice even before she turned. If you'd ever heard it once, you had it.

Sure enough, it was Bill Carroll with "The Big One!!!!"—the TV game show host. The man couldn't have been five-five even with his lifts. He was wearing flip-flops poolside.

Sam had met him once in San Francisco at a museum benefit. Her impression then: She'd rather buy her used cars from Richard Nixon.

"Billy!" the woman at the table with Carroll snapped. "You don't have to be so rude."

The look Carroll shot at the woman said he'd like to give her the back of his hand.

Sam saw that even when he did a quick turn like that, Billy Carroll's hair didn't move. Did he take off his blond-gray helmet when he got in bed, or did it stay that way when he bounced around?

Of course, with Billy's attitude, his wife probably didn't go in much for bouncing—at least with Billy. Now, *she* was quite something in her gold lamé swimsuit. She sported megadiamonds on her fingers and wrists. And she was wearing high-heeled sandals and lots of makeup. You hardly ever saw anybody with that look anymore—pale lipstick, dark lip liner, multicolored hair twisted up into curls on top, falling in a wave over one eye à la Betty Grable—except in LA. But your eyes didn't stay on her face long. They slid down to her chest, her nice little fanny, still-good legs, brightly painted toes.

"I hope you two aren't going to start." That had to be the daughter. Take the mother back to fifteen, dress her all in black, make her up like Vampira, tease her frosted blond hair out to Delaware.

Sam knew the waiter thought the daughter was quite something, even if her father was a horse's patoot. He was shifting from one foot to the other, standing there.

"We're not gonna start. We're gonna eat." Then Billy Carroll chuckled.

"It's the laugh track on TV," Harry said out of the corner of his mouth. "Makes him think he's really funny."

"Since when do you watch daytime TV?"

"You'd be amazed what I have to do when I'm tailing somebody." Harry was still working part-time for his uncle Tench as an insurance investigator while he and Lavert put together their restaurant. "I've caught his show. He sucks eggs. You want some more water when this young man gets the use of himself?"

But their waiter had taken the Carrolls' order and dematerialized. Harry said he'd go get his beer and her San Pellegrino himself.

Sam loved watching Harry walk. He had an athlete's broad-shouldered, strong-legged gait. Not too cocky, but like he knew where he was going, knew how to get there. He knew how to get to her, that was for sure.

Over to her right, the Carrolls began warming up again.

"So, are you going to see her?"

"Darleen, I'm warning you."

"Well, are you?"

"It's nothing. I told you."

"You always say that."

"We were just talking."

"Standing and moving to the music. I'd call that dancing."

"Okay, we were dancing. What's wrong with that?"

"They're not supposed to be dancing. They're supposed to be locked in their rooms getting their beauty sleep. They're not even supposed to be talking to men."

"You're crazy, Darleen. They can *talk.* And I'm TV, for Christ's sake. They *know* me."

"TV. Ha! Does that mean you checked your dick at the desk?"

"Darleen!"

"I'm outta here." That was the daughter.

"Sit down, Rachel Rose! You're not going anywhere." Billy Carroll was wrong. The daughter was already strolling off to the left down toward Jail, not even pausing for Just Visiting. The whole Monopoly board was reproduced in tile around the pool. Rachel Rose turned the corner, headed up toward the bar, Free Parking.

"You could have left it downstairs, for all *I* know." Darleen wasn't going to drop the subject.

"What?!"

"Your dick, darling."

"Would you stop? I told you we're just friends."

"I find that difficult to believe since you have zero, zilch, no, *nada, niente* buddies, Billy. So now you're practicing the art of friendship with a twenty-two-year-old girl with great lungs? Puh-leeze. Give me a break."

Over at the bar, Harry was signing a check, nodding at Kurt Roberts, who was saying something to him. Cindy Lou tossed in her two bits. Laughing, she threw her head back, all the while holding on for dear life to Roberts's arm. Rachel Rose was walking very slowly with her cute little body in a black bikini, chewing gum, pulling even.

Just about then a gorgeous black youngster, Sam would put him at about sixteen, skated into the pool area at the entrance designated B&O Railroad. Wearing black spandex shorts and nothing else but his bright red rollerblades and a headful of braids, he was *built* for a kid. Rachel Rose stopped dead in her tracks, only her jaws moving.

Harry nodded to the kid, then started past him. Cindy Lou leaned over, her breasts leading, and said something to the kid, who grinned and answered. Whatever he said, Roberts didn't like it. He came off his barstool, arms waving.

Harry was still moving away with his back to the action.

Rachel Rose was into it now, laying some opinions on Roberts, stabbing a little hand with lacquered black nails in the air for punctuation.

The kid said something else, was backing off, or was he? With the skates to-ing and fro-ing, it was hard to tell. The kid was off balance now. He reached out to steady himself.

Roberts grabbed him like he was helping him straighten up, but no, he wasn't. He gave the kid a big push. The kid rolled right off into the deep water. *Kersplash.* Then nothing but bubbles.

Sam's head snapped up toward the lifeguard's chair. It was empty. He'd gone to grab a soda, call his girlfriend, tell her some lies.

The kid was well over his head, weighted down by his skates, and who knew if he could swim anyway?

Harry had turned around at the splash and Rachel Rose's yelp. Now he squatted, lowered his beer and Sam's bottled water to the pool apron, and then, continuing in one graceful motion, dived in from the side. He hardly made a ripple.

One, one thousand, two, two thousand, three, three thousand, four, four thousand, five, five thousand, six, six thousand, seven, seven thousand, Sam counted the seconds, then Harry and the kid were back on top, the kid snuggled in a life-saving hold, but fighting.

And it was all over but the shouting.

The lifeguard raced up. He and Harry turned the kid over. One, two, up came the water—and lunch.

Cindy Lou was yelling something at Roberts.

Rachel Rose was right in his face. "You could have killed him, you big bully! Why don't you pick on somebody your own age? Are you crazy?"

Darleen raced around the other side of the pool, passing Go, but not stopping for her two hundred dollars. Now she had her hands on her daughter's shoulders. "Come on, Rachel Rose!"

"Jesus Christ!" muttered Billy Carroll, still beside Sam, watching the action. He and his hair hadn't moved. "Jesus H. Christ. If it's not one thing, it's another. They hear about this, my sponsors, they'll hate it. Notoriety is not good."

The kid was coming around with Rachel Rose down on her pretty knees bent over him. She was saying something to him, then looking back up with stars in her eyes.

Roberts, white-faced, stalked away with Cindy Lou following.

And here was Harry, dripping wet, holding two drinks on a small tray. "Your San Pellegrino, signorina." He bowed.

"Bravissimo." She reached up and gave him a big kiss, remembering at the last minute to be careful of his lip. "You're a hero, Harry."

Harry shrugged off the compliment, but now he felt a lot better about having taken the sucker punch in the lip.

Over at the other side of the pool, two plainclothes security men and a hotel manager were talking with the roller-skater who was sitting in a chair now, swaddled in hotel towels. One of them was taking notes. Rachel Rose was still hanging in there, explaining ninety miles a minute how it all happened, while her mother was trying to tear her away. The skater said something, and the three men broke up laughing. Then one patted the boy on the shoulder, closed his notebook. It looked as if they knew him. Another was reaching for his walkie-talkie, speaking into it.

"Maybe they'll send for the cops, arrest that Kurt Roberts for attempted manslaughter," said Sam.

"I doubt it. It'd look bad for the hotel. They'll call it an accident, since nobody was hurt."

"He's *such* a creep."

Harry read her face carefully. "Did he say something to you, Sammy?"

She looked at his bruised lip and then at his hand, which he'd scraped on the bottom of the pool. He hadn't even noticed it was bleeding. No, she didn't need to tell Harry that Kurt Roberts came on to all the ladies. Not today.

Over at the other side of the pool a woman Sam knew had joined the security men, the manager, and the youngster. Sam watched them over Harry's shoulder for a minute and then said to him, "You know what happens when you save somebody's life, babe?"

"They live."

"The Chinese believe you're responsible for them forever. So I guess old Malachy Champion's responsible for me and you're responsible for that young man."

"No way. Besides, I didn't do that much. If I hadn't jumped in, someone else would have."

"I don't think Gloria thinks so."

Harry turned to see what Sam meant and came nose to nose with Big Gloria, who grabbed him up in a bear hug.

"I don't know how to thank you," she cried. "You've already been so generous—" Her voice broke. "And now saving my Junior's life. But I will repay you! I will!"

. . . 4

WAYNE LOVED SITTING IN HIS STUDIO IN FRONT OF ALL THE monitors. The third floor of the Monopoly, Action Central, that's what he called it.

He had eight screens going. On a table in front of him, three double cheeseburgers were lined up along with a large order of fries and a half gallon of cola. Wayne really loved pop. And a superlarge box of Cracker Jacks. He couldn't wait for the prize, but work came first.

He'd already reviewed the stuff from that morning through early afternoon. There hadn't been anything useful. The cameras were triggered by motion in the rooms. So there were the maids, making beds, cleaning bathrooms. That was a waste. But he couldn't rig to timers, because you couldn't tell when the guests might pop in and out.

Eighteen oh one, the man was shaping up to be a player—the one he'd punched in the mouth. Wayne grinned at the memory of his fist connecting. The room was registered originally to the tall brunette. The little dog and the boyfriend were extra. She was worth watching, for sure. But the dog was a real pain in the ass. Twisting, turning, twitching even in his sleep, setting off the camera. There he went, up for a drink of water, over to the floor-length window. Short little sucker, what did he think he was gonna see? A Mighty Dog train pulling into town? Wayne laughed at his own joke. Now the dog was rolling over. Licking himself. Bor*ing*.

Then, uh-oh, middle of the afternoon, here comes the brunette. Had the boyfriend told her somebody had been fiddling with their room? Naw, she didn't have that look about her, like she was afraid, paranoid, checking things out. Nope, she swooped in, big smile on her face, talking to that stupid little dog, kissing him, then talking to herself in the mirror. Kind of strutting back and forth like *she* was Miss America.

A little old, honey. Not bad, but hidey, hidey, ho. What was she up to? All *right!* Changing clothes. Off with the skirt, the blouse, keep going. Not bad. Absolutely not bad at all for a broad with a couple years on her.

Oh, *yeah!* Now, *that* was more like it. Off, off, take it all off, honey. Bonanza! Uh-huh. What now? Want to parade around a little while? Nope. Into the bathroom. No problem. Wayne punched a button and the bathroom camera switched in. There she was, turning on the shower. No time for a long soak in the big tub, honey? Too bad—and too bad about the shower door. It was clear, not frosted, but the water and the steam clouded it just enough so he couldn't get a clear shot.

Then out, toweling, baboom, baboom, slipping into that pretty red swimsuit. Gonna knock 'em dead at the pool, honey. Go get 'em. Why don't you take that squirmy little dog out there with you?

A little while later, there'd been some even better stuff in 1803.

A twofer: 1803 and 1805.

Not combining their suites. They *could* have if they'd had the keys to the door between them. But rooms wasn't what they were interested in joining.

They did it in 1803, his room. He stormed in first, slamming the door open. He was mad as hell about something, but not saying a word. Eighteen oh five jawing a mile a minute. "Kurt, honey." Wayne could read her lips. He could have turned the volume up and heard every word. But he had the audio recorded anyway.

It was a little game Wayne liked to play, watching with the sound turned off, trying to figure it out. He was pretty good at it, usually. Especially when the actors, that's how he thought of them, actors playing out scenes just for him, were really into it. When they weren't talking about something dumb, like the stock market.

There was nothing like that on 1805's mind. No sirree. She was a real tall, pretty woman, nice set hanging out of her little blue bikini top, pleading with 1803, "I didn't mean it. I was just joking." She followed him into the bedroom.

Eighteen oh three was playing the tough guy. Quiet. Not a word. The Sly Stallone part. She pulled on his arm. He flung her off and gave her a stiff arm, just to make sure. She landed on the bed. Big boo-hoo. Sly stepped into the head and slammed the door.

Wayne flicked on the bathroom camera, just to make sure. There was nothing happening, except that Sly wasn't the least bit upset, playacting in the bedroom, checking himself out in the mirror. He got up real close so he could see his pores. Gave himself a big smile. Looked this way and that, right profile, then left. He ran his hand over his jaw, feeling a couple of days' growth. Winked at himself, deciding to leave it. Then he peeled off his white trunks and headed for the shower. Wayne switched back to the bedroom.

Miss Boo-Hoo had gotten ahold of herself. She was over at the dresser with her big bag, pulling out her makeup. Pat pat, slick, lick. Polishing herself up.

That was the one thing you noticed about these people this week. All of them were good-looking, well, almost all of them, and dead set on staying that way. Wayne could understand the girls, that's why they were there, but the judges? Go figure. Maybe whatever the girls had, it was catching.

Anyway, Miss Boo-Hoo finished with her lipstick. Checked her teeth. Fluffed up her hair. Adjusted herself in her swimsuit. Got 'em just how she wanted 'em, checked herself out back and front, looked down, picked up 1803's red judging binder. Flipped through a few pages. Flopped down in a chair to take a closer look.

Wayne zoomed in. He wanted to look too. It wasn't every day you saw something like this.

Wasn't this great? He could read every word: Homecoming queen. Graduate nursing school. 23, 5′7″, 117.

Now here came trouble slouching back into the bedroom like Mr. Cool. He was wearing a towel and carrying something in one hand, kind of hidden behind him. Wayne couldn't quite see it from this angle.

Damn! There was 1801 and that stupid little mutt. Now 1801 was making a phone call. Should he listen in? Naw. The tape'd get it.

But back to 1803. They were laying across the bed. Hadn't pulled the covers back. He had her all snuggled up. They were flipping through the red binder.

Look at *that* dog, he was saying. Ahwooooo! Flipped a couple more. Now, *that's* more like it. Who's this blonde? Miss New Jersey. She looks a little like you, Cindy Lou. He reached over and gave her boobs a lift. Or like you *used* to.

She swatted him one. She does not!

Then they were fooling around too much for him to read their lips. This could be important. Wayne flipped the volume up.

Sly was still turning pages, looking at girls.

I *like* her, Cindy Lou said, pointing at a titian-haired beauty with big brown eyes. I think she's got it. I gave her a ten in the interview.

Sly shook his head. No way.

Old Cindy Lou wasn't giving up. Listen to me, Kurt, she said. I *know* what I'm talking about. This girl's got it. She tapped the picture again.

He still wasn't buying it. Give me a break. The state's had too many winners. And look at that mole.

Cindy Lou rolled her eyes. It's a beauty mark. Don't you know anything? Don't you know that model Cindy Crawford, Madonna? Beauty marks are *in*.

He grabbed her by the arm. Don't tell me, you stupid twat. Modeling? You're talking about my business. And you don't know diddle. I wouldn't vote for this girl if she were the last piece on earth. You like her? Then *I'm* giving her all ones. Cancel you out. She'll never make ten.

Cindy Lou pouted. It looked to Wayne like something she had practiced a lot. I don't think that's fair, Kurt. And I don't think that's any way to talk about a lady. In front of a lady. Especially a lady who made ten herself.

Kurt almost fell off the bed laughing. Lady? Lady! Then he pounced on her. It didn't take but about two seconds for that little blue bikini to hit the floor.

Red lights were flashing on the monitors of 1804, 1806, 1807. Everybody was coming home. Forget 'em, thought Wayne. They could shower, get dressed for dinner by themselves. Tape would get 'em. Wayne wasn't leaving *this* picture show.

Damn. While he looked away, Kurt had already spread-eagled her across the bed, doing it to her. Bam. Bam. She was rolling her head back and forth, saying something. Wayne flipped up the volume some more.

"No, no, no, no. You're hurting me, Kurt."

"You don't know what hurt is, baby. Making a fool of me out there, you sticking your chest in that kid's face like I wasn't even there."

"That was nothing! It was—"

Then he really put it to her. The man was a jackhammer.

"Stop it! Stop it! Let me go!"

"I *told* you I wasn't in the mood. I *told* you I'm into the room downstairs for ten—" As if to emphasize the word, Kurt slapped her with the back of his hand. Cindy Lou's head rolled. "—I don't have. Guy I usually borrow from, I've already tapped for two. *He's* leaning on me. I'm bleeding to death here, Cindy Lou." He slapped her again. "Dice table's killing me. I gotta get out of here. And I *don't* need any more crap from you."

"It's not *my* fault. It's not my *fault.*" She was screaming at the top of her lungs. Cindy Lou was losing it.

"Yeah, and it's not my fault that my building back in New York needs a new elevator either, but who's gonna pay for that? *Somebody's* got to."

"But not *me,* Kurt. Not me."

Kurt was still inside her, still putting it to her, his hands atop her wrists like straps. He leaned his face down real close to hers. "What a disappointment you've turned out to be, Miss Ohio. Miss Used-to-Be. Miss Washed-Up."

That *really* hurt. Cindy Lou started to wail big time, calling Kurt things Wayne had never even heard of. Misogynist? What kind of curse word was that? Motherraper—now, there was one he knew.

That's when Kurt reached behind him and pulled out the thing Wayne couldn't see before. A razor strop. Kurt let her have it good a couple of times before she got her bearings, started fighting back.

And she was a *big* girl. Easily as tall as old Kurt. He probably didn't have ten pounds on her, if that. And she was pretty broad-shouldered. She was giving it to him good.

Wayne was jumping up and down now, shoveling Cracker Jacks so fast he almost ate his prize. Oh boy oh boy oh boy. Wayne knew he'd done good.

Kurt had said exactly the kind of thing Mr. F wanted to know. Wayne was going to hustle it up to him right then. And now this! The man was absolutely going to *love* this show.

. . . 5

AROUND EIGHT, JUST ABOUT THE TIME THE SHOW WAS STARTING over on the big stage, Big Gloria got a call from Clothilde. Clothilde's voice, real tight, said: "Bee Gee, I think you better get on up here to 1803."

Oh, Lord. What was it *now?* She ought not to be here anyway. She ought to be home having some supper with Junior, pretending they were some kind of nuclear family like Bill Cosby on TV, instead of supervising turndown. But, when they asked her, even two days in a row, it was hard to pass up the extra shift. Especially with the car payment due and Junior spending money like it grew on trees.

So what was it now? Another drunk had punched his hand through a wall? That was nothing, but multiply it times six thousand rooms in the casino hotels alone, if she had any sense, she'd be in the dry-wall business. Her daddy and her brothers had taught her how to do all that when she was growing up back in Bastrop.

Of course, it wasn't as if she hadn't tried. People just didn't want to give construction work to a woman, especially a black woman, even if she was as big as Gloria. So here she was, messing around with a bunch of white people's bedsheets.

All the way up in the service elevator Big Gloria was thinking about how much she loved getting her hands on a bunch of brand-new two-by-fours, the clean, piney smell of them reminding her of home, of building kitchens with her daddy. It wasn't until the elevator stopped at eighteen that Gloria remembered who was in 1803.

"What you doing out here, girl?" she said to Clothilde, who was standing in the hall staring at her. "Come show me what you're talking about. It couldn't be *that* bad."

It was a mess, though.

. . . 6

SHAME! READ THE PLACARDS, BIG RED LETTERS PRINTED ON white. SHAME!

"Who they?" Harry asked Sam, who didn't know.

The thirty young women carrying the signs shuffled in a single line outside the main doors to the Convention Hall. They were dressed in long robes of brown burlap, and on their chests hung silver crucifixes that looked suspiciously like aluminum foil. The crowd had to pass through them to get inside. Security police were giving the women hard looks.

"Disappointed also-rans?" Harry joked.

Hardly, thought Sam. These pale, grim-faced girls didn't look as if they'd ever practiced their smiles, much less paraded in swimsuits. And none of them were pretty, though, of course, that would be tough, wearing a long potato sack.

Now they were shaking tambourines, shuffling in their single line, chanting: *Shame, shame, shame.*

Chain, chain, chain, Harry sang, taking Sam's hand and juking to the opening words of that oldie.

One of the girls cast her ice-pale eyes on Harry and said, "God sees what you do."

He shivered in mock fright and hurried Sam into the auditorium. There they were sucked into a buzzing, glittering crowd where *no one* wore burlap.

"Who'd of thunk?" Sam stared amazed at men in black tie, women in sequined gowns. Of course there were elderly day-trippers too, who hadn't changed from their ice cream–

colored polyester and sensible shoes. And gangs of New Jersey boys in T-shirts, jeans, and running shoes who'd come to punch one another and leer.

The seating in the mammoth space spread across the floor, up tiers, risers, and then two levels before disappearing into the rafters. They found Harry's seat near the ramp with the Louisiana delegation. His friend Lavert hadn't yet arrived.

Sam was in the press section nearby, directly rampside. The seat itself was of the orange padded plastic 1940s kitchen chair variety, but there was a ledge for her laptop computer and an electrical outlet. The *Inquirer,* on Sam's right, was carrying her own phone.

Sam hadn't realized the girls would have cheering sections. Each state marked its territory with banners and flags. The fans wore huge badges with color photos of their favorite girl trailing red, white, and blue ribbons. Hawaiians boasted orchid leis, Texans were in ten-gallon hats and boots. Alaskans were in furs.

"Some of the state delegations bring a hundred people. So you could easily have five thousand groupies here," the *Inquirer* informed her.

It was hard to believe.

"Oh, they're real enthusiasts. They do pageants instead of football, or gardening, or torturing small animals—whatever it is Americans out there do."

"Look at all the spangles!"

"They're bugle beads." The woman on Sam's left corrected her. "That's what their dresses are done with, hundreds of thousands of hand-sewn bugle beads—just like the girls' gowns. But tonight's nothing. It'll get dressier tomorrow and Thursday, but Saturday's when you see the *really* fancy duds."

The woman's own scarlet suit was aglitter with the dancing lights of intricate beadwork. She had snow-white hair and a beautiful face. She was quite something.

"I'm Sally Griffin." She had a firm handshake. "I'm an image consultant from Raleigh, North Carolina. I just finagled this press seat because I want to see close up what my girls do."

Image consultant? Her girls?

"Sally does figure and wardrobe analysis for pageant contestants," explained the *Inquirer.*

"And interview coaching," added Sally. "I'm full-service. I also recommend speech coaches and designers, hairstylists and makeup artists, and workout coaches for swimsuit. And, of course, I have my pageant workshops."

Workshops?

Sally laughed. "Your first time? Well, most girls are as naive as you when they first enter pageants, but once I get my hands on them, they learn fast. They have to, if they're going to get anywhere in this business. Listen up and work hard, I tell them. I do a workshop on looks, on interview, on first impressions. I also hold one for judges."

Judging school?

"Oh, my, yes. You know, pageant officials and judges want to move up in the rankings, too. You start off as a volunteer on the local level, doing whatever you can to help your pageant, and then after a while you want to go to state. Once you're at the state level, you start to get into the nationwide network of pageant people. And, of course, the ultimate is to judge Miss America.

"For that, you need years of experience, and that extra something, just like the winning girls have, to catch the attention of the judges chairman and make him pick *you.* I've judged and emceed pageants for years. And I used to participate, of course, when I was younger."

Sam looked at Sally carefully as the music rose, the lights lowered.

"I was Miss North Carolina in the Miss America Pageant ages ago." Sally smiled, feeling Sam's scrutiny. "I'm fifty-one." She patted Sam's knee in that way southern women do. "Better to be over the hill than under it. No shame in getting old."

At that, Sam remembered the Shame Girls outside. But it was too late to ask the *Inquirer.* "Here we go!" the young blonde said.

The curtain rose on the Miss America dancers, young men in white pants and white pullovers. In their midst strutted a figure in devilish black.

"Nickie Brasco. He works the casino circuit the rest of the year," the *Inquirer* whispered.

The gentlemen soft-shoed and sang their way through a verse and chorus of "Tonight." Then a back curtain lifted and there they were in all their glory: the Miss America finalists.

The fifty of them sported short, tailored dresses in fuchsia, blue, and off-white, no two dresses quite the same. The girls posed and modeled their way through another chorus and verse of "Tonight," then sang a chorus of "There She Is." They did a quick turn down the runway and back, singing, smiling, waving all the while.

"Let's meet them face-to-face," Brasco called, the signal for the Parade of States to begin from the two sides of the great stage.

"I'm Miss Alabama, Ashley Dunbar, a graduate of Auburn University," announced a big redhead with a booming voice from stage left, then strutted down the runway.

Miss Alaska, a brunette with quite a bounce, declared from stage right that she was "Tricia Lewis, bringing you greetings from the frozen North. I'm a graduate of the University of Washington and a speech therapist." She bounced behind Miss Alabama.

They all had the same walk. The Miss America Suck-and-Tuck Glide, said the *Inquirer*. They suck in their tummies and tuck their buns under. Swing their arms like wings to alternate with the legs. It covers thunder thighs.

"You're looking wonderful," Sally Griffin shouted to Miss Arkansas as she sucked-and-tucked above them on the runway. It *was* rather dazzling to be so close. "One of mine," Sally said to Sam. Miss Arkansas beamed and waved and shot Sally a thumbs-up.

The *Inquirer* shouted to Miss Colorado, one of her personal favorites. So when Miss Georgia paraded by, Sam called, "Hey, Rae Ann, looking good."

Rae Ann was flying. Her eyes sparkled and her color was high.

It was tough not to be excited. The enthusiasm in the hall was wildly contagious. The evening felt exactly like the semifinals of any sporting event—the music, the fans, the lights, the banners, the shouts, the applause, and the players themselves, pumped within an inch of their very lives.

Sitting right at the edge of the runway, Sam almost could have reached over and touched the girls. And she found herself wanting to, they were so vibrant, so alive. And though they weren't all beautiful, not what you might think a Miss America ought to look like (whatever *that* was), when she was prancing down that runway, each girl looked like she held the title to that long, narrow piece of Atlantic City real estate.

Now here was Miss Louisiana, Lucinda Washington, Lavert's drop-dead-gorgeous cousin. One of two black contestants, she had the queenly bearing of Jessye Norman—though she'd spot the diva a hundred and fifty pounds.

There were bouquets of long-stemmed blondes. More brunettes. A few redheads.

What Sam noticed most was their bodies: how tall they all were—though of course she was looking up—and how thin, with long, shapely legs, not much fanny, and considerable chests. Their heads were different, but the bodies were all by Barbie. This was it: the Role Model. The Golden Mean. Twenty-two years of age, 35-22-34, 5′7″, 117 pounds. No wonder the average American woman wanted to kill herself and was perpetually dieting.

Following the Parade of States was some banter between the emcees Phyllis George (Miss America 1971, former pro football commentator, wife of a former governor, and now a chicken entrepreneur) and Gary Collins (NBC game show host and husband of Mary Ann Mobley, Miss America 1959).

They introduced the reigning Miss America, Lynn Anderson, who was stunning in a low-cut dress of gold and silver. As Lynn paraded and waved to the roaring crowd, Sam, swept away by the moment, actually found herself tearing up.

Ridiculous! Though she did remember crying along with the winner of every Miss America Pageant of her girlhood.

Beauty pageants have always been especially popular in the South, and growing up in Atlanta, Sam had loved the Miss America Pageant even more than the Oscars. The second Saturday in September, it was timed just perfectly, right after the opening of school. She and a dozen of her friends had huddled together in their pj's, draped over one another like so many cats on her bed before the television.

"Yeeeeeeew! *Ugly!* Too fat! Look at those thighs!" they'd screamed. Or, "Wow! But get up in front of all those people, play the piano, answer questions, I'd diiiiiiie!"

They'd stayed awake until midnight—and past. However long it took, they were there when Bert Parks announced the first runner-up, and it dawned on the other one, the girl whose name wasn't called, that she was IT!

There she is. They'd sung along as *she* paraded down the runway, each and every one of them fighting a big lump in her throat, squeezing her eyes tight trying to imagine what *she* must feel like. To be the fairest in the land, smack-dab in the middle of a fairy tale. An ordinary girl from an ordinary family in an ordinary town—now crowned like Cinderella. And it was *permanent.* You *always* would be Miss America. Always and forever. No matter what.

But then Sam had grown up and gone on to Real Life, and the pageant hadn't. The girls on TV, if she happened to flip past them on that September evening, were exactly like these girls before her now. Looking older than their peers because of the makeup and silly hair, they were plastic Barbies mouthing platitudes. Real women had thrown away their pushup bras along with the old second-class ways of thinking.

Yet here she was, and there they were, and she was the one with tears in her eyes.

Go figure. She surreptitiously blew her nose. But the *Inquirer* never missed a trick.

"Getting to you already, I see." She rubbed her hands together. "I can't wait to collect."

"The day I become a pageant junkie, I'll not only give you the hundred, I'll buy myself one of those spangled gowns," said Sam, pointing at Lynn Anderson's rear as she made her way offstage.

"Bugle beads," said Sally Griffin. "You've got to get the terminology right."

Where did they find those dresses anyway?

"In pageant stores, when they're beginners. Further along, most girls get them custom made from designers like Stephen Yearick, Jeannie Carpenter, or Randy Dimitt. Jeannie and Randy both have stores in Russellville, Arkansas. Girls fly in from all over the country for fittings. And then some go to designers like Bob Mackie, who designs for Cher."

Pageant stores? Sam hadn't gotten past that.

"Sure," said Sally. "They have everything, the beaded gowns, the acrylic rhinestone pumps. Come over to the trade show in the Trump Regency, you'll see everything—but wait, I want to hear Susan Davidson." Trade show? Did she say trade show?

A Miss America first runner-up from several years past sang "With a Song in My Heart" in the spot where a commercial would be on Saturday night.

Then the panel of preliminary judges, who sat in a V between stage right and the runway, was introduced. Mimi Bregman was in red sequins. Eloise Lemon had chosen blue metallic. The men wore handsome evening clothes. Julian Peacock's ruffled shirt and cloth-of-gold vest stood out in the field of black and white.

Cindy Lou Jacklin took her bow in apricot chiffon and sunglasses. "Is she afraid she'll be blinded by the spangles, I mean bugle beads?" Sam wondered aloud.

"It's her shiner she thinks she's hiding," said the *Inquirer.*

Shiner?

"Yeah, wait a minute. I want to see how they handle this. You notice someone's missing?"

Sam took a closer look. Why, of course, that slimebag Kurt Roberts was nowhere in sight. But there'd been no mention of his absence. "Where *is* he? What happened to him?"

USA Today on the other side of the *Inquirer* couldn't keep out of it. "What *I* heard is that he rang up Barbara Stein very late this afternoon and said something had come up in New York and he had to go home."

That was preposterous. If you'd agreed to be a judge for the Miss America Pageant, for pete's sake, you'd clear your calendar months in advance.

"That's the skinny," said the *Inquirer*. "Of course, Barb was fit to be tied, but I guess they just decided to go ahead with the six. What're they going to do, bring in somebody else for these three nights, after they've already done the interviews?"

"His mother died? His girlfriend threatened suicide? What could have happened?" Sam asked.

"Taking this business awfully serious already," warned the *Inquirer*.

"I just think a deal's a deal. You tell somebody you're going to do something—"

"That's exactly what I teach the girls," said Sally. "You agree to make an appearance, then you darned well better show up on time with every hair in place, your shoes shined and color-coordinated to your outfit, nails polished, yourself fed, fragrant, bathed, fresh-breathed, with your clothes clean, good-looking, pressed, and accessorized."

The three reporters stared at one another, and finally *USA Today* giggled, "I guess Kurt Roberts didn't do any of that."

No, Kurt didn't. He definitely wasn't fed, bathed, or fresh-breathed, though he was becoming a little fragrant. Or perhaps ripe would be more accurate.

His clothes were a mess. There was blood on his peach-colored T-shirt, and even the best cleaners would play hell trying to get the stains out of his creamy Armani suit. Roberts was no Jay Gatsby at this juncture, though Gatsby, if Kurt had been the kind of guy who read, would have been one of his heroes. He'd have loved Gatsby's style—his tailoring, his great house on Long Island, his heavy saloon of a car—for style was Roberts's whole life. He wouldn't have appreciated Gatsby's adoration of Daisy Buchanan, however. Women? Women were playthings. They were like Kleenex. You were finished with one, you threw her away.

But speaking of disposable, look at Roberts now.

"What about Cindy Lou's shiner?" asked Sam.

"Well." The *Inquirer* leaned closer. "I just happened to worm my way into a table beside the judges at dinner in Monopoly's steakhouse. Somebody popped her one good, all right." She nodded with the certainty of a reporter who had her facts straight. But in this case, she might know the what of it, but she didn't know the who, when, why, where.

"Interesting, huh?" She cocked an eyebrow. "One judge splits, the other's sporting dark glasses. Especially since they seemed to be, shall we say, cozy?"

So others had noticed, too. But of course they would. That's why the press was here, to sniff out, in the great tradition of pageant coverage, every little trace of scandal and innuendo.

But what Sam had witnessed—and as far as she knew, no one else from the press corps had—was Kurt Roberts's attack on the young boy at poolside and his subsequent departure from the scene arm in arm with the lovely Cindy Lou. He seemed to have called Barbara Stein with his apologies soon after.

So what did that mean? Anything, nothing? Were the two events related?

But there was no time to ponder such intrigue, for Gary and Phyllis were explaining the judging.

The girls were divided into three groups: Alpha, Mu, and Sigma. Tonight Alpha did talent, Mu did evening gown, Sigma did swimsuit. Then they rotated events each of the other two nights until they'd been judged in all three categories. Sam punched the information into her laptop.

This beauty business was foreign territory with its own lingo, and she wanted to get it straight.

"The girls will be judged on *physical fitness* in swimsuit, on *talent,* and on *onstage presence* in evening gown."

Interesting word choices. But then, if you listened to the official pageant line, here were the priorities:

Talent
Intelligence
Olympic ability (whatever that was)
Energy
Communication
Poise
Attractiveness

Pretty is as pretty does, and beauty was dead last, or so they said.

"The swimsuit and evening gown are going to go very quickly," warned the *Inquirer.* "If you want to score, use whole numbers. Ten's the top."

When Price Waterhouse did the tabulations, talent counted forty percent. The interview conducted earlier in the week was thirty. Evening gown and swimsuit were each fifteen.

Sam didn't get it. "Swimsuit's only fifteen? Then why do swimsuit winners take the crown so often?"

"She's been doing her homework," sighed Sally.

"But don't they?"

"Yes," said the *Inquirer.* "Nine of the last twelve Miss A's were preliminary swimsuit winners."

"So?"

"I guess you'd prefer they didn't *do* swimsuits?" Sally didn't try to hide her irritation. The controversy over the swimsuit competition was an old wound, reopened every year.

"Hey," said Sam, both hands up. "I'd probably prefer they didn't do Miss America, if you want to know the truth."

"It wouldn't be the pageant without the cynicism of the press. *You* all are as much a part of the tradition as the damned swimsuits you're so high and mighty about."

"Now, wait just a minute—" But Sam didn't finish as the curtain rose on a stage set that replicated the Boardwalk outside. While strains of "Summertime" filled the air, fifty girls in gold lamé beach togs thrown over their white swimsuits perambulated down in roller chairs, played volleyball, built sand castles in the pseudo-sand.

Then they did some more dancing, singing, and posing with the Miss America dancers.

What did Sam think? She thought they looked terrific. They looked like showgirls, even if they couldn't dance. And she couldn't help it, she wished she looked just like that.

But see? That's what this kind of crap did to you. Beauty pageants and girlie magazines, starlets, they made you think that's what women really looked like. And how many women felt rotten about themselves because they didn't? Even women who came close would call themselves old hags the moment their breasts began to migrate south.

She said as much to Sally, who replied, "Barbara Stein has been campaigning for years to try to drop the swimsuit category—and you know what? If they did, people out there in TV land would scream their heads off. Watching beautiful girls parade in swimsuits and then bitching about it is as much a part of the American way of life as—"

"—the cynicism of the press," said Sam.

"That's right." Sally laughed.

The emcees held forth about the judges' looking for fitness, grace, an all-over statement of health. The American woman worked out and was in better shape than anytime in history.

What it sounded like was an apologia for a T&A show.

However, up on the stage, no matter what *anyone* thought, the girls of the Sigma group were ready to strut their stuff. One by one, and much more quickly than Sam had imagined, each girl—wearing only her white swimsuit, her taupe pumps, and a big smile—made the trek down to center stage, where she paused, turned to show her full backside, stopped for a count of five before the judges, and hit the runway.

There, close up, they looked great. Again Sam thought of athletes pumped up for the big game. Because, she'd have to give it to them, for whatever demented reason, these girls had worked hard, sacrificed God knows what to arrive here at their peak. Their bodies were toned drum-tight, their skin flawless, their ample bosoms high, their waists tiny, their buns bounceless, their racehorse legs went on and on. They were nigh unto perfect. They were all tens, by God, and proud of it.

Or so Sam thought.

Had Kurt Roberts been there, he would have told Sam she knew nothing about womanflesh, not the way a pro like himself did.

That's what a big-time fashion photographer did for a living, coax beauty from girls who came in on the Greyhound from Paducah with their heads full of silly notions of what modeling was all about.

They didn't know it was hard work. They didn't know they needed more than a little turned-up nose, nice boobs, and a face that made the "beauty" section of their high-school yearbook.

They didn't know that if they were extraordinarily lucky, what they had for a face was a blank canvas. A face you could make into a thousand different women. A face that if you laid your portfolio open, the client would say, "That's her? And *that's* her, too?" Look at Marla Hanson. Not that she would have ever been as famous if those geeks hadn't gone after her face with a razor. Talk about your free publicity! But she had the basics. A face you wouldn't look at twice walking down the street. A blank canvas, as he said, for the genius of someone like himself who, along with a good stylist, could coax her, and coke her, and kiss her, and baby her into making love to that camera.

That's what it was all about. Doing that camera with your face. Doing those judges, giving it to them, oompah-pah, oompah-pah, ooh ooh ooh.

That's what the famous fashion photographer Kurt Roberts would have said to Sam about beauty, if he could have, if he'd been there.

"Oh, God," said Sally. "Look at that makeup."

Sam stared at the leggy brunette on the ramp. Her face looked fine to Sam. Overdone, of course. But they were all painted for the stage.

"No, on her legs. See that?" Sally pointed. "She tried to sculpt them, to make them look thinner by using a darker shade of makeup down the outer and inner sides of her legs and a lighter shade in one straight line down the middle. But you can *see* it. That's a no-no." She gave the girl a three.

"And look at Miss Arkansas's tan line," said *USA Today*. "They should tan in the altogether to avoid that." Another three.

Leg makeup, Sam wrote. Tan lines.

"Oh, my God. Check out those pads," said the *Inquirer*.

Where?

"Right there." Sally pointed. "Miss Colorado. You can see her bust pads through that white swimsuit. With white you have to be *so* careful. That's why the girls hate it. But you do what the pageant tells you. Another three. Next."

It was okay to wear falsies?

"Oh, Sam!" cried the *Inquirer*. "Honey, what century do you live in? They use the latest in silicon mastectomy pads. Eighty bucks apiece."

She was as shocked as Hoke had been when she had implied the same thing as a joke.

"There's no rule against breast augmentation—"

Were we talking boob jobs too?

"—of any sort in the Miss America Pageant. Now, Miss Universe is different, but it's a different pageant." Sally added that last, looking down her nose.

"What about noses?" Sam stared up at Miss Texas. She was a gorgeous willowy redhead with a nose as straight as Sam's had been before Skeeter Bosarge had whacked her. The jury was still out on whether or not Sam's was going to need rehauling when all the swelling finally subsided, and she'd found herself paying special attention to schnozzes lately. She gave Miss Texas a ten.

"Many of them do have rhinoplasty. But many people *you* know do, too," said Sally.

That might be true. But they didn't do it to win beauty contests.

"Why, then? To win husbands?" Sally was on her high horse again.

Well, but—

"Most of them don't have *any* surgery," said Sally. "But what they *all* do is work out like crazy to get bodies like that. The swimsuits can be custom made so the girl looks as good as possible with what she's got, but the swimsuit's not going to do anything about what's hanging out of it, about muscle tone. That's why they eat right and train like the dickens."

"Body by Weisbeck," said the *Inquirer*.

A swimsuit designer?

"A body designer," said *USA Today*. "Chuck Weisbeck and Artie Richards have trained Miss America 1989, Miss USA 1989, and lots of state winners at the Butcher Shop, their Texas health club."

"Their slogan's 'We trim the fat,'" Sally added. "And they do. When they take a girl on, they do a total program. They teach her how to eat. If she can't stick to it, she'll have to move in with Artie. She's one tough cookie." Sam was taking notes like crazy.

"And then there's tape," said the *Inquirer*.

"You had to tell her that, didn't you," Sally sighed.

To prevent their swimsuits' riding up?

"Nope," said the *Inquirer*. "For that they use Firm Grip, a spray you can buy in any sporting goods store. But to get cleavage like that"—she pointed at the nearest girl—"you bend forward and use duct tape beneath your breasts, pulling them together. See, the swimsuits are backless, so you wrap back and forth."

"You can cinch in waists and hips with tape too," said Sally. If the *Inquirer* was going to give Sam all the secrets, she might as well get them right. "That makes breasts look higher, fuller, and rounder by contrast."

Sam stared up at the last girl down the runway, Miss Louisiana, Lavert's cousin. She was a ten in her swimsuit, for sure, but what was she *out* of it?

"Interview slips?" It was one of Barbara Stein's assistants moving behind them in the dark. They filled out requests for the girls they wanted to interview in the pressroom after the show.

Talent was next. "This is very tough," said Gary Collins, who seemed to Sam to be growing paler as the show went on. He had a pinched look around his mouth, as if his stomach hurt. He explained that one of the things that made judging talent so difficult was that a singer might follow a dancer who followed a pianist, and they all had to be judged on their own merits.

Yeah, yeah. And this was the part of the competition where the folks at home, come Saturday night, would be rolling in the aisles.

"The reason for dividing them into Alpha, Mu, and Sigma groups by talent," Sally said, "is so we don't get twelve piano players in one night."

Or six ventriloquists, thought Sam, remembering acts she'd seen on TV in her youth. Or three girls riding their palominos, though all animal acts had been verboten since the birds got away and the horse almost landed in the orchestra pit.

That was really a shame. Part of the fun of the pageant in the old days were acts like the girl who showed America how to pack a suitcase. Or the girl who sang and smiled like crazy while simultaneously wailing on the accordion and the snare drum. The tap dancer who did her routine standing on her head in a specially constructed box. The hand wringers doing Joan of Arc. The singers who knew only that one song—and forgot the words to it. The Miss A whose talent, for pete's sake, had been sewing her own wardrobe. The fire baton twirlers—though fire had gone the way of the palominos, alas, along with the ice skaters.

"Also, the top girls are seeded throughout the three groups so they don't kill each other off in early competition," the *Inquirer* said in Sam's ear. She was proving to be such a fund of information. Was she looking for a job in Atlanta?

The first girl out of the chute was Miss Mississippi, a brunette in a gorgeous long red gown who sang a tune from *Phantom of the Opera.* She wasn't bad.

Next came a ventriloquist with a dummy who looked like Big Bird. Now, this was more like old times. Miss Montana did a tap routine. Miss Michigan was a hand wringer: her monologue (she wrote it herself) was about a little girl waiting for her daddy, who was never coming home.

Barbara Stein's assistant was back whispering, "Texas, Miss Texas."

What?

"Texas took swimsuit," the *Inquirer* explained. The press got the news first. Swimsuit and talent winners were announced at the end of the evening. Evening gown remained a secret.

Miss Texas was the tall redhead with the great nose. Sam had scored her ten. As a judge of horseflesh, she wasn't doing badly.

Pianist, torch singer, pianist, ballerina, pianist, and then it was Rae Ann's turn. Sam found herself rooting for the born-again Georgia peach.

She wondered if Rae Ann had the rabbit's foot Hoke said he'd given her tucked somewhere under that beautiful blue gown. Two steps out, she looked fragile as a china doll. Yet Rae Ann strode right out like a pro and *took* that stage.

This girl had weighed two hundred fifty pounds? This girl had had nothing bigger in her life than paint-by-the-numbers and TV soap operas? This girl with the angelic voice, the graceful hands, had been a victim? This girl with the dreamy look—you could *see* the tear in her eye through Sally's binoculars! This beauty had been a one-girl disaster area?

* * *

Kurt Roberts knew *that* was one of the formulas for success, finding a girl convinced she was really rotten. Find yourself one of those, you've got a girl you can mold.

On the other hand, a girl who comes from a supportive family that's given her love, what does she need you for? She's already sporting a strong self-concept, and those girls are trouble.

He wanted a girl who's been abandoned, pushed into a corner, a Ping-Pong ball between one parent who dishes it out and the other who laps it up.

There's a girl who, once you get her attention, and give her just enough of a taste of what *might* be, will do anything you tell her to. She'll be more than happy to pay the price. Sacrifice is her middle name.

She'll starve herself. She'll do those reps till her nose bleeds. Tell her to smile, she'll glow. Give her a plan, she'll follow it to a T. She'll start to see the angles herself. Girls around her are wearing their hair up, hers will go down. They're wearing black, she'll show up in white. She'll do anything to please, to make you proud, to stay out of that hellhole she used to call her life.

Just like Rae Ann.

He could smell a Rae Ann a mile off.

He'd given her a ten in interview because he knew she was a survivor.

What Kurt didn't know was if he was, now, himself.

It was the best version of "Don't Cry Out Loud" Sam had ever heard. She didn't know how Cheryl Prewitt, Rae Ann's idol, had delivered it when she won in 1980, but in Sam's opinion, Patsy Cline couldn't have done it better, and that was her ultimate compliment.

"She'll take it," said Sally. "No question."

Really? Way to go, Rae Ann!

"You better watch that stuff," said the ever-vigilant *Inquirer*. "Pulling for a girl is the first sign of involvement."

"I'm *covering* her," Sam protested. "That's why I'm here."

"Uh-huh."

Onstage presence in evening gown was next, after another forgettable number by Nickie Brasco and the dancers. "They do different production numbers each night?" Sam hoped.

Her new friends hooted. "No, honey," said Sally. "This is dress rehearsal for Saturday. Not only are you going to see the same songs, but you'll hear the same patter from Phyllis and Gary. Tomorrow, come half an hour later and skip the opener."

Then the *Inquirer* shushed them. Miss Florida, a petite blonde, was first in a shimmering dress of crystalline pink. *Bugle beads,* wrote Sam in her notes.

The drill went like this: each girl floated through the set, down some stairs, and took her place beside Phyllis George, who didn't look bad herself in black sequins. Phyllis and Gary had already explained that each contestant had written a one-page "issue-oriented essay for women of the nineties" and that her impromptu question would be taken from that.

Miss South Dakota, a brunette in a hurt-your-teeth-orange gown, must have written something about alcohol and drug abuse among the young. "What I, as a future state superintendent of schools would do, is make sure that each of those students with a negative experience be identified, and those negative experiences traded in for positive ones."

"Hey, sounds easy," Sam whispered to the *Inquirer.* "I'm all for that."

"They're a little naive," agreed the *Inquirer.* "But on the other hand, think about it. In front of thousands of people, and on Saturday night, *millions,* you've got thirty seconds to be intelligent, if not brilliant. And you're twenty-one years old."

Okay, she'd give them a little slack. But, on the other hand, they'd asked for this.

Miss Rhode Island, in a purple and black number, was holding forth on citizen involvement. Patriotism was a favorite issue in these circles, the Jaycees being the prime sponsors at the local level.

Phyllis thanked her, and Miss Rhode Island glided over

toward the judges, stopped, did the same sort of slow, big smile the girls did in swimsuit. Then she hit the runway. "Walk it, girl," said Sally.

"Georgia," Barb's assistant was whispering again in the dark. "Miss Georgia."

Georgia? Georgia! She'd done it! Rae Ann had won talent! Forty percent! Hoo-boy! Sam was bouncing up and down in her orange plastic kitchen chair.

Then she checked her watch. Deadline was forty-five minutes and counting.

"Back out that way"—the *Inquirer* pointed to the exit behind the refreshment stand—"are the pay phones. And don't forget the interviews after the show."

Sam missed the rest of the show and the interviews. She didn't get to see Rae Ann's victory strut down the runway. Harry said she got to going so fast she almost blew right off the end of the ramp past Miss Texas, the swimsuit winner, who was no slowpoke herself.

Sam had sat on the hallway floor and dashed her story off in twenty minutes. But then, when she tried to modem it over the phone, she got line noise. *No carrier No carrier,* her screen flashed. The guy in Atlanta couldn't read it for the distortion. So, in the end, she had to talk it to him.

Hoke, who'd told Lois he had to work late, got on another line, hurraying and huzzahing.

"What'd Rae Ann do? What'd she say?"

Sam didn't have the slightest. She would have to do the follow-up tomorrow, beg, borrow, or steal Rae Ann away from her schedule.

"Now I guess you're off to the Georgia victory party?" asked Hoke. "God, I wish I could be there."

"Now," said Sam, whose day had been fuller and richer and more confusing and exhausting than she'd thought possible, "I'm finding Harry, and he and Harpo and I are hitting the sack, pronto."

. . . 7

WAYNE LEANED BACK IN ACTION CENTRAL IN HIS BIG LEATHER chair, an exact copy of Mr. F's. He was feeling very pleased with himself.

There was nothing in the world like the pride of accomplishment at the end of a long day.

Not that the days ever seemed that long, working for Mr. F, who made everything easy—and exciting.

Like one day he might ask you to meet him at the train station, and he'd be dressed up in his conductor suit. Mr. Franken *loved* trains. He had the biggest collection of toy trains in the whole world.

Or there was the time he sent Wayne a ticket to the circus, in *Chicago.* And a train ticket, of course. Wayne had a front-row box seat, was having a great time—he especially liked the lions and tigers—when halfway through the second clown act, the bozo in an orange wig with a purple nose pulled him out into the arena to be part of the show. He whispered in Wayne's ear just as he stuffed him in a barrel. It was Mr. F.

Mr. F said he liked kid stuff—games, toys, playacting, dressing up—because he had been raised so poor, he and his sister, by an aunt in West Texas. So when he got to where he could afford it, and he could afford *anything* now, he was one of the richest men in the country, he played all the games he wanted. He said making money was game-playing too, especially if you had a gift for salesmanship—which Mr. F did. He learned it from his aunt Gracie, who ran the only general store in Crockett County. Wayne loved to hear Mr. F talk about when he was a boy, selling Bibles door-to-door. Mr. F dropped out of high school at fifteen, bought an old Ford, made himself a small fortune selling vacuum cleaners, even to them as didn't have electricity. He said not to worry, they would. They did, eventually.

Mr. F invested his earnings in real estate, just like in the game Monopoly, buying big pieces of cheap property, like Baltic and Oriental avenues, building warehouses on them. Then he moved on to houses and hotels and office buildings. He said he'd figured out the way to make *real* money was not selling, but developing and holding on.

But Mr. F's favorite was his FrankFairs. He'd started buying up tracts of land in West Texas, especially near dead-ass little towns, put up these big stores on 'em, giant versions of his aunt Gracie's store. He sold almost everything you could think of. And sold it cheap. He insisted his FrankFairs have *big* cheap toy departments. They gave each kid whoever came in a prize for walking through the door. Mr. F figured soon every kid in America'd be whining for his parents to take him to FrankFair. And he was right.

One of Mr. F's favorite things was to play dress-up, wear disguises, show up in FrankFairs unannounced and take a serious look around. Incognito, he called it—one of Wayne's very favorite words.

Mr. F'd been on one of those unannounced incognito visits two years ago to a store in Cherry Hill, not too far from Philly, when he'd found Wayne.

It was on his way to the FrankFair, actually. Mr. F was riding his bike. That's what he'd do, sometimes. Ride the train till he got to a town, then take his bike out of the baggage car, pedal along incognito, pretending he was just another guy down on his luck, couldn't afford even a beat-to-crap Plymouth, going to do his shopping—nickels and dimes squirreled away in one of those little red plastic cases that looked like a mouth opening when you squeezed it.

There was Wayne, up in his tree house in a good stand of oak, watching this dude, pedaling away in his jeans and blue workshirt, watching on the monitor that fed in from the camera he'd planted down at the south end of this little road. He had one at the north end too. Wayne fed the power out of lines, camouflaged real careful, he'd run from that shed over there, where a man named Huckaby played with his woodworking tools when Miz Huckaby got on his nerves. Wayne knew that 'cause he'd bugged their house, just for the practice. There was nothing much interesting going on there. Though their niece had been coming to visit the next week, and he'd thought that might be worth another little camera—in the bathroom. In the meantime, Wayne was just riding high, living off the fat of the land and what he stole from the Grand Union, Radio Shack, and the FrankFair.

He was happy as a clam to be out of that halfway house. Halfway between what and what, he used to ask. Old Miz Mizery—that's what he called her, the woman who ran the place, didn't have the sense God gave a duck, just knew how to cash those government checks—she didn't have any answers.

Wayne did. Wayne knew the answer to most problems in his world was to walk away. People didn't want to deal with love, pain, need, dreams—the things that cut too close to the bone. It was easier to scram. Nobody gave a crap, not really, not about another crazy, which is what Wayne, most days, knew he was.

'Course Miz Mizery cared in that she liked to keep up the head count, keep those checks rolling. But like his friend Thelma Thirty, that's what they called her 'cause she had that many fingers and toes, used to say, They care so much about us, how come they cut us loose? Threw us out of the crazy houses that used to at least give us three squares and a cot, keep us out of the rain and snow, Christmas party every year with the do-gooders singing songs, bringing green punch and cookies with red sprinkles?

Wayne had walked away lots of times. He'd let himself get picked up, shipped back to some kind of shelter or halfway house every once in a while, when he was sick or just needed to rest up.

But this hadn't been one of those times, this day he saw what turned out to be Mr. F pedaling down the road. It was early May, the weather getting to be real nice, and Wayne was feeling good. He hadn't had any flashbacks in quite a while from those bad Mexican drugs that had near about fried his brain. And the electric shocks, well, there were those blank spots, but you could get used to anything, Wayne had learned. So there Wayne was, having a good time living up in his tree house, practicing all that stuff he'd learned about electronics and surveillance courtesy of the United States Army—a class A outfit until you wanted out.

Then you had to walk away from that too. 'Course if somebody got in your way, somebody *had* got in Wayne's way, you might have to close them down.

Eliminate them. With that thought Wayne had zeroed in through the telescopic sight of his rifle, closed in on the bicycle man pedaling down the road, thinking about zapping *him.* But why? Why not? Why? Why not?

The bicycle man was getting closer now; Wayne could see he was blond and round-faced. He looked kind of like John Denver. He was wheeling along, whistling something kinda out of tune. Whatever it was it reminded Wayne of when he was a little kid, sharing a crib with brother John. Now, *that* made him nuts.

The very thought of John made him think he might decide to zap this bicycle sucker anyway, when all of a sudden the bicycle man, hidden down there somewhere under the spring-green foliage, Wayne couldn't see a thing, hollered: You gonna blow me six ways to Sunday or you just fooling around?

Next thing you know, Wayne never did *know* exactly how it happened, the bicycle man's up the tree with him—*that's* when Wayne first saw he was missing his right arm, *how* could he climb—watching both ends of the road on the monitors, listening in to Miz Huckaby in the house talking to her dog, like either one of them had good sense. The man's bright blue eyes were all lit up like Christmas. He said, I think I've got a use for you, my good man, in my stores. Of course, Wayne thought, here's another member of the club. Another crazy. What was a one-armed bicycle man talking about, My stores?

As it turned out, he was talking about one hell of a lot.

The man owned half the world. *Furthermore,* he immediately recognized Wayne's innate worth.

Mr. Tru Franken told him all about that, about how

valuable each and every human being was. From little acorns great oaks grow. (Wayne thought, yeah, except my brother John, but he didn't tell Mr. Tru Franken that.) He *understood* about Wayne wanting to live in a tree house, be left alone to play with his electronic toys.

He said the world's your oyster, you can live anywhere you want, and I'll give you a super-duper bunch of gadgets. And Mr. F had always been as good as his word. He worked Wayne in surveillance in FrankFairs for a good long time, then moved him here to the Monopoly—which Mr. F had up and bought one day, the way other people might buy a new TV.

Of course, a man like that wasn't happy when people didn't return the favor.

Just like real late this afternoon when Mr. F had called him in and said he'd reviewed the tape Wayne had thought he would find interesting, Thank you very much, Wayne. Mr. F was always very polite. You did great, he added.

That made Wayne *feel* great. So there he was, ready and waiting, standing on his tippytoes, to see if there was anything else Mr. F wanted him to do.

Especially since Dougie had showed up from Wharton, the same business school as Donald Trump, Wayne had felt like he really had to hustle his butt to prove to Mr. F he was the truest, bluest, most loyal human being he'd ever saved, with probably the most innate worth—stuff you couldn't learn in some fancy business school. He was hoping against hope Mr. F didn't lay a lot of store in blood being thicker than water.

If he did—well.

Mr. F pushed the remote control in his left, and only, hand and rolled the tape. When he got to what he wanted to show Wayne, yep, it was the part he thought Mr. F'd want to see, he did a freeze frame. Then he backed it up and played the audio again.

"You hear what this man's saying?"

Yep. That's why he'd brought it to Mr. F's attention.

"That's the kind of behavior we have to guard against," said Mr. F, his blue eyes very serious behind his glasses.

Then Mr. F walked up to the monitor and put his left, and only, forefinger on the screen. "I'm going to have to think about this. This is good, Wayne."

"Anything else you'd like me to do, Mr. F?" Wayne touched the bill of his black Monopoly Special Staff cap Mr. F had given *him* and nobody else.

Just about then, Dougie had walked in the door. Waltzed in, big as you please, without even knocking. Took a seat. Poured himself a glass of the orange pop Mr. F was partial to. Mr. F always kept a few bottles on a silver tray, along with an ice bucket, crystal glasses, Mr. F being a gentleman of class and distinction. Dougie didn't say a word, but he had that smirky look on his face, like What's happening, scumbag? You could feel that he thought he was Mr. F's only begotten heir, being Mr. F's only sister Vivian's only son. Which meant his name ought not to be Franken, unless he was illegitimate, which wouldn't surprise Wayne one bit, but when he'd asked Dougie about it, Dougie had just given him a look. Like that's for me to know and you to find out, sucker.

Mr. F turned and Dougie started talking with him about something—market share, recession, numbers of players down, same thing in Vegas—Wayne didn't understand. It made Wayne feel stupid. So he hadn't wanted to ask Mr. F the question again, What did he want him to do, if anything? not in front of Dougie.

But Mr. F, God bless him, had picked up on his hesitation, and he'd said one word to Wayne.

Just one.

Erase.

So Wayne did.

He did exactly what Mr. F told him to do. And now, at the end of the day, he was feeling just great. He was going to close up here, go home, and sleep like a baby.

On the other hand, Big Gloria was wide awake, pacing the floor. She'd come home after working her extra shift, about as bone tired as a person could be and still be living.

And what did she find?

Nothing, that's what. An empty house. Junior long gone. She'd laid a hand on his favorite chair. It wasn't even warm.

Oh, Lord. She'd thrown herself down in that chair and eased off her shoes. In a few minutes she'd get up and go run a pan of hot water with some Epsom salts in it and give her dogs a soak, but first she had to sit there for a few minutes.

Sometimes she wished the Good Lord hadn't made women so strong. She'd sure like to lay some of her burden down. But He knew she could carry it.

Otherwise, how'd you explain a day like today? She was late to work in the first place, having to go visit Aunt Baby in the hospital, then that crazy Wayne Ward being bad on eighteen, busting that handsome Harry's lip, the one who'd given her the money. Now, *that* was a bright spot. Not the lip, but Lord knows the money was. Then that white lady, the Kewpie doll, trying to sneak into a room. For all Gloria knew, she was a burglar. Gloria probably ought to have reported her.

But then, that wasn't the least of what she should have reported.

Thinking about that was when she got up and started pacing the floor, forgetting all about the hot water and Epsom salts.

Gloria, she said to herself, have you lost your mind? Clothilde called you into that Kurt Roberts's room, the one who tried to drown your Junior, room was tore up six ways to Sunday. What'd you do? Did you call security?

No.

Did you know you ought to?

Uh-huh.

So why didn't you?

Well, his bags were gone—all his stuff. I thought the man was just a slob, like the rest of them. You think I don't see lots of messy rooms? You wouldn't believe how people behave, paying one night's rent.

Uh-huh. He tore his sheets all up and bloodied some of them 'cause his mama didn't teach him any better?

Or, it could have been that old man with the limp who came by earlier came back again. Slipped me a phone number to call if I saw Roberts, said he'd make it worth my time. I think he used to be a friend of Nickie Scarfo, you know who I mean? He could've have found Roberts, beat him up, cut off all his fingers and toes. They do things like that.

Old man, huh? With a limp? How many times you seen *The Godfather Part III,* Gloria?

Well, I know who that old man is, and furthermore, I didn't *care* what happened to any Mr. Kurt Roberts, you want to know the truth. He's the one who tried to *kill* Junior.

Uh-huh. So you thought, whatever, he deserved it. No matter that he was a pageant judge, it seemed kind of strange he'd be leaving right in the middle under his own steam, you weren't gonna worry your head about it.

Something like that.

What else, Bee Gee?

Nothing.

No? You sure?

Uh-huh.

He didn't leave not one little thing in the room that you might have ought to have turned in?

Who're you? The Good Fairy?

Gloria Sturdivant, your own mama'd be turning in her grave if she could see what you've come to.

Yeah? Well, I bet she wouldn't. I bet she'd do the same thing.

She'd take a man's tickets on a horse race—someplace down in Florida is what the man said when she cashed them in, someplace called Exacta, or something like that—and *keep* the five thousand dollars?

She would. She most certainly would, if she wanted to get out of this hellhole as bad as I do. I know my mama. She'd call it grabbing opportunity by the foreskin.

She would do no such thing.

Oh, yes, she would. A woman gets up against it, she's liable to do anything. What do *you* know, voice of the devil?

Unh-uh. You talking 'bout the wrong channel there, girl.

Oh, yeah? You telling me the Lord thinks I ought to give that money back to that man who tried to kill my son, when I could use it to get Junior *out* of here before he ends up like all those other mothers' sons—in jail?

Isn't that what you're really afraid of now? Isn't that why you're walking the floor? Afraid that what Junior did, he was so mad at that man, was go up to his room and give him what-for? And then? Then? You don't want to think about what might have happened then, do you, Gloria, that might *really* put Junior in jail?

No, she didn't want to think about it. But she couldn't help herself. She didn't know where Junior was, how long he'd been gone, what he'd been up to. All she could do was what women had done for as long as there'd been men to trouble their minds, keep walking that floor.

"Harry?"

"Hmmmmm?"

"Did I hurt your lip?"

"Nuunh-uh."

"Are you going to tell me what happened to your lip?"

"Unh-uh."

"Are you asleep?"

"No."

"You know what?"

"What, Sammy, what?"

"Jeeszt. You don't have to be such a grump."

"I'm sorry. I was just drifting off. What, honey?"

"Nothing. Go back to sleep."

Harry sat up. "I can't now. Tell me, *what?"*

"I was just wondering, do you think it would be *fun* to be Miss America?"

"I think it'd suck eggs."

"Really? If you were that young—it could be pretty exciting. Traveling for a year. Meeting the president—even if *he* sucks eggs, it's still pretty impressive to a little girl from Oshkosh, or wherever. Earning all that money."

"You sorry you were never Miss America, honey? Ow! That hurt."

"*I* could never have been Miss America."

"Why not?"

"I'm hardly the type."

"You mean you weren't malleable enough—even as a girl? No, you're right. Probably not. Probably had a head hard as a rock even then."

"Not pretty enough, either."

"You're a hell of a lot prettier than any of those girls."

"Oh, Harry. Don't be silly."

"You are!"

"I'm old."

"You are not old. You're forty."

"Thanks a lot."

"Why do I have the feeling I'm going to lose no matter what?"

"You're right. I'm sorry. Being around this beauty queen stuff makes me crazy. Jesus. As if being pretty were the most important thing in the world."

"Well, you know it's not."

"But it *is* important."

"What?"

"Being pretty."

"It's not important. It's—it's nice."

"So, you don't love me because I'm pretty."

"I love you because you're you."

"Even if I were ugly, you would."

"Yes."

"Even if you were just as cute as you are now, you'd love me if I looked like an old hog."

"Yes."

"Harry? You're full of crap."

"I know. Listen, now that I'm wide awake, I'm going to get a beer from the minibar. You want a glass of milk? Some water?"

"Water, please. Hey! You know what? I just remembered what I wanted to tell you."

"Good. I hope it takes a long time. Here's your water. I hope we stay up all night and feel like doo-doo tomorrow. That's what I really love, is dragging around feeling like a dead dog on my vacation. Sorry, Harpo. I didn't mean to say that."

"Hush, Harry. Listen, what do you think happened to Kurt Roberts?"

"Who he?"

"The creep, the judge, out at the swimming pool. The one who knocked the kid in, Junior, you saved his life, remember?"

"It's all coming back now."

"Roberts didn't show tonight. Did you notice?"

"Unh-uh. You mean he didn't show for the judging? Where was he?"

"Nobody knows. He said he had to go back to New York."

She didn't tell Harry about the itch, the one she got at the base of her neck, that sure as an aching behind her knees had always been the first sign of flu told her something absolutely hideous was about to go down—or had. The timing wasn't always precise.

Sam scratched her itch and wondered about the size and shape of this particular piece of fresh hell. It made her edgy, as if somebody had whacked her with a giant bag of PMS.

"That's weird," said Harry.

"That's what *I* said. It's also weird that Cindy Lou Jacklin, one of the other judges, remember the big blonde in the blue bikini at the swimming pool with Roberts—*left* the pool with him?"

"Vaguely. Very vaguely."

"Yeah, I bet, former Miss Ohio. Well, anyway, she was wearing shades tonight. Like maybe she was hiding something."

"So what you think, Ms. Big Time Investigative Reporter with a Specialization in Crime, is that Kurt took Cindy Lou back to his room, and in a fit of pique because he didn't succeed in drowning the kid, he beat her up, and then—God, you have a devious mind."

"She killed him and dumped the body in the ocean."

"Good. It's good, Sammy. A great scenario. Now can we go back to sleep?"

"Something happened to that man, Harry. Maybe not that, what I said, but something equally awful."

"Please don't tell me you have a really strong intuition about this thing. We're here for you to do a simple story—not to solve a crime. And *stop* scratching!"

"Harry. I'm telling you. Something happened to Kurt Roberts. He did not simply check out and go home and leave the Miss America Pageant. That doesn't make sense. Slimy guys like him do not go to all the trouble to get here, which has got to be a *major* feather in his little fashion-photographer cap, and then up and split."

"A thousand bucks says you're wrong."

"What?"

"A grand. It's late. Put up or shut up."

"Have you lost your mind? We're talking about a man's life here and you want to *bet* on it? Is this what happens to semi-normal people when they come to Atlantic City? They make wagers on life and death?"

"This is what happens when you wake people up. *You're* betting on disaster, Sammy. I'm betting a thousand the man's back in New York shacked up with some sixteen-year-old model, wait, twin models, having the time of his life. That, or something equally normal."

"Sixteen, huh? Sixteen would be the time of his life? Sixteen's your idea of hot stuff? *Sixteen?* Give me a break! You're on, bub. Put it right here."

"Where?"

"Here. Not there. Unh-uh. Stop it, Harry. Now, you stop that right now. I'm going to count to a million, and you better—"

...8

THE NEXT MORNING IN THE MONOPOLY COFFEESHOP, LAVERT pushed all six foot six of himself back from the table and asked, "*How* long you said ya'll been here?"

"Monday afternoon late," said Harry. "Less than forty-eight hours. Why?"

"I just wondered how long you can eat garbage like this before you have to check into the hospital."

Sam laughed. "Lavert, you've turned into a food snob. Just because you're a great cook doesn't mean—"

"Great isn't the issue here. We're just talking about survival, Sam. Honey, you know if G.T. was here," General Taylor Johnson was his voudou-practicing ambulance driver of a girlfriend and one of Sam's favorite people, "she'd put a hex on this kitchen. Close it down. Only way of saving people from the ptomaine."

"You're right, Big Man. There's no decent food in this whole town," mourned Harry. "The worst dive in New Orleans would be ashamed to—"

"Hey, bubba," Sam interrupted. "Who wanted to come to Atlantic City? *I* could have weenied out, you know. We could be eating lobster in Edgartown—"

"Wait," said Lavert. "Hold the boat. You don't think I left home without a few recommendations from our friends in the business."

"This is my man," said Harry, attempting to throw his arm around Lavert, who'd been his friend since their days at Grambling, where Lavert had played football. "I knew he wouldn't let us starve. Who'd you get these from, bro?"

"Well, actually"—Lavert shifted in his seat, feeling Sam's eyes on him—"it's only one."

"Some mob hangout Joey the Horse turned you on to, am I right, Lavert?" said Sam.

"This woman is bad," Lavert said to Harry. "Anybody

ever warn you about her? Bad. Not a drop of the blood of Christian fellowship in her entire body."

"Cut to the chase." Sam grinned. "Where are you taking us for lunch, and what's the password?"

"It's dinner actually, early, before the show. Ma couldn't make it for lunch."

Ma? Lavert's mother was in town?

"Naaaw. Ma's Michelangelo Amato."

"What'd I tell you, Harry?"

"Ma's not mob. I swear to God. He's in the pizza business."

"Right. What else does he do? Pick up things that fall off the backs of trucks? Save the sanitation department the trouble?"

Lavert shook his head at Harry. "You let her put you through changes like this all the time? I'd fling her pretty bones across the table." At that they all laughed, for Lavert—despite the time he'd spent at Angola, Louisiana's state penitentiary, for removing tourists' extra weight, as in wallets, pearls, and gold watches—was the gentlest of men. "And he *owns* a bunch of trucks."

"Pizza parlors and trucking in AC and he's a friend of Joey the Horse. Come on, Lavert."

"You know what else?" Lavert's face beamed. "He's a great painter."

Both of his friends cracked up.

"No, really. Nudes. There are a couple hanging in the dining room of Va Bene, his club. You'll see."

"I can't eat dinner with a mobster," said Sam.

"How many times do I have to tell you? He's *not* a mobster. You're suffering from a common problem of WASP debutantes, you know that? Going around categorizing folks. I guess you think everybody who's black's gonna mug you?"

"Give it up, Lavert."

"And you think all Italians are mob? I have some Italian friends who get awfully sick of that stuff."

"I'm sorry. I'm sorry. I didn't mean to—" He was making her a little uncomfortable.

"I'm telling you, I bet more than one of the august members of the Atlantic City police force has tied on the old feedbag with Ma, and been damned grateful for it. Maybe you'd rather have another meal in this hotel."

"Cripes! Enough. You're making me sound like a card-carrying member of the Klan. You're right. Forget what I just said. What'd you say the club's called?"

"Va Bene. Means 'all right.' Like—how ya'll? You say, *va bene.* It used to be called Tiro a Segno, but there was a falling out among some of the members, and they went away and formed their own club and took the name with 'em, so—"

"That's pretty," said Sam. "Tiro a Segno. And it means—?"

"'Shoot the target.'" Lavert held up a huge hand, but it was too late.

"Uh-huh." Sam nodded. "Uh-huh. Uh-huh."

"It's not what you think. It's a hunting club. There are chapters all over Italy—"

"Forget it, Lavert. Just shut up and take us to dinner and we'll be grateful," said Harry.

"They don't hunt anymore, though there's still target shooting in the basement." Lavert couldn't let it go.

Sam was shaking her head in disbelief, still laughing. Harry said, "Look at her. You're just making it worse, man."

"I already talked with Ma, and he really wants to meet you, Sammy," said Lavert.

"Meet *me?* He wants me to ghost his autobiography *I Was a Close Personal Friend of the Mob?*"

"Maybe, if you're good. Naw, he likes to talk about all this Miss America stuff."

"Michelangelo is a Miss America buff? And he paints nudes? Oh, my God! I know you didn't make this up. It's too good."

Harry and Lavert just stared at her.

"Are you through?" Lavert finally asked.

"Yes." She blew her nose. "I'll try to stop."

"You might say he has a special interest in Miss America."

Sam gave him a long look while she considered the possibilities. "His daughter's a contestant. No. Wait. He owns a Miss America franchise—Miss New Jersey. No. Oh, he's a bookie, right? He's making book on Miss America? Is that what you're saying?"

"I didn't say that."

"He is, isn't he?"

"I don't know."

"Is he a bookie?"

Lavert stared off into the distance for a long time. "Maybe he's been known to place a bet now and then."

"Yeah. And maybe he makes a loan now and then too. To his best friends. Am I right? Am I right, Lavert?"

"She can really get on your nerves, can't she, Harry?"

"She tries. And it's not as if *she* hadn't ever placed a bet before. She's got a hundred down with the Philly *Inquirer*—and she's about to be into me for a thousand."

"Whew! That's going some. Stakes too rich for my blood. High-rolling, Sammy."

"Don't be absurd. Harry's not telling you the whole story."

"What's Miss High and Mighty betting the grand on, Zack?"

So Harry told him the story about Kurt Roberts.

"I'm with you. Sammy, you want to give me a piece of that action? Let's say, five hundred. Me and my main man here love to take money from a debutante. And all we have to do is find this Roberts safe and sound."

"I was *not* a deb, and you know it."

"Sammy, Sammy. Don't get your blue blood in an uproar. You going to need your wits about you, 'cause you know what a mean team we be, little Robin here with me his Batman. Like back home, when we were investigating Church Lee's untimely demise for you. Saved your bacon."

"Saved *my* bacon? I beg your pardon. What you two did was create a royal cock-up, ending with that shooting—"

"Did you do any shooting, son?" Lavert asked Harry.

"I didn't do any shooting. I don't even own a gun."

"Me neither. Sammy does though. That little .38. You

reckon that's why she thinks she's the cops, seeing danger everywhere, getting herself all upset over a man checking out of a hotel, going home, thinking he's been killed? Willing to bet perfectly good money on it, we're happy to take out of her hands? That's how cops are—suspicious—whoowhee!"

"I didn't mean killed—literally. Well, maybe not, I'm not sure. I just think—I *feel* so strongly—something happened to Roberts. The man did not just go home."

"Well, you're the smart lady. I guess that's why it's gonna take the two of us big, strapping, stupid boys, to prove you wrong, relieve you of some of your trust fund." Lavert checked his watch. "This contest start now?"

"Anytime," Sam said. "Clock's running. Speaking of which, I've got to get moving. Either of you big spenders interested in a stroll down the Boardwalk, walk off some of this ptomaine? I've got about an hour before the Fruit of the Loom Award press conference. Rae Ann has a shot at being Do-gooder of the Year. Ya'll want to bet on that too?"

"Nawh. I don't want to bankrupt you, Sammy," said Lavert. "And as much as I enjoy jawing with you, I'm going to let you guys get on with your day. I've got lots of stuff to do putting together the celebration for Lucinda tonight."

"Oh, really? Celebration for what?" asked Sam.

"She's gonna take talent breezing. You'll see. You ought to talk to her, Sammy. Magic's a great girl, and I'm not saying that just 'cause she's my kin."

"Magic? Miss Louisiana's called Magic?"

"That's her talent. Wait till you see it. You talk with her and her friend, Miss Texas, that redhead won swimsuit last night? They're a trip. Not your garden-variety beauty queens. Did you see Texas, Harry?"

"I saw her, Lavert. And she's got nothing on Sam—"

She punched him in the ribs. "Shut up, Harry. The girl's half my age. Don't start that phony baloney—"

"Honest to God, Lavert. If you ever saw Sammy naked, you'd think—"

"I'm out of here," said Lavert, standing and grabbing the check. "That woman's gonna stab you with a fork, about half a minute. You not gonna have to wait for Ma to shoot you, Zack, at dinner tonight when Sammy asks him in that pecan-pie voice of hers, 'Tell me more about your bookmaking business, Mr. Amato.' "

"Aw, man. Don't you know better than to say that kind of thing in front of her?" Harry groaned. "She'll do it, in between the cheese course and the espresso. I'm too young to die."

"And too cute," said Sam. "And I bet you don't even have any life insurance."

"Me? The big-time part-time insurance investigator, no life insurance?"

"Not a cent." She turned to Lavert. "Son thinks he's going to live forever. Youngsters always do. I may have to take him upstairs and pummel some sense into him."

"Pummel me. Pummel me. I'll give you every penny I've won," he said to Lavert. "I'm up to two thousand, playing blackjack. Did I tell you that?"

"I figured you must be on a roll, you stopped shaving. Isn't that your private little magic trick?"

"Shhhhhh. Don't say it out loud. Put the hex on my deal, lose Big Gloria's rescue fund. Me and the Big Gloria, splitting even, I'm going to have her and Junior back home in no time. I'm hitting that twenty-one just like I had a crystal ball."

At the talk of magic, Sam stared across the room, seeing in the far distance the face of that crazed magician Skeeter Bosarge. With his knife tricks and his rope, loop-de-loop-de-loop. But that was bad magic. They were talking about good magic. Good times. Good luck. Now, if only she could scratch her itch. *Damn* intuition.

...9

IT WAS A CUTE LITTLE HOUSE, ESPECIALLY SINCE GLORIA HAD LAID her strong hands on it, shoring up the sagging porch, installing new plumbing, painting every inch of it a nice cream, the trim a soft blue. But the rooms were small. So Junior, getting dressed for school, was having a hard time running from Big Gloria, which he would have anyway even if she hadn't picked up a broom.

"Mama, what did they do to you at work? You lost your mind?"

"Just tell me where you went last night, son."

"I *told* you. Nowhere. I went to sleep." She whacked him hard with the broom handle. He backed away, hands up, saying, "They're gonna get you for child abuse."

"They're going to get me for first-degree murder if you don't tell me. I called around nine, you're supposed to be here. You think I don't check on you?"

Well, no, he didn't. She didn't used to. He told her that.

"Yeah, and you didn't used to be a juvenile delinquent. You think I want to wake up some morning and see your name in the papers? When you reach your goal, life of crime, kill somebody? 'Junior Jolted!!!' That's what the headlines'll read when they strap you in the chair and stick the juice to you."

"Aw, Mama."

"Don't you aw-Mama me. Just tell me what you were doing, Junior."

"Hanging."

"Hanging where?"

Junior ran his hand over the little twists that covered the top of his head. The hair beneath them was shaved close. Baby dreads is what they called his do. He said, "On the Boardwalk."

"With who?"

"Some guys."

"What guys?"

"Guys, Mama. You know, guys from school."

Big Gloria reached for a pencil and paper. "Names?"

Junior fell back on the blue and gold paisley sofa, arms wide. "What you gonna do? Call their folks before breakfast?"

"I most certainly am." She was standing over him now, leaning down, putting her face right close to his. He could smell her talcum powder. "I am not standing by and watching you turn into a hoodlum like every other boy around here. You're not stupid. You do fine in school. And I've raised you better. Just because you turned sixteen, your hormones got you all in an uproar, does not mean I'm setting you loose. I've told you a million, jillion times, you're going to college, boy—"

"I know, I *want* to."

"—or I'll know the reason why. You're going to make something of yourself, support me in my old age." She poked him in the chest right at the green line on his T-shirt that said FILL TO HERE WITH MARGARITAS. "And I want you to stop wearing this stupid stuff. Where'd you steal this, anyway? You keep going this way, you'll run up on some security won't call me, is going to send you straight on to juvie. It'll probably do you some good. Let you practice up for prison, the big time."

"Aw, Mama."

"Your record's stuck, boy." She tapped pencil to paper. "Names?"

There was no getting around a woman who thought she was big as the Taj. She almost was, too. And stubborn as all get out.

"Rachel Rose," he mumbled.

"What'd you say, Junior? Speak up."

"Rachel Rose," he hollered.

She stood staring at him, hands on her hips, staring in amazement. "Who?"

* * *

From there it was easy, making up the rest of the story. Not that that part wasn't true, being with Rachel Rose.

It was true too that they bumped into each other in front of the arcade. Rachel Rose looked like a million dollars wearing an off-the-shoulder black midriff top that clung to her sweet chest, cutoffs over black tights ending in lace at her little ankles, high heels.

She said, God, how're you feeling? He shrugged like he almost drowned every day, no biggie.

Then they'd hung out for a while at Aladdin's Castle, the arcade at Bally's, playing pinball. Rachel Rose had thought he was some kind of wuss at first, said she never saw a pinball machine before. She said it was nothing at all like video games—NARC, Gauntlet II.

Which gave Junior a chance to be the man of the world. He explained to her how pinball was back. How these new machines in the arcade, Big Betty's Truck Stop, Monday Night Football, had high-tech thumpter bumpers, stereo sound, modular plug-in boards. How when he went down to visit his great-aunt Beautiful in New Orleans, his second cousins took him to a pool hall that had about a dozen old pinballs, the kind that go *ka-chunk* when you knock a row of targets down. The kind you finesse, hitting it on the opposite side when a ball's about to go out.

He told her about his favorite, an antique from the fifties called Central Park. It had a monkey that hit a bell, a horse and carriage, a man on a bench feeding pigeons, a cop, a garbage man. He didn't tell her that Jake, the man who owned the pool hall in New Orleans, had painted all the faces black—except for the garbage man's, he left it white. He did tell her he'd been to New York, where he saw the real Central Park, which was really cool, most parts of it. Especially the little zoo. They had penguins, polar bears, the coolest little monkeys, so tiny their little hands almost broke your heart. And all over the place people were doing their thing, one heck of a lot better than here on the Boardwalk. He saw rappers, rollerskaters, jugglers, pretty girls in little bright-colored skirts jumping two ropes. They were so good, people gave them money. But the park was dangerous too. There were bums all over the place. People living in cardboard boxes. Gangs of kids wilding scared *him*.

Rachel Rose shivered. She was from LA, Newport Beach, where she said it was a lot safer.

It was a lot whiter too—as in totally. If a black person came on the island who wasn't a maid or a handyman, patrols were all over them like a cheap suit. That was her daddy's expression.

But she didn't tell Junior any of that. Instead, she said, wasn't it funny, they both lived on islands on opposite sides of the continent, facing the ocean. But her life was so boring, she said. Kids did nothing but go to movies, hang out in shopping malls, South Coast Plaza, places like that. Sometimes, if they wanted some LA night life, they called the Bat Lady on the Batline to see where the latest floating underground party was. Then they had to go shopping again, depending on whether the scene was mod, skinhead, cowboy punk, beach funk, or jock chic. In California you had to go cruising around *looking* for fun. Whereas Junior had it all, right here, every night.

Junior thought she must be putting him on. AC had to be one of the deadest places on earth. *Used* to be something, that's what the grannies said, back in the twenties, when fancy rich people drove great old cars like Stutz Bearcats down from New York. Now all you saw every day were thousands of tour buses full of old, *old* people holding on to their free coupons like you were gonna steal 'em and their plastic cups full of quarters.

His best friend, Rashad, he'd told her, enjoying talking with her a lot, used to wait tables at one of the casino coffeeshops till Rashad got to where he flat *hated* old people. He said, first of all, they give the codgers these coupons on the bus worth ten dollars for lunch. Rashad sat down with the menu, put together every combination on earth, and there's no way you can come out an even ten, excluding tax and tip—and *there's* a joke, that last word.

Rashad told the old folks that from the get-go when they put their coupons on the table, but did they believe him?

Nooo, said Rachel Rose.

They tried the hamburger, fries, cole slaw, giant Coke. That was $9.50. The deluxe turkey club and coffee was $11.25. And on it goes, until finally they ordered, always *under* what the coupon was worth. And then they wanted change.

Like the casino *owed* them that back. No way, Jack, Rashad told them. So then they got mad and what did they do?

Stiffed *him,* said Rachel Rose.

That's right, said Junior, loving the way she looked when she laughed. Plus they take everything that's not nailed down. They bring plastic zip-up bags, dump in the whole bucket of pickles. All the crackers and bread and Sweet'n Low. It made Rashad so frustrated, it's no wonder, said Junior, that sometimes the two of them, after Rashad got off work, they'd find themselves a couple of people who look prosperous, not the codgers, but regular tourists, lady wearing gold chains and diamonds, and—

"And what?" said Rachel Rose.

Uh-oh. Junior realized he'd gone too far with this story, making up most of it as he went along. Rachel Rose was giving him this look.

"And what?"

"Well, you know."

"You *rob* 'em?" Rachel Rose's big blue eyes were even bigger. And softer. Her voice was whispery and really low.

"Well—"

She stepped a little closer. He could feel her warmth, see every eyelash. "God, that's exciting," she said.

There you were. It just goes to show you. There's no way to know what's going through a girl's mind.

That's what Rashad, who was always studying people because he was going to be a movie director like Spike Lee, said. He said, Boy, you're just humping along, doing your stuff. Half of it makes girls mad as hell, but *some* of it, and there's no predicting which part, makes 'em look like that. Like starlets in the movies, faces all soft, ready for their close-up.

Just like Rachel Rose looked now.

"Well, yeah," Junior said, giving his dreads a little shake, puffing his chest, shifting his weight.

"How do you do it?"

Junior stood off and looked back at himself. "Actually, we have several different methods." Sounding like an expert. Trying not to crack up.

"Like what?"

"There're different ways—"

"Show me one," she breathed. "Show me one *now.*"

She was begging him. He had to pull this off—and make it look like he knew what he was doing.

"Well, okay." He shuffled around, staring at the laces on his hightops. "Here's one. First off, we buy ourselves a couple of hot dogs. We put lots of mustard on 'em."

He and Rashad had read about this gimmick that slick dudes did in New York. They were thinking about using it in a video Rashad had started working on, Junior providing the background music with his harmonica, and technical assistance. They'd finish it someday. Someday would be when they had some money, new equipment, better than Rashad's old broken-down—

Uh-huh, she said. He could tell she thought he was crazy, but she stepped right up to the counter and ordered the dogs.

"Now grab yourself a whole bunch of napkins. Good, now give them to me. No, hey, wait, girl. You're not eating that thing. Just come with me. Let's stroll."

Off they went, down the Boardwalk. It was still early, a little after ten, but there were plenty of people all over the place because the Miss America show had just let out. People were dressed up like *they* were trying for Miss America. Women in spangles and pearls with fancy hairdos were giggling when their high heels stuck in the Boardwalk. Mixed in with the pageant crowd were the geezers from the tour buses who ate their dinners about five o'clock, then went back for some more gambling. They were out now for a nightcap: an ice cream cone and a little stroll. And there was that bunch of ugly girls with their stupid signs that showed up with that crazy Reverend Dexter Dunwoodie. There was the rev now, with his fat-assed self and his silly, greased-up hairdo.

Rachel Rose pointed at them. "Who's that?"

Junior pretended he didn't know. It embarrassed him, explaining about a black man who was a fool like Dunwoodie, always stirring people up instead of helping them out. Dragging this pitiful bunch of white girls around like they were something. Proved something. Protesting the pageant. Now, did that make sense? Somebody ought to protest his ass. Ask him what he did with all that money he collected *last* year, his mama said every time she saw him on the local news, supposed to be building a special high school for street kids, help them out.

They walked on past Eddie and Louie. Eddie, a huge man singing "I'm Just a Prisoner of Love," had a soft, womanish face. His big old privates were about to fall out through a hole in the crotch of his checked pants. Louie was a hundred-year-old twisted-up arthritic wearing a thousand-year-old Hawaiian shirt and playing the keyboard.

Gathered around them were a circle of middle-aged white men in bermuda shorts or baggy pants, those stupid white hats. Their ladies were dressed in colors like aqua and peach. But they weren't who Junior was looking for.

To do this right—and why not, if he was going to do it—he needed a couple dressed nice. They'd be headed for one of those casino restaurants that didn't have prices on the menu—you cared what it cost, forget you. They'd played some baccarat and were out for a breath of fresh ocean air just like the codgers.

"What are we gonna do?" Rachel Rose whispered.

"Be cool. Stop fidgeting." He nudged her over to his left side. The ocean was on his right. They were walking up toward the Taj. He dropped a little behind her. She stopped, turned around, and gave him the big eyes. "Nope. Don't look at *me*. Keep going. That's right. You're doing great."

I'm doing terrible, he'd said to himself. How'd I get myself in this spot? This isn't a little shoplifting. This is

Boardwalk robbery. I could get myself arrested for real. But he didn't know how to back off without making a fool of himself.

So they strolled on past Fred, a beggar who'd held out a cup so long his hand had frozen like that.

There was no one who looked exactly right to Junior, who didn't look like they'd scream and call the cops. Maybe he didn't have the stuff it took to be a mustard chucker. Maybe he'd have to admit to Rachel Rose he was just jiving.

Then, there they were: two white ladies loaded down with purses, jewelry, pearls, gold earrings, probably the real thing. They were yakking ninety miles a minute. One of them, the woman closest to Rachel Rose, was tall, very skinny, with lots of frizzy red hair. She looked like an old stork, except she was carrying a briefcase instead of the baby you saw in most pictures of storks.

It was now or never, thought Junior, his heart pounding, wondering if maybe he really was cut out for a life of crime. Consider the possibilities. Bank robberies? Maybe. Or he could be a cat burglar, sniffing out safes behind family portraits. Go, he said to himself, go! Quit daydreaming. So when they pulled just about even with the two ladies, Junior shoved Rachel Rose hard.

"Oh, my God, I'm so sorry." Rachel Rose sounded truly concerned. The girl was a natural. Of course, she didn't know what was going on.

The Stork Woman, staring down at her white linen dress splattered with mustard, teeter-tottered on the edge of tears.

"Here, ma'am, let me help you." Now Junior was Johnny-on-the-spot, wiping at Stork Woman with a handful of napkins, dabbing her this way and that.

"I am *so* sorry," Rachel Rose kept saying, wringing her little hands. "I feel so bad. Can I pay you for your cleaning?"

Now, that was going *too* far.

Then the Stork Woman's friend pulled at her arm and said, Come on, Mary Frances, let's go back to your room and wash it off.

Sorry, so sorry, Rachel Rose echoed. Junior gave the

ladies a last big so-sorry smile and pulled Rachel Rose on down the Boardwalk, which wasn't easy with her spike heels.

Then he pushed her through the doors of the Showboat, down the long center hall, past the band playing Dixieland, past the casino waitresses in those short little purple and black outfits that pushed their boobs up, the bottoms cut so high you could see their behinds, past security, giving them the eye. Junior gave the man back a big smile—though not too big. Actually, Junior was terrified.

"What's going on?" Rachel Rose sounded a little pissed. Then she turned and whispered to him, "When do we do *it?"* The girl really didn't know.

"We *did* it."

That stopped her dead in her tracks.

Junior took her arm—he was afraid to stop—and led her out the casino's back door, out onto Pacific Avenue. He turned left, heading back down past the back of the Taj, Resorts International, down toward the Monopoly, hurrying her along.

On top of everything else, it wasn't safe back here off the Boardwalk. Somebody could hit *them* in the head, take their stash. He didn't want to tell Rachel Rose that.

But then she stopped again, right in the middle of the sidewalk. "I'm not going another step until you explain to me what happened."

What happened? What happened, he said, was she chucked the mustard on the Stork Woman, he wiped it off her, along with—he held them up—her wallet and her miniature tape recorder.

"Holy Jesus!"

Junior grinned. "I wouldn't go that far. Junior Sturdivant'll do."

"My God!" She couldn't get over it. "What if you get caught?"

"You? Who's this *you? We* did it."

Then the little girl threw her hands up in the air like somebody was holding a gun on her.

"You were the mustard chucker," he said.

"The what? The *what!"* And Rachel Rose sat down, just like that, on the sidewalk. Her shoes fell off. She doubled over, holding her stomach. Junior thought she was having some kind of fit. But she wasn't. The little girl was laughing her butt off.

Well, hell, he thought, the deed was done. So he plopped down too, and before he knew it was wiping tears and snuffling. What he *really* wanted to do was cry, he was so scared inside.

Then, just as it was getting good—Rachel Rose turned and threw her arms around his neck, she felt so soft, smelled so good—a car at one of the Monopoly's service doors, he hadn't even seen it before, someone slammed one of its doors, then after a minute, slammed the trunk, now a door again, and cranked up, flashing its brights.

Junior froze, guilty, red-handed, feeling the loot still warm from the Stork Woman. Whoever was in the car had seen the whole thing—Junior holding up the stash.

What? said Rachel Rose, nuzzling against his T-shirt, the one that said SHUT UP AND KISS ME. And she was about to, he could tell that, except he was so scared somebody, plain-clothes probably, was about to get out of that car and slap the cuffs on him, he pushed her away so he could keep an eye on them.

The engine roared. The driver slammed the car into reverse. It screeched back, forward, came on, blinding them, till Junior thought they were dead for sure. The sucker's gonna squash us flat right on the sidewalk, arms around each other like Romeo and Juliet Miz Abrams made us read last year. The headlights were dazzling, blinding him, he was going to die. Then they slid on by.

Junior's attitude did a 180-degree flipflop. He was mad as hell they scared the bejesus out of him, made him look like a fool in front of Rachel Rose, who'd been about to lay a wet one on him. If he ever got his hands on . . .

But the night was too dark and the lights were too bright. Junior couldn't even get a good look.

If he had, it was Kurt Roberts whom Junior would have seen staring out of the passenger seat before he was jerked out and shoved into the trunk. Kurt Roberts, the very man who had pushed him into the pool. With dried blood on his face, eyes puffed and swollen into slits. His long, thin nose broken and askew. A couple of shiny white capped teeth were missing. His mouth gaped open and closed. He looked like a big fish who'd done battle with an outboard.

Saying, *Help. Help. Somebody help me, please. Oh, God.*

But Junior didn't see him.

And none of that was what Junior told Big Gloria. How could he? She'd kill him. Instead, he made up this nice little story about running into Rachel Rose, did Mama remember her from yesterday afternoon, the pretty little girl by the pool?

That didn't make her happy either. What are you doing messing around with her? You'll find yourself killed when her daddy gets ahold of you.

There was an awful lot of threatening to kill his young ass around these days, thought Junior. Then he told his mama how he and Rachel Rose had played pinball, ate hot dogs, walked down the Boardwalk. He walked her home to her hotel. That was the end of it.

Later, at school, Junior would think how stupid he was for telling her that much. Placing himself and Rachel Rose on the Boardwalk wasn't the smartest thing he could do. You never could tell what might pop up. The Stork Woman could describe them, then the cops would come looking for them. But it was *hard* to lie to Mama. There was something about her that made you want to tell her everything, even stuff you were ashamed of.

And Big Gloria would worry herself crazy knowing that Junior had told her *some* version of the truth.

Gloria had spent her entire life listening to men tell lies, and she knew one when she heard it.

What she wanted to know was, son of mine, only child of my womb, did that white man make you so mad, the one who pushed you in the pool, that you broke into his room, beat the tar out of him, killed him with your bare hands, and dragged him off somewhere?

Son of mine, only child of my womb, could you do that? Did you do that? Have I already lost you?

. . . 10

After breakfast Sam and Harry had walked so far south on the Boardwalk, the casinos were huge ships in the mist behind them. It was a sweet time. They held hands and laughed, the color in their cheeks the same cherry red as Sam's sweater.

"Do we look like a television commercial?" she asked.

"For some soft drink. The good life."

"Rather have bottled water."

"Oh, that's right. You're *that* one."

"Uh-huh. I bet you do have trouble keeping track of who you're with—those cuties you've stashed all over the Quarter."

"One way to find out. Come live with me."

"In that tacky little place?"

"You love my apartment."

He was right. She did. She loved his big brass bed upstairs in the tiny slave-quarter cottage overlooking a courtyard. She loved the jazz from Preservation Hall drifting across his little balcony, through his window, across their bodies, which always seemed to be naked, or semi-naked.

It was a great place to visit.

"Now what's that you're whistling?" she asked.

" 'May I Have This Dance for the Rest of My Life?' " Then he took her into his arms and waltzed her around and around on the Boardwalk. "What do you think?"

"Oh, Harry."

Suddenly a wolf whistle split the air, followed by a round

of applause. "You two want a ride?" It was a young blond man pushing a wicker beach chair, Atlantic City's version of a rickshaw.

"Get out of here," Harry waved him off.

"Five dollars'll get you all the way back to the casinos."

"Vamoose. Am-scray."

"Jeeszt. You don't have to get hostile about it, man."

"Jeeszt, you don't have to get hostile about it, lady," Harry said to Sam as the man and his chair pushed on down the Boardwalk.

"About what?"

"About my invitations. Two. Living and dancing."

"Harry, dear heart—"

"Special offer today. I don't think you want to miss it." That wasn't Harry. It was *another* beach chair.

"What's *with* you guys?" Harry barked.

"I'm no guys, sir. I'm your Super-Duper Buggy Pusher also known by the appellation of Rashad." The young black man performed a deep bow in his white tie and tails—above a pair of cutoffs. "I've been employed in this profession only two days, so as you can see, I'm still fresh as the proverbial daisy—*Chrysanthemum leucanthemum.* I'll perambulate you up and down, deliver you a son et lumière show—if that's your pleasure, m'lady."

"Maybe we ought to, Harry."

"Are you nuts? I don't want to do this."

"It's part of the Atlantic City tradition," said Sam. She'd read that in her press kit.

"Perhaps you should listen to the pretty lady—meaning no offense, sir. Perchance she's fatigued."

"She's just old," said Sam. "And she doesn't want to be late."

"She wants to change the subject is what she wants," said Harry. "You think this guy's gonna push us faster than we can walk?"

"I'm known for my speed," said Rashad. "Faster than the proverbial bullet. But safe. Oh, yes, surety is my middle name."

"Surety, bull. Shuck and jive, you mean," said Harry.

"You're being rude, darling." Sam stepped into the rolling chair and extended a queenly hand to her consort.

"Do you know the derivation of that phrase, shuck and jive?" asked Rashad from behind them once they'd both tucked into the chair and he'd headed north.

"No, we don't, and we don't want to," said Harry.

"I'd love to know," said Sam.

"Well, you see, down in New Orleans, in the oyster bars, there are these good fellows who earn their livelihood opening the local bivalves—"

"I'm *from* New Orleans," Harry groaned.

"Then I defer to your superior wisdom," said Rashad. "You must certainly know the anecdote."

"Tell us the story, Harry," Sam said.

"I don't know the damned story."

"Then hush. Go on, Rashad." She sounded just like a contestant, with a smile in her voice.

"These oyster shuckers, I met one, actually two, who were here in Atlantic City enjoying a weekend of recreation. Michael Broadway is in the employ of the Acme Oyster House—"

Harry groaned again.

"That's right around the corner from Harry's house. I'm Sam. He's Harry."

"Charmed to make your acquaintance. And Harry doesn't like New Orleans?"

"Harry loves New Orleans," said Harry. "Sam doesn't."

"Sam *loves* New Orleans," she protested.

"But Sam doesn't love Harry," said Harry.

"Sam loves Harry. Sam just doesn't know if she wants to love Harry *in* New Orleans. Full-time."

"She'd rather love him from Atlanta," Harry explained.

"Long distance, as it were," said Rashad.

"As it were," sighed Harry. "Go on with your story, Rashad. You were at the Acme."

"The other bivalve professional was known as Robert Washington. He's in the employ of Casamento's—I believe he said."

"Out on Magazine. The little place with the great tiles," Harry reminded Sam.

"Robert Washington. Is he a cousin of Lavert's?"

"Probably. I think everybody's a cousin of Lavert's."

"Anyway, these gentlemen were telling me how they ply their trade."

"Are you an English professor in your spare time, Rashad?" asked Harry.

"No. Why do you ask?"

"You speak rather precisely."

"Rather? What do you mean—rather? I thought I spoke precisely in the main."

"I think you're shucking us, Rashad," said Harry.

"Or at least jiving," said Sam.

"Jiving is correct," Rashad agreed. "Now, jiving is what I was attempting to explicate. As I was saying, I encountered these two bivalve professionals here in a local bar one evening, where they were attempting to explain to a local bivalve amateur how to properly open a mollusk."

"Which is?" asked Harry, finally loosening up a little. "I've seen it done a million times, but—"

"That's what Messrs. Washington and Broadway said. Seeing and doing are two different things. What they demonstrated went like this: Now, there's a hole in the smaller end of the oyster, and that's where you insert the tip of your oyster knife—which is *not* a sharpened blade. Then you lean all your weight on the oyster, not the blade, and twist your wrist."

"It's all in the wrist action?" asked Sam.

"As in many things," answered Rashad, "it's a matter of finesse. Then you peek inside the oyster and slip the knife around and cut that top muscle. Flop it over, cut the other. Wiggle the oyster around, get rid of the debris. The gentlemen made it look so easy, the same way a fine pianist does, playing the *Moonlight Sonata* or the dirty boogie with equal dexterity."

"Actually, we had a fellow who did that. Opened oysters, that is, in the movie I worked on recently. He shucked, *I* played the dirty boogie," said Harry.

The rolling chair lurched to an abrupt halt.

"Did I hear you say *movie?* As in *film?* As in *cinema?*"

"As in picture show, Rashad," laughed Harry.

"In New Orleans? You worked on a movie in New Orleans recently?"

"Yeah. With Spike Lee."

At those words, the entire rail-thin six-foot length of Rashad plummeted backward to the Boardwalk like falling timber. He landed belly up, paused a moment, then flopped over and knelt, facing the Atlantic. "Allah is good. Allah be praised."

"Allah isn't in the business, Rashad," said Harry.

Rashad popped back up and leaned over, almost in Harry's face. "You *know* Spike Lee?"

Harry shrugged. "Not really. I just did the background, me and the guys I play with. Mostly some other guy told us what the scene was, what mood they wanted, and we fooled around till we had something they said was okay."

Rashad did two cartwheels.

"Pretty amazing," said Sam.

Harry had to agree.

"But you *met* him," Rashad crowed, now upright again. "You met Spike!"

"Yes, you could say that."

"And what *I* could say is that if we don't get going here, I'm going to be late for my press conference. Or shall we get out and walk, Rashad, until you get the use of yourself again?"

"So sorry, I'm so sorry." And then Rashad propelled them lickety-split, slowing only slightly for codgers, other rolling chairs, and ambling dogs.

In front of Convention Hall he refused to accept more than the most minimal payment from Harry, and waived the tip altogether.

"Why do I think I'm going to be seeing you again soon, Rashad?" asked Harry. "Perhaps with a film can in your hand?"

At that, Rashad's head began to bob, and he could hardly

control his feet, which seemed to have many miles to hustle before sundown. He tried to control himself, but then his exuberance won out and he did six backflips. Three passing tourists tried to give him small change, and he kissed their hands.

"Now, Rashad, I doubt that I can help you much," said Harry. But then he heard himself saying those words and remembered how many times he'd heard the same ones in Nashville. How many times he'd stood just outside the door when the man on the other side could have extended a hand, given a nod, and it could have made all the difference in the world to a young songwriter. "But I can try. I'll do what I can. . . ."

Rashad did four forward flips, six backward, and a small crowd cheered.

Sam laughed. Oh, God. Wasn't it fun, being with Harry? Crazy things were always happening to him. Crazier even than a press conference to announce the Fruit of the Loom Award, which is where *she* was headed.

She said her good-byes to Harry and Rashad and then remembered. "You never finished explaining the jiving part of shuck and jive, Rashad."

"That's what the bivalve professionals do while they shuck. Chat up the customers."

"That's the jiving of shucking and jiving?"

"That's the jiving," Rashad nodded.

"That's the jiving," said Harry, pointing at the Undisputed Jive Master of the Boardwalk, Monsieur Rashad.

. . . 11

ON HER WAY THROUGH THE LOBBY TO THE PRESS CONFERENCE, Sam caught sight of Cindy Lou in a bisecting hallway. Thank God for small favors and good timing.

The former Miss Ohio was wearing a powder-blue suit,

her shoulders hunched in a posture that would have never won her a rhinestone tiara. She was still hiding behind those shades.

Was that because Kurt, the mean, mysterious Kurt, had popped her one good, as the reporter from the *Inquirer* had surmised? Sam called after the former Miss Ohio.

Cindy Lou turned and spotted Sam. She hesitated for a count of one, then raced on, her heels clicking on the terrazzo.

But Sam didn't walk miles every day for nothing. "Hi!" she said as she pulled even with Cindy Lou, who didn't look the least bit pleased.

"Sam Adams. Atlanta *Constitution.* I'm the one who did the interview yesterday in the press—"

"I know." Cindy Lou hadn't slowed.

"I was on my way to ask a couple of questions of Barbara Stein, but I saw you and thought, What the heck, I bet you know more than she does. After all, you've *been* up on that big stage, haven't you?"

Cindy Lou pointed the dark glasses straight at her. If she lifted them, her eyes would read, Cut the crap.

"I was wondering, do you and the final judges sit down and have a powwow?"

Cindy slowed a tad. "Yes, we do. We get together on Saturday morning."

"And you tell the celebrity judges all the poop from the past week? Like who has the biggest sob story, gimp points—"

Cindy came to a full stop. A little smile played around the corners of her mouth. "You're picking up the angles."

"I'm a quick study. Another thing, has it made any difference with one less judge?"

Cindy stiffened. "Dividing the totals by six is no more difficult than dividing by seven. The pageant uses computers, you know. Now, if you'll excuse me—"

Sam stepped right in front of her. "Rumor has it that Kurt Roberts was kidnapped by the delegation from—" Which state would make sense? It helped to have these lies worked out in advance. Kidnapped by whom? The mob. New

Jersey. It'd play. "—New Jersey because they got the drift that Kurt didn't like their girl."

Cindy whirled. "That's the most ridiculous thing I've ever heard."

Well, at least it got her attention. "And I couldn't help but notice, I saw you and Kurt Roberts out at the pool yesterday afternoon, and it seemed as if you two—I was just wondering—do you know where he went? I was thinking of doing a sidebar on judges and the judging process." Actually that wasn't a bad idea. "And it'd be interesting to know what could drag a man away from—"

Cindy Lou bobbled her head above a rigid neck, her lips in a pout. When Goldie Hawn did it, the gesture was cute. "He went back to New York."

"That's what I heard, but it seems strange. Is that what he told you?"

"He didn't tell me anything."

"Really? He just up and left without saying good-bye?"

"He—I—" Suddenly Cindy Lou's composure crumpled. Her mouth trembled. "Get away, leave me alone," she snapped, then wheeled and bolted down the hall.

Sam could have caught her again, if she'd really wanted to. But there was the siren call of the press conference. She'd give Cindy Lou a rest.

Darleen Carroll stared in the mirror of the dressing table. It was almost noon, and she hadn't put her face on yet. Here she was, barely thirty-six, and an old hag.

At least, that's what Darleen thought. Actually, she still looked rather like the eighteen-year-old only daughter of the only Jewish jeweler in Eureka—way north of San Francisco, on the cool redwood coast where the fog made for good complexions—when she left off the two inches of makeup.

If she looked hard, she could see that young girl yet, the Darleen who'd hitchhiked her way south across the border to an abortionist in Tijuana before she chickened out at his front door, where pigs were rooting in garbage she didn't want to think about. It was in Los Angeles that she, still pregnant and hitching her way back toward Eureka, met

Billy, who was pumping gas and waiting for a break into the Big Time. Billy thought he had the stuff to be another Old Blue Eyes. He'd done some little theater, and he had the eyes and the best baritone in Sioux Falls.

Those had been the sweet days. He'd said she reminded him a lot of the little sister he'd left back home in South Dakota, and he'd let her sleep on his couch. It wasn't long before she'd moved into his bed, and then she had a miscarriage, losing the baby of that other Billy, Billy Barnes back in Eureka, who couldn't have been much of a man, said Billy Carroll, whose real name was Billy Karczewski, to let her run off that way by herself.

Darleen had straightened up Billy's little apartment, made some curtains out of flowered sheets she found on sale—she'd liked to make things pretty since she was a tiny thing—and before you knew it, they had a sweet little home, and Billy did get a break. They honeymooned on the proceeds from his deodorant commercial, and then there was a walk-on on a soap. Next came a small speaking part in a James Garner film, and they thought the sky was the limit.

But before too long, it became apparent that Billy would have to aim a little lower.

"Too short, next!" casting directors would say, *right to Billy's face.* Hey! What about Alan Ladd, he'd scream as he threw things through the windows of the little house they'd taken in Santa Monica. *His* leading ladies stood in a trench. A few inches didn't stop *him.*

Darleen never said, Yeah, but maybe he was more talented, though she was beginning to think that. But it was too late to make noises like that because Rachel Rose was on the way, and she definitely wanted this baby to have a daddy.

So she kept telling Billy he was the greatest and went right on with the decorating classes she'd started taking at night. It wasn't long before Darleen could render you a perspective of what your house was going to look like along with color swatches to beat the band, and she found it real easy to get along with the Haute Queen antiques dealers at the Design Center who gave her special deals and turned her on to superrich clients in return for a little kickback.

Darleen had done *very* well, and Billy's career had eventually picked up. He'd found his way into the emcee market—and occasionally got to sing a song or two. Then "The Big One" had come along, and it was the Big Time—for Billy. It paid bushels of cash, and the set was always plump with cute little dollies.

Darleen stared hard at her face in the mirror and wondered, What would happen if I had a chin implant? Would that pull out those little grooves that are starting from my nose down to my mouth? Or are we talking full-scale lift here?

She'd have to ask her friend Maureen, who had had the whole thing done when she was forty. Maureen said there was no such thing as too early, and besides, you could always have it done again.

But what Maureen couldn't tell her, and what she wanted to know right now, was whether or not Billy was sleeping with Miss New Jersey.

He played AC once a year, just to keep his hand in, he said. His hand in *what?* Last night Darleen had passed on watching Billy's act. After all, she'd seen it a million times before, both onstage and in their living room, and besides—it wasn't in the main room. He was just another singer playing to a bunch of drunks and losers, and the combo couldn't ever seem to get the intro to his theme song, "Send in the Clowns," to go just right.

Frankly, the show embarrassed her.

Actually, Billy was beginning to embarrass her.

Aw, come on, Darleen, she said to herself in the mirror. Admit it. Billy has embarrassed you for years, and humiliated you with other women, and what you're trying to do now is get up the nerve to leave him.

That's right, she whispered back. But it's hard to do, after all this time, and you're afraid of spending the rest of your life like all those divorcées you know back home in Newport Beach, Brentwood, Beverly Hills, doing your house and your face over and over until your face looks Chinese and your house looks like Versailles. So what you're looking for is some Grand Finale, some Huge Scene, some in flagrante delicto so flagrante that it will force you into declaring it the coup d'état—Darleen having learned more than a soupçon of French from the Haute Queens.

For a long time she'd hung in because of Rachel Rose. But she couldn't use her as an excuse any longer. Rachel Rose was just about grown, and she was wise to her dad, though she still loved him. As did Darleen—a little. After all, he had taken her in when she was young and desperate. They had known each other forever, and knew each other's warts. On the other hand, there was her pride.

The song was right. Breaking up *was* hard to do.

Just then, Billy stumbled into the bathroom.

"Oh, Jesus," he said. "My head."

Darleen gave him a look of cool appraisal. After all, she wasn't a jeweler's daughter for nothing. "Four A.M., I'd say. And at least half a bottle of Cutty Sark."

He held his head. "Ooooooh. Don't remind me."

"I waited for you after the show, Billy. Right where we agreed, in Uncle Pennybags."

Billy lifted his face from the sink, which he'd filled with ice from the wet bar. His theory was that a faceful of ice cured any multitude of sins and hid them from the camera. Darleen didn't know why he persisted in this belief, since he looked easily five years older than she, and they were born two weeks apart.

But then, she didn't drink.

And she didn't screw around.

"No, darling, I didn't get your message." She shifted into her cheerful voice, which Billy detested in the morning, if you could call noon the morning. "Did you leave it with one of the sweet Guatemalan waiters who couldn't deliver it because he doesn't speak English so well, bless his heart?"

"No, I left it with the hotel answering service."

"Oh, damn that hotel answering service."

Billy lowered the ice from his face. "Sarcasm is not becoming, Darleen."

"Oh, double damn," she said. "And to think no one told me that before now."

* * *

Billy was worried about Darleen. She didn't seem like herself lately. A little more snippy. A lot more outspoken. He wondered if she was going through the change of life early. His aunt Thelma back in Pierre had done that. At least that's what they said when she went out into the barn early one morning and castrated all the bulls.

The thought made Billy shiver. He reached for the bottle of Maalox.

"Bad stomach?" Darleen cooed.

Yeah, maybe it was the change. Maybe he ought to talk to her about going to see that gynecologist of hers. Of course, Billy was convinced that the gynecologist was a dyke. How else did you explain a woman wanting to stick her hand up other women all day? And he didn't want any dyke putting any more ideas in Darleen's head. She came up with enough of them by herself—and talking to her crazy friend Maureen.

He didn't know what had gotten into women these days. *Nothing* ever seemed to make them happy. That's why he preferred 'em young.

Of course, preferring and having were two different things. If you'd been around the block more than once, you really had to show the girls something.

Something like a Mercedes 560 SL, for starters. Access to swanky clubs, hideaways down in Florida like Gary Hart—though you tried to use a little more finesse than that bozo. A lot of disposable green to throw around.

At that thought, Billy shivered again.

It was trying to make that disposable green to impress the dollies that had gotten him into the fix he was in.

Oh, Jesus.

He didn't know why he'd let himself get snookered into that poker game in the first place. Poker wasn't his thing. He favored the ponies.

He stared into his sunny-side-up eyes above the sink and thought, Who're you fooling, Billy? Everything's your thing. Everything you can lose money at. Football. Cards. The track. Basketball. Baseball. Hockey. Tennis. Hell, once he'd even bet on Ping-Pong when the Olympics were on TV in a bar.

The girl who was with him at the time, a silly little redhead not much older than Rachel Rose, which shamed him if he thought about it—he tried not to think about it—said: Billy'll bet on anything that has balls.

There was some truth in that. The whole truth was, Billy would bet on anything, period. He was the kind of guy, the fellas in Vegas liked to say, his mother was dying, Billy'd bet which way she'd fall.

Yeah, Billy was a Vegas kind of guy.

The kind they loved to see coming.

And coming and coming and coming.

Yeah, Billy was a real spurter all right. And a bleeder and a sweater and a crybaby, and right now he felt like he didn't have a single drop of liquid left in his body.

He'd pissed it all away on the cards last night.

And why had he gone into that back room at Tommy's for that very private little game with the high rollers? The big boys?

Because they asked him, that's why.

It made him feel like one of the gang. It made him feel like a big man, Billy Carroll of "The Big One." Little Billy Karczewski was left behind in Sioux Falls, never to be thought of again.

It made him feel like the kind of guy who would always be lucky, and who would *get* lucky every night, with a different beautiful babe on his arm—many of them *tall.*

But then, when it was all over, and he'd lost, lost Big Time, he'd turned to old Angelo Carlo, called Angelo Pizza because he ran a chain of pizza parlors for Ma Amato. Angelo was very big in Ma's various businesses, not the least of which was loan-sharking. "Angelo," he said, "I'm gonna have to ask you for a favor."

"Don't do it," Angelo had said, shifting his weight to his good leg. "It won't be no favor."

"I need ten thousand."

"I can see that. But I can also see that the last time you

had trouble paying the vig, and it got nasty before it got nice, and I don't like having to do that. It puts me in an awkward position, Billy. And I'm in a bad mood already, got a guy who skipped, just like you, always behind."

"Please. You know I never skipped on anything in my life. What's skip? As if you couldn't find me in a second. Please, Ange." Billy hated hearing himself beg like that. But he didn't have much choice. He had to give the players the money, or he wasn't getting out of the room alive. Better to be alive now and worry about being dead tomorrow was one of Billy's philosophies.

Eventually, Angelo made him the loan.

But now Billy looked at his eyes in the mirror, and they made him want to puke because they were so scared. The vig, the vigorish, the interest on ten thousand, was three hundred a week, or three percent. That was what he had to come up with, just to stay even, paying nothing back on the principal. That was one hundred and fifty-six percent interest a year. Which would make it fifteen thousand six hundred dollars—plus the original ten thousand.

"And," Angelo had said, "I'm giving you a break on the vig 'cause I know you. And I like your singing. Anybody ever tell you you sound a little bit like the Crooner?"

Yeah. Yeah yeah yeah. Billy knew all that. He also knew that Angelo could charge up to five, six percent on a short term and nobody would really holler. Nobody desperate, that is. And who but somebody desperate would borrow money from Angelo Pizza in the first place?

Just then, Darleen came up and put her face right beside his. She'd slapped on her full war paint.

Did that mean she was about to scalp him?

Yeah, maybe. She was running her fingers through his hair, or trying to.

"Billy, did you ever think you might bring your do into the twentieth century?"

Billy stiffened. He hated talking about his hair. He hated talking about almost anything *personal,* but especially his hair. This was his lucky hair. He'd been wearing this hairdo when he got his shot at the Big Time on "The Big One" and he saw no reason to mess with success.

"Get out of here, Darleen," he said.

She pinched him on the behind through his pink boxer shorts. He stared at her, big-eyed in the mirror. She used to do that when she was in the mood.

"Do you have something in mind here, Darleen?"

She did. She didn't know why, but every time she got right to the edge of leaving Billy, she wanted him like crazy. Maybe it was realizing that once he was out of the picture, loving might be scarce for a while. Maybe it was old times. In any case, she leaned over and kissed him on the back of the neck. "Why don't you slip into the shower and I'll sit outside here and tell you all about what I've got in mind."

He couldn't believe it. That's what they used to do, back in the old days, before they lost it. He'd shower and Darleen would talk dirty to him, and sometimes they couldn't even wait until he finished showering. Sometimes she'd jump inside and they'd make love standing up with the suds and hot water running all over them.

"Darleen—" he started, and then changed his mind. Better not to talk. He ripped his shorts off, adjusted the water, and stepped inside.

"Do you remember," she purred, "that weekend we spent in Acapulco?"

How could he ever forget it? Darleen hadn't worn any panties the whole time, and he'd felt like the biggest stud south of the border.

"Do you remember that afternoon when we sat by the pool and sucked down about forty-two margaritas and then in the elevator on the way to the room—"

Oh, yeah. This was more like it. Like old times, when they still liked each other, before he . . . The phone rang.

"Don't answer it," Billy cried. It was probably somebody he owed money, and whoever it was, he wasn't in the mood. What he was in the mood for now . . . "Please don't answer it, Darleen."

But she did. Who could tell? Barbara Bush may have

decided she needed a redo on the house in Kennebunkport. Get rid of all that frumpy old chintz and think about—

But it wasn't Barbara Bush. Or Nancy. Or Rosalynn. Or any of the other First Ladies Darleen had fantasies about.

Though it was *a* Barbara. Barbara Stein. Who seemed desperate to speak with Billy.

Darleen handed the receiver into the shower.

Billy listened for a moment, then turned down the water. "You said he did what? He can't? You what? *Me?* You're sure? Well, of course. I'd be delighted. It's wonderful. I mean, it's too bad for Gary, and nobody can really replace him. Yes, I know, Phyllis will be a big help. *She's* wonderful. *It's* wonderful. *You're* wonderful. And, yes, I agree, NBC's wonderful for thinking of me. I know, the most convenient thing in the world, that I'm right here! Yes indeedy, the show must go on."

After it was over, Billy leaned against the back wall of the shower, ignoring Darleen outside yelling *What? What? What?* and turned the water back up, letting it pour over him like a baptism.

For he was saved. Yes, he was.

Gary Collins was sick as a dog, puking his guts out, and they wanted *him*. They were going to pay *him* one hundred thousand dollars for the three nights, tonight, tomorrow, and the Saturday night live on TV, more than enough to pay off Angelo Pizza and any vig he might dream up.

Miss America had saved Billy Carroll's sweet patootie.

Way to go, Miss A! Billy screamed, standing ankle-deep in hot water.

...12

"OKAY, FILL ME IN ON THIS THING." SAM FLOPPED HERSELF DOWN in the pressroom beside the *Inquirer*.

"You noticed on the girls' bios how they all do good?"

"Never seen such helpful little munchkins. Seeing Eye

dogs, hospital hopalongs, rest home regulars, funding for AIDS, they do it all. A pageant requirement, right?"

"Uh-huh." The *Inquirer* was sucking down a giant lemonade. She looked a little shaky. "Since the pageant itself depends on jillions of volunteers to put together the shows on the local and state levels, mostly Jaycees, they're real big on volunteerism. This scholarship's winner is usually a girl who's a victim. Like she had cancer and talks with cancer patients. Gave a lung to her brother, works with transplants —that kind of thing."

"You're sounding awfully cynical today for a pageant groupie."

"I could use a brain transplant myself, if not a whole new head. Too much partying with those Texans. You missed some righteous hooting and hollering."

"I can imagine. Did you have your stomach pumped last night or this morning?"

"I wish," moaned the *Inquirer*. "I'd feel a hell of a lot better. Promise me you'll go to the Old South Ball Saturday if I can wangle you an invite, so you'll feel as bad as I do."

Not a chance. But what was it?

"It's the best of the parties. Right before the final judging, the southern delegations put this one on. Complete with color guard in Confederate uniforms, flashing swords, stars and bars, hoopskirts, enough bourbon to drown in."

"Must be hell on Miss Louisiana."

"Would be. Except contestants don't go. Press doesn't either, usually. Let me know if you're interested." That said, the *Inquirer* snuggled down for a few winks while Barbara Stein went on about the award, volunteerism, and the wonderful young lady who was this year's first-place winner.

Sam punched her awake. "Hey, hey, hey! It's my girl! Rae Ann's Miss Fruit of the Loom."

Then Miss Rae Ann Bridges, Miss Dogwood Festival, Miss Georgia, and Miss America preliminary talent winner, stepped right up and took that microphone just like she'd taken the stage the night before.

"This is the proudest moment of my life," she drawled, letting a little more of her Southern creep in than usual.

Sam knew that one. You turned it on and off with Yankees. A little was charming. A tad more, they thought you were mentally retarded.

"I don't think there's anything that could make me prouder. Even if I were to become Miss America, that moment just couldn't make me any prouder and happier than this one."

"You need a hankie?" The *Inquirer* gave it her mid-Atlantic drawl, her eyes still closed.

"Hey, I cry at AT&T commercials. The one where Mama picks up the phone and it's her kid telling her he loves her. Doesn't mean a damned thing."

"Uh-huh. Uh-huh." The *Inquirer* leaned her head back on the top of her chair. "Tell me another one. That Ben Franklin's dying to jump over into my pocket. Why don't you just go ahead and pay up?"

"Why don't you go take an Alka-Seltzer? Now, if you'll excuse me, I've got to go file this little tidbit." This kind of thing kept up, Hoke was going to give her a raise when she got home, if she didn't quit first.

Harry found Lavert at poolside, where the big man had commandeered a table, two lounge chairs, a waiter, and a telephone with two lines.

"What's the matter? They didn't have a fax?"

"Man's working on it. He's cool."

"You tell them you're James Bond?"

"Naw. It's easy, you know folks in the business."

"I thought you were getting out of the business. You better, if we ever hope to get a liquor license for Lavert's."

"Not the Joey business. The restaurant business. Nicest people in the world."

"Great, Lavert. Now, could we get down to it here?"

"Stealing your pretty girlfriend's money? That's what you mean?"

"Winning our wager, yes." He pointed at the phone. "What've you got?"

"Not much. A little something. How about you?"

"Zero. I started with Roberts's office. They told me he was here in Atlantic City, judging the pageant."

"And his house?"

"Answering machine with a message saying the same thing—like the man was real proud of himself."

"Well, I put myself in touch with a couple of friends who have access to credit records—"

"Lavert—"

"And they said there's been no activity on any of his charge cards or his bank accounts since yestiddy afternoon, when he bought himself some suntan lotion, a new razor, and some rubbers at the Walgreen's on Pacific."

"But that couldn't be right. What about his hotel bill when he checked out?"

Lavert grinned his run-around-the-tight-end grin. "That's the little-something part. The man didn't check out."

"What?"

"Nope. He's still registered. Which means he's probably just shacked up with some lady somewhere, living off her."

"But wait, man. I'd have to agree with Sammy on this one. Why toss over the pageant for some—"

"We don't have to worry our pretty little heads about that. All we've got to do is find the dude alive and well. Isn't that the bet?"

"Yeah, but there's got to be some logic to this thing."

"Man, you think there's logic when a lady's involved? Since when did a man be talking logic to his Johnson?"

Lavert did have a point there. After all, *he* was the man who'd ended up in the Angola State Penitentiary because he had fallen for a little girl named Sharleen, a maid at the Hotel Monteleone on Royal Street who had access to lots of pretty things in people's rooms her ownself but asked Lavert would he be so kind as to carry them for her. It had been Sharleen who was screaming at the top of her lungs when the hotel security came busting into that last hotel room, Sharleen already had clean sheets on the California king: *He's the one, the one made me do it, said he'd beat me up, big old boy like him, little thing like me scared to death.*

Lavert reminded Harry of that scenario in an attempt to convince him to *cherchez la femme,* and Harry's face lit up like it was his birthday. "Shazam, Batman. You've led us to the source of all knowledge, inadvertently."

"Lavert don't inadvert, man. Tell me what brilliance I've zeroed in on."

"Big Gloria. Queen of Monopoly Housekeeping, Big Gloria's got her finger on the pulse. *And* she owes me."

. . . 13

LAVERT WAS RIGHT ABOUT THE GIRLFRIENDS. THEY WERE SOMEthing all right—both absolutely beautiful and stunningly tall. Texas was the voluptuous one. Louisiana, whippet thin.

All conversation stopped when Sam and the two contestants and their chaperones strolled into the White House Sub Shop.

The girls were wearing white shirts, neatly pressed jeans, and cowboy boots with high heels—Texas's were red, Louisiana's silver.

"Never walk into a room under six feet is my motto," said Texas, who would have been impressive at half a foot less with her dark-auburn hair, golden-brown eyes, and magnolia complexion. Louisiana, also a knockout with a ruby-red smile and skin of mahogany velvet, nodded. "Anything less, they don't notice you."

Then both girls laughed. They reminded Sam of two old ladies she knew in New Orleans, another salt-and-pepper couple of friends, both still beautiful in their eighties. When they stepped arm in arm into the dining room at Galatoire's, mouths dropped.

Lucinda "Magic" Washington, Miss Louisiana, and Connors McCoy, Miss Texas, were giving their pageant hostesses fits as they settled into an orange plastic booth.

"This is not according to the rules," said Miss Louisiana's chaperone, a middle-aged blonde with frosted hair who looked like she'd be more comfortable at a Junior League tea. Miss Texas's companion was her twin.

"Look, ladies," said Magic, "why don't you just sit yourselves in this booth right behind us here, order yourselves something sinful on us, like the cheese-steak sub, and kick back for half an hour? Enjoy yourselves. You can hear every word and slap the cuffs on us if we get too far out of line."

"You *said* you were going to satellite interviews," said the Miss Texas chaperone, tight-lipped. "This is not a satellite."

"Nope," laughed Connors, "it sure idn't. But let's pretend it is for the time it takes me to get myself on the outside of a White House Special with extra salami, provolone, ham, and cappacolla."

"How can you eat like this and look like *that?"* asked Sam, ordering half a Special herself.

Connors said, "I figure, a big girl like me, six feet and not half stupid, I've got to keep my weight up to my IQ at all times."

"Which is what?" teased Magic. "One-ten?"

"One-fifty, and you know it. One-ten's more like you, Miss Slim and Trim National Merit Scholar. I hate your guts."

Magic grinned. "I like being skinny. Always have, since I was a little kid."

"Oh, Lord." Connors rolled her eyes. She'd heard this routine before. In fact, she finished it for Magic—"That way when they were kids, her cousin Lavert kicked her butt, she didn't jiggle. Whereas a fleshy girl like me—"

"She jiggles in the back. She jiggles in the front. She jiggles in the—"

Harrumph. It was the Pageant Police.

"No kidding," said Magic, "you let one of those mean workout devils get ahold of your body two hours a day, you need something to keep your strength up."

"Don't lie to the nice lady. She's homefolks," said Connors. "You know you live on bean sprouts and whole grains."

"Uh-huh," said Magic, adding a chocolate malt to her order. "And crayfish étouffée and jambalaya, and I'm about to die for some beignets."

"That's it. I'm heading straight to New Orleans from here to get myself a decent meal," said Sam.

"Ain't that the truth," Magic agreed. "A person could starve. And I do think this is the ugliest place I've ever been in. Town makes the projects in New Orleans look like Shangri-la."

Behind them, the chaperones sniffed *and* harrumphed.

"Now, tell me what two girls like you who seem to have good sense as well as a fair-to-middling sense of humor are doing in this pageant," Sam demanded.

The chaperones sniffed again. Well, as long as they didn't faint or take to screaming.

The Girlfriends laughed. "I originally got into this silly business as a joke on my mama," said Connors. "And when I started winning money, I fairly fell in love with it."

Sam liked it so far.

"Well, I'll start back at the beginning."

Uh-huh. Sam knew there was no other way for a Texan or a southerner to begin, and by the time they were through, you'd be glad they had.

"When I was little, my daddy was a land-poor rancher trying to make a living on a spread south of San Antonio. We barely had a pot to piss in—*excuse* me, ladies. My mama used to make my dresses out of remnants from the Ben Franklin. Just like her mama made hers out of feed sacks—like those poor, pitiful little girls out there on the Boardwalk carrying those stupid SHAME signs. Have you seen them? Well, *anyway,* I was about ten, the natural gas got to coming in like gangbusters down on the edge of the property, any further south we'd of had to give it back to Mexico, and we moved over into Houston and tall cotton.

"First thing my mama did was take us both over to the Neiman-Marcus to the couture collections, me to the junior couture, and she said, 'Just start bringing it out and ringing it up. You get tired of writing, bring in a relief.'

"She'd been poor her whole life, and so she had pretty much the same attitude about the disgustingly big house she had Daddy build us over in River Oaks, right down the street from Lynn Wyatt and about a stone's throw from the River Oaks Country Club. When my friends and I got on her nerves she'd say, 'You girls go on over to the club and get yourselves an orange juice.' And so we did. We'd go suck down some five-dollar citrus and watch the rich ladies work on skin cancer at the pool.

"Time went on, Mama forgot where she'd come from, and she got to working on Daddy about how nothing he did was classy enough. 'J.T., that Cadillac with that steer-horn ornament on it looks like white trash,' she'd holler, and then order him up a black Mercedes sedan he called the Hearse. He drove it, though. But he was just biding his time, putting up with her nonsense until he could figure out something that would *really* get her goat." Connors spread her arms wide. "This is it."

Pageants?

Connors smiled the big smile, reminding Sam of a news filler she'd read recently: *Working Woman* magazine was advising a businesswoman to improve her telephone voice by constantly smiling when she speaks. *Say cheese.* Said it conveyed interest and energy. Talk about ought to be ashamed, that feminist rag—but then, look at Connors. She sure had plenty of energy.

"I was already through college, finished at Rice with a business degree, and Daddy and I were dabbling in the stock market, doing a few real estate deals when—well, you know what happened. Recession City. Anyway, he came in the office one day with a grin on his face and a piece of paper in his hand and said, 'Sugar pie, there's a little favor I want you to do me.' Well, I've always been my daddy's girl, and even though it was an application form for the Miss Blue Bonnet Pageant, which was about the silliest thing I'd ever heard of, I thought, what the heck? I wasn't doing anything except my nails and the crossword puzzle day after day, business was so bad. I thought it'd give Daddy a giggle to see Mama's face when I hollered out a few country and western tunes and strutted across that stage in a swimsuit, those slime-faced judges staring at my crotch. It'd be worth the humiliation."

"Not a clue you'd win?" asked Sam.

"Are you kidding? I didn't even know how to walk. I just galloped up there like I was a palomino in a parade hurrying up to get this thing over with so I could get back to the barn and my oats, and the next thing I knew, I was on my way to Miss Texas."

"So how'd you take that title, given your attitude?" Texas, Arkansas, Oklahoma, Louisiana, Mississippi were the biggies. The further south, the stiffer the competition.

Connors laughed. "You mean 'cause I know this is all bulldookie? That it is not a 'strong value' to think you're hot shit because you've got big bazooms? That winning another pageant really ain't going to win the war on drugs or do anything to salvage crack babies, stop world hunger?"

"Exactly. If those girls work so hard, and you just—"

"Flounced myself around up there like I had good sense? I tell you, I'm not sure. Except they say, you know there's this pageant consultant named Sally Griffin—"

"We've met."

"—well, she came up to me after I won Miss Texas and she said I was the most natural winner she'd ever seen. Like that was a style of winning. She said you've got your Natural, like me, your Obsessive Goal-focused, that's your nut cases, and your Self-motivated, most girls, who work real hard and hope for the best. I told her I was a Texas woman, and we're among the most independent women on earth. We just can't help ourselves."

"So why didn't any of those other Texas women win Miss Texas?"

"Because they didn't have bazooms as big as Connors's." Magic laughed.

The chaperones were into throat-clearing now, and Connors pointed a finger back at Magic's chest.

"Unh-uh." Magic shook her head. "That's not why *I* won. Honey, I am your David Duke backlash contender."

"Explain to the nice lady."

"Well, those rednecks back home in Metairie and up in

North Louisiana have been hollering to that Klansman David Duke who almost won governor, 'Mr. Dukes, those last three Miss Americas wuz nigger or part nigger. I just don't know when we gone have us a white Miss America again.' Well, the two or three liberal-minded folks in the state got together, and they must have all been at the pageant, 'cause the next thing you know, here I am."

"Not a thing to do with being pretty or talented?" said Sam.

"Nope. I'm your dark horse candidate through and through. Only black in the state pageant. Those two or three liberals said, 'Okay, we'll show 'em.' "

"Nothing to do with your blowing them off the stage with your act?" said Connors.

"Unh-uh. They don't think magic's a talent anyway. They think I'm up there doing voudou."

"And?" Sam had seen enough of *that* with General Taylor Johnson, Lavert's girlfriend, to know it was a possibility.

Magic just grinned.

"So what's this Girlfriend business?" They'd called themselves that in a couple of interviews.

"We're just kind of goofing on this whole thing. Having a good time. Fooling around," said Connors.

"You took swimsuit. Not too shabby."

"An accident if I ever saw one."

"What if you win?"

"Give me a break."

"We're just acting like we're in junior high school," said Magic. "Playing dress-up, being fools."

"This is just a big yok to you too, Magic? I don't believe it. I bet *all* the girls say they don't care if they win. *I'd* care if I worked that hard."

"Well—if I made ten, it couldn't hurt my career," Magic admitted. "Getting the exposure on TV, come Saturday night. So I'm paying a little bit more attention to what's going on than my friend here. 'Course, if I won, I wouldn't turn down earning that two hundred grand for personal appearances."

"Hoping to parlay this into something bigger?"

"I don't know if you ever noticed, but it's not the easiest thing in the world for a black girl with a magic act to get herself booked into gigs. I'm a high-school speech teacher. I do clubs back home when I can get the work. Had a couple of weeks at the Blue Room at the Roosevelt once. But drunks are a tough audience, and most tourists in New Orleans are bound and determined to stay that way till they get back to the airport."

Sam knew what she meant. But she wanted to get back to this winning question a minute. "Every time I've seen the pageant, after the winner's announced, all the other girls crowd around and pretend they're thrilled for her. Were *you* happy for a winner?"

The girls stared at each other for a minute. Then Magic shrugged. "Neither one of us ever lost, not in this business. First time either of us tried, and we just sailed through."

"Yeah, but losing in general, losing in life?" Connors said, "Don't believe those smiles for a minute. It's the same thing as anything else. You try real hard for something, sure you want it. Even if it's one of your friends who gets it, are you really thrilled? Not unless you're some kind of modern-day Christian martyr. Which *I* ain't."

Now, *that* was the truth. Sam had felt it herself when the journalistic prizes were handed out. And she'd done her share of winning. But you always wanted it. Everybody did. At least, everybody *she* knew. Maybe they were all competitors.

These two surely were. "Where'd ya'll meet, anyway? Here?"

"Oh, no. Lord. We met at the Miss Texas Pageant," said Connors. "Magic had already taken Louisiana, and she was doing a guest number at our pageant. After you win state, you have to give up your job or your schooling just to do all the running around to other pageants, opening up supermarkets, laying across the hoods of Jeep Cherokees, ribbon cuttings every other day, talking with the Jaycees in West Armpit, and getting yourself ready to come here."

"Yep. You spend your time getting pretty or being pretty and smiling," Magic agreed.

Had any of it been fun?

"Are you kidding?" said Connors. "It's a hoot. This pageant thing's just like men, can't take it too seriously. And some of the other girls are kind of trippy."

"Anybody in particular?"

The two girls looked at each other and said in chorus, "New Jersey."

Sam couldn't remember which one she was. "Why?"

"Just take our word. You don't want to miss her."

Sam made herself a note. "Now, what did you mean, the pageant's just like men?"

"You can't be yourself—with men or in pageants. You'd scare them to death," said Connors.

"Avoid sudden movements of any kind," said Magic. "Judges and men—they're skittish and easily frightened."

"I practice for being with men a lot," said Connors. "Same way I practice for the pageant. I pretend I'm a soft, mysterious cat. They eat that stuff up. And I am *never* sarcastic with men."

That sent the two girls off into fits of laughter.

"Tell me the most interesting thing that's happened to you since you started this pageant business."

"Seriously?" said Magic. "I've already had a feature article in a couple of magazines, one in *Ebony* that got me an agent."

Connors thought it was the people. "I make fun, but people really have been nice. They want you to succeed, and they pull for you. It's kind of heartwarming—I mean their hearts are in the right place even if their brains aren't."

"Especially when they're millionaires," teased Magic.

"Millionaires, Connors? Like the Donald?"

"Oh, you know. Bunch of guys own oil wells, car dealerships. There's still *lots* of money in Texas even with the bust, some of them come sniffing around. Want to buy me another sable. Make sure I have enough Mercedes to get me from one mall to the next. No strings attached, you understand." And if you believed that, she'd tell you another one.

"Georgette Mosbacher." Sam suddenly realized who Connors reminded her of. "You've heard that before?"

"Yeah, yeah. Matter of fact, I've got this secret admirer, sends me flowers every day, said that in a note. Of course, he probably sends posies to *all* of us, hoping maybe one of us'll roll over."

Trolling, like Hoke Tolliver with his line, *Wanta do it?* Or like Kurt Roberts—?

"Ever get any offers from the judges?"

Connors rolled her eyes. "Well, you know we had that mess back in Texas a couple of years back."

The Texas pageant director had been accused of making improper advances to the girls. "Either of you see any of that?"

No. "Lots of the guys in the business are gay anyway, you know?" Magic said. "For them it's just another drag show, another brand of show biz."

"How about here in Atlantic City? Any of the judges—?"

The hostesses both cleared their throats.

Connors went right on. "I see you've met the *wonderful* Kurt Roberts."

Did he hit on the contestants?

"What was that line about that Watergate reporter, whatsizname, the one who fooled around on his wife when she was pregnant—he'd screw a venetian blind? That's your Mr. Roberts. He's a total joke."

"You don't think any girls would be tempted to take him up on it, seeing as how he could do them so much good—?"

"Maybe." Magic shrugged. "*I* don't know any who would, but you never can tell. But what's the diff? I mean, he seems to have exited stage right, you know?"

"You sure you didn't disappear him, Magic?" teased Connors.

"I wouldn't waste the energy."

"Now, that's an interesting idea—" Sam was thinking aloud. What if he made promises to more than one girl in return for her favors, and they compared notes and caught on to him?

"We're great at poking our noses in other folks' business," said Connors. "You want to know if we hear anything?"

"Girls—" The hostesses were signaling. It was time to go. Sam signed for the check.

"Yeah," said Magic, back out on the sidewalk. "I've got to get up to my room for a few minutes anyway, see if Eddie Murphy sent me roses again."

"She's just pulling your chain," said Connors. "Though you'd be surprised who turns up if you make it this far. Every man with a roll of hundreds in his pocket and his age bigger than his waistband thinks he can own one of us, he throws a little gold around."

"And you don't intend to be owned?" said Sam.

"I don't even intend to be rented. That's one thing about growing up a Texas woman, you learn quick, you got any wits about you at all."

"That Lady Day knew what she was talking about," added Magic.

"What's that?"

God bless the child who's got her own, they whistled. The Girlfriends were a mean duo.

...14

"SO, MY MAN," SAID DOUGIE, PLOPPING HIMSELF DOWN BIG-AS-you-please beside Wayne in the Monopoly employees' cafeteria.

Dougie had a way of just making himself at home that really scorched Wayne. He thought it was rude.

"How they hanging?"

Wayne didn't even bother to answer. He just kept on eating his hamburger, washing it down with gulps of cola. He'd think about something he liked, fountain cherry colas and french fries with lots of ketchup at the Walgreen's when he was a little kid, that'd do it, keep his mind off Dougie so he didn't turn around and put his fist through the wuss's mouth.

"So." Dougie leaned closer. Wayne could smell his breath mints. In Wayne's opinion, only drunks and fairies used the things. He thought the Certs people ought to be bombed. If he could ever find their factory, he would—by remote.

Or maybe he'd blow up Dougie. Now, that would be a sight. Little bits of Dougie so fine you'd think somebody just sneezed on you, left a few globs. The thought made Wayne grin.

"Glad to see you feeling so good." Dougie slapped him on the back. "I guess you *love* working for Uncle Tru."

Uncle Tru. He always called Mr. F that. In case you'd forgotten that *he* was the Only Begotten Nephew.

Just about then Big Gloria strolled by.

"Hey, Gloria," Wayne called to her. He liked Gloria. She made him laugh. And, he thought, she probably had the hots for him since she'd seen him land a good one on that pretty boy out in the hall yesterday. She'd probably want to be laying something sweet on him. He ought to chat her up. Besides which, he'd do anything so Dougie would stop talking to him.

But Gloria shook her head and kept moving. Her face had a great big frown on it. What the hell? Probably her time of the month. Women. All in all, they were more trouble than they were worth.

"So?" Dougie *always* started that way. So? So? So? Wayne really wanted to belt him. "So I guess you get lots of good stuff on your tapes, huh, Wayne? You keep copies of the really hot ones, or you just erase them after you've checked them out?"

Dougie had that look on his face like he'd like to come up and watch Wayne's tapes. All of them. Any of them. Yeah, Wayne had seen his kind before. Just liked to watch. Wayne liked to watch, too, but he had a purpose. It was his job, part of his innate worth to Mr. F.

"Uh-huh," Wayne grunted. "I got every high-roller suite in the whole place wired. Mr. F keeps his finger on the pulses that way. You know, you see the guys practicing, the ones who count cards. It's not just stealing towels, you know." Maybe if he threw Dougie something, anything, he'd go away.

"Uncle Tru says you can make people do things, too, with that subliminal stuff. He said you're a regular electronic wizard. Tell me about it." Dougie cozied closer, close enough to kiss him on the mouth.

Wayne jerked back. Guys around them were gonna start moving away too, maintenance guys over at the next table'd think Wayne was some kind of fruit.

"It's nothing," Wayne mumbled.

"What'd you make them do, Wayne? Come on, tell Dougie."

Tell Dougie. Tell Dougie. He'd tell Dougie, all right. "I work magic. I make 'em think they can do anything," Wayne blurted.

"Really? Gee, Wayne." Dougie scratched the top of his pointed little head. "Like what?"

"Like break the bank. Like walk on water."

"Walk on water, that's great."

"Yeah, just like you. I make 'em think they're Jesus Christ, Mary, and Joseph rolled into one worthless little fart."

It took Dougie a minute to get it, to realize that Wayne had actually had the nerve to insult him. With that, Dougie jumped up and stomped out of the cafeteria on his short legs, his shoulders stiff and huffy in his navy blue blazer. Wayne and the guys from maintenance over at the next table, who'd also had a bellyful of Dougie's guff since he'd come on staff, were laughing like crazy.

"Way to go, Wayne," one of them hollered. Wayne gave him the high sign, then went back to his third burger. He was seriously thinking about getting up and grabbing another order of french fries with plenty of ketchup.

Then his pale blue eyes narrowed into slits as his mind slid back to what he'd said to Dougie. Yeah, he had. He'd worked some magic, all right. Or almost. It was tougher to do in actuality than on the video monitor.

Oh, well. So sometimes things didn't work out *exactly* as you'd planned. He took another bite of his burger.

. . . 15

"THIS IS HIGHLY IRREGULAR," SAID THE BIG WOMAN IN THE MISS America sweatshirt posted at the door to backstage. "I'll have to call Barbara Stein. You know, the governor of New Jersey was thrown out of the wings a few years back, and all he wanted was a soft drink. *No one* is allowed back here."

Now, that was a crock. "There've been press tours all week." Sam held her ground.

"Last week. And on Monday."

"I wasn't here last week or Monday."

"Sorry about that."

"Could you call Barbara Stein, please?" Sam pointed at Florence's phone. That's what her name tag said.

Florence stared at the phone, then at Sam, back at the phone, and finally made a top-level security decision. "Barb's very busy," she muttered as she dialed, turning her body so Sam couldn't see the number—in case she wanted to call up Barbara and squander her time chatting about bugle beads, Sam supposed. "Uh-huh, uh-huh. Okay. Roger." She glared at Sam. *"June* will take you."

After all that, the dressing room was hardly worth the ruckus.

Sam didn't know what she was expecting to see—caribou-trimmed dressing gowns, sweating silver champagne buckets, ladies' maids in little black and white ruffled uniforms sneaking smokes while their charges weren't around. But that was old Hollywood. This was a long narrow room filled with three rows of battered wooden dressing tables, rickety chairs, iron-pipe clothing racks. Chopped celery and carrots and yogurt and granola littered a snack table—along with a respectable showing of junk food. Garment bags hung about. White swimsuits dangled from clothes hangers, their bosoms puffed like pouter pigeons. Despite the feminine footprints through spilled face powder, the blue boxes of Tampax everywhere (since every girl got her period the minute she hit town, according to June), there was something about the place that reminded Sam of the boxing gym where she'd once interviewed a contender. Maybe it was the depressingly dim lights, the steam pipes, the seediness. More likely it was the smell of nervous perspiration that lingered behind the girls who were now up on the big stage practicing their smiling, turning, posing, prancing.

Sleepy Hollow, another flight up, was a large dark room with shades drawn over large windows overlooking the ocean. It held twenty single iron beds covered with pastel blankets where the girls, worn out by smiling, turning, posing, prancing, grabbed catnaps.

"Looks like a women's shelter," Sam said to June.

"A what?"

She couldn't believe June had never heard the term before, but then she took a closer look at the shiny pageboy, gray silk dress, nude stockings, neat black pumps, diamond studs. Anything was possible.

June blinked, then said brightly, "I've been doing this for fifteen years. I'm the chief backstage hostess. I started out doing seating at the luncheons."

"So you worked your way up?" Oh, the worlds and worlds and worlds.

"Yes, along with the head of the dressing room crew, I'm in charge of all this." She waved a hand at her empire. "And solely responsible for Sleepy Hollow."

Standing guard at the door. Making sure no one disturbed the Goldilocks' dreams. Women's shelters could sure use somebody like June, yes indeedy. But Sam didn't say that.

She asked, "Anything very exciting happen back here?"

"Oh, yes. Of course, *we* think it's all exciting. But once," she paused dramatically, "a couple of years ago, the girls were about to go onstage for a big production number at the

Saturday night finals, and we suddenly realized Miss California was missing. We looked high and low for her and were really getting worried, when I thought, Sleepy Hollow. We hadn't looked there because how could a girl take a nap during the final judging? Well, there she was. And she wasn't asleep. But she had ducked in for five minutes, she hadn't made the final ten, you understand, so she had some time. Well, that night there was this thunderstorm, with ferocious thunder and lightning. And this dear girl, well, I didn't know they don't have thunder and lightning in northern California where she was from, but I found out they don't, and she was standing positively transfixed at the windows watching the lightning out on the ocean."

Wow! said Sam. Wow!

She said it again for real when she got back downstairs and saw the line of people waiting outside Barbara Stein's office.

Later days. Sam didn't want to hang around in line. She could call Barbara on the phone and ask her to recap Roberts's last phone call to the pageant office, something she'd been meaning to do.

Then the door to Barbara's office flew open. "I do not understand why you are not taking this more seriously!" The woman shouting was very tall and very thin with a mane of flaming hair. She was wearing a severe black suit. "They took my tape recorder with a tape of my very best interviews! I cannot *possibly* duplicate all that work! I've told you what the hoodlums looked like who stole my tape recorder—*and* my wallet!"

Barbara Stein joined the woman in the doorway. She rolled right on. "You don't *care* if I get my article done. You don't *care* about serious scholarship and the evolving role of the beauty pageant in postmodern feminism."

"Miss DeLaughter." The fact that the woman in black was a foot taller than Barbara didn't seem to faze her. The petite redhead delivered a right jab with a scarlet fingertip to DeLaughter's forearm. "I told you before, and I'll tell you again. We are delighted to have you here. We are very sorry that your tape was stolen. We are equally sorry you got mustard all over your nice white dress. But we are not the Atlantic City Police Department. *That's* who you should be talking to."

"You want *me* to go to the police?"

"I assure you they're a very respectable organization, full of delightful young men who would be more than happy to help you."

"I think you're being sarcastic, Miss Stein."

"I don't have time for sarcasm."

The police, Sam thought. Should she go to them about Kurt Roberts? Did her friend Charlie back in Atlanta know anybody on the Atlantic City force? Maybe it was worth a phone call. But in the meantime, maybe she'd see if Cindy Lou was over her snit and ready for a cup of coffee and a heart-to-heart.

It hadn't taken her long to find Cindy Lou. She wasn't in her room, but a fiver to the bellman bought her the name of Cindy Lou's favorite hangout. She could forget the coffee.

"Hi," Sam said to the lanky frosted blonde with the dark glasses. Her long legs were tucked into the dark red booth. Uncle Pennybags was convenient for a woman who didn't want to drink alone in her room. Cindy Lou had changed into a pink two-piece pants outfit with whorls of embroidery and little bows and sequins on the top. "Fancy running into you here."

"Uh-huh." Cindy Lou wasn't buying it. She didn't invite Sam to join her, though Sam slid in anyway, pretending the other woman had forgotten her manners.

"This round on me?" Sam offered. Not exactly prescribed AA behavior, but she somehow doubted Cindy Lou had ever even considered getting sober.

Sam ordered bottled water. Cindy Lou signaled for two doubles, vodka on the rocks, and she downed them. Two empty glasses were already sitting on the table.

Sam had been there. She knew that old one-two-three-four punch and how comforting it was to a serious drinker to get those belts down fast so she could regain some kind of control. Well, it *felt* like control.

In any case, Cindy Lou could now light her own cigarette without her hands wobbling all over East Jesus. She sucked the smoke down hard, then exhaled through her nose—not exactly the prettiest personal habit for a beauty queen, but those days were long gone, weren't they, Cindy Lou?

"What do you want?" The former Miss Ohio wasn't even trying to be nice.

"Same thing, I—"

"You want to talk about Kurt, don't you?" She wasn't looking at Sam, but across the room.

"I do. I just can't find anybody who knows where he got off to. You know how we reporters are—" It couldn't hurt to include Cindy Lou in the sisterhood, even if she were a weatherperson, a talking head on the TV. "—Just can't seem to let go when there's even a hint of a story."

Cindy Lou turned, facing her head-on. "Did he come on to you?"

"No. He—I barely even talked with him."

"Kurt could come on to you in half a second." Cindy Lou tapped the ash of her cigarette. "I don't know why I get involved with guys like him." The vodka was starting to talk. Sam waited. "You know how it is. You're pretty, I mean, *you're* pretty, you like good-looking guys, don't you?"

Sam nodded. Yes, she said, she'd always been a sucker for a pretty face. That was true. Her very first broken heart—back in Atlanta—now *that* was a pretty face. Her ex, Jim, was a Jeff Bridges look-alike. Sean, who'd been run down on a San Francisco street like a dog, he'd been a handsome man. Harry was as cute as they come.

Cindy Lou went on. "I've always wondered, do ugly women like lookers, too, or do they just figure they're lucky to get anybody. I'd hate that." Cindy Lou paused. She stared at the end of her cigarette. "I'd hate getting up in the morning and looking at myself in the mirror and knowing that I was ugly." Then in a small voice she added, "Some mornings I think I *am*. Everything's falling down. And it's not going to get any better, is it?"

Cindy Lou slumped against the red Leatherette of the high-topped booth and slid her head back. Her eyes were probably closed behind the big shades. She was in there feeling sorry for herself, thinking about old disappointments, flaccid skin tone, things that had gone wrong.

Why would a former contestant like Cindy Lou want to come back here, anyway? It had to be depressing. If beauty were what you pinned all your hopes on, why return to Atlantic City to watch this year's crop of tight young things try for the same gold ring that had passed you by?

"It's not only that I pick guys who are cute, but they aren't very nice, either. You know?" Cindy Lou was talking about men again.

Sam allowed as how, Yes, she'd known some bad guys in her time. Of course that was mostly when she was drinking, but she didn't say that to Cindy Lou. The former Miss Ohio, beginning to show some wear and tear from too much booze, didn't want to hear any AA philosophy right now, that was for sure.

Sam watched her chug down another double. She thought people couldn't smell the vodka on her breath.

"But whatever Kurt did, I don't think anybody ought to have hurt him."

Hurt him? Sam's heart rose. Aha! Then she was disgusted with herself. Was she really so set on winning the bet with Harry and Lavert that she *wanted* this? No, of course not. But her intuition *was* on track. And, well, okay, Roberts was a rotter. . . . She handed Cindy Lou a tissue. "What makes you think somebody hurt him?"

"I've been thinking about what you said about the New Jersey delegation kidnapping him."

Uh-oh. Was that what this was all about—the story Sam had made up?

"But that's not what happened. And he's not all *that* terrible. You know what I mean? He can be real sweet. *Really* sweet."

"I know what you mean."

"*Sometimes* he's a little rough, but—" Cindy Lou shrugged. Men. What were you gonna do?

"Cindy Lou, what exactly are we talking about here?"

The former beauty queen was going to tell the long version. "After we went back to Kurt's room, Kurt was *really* mad because he thought I was flirting with that young black dude. D'you know the one I mean?"

"The one Kurt pushed in the pool."

"Exactly. Actually, I thought that was kind of cute. I mean, I'm glad the kid didn't drown, but it makes you feel kind of good when guys fight over you. You know?"

Sam's nod was a lie. When she was in high school, her boyfriend had slugged out another boy at somebody's lake place one summer's night after too many Salty Dogs. He'd misunderstood what the other boy had said to her and thought he was being chivalrous. For about a minute and a half she'd thought she was pretty hot stuff, young bucks butting heads over her and all that, until she heard the crunch of that first punch, saw the scarlet gush of blood. Suddenly it was about as romantic as a car wreck, and just as terrifying.

"So, anyway, he was really jealous, but then we made love, and he was *really* wonderful. He's a *really* wonderful lover, and he can be *so* tender. You know what I mean?"

Sam nodded. She did indeed. She had herself one of those. But why didn't she believe Cindy?

"So we made *wonderful* love, just like nothing had ever happened, and he told me he loved me—"

"How long have you known Kurt?" Sam couldn't help asking.

"Since Saturday," Cindy Lou nodded. "Isn't it great, when you just know immediately like that? That the two of you are—and anyway, I went back to my room to get dressed for dinner. The judges all eat together, y'know, every night. And"—big tears welled up, and Cindy's voice choked—"that's the last time I saw him."

"He didn't come down to dinner?"

"No. He never showed. I even got up from the table and called him, I thought maybe, well, he was exhausted from making love and maybe he'd fallen asleep, but there was no answer. Then Barbara Stein got a call from somebody in her office who said Kurt'd called and said something had come up and he had to go back to New York." Her lip wobbled. "He would have called to say good-bye. I mean, I was right next door. We'd just made love." She picked up her empty glass and stared into the bottom.

"Did Kurt hit you, Cindy Lou?" Sam tried to ease the question in.

"No! What makes you think that?"

Sam pointed at the dark glasses.

"Oh?" Cindy Lou laughed. "These?" She reached up and touched the shades, but she didn't take them off. "No, I have a terrible eye infection. It's really unattractive."

"Uh-huh. Have you seen a doctor about it?"

"Sure. Kurt was really concerned. He called his doctor in New York, who gave me a referral to someone here."

"I see. So what do you think happened to him, Cindy Lou?"

"I—I don't know. I just know something happened."

"Because he wouldn't leave without saying good-bye?" This was going nowhere fast, just drunken rambling. And she needed to spend a few minutes with Rae Ann before the girls went to dinner. She'd call her from the phone in the ladies room.

"Yes, that. And because of the voice."

The voice? Sam's attention snapped back.

"I told Mimi and Eloise—you know, the other two women judges. You spend that kind of time with people, you think you're getting close to them. But I told them about the voice and they just said I need to lay off the sauce." She ran her tongue around the rim of her glass and then signaled for the waitress. "Maybe I do drink a little too much."

And maybe you're having hallucinations. It happens when the booze has really gotten to your brain. "When did you hear the voice?"

"Last night. And again today. Every time I go to my room."

"The voice is in your room?"

"Another." She pointed at her glass to the waitress. Then

to Sam, "Uh-huh. I'm lying on my bed or in the tub, and I hear it."

She hadn't realized until now that Cindy Lou's alcoholism was so advanced. She was probably blacking out, too. Maybe she didn't remember Kurt hitting her. Or, maybe *he* hadn't. Maybe she didn't even remember who had.

"What does the voice say, Cindy Lou?"

Cindy Lou leaned closer. Her breath was fierce. "He says that if Miss X doesn't make ten, I'm going to get hurt. Just like Kurt did."

Oh, Christ. "Who's Miss X?"

Cindy Lou put a finger to her lips and shook her head. "I can't tell you. They'll hurt me."

"Wait. The voice says it has done something to Kurt?"

"No, but Kurt didn't like Miss X, and I know that's what happened to him."

Great. That was just great. A voice had disappeared Kurt because he didn't like Miss X.

At that, Cindy Lou broke into loud sobs. Wet ones, with lots of tears and drool. A couple of well-dressed men at the bar turned and stared. Then one of the men said something, and they both laughed.

Sam reached over and patted Cindy Lou on the arm. God, was there anything more disgusting—and unreliable—than a falling-down drunk?

Sam knew the answer to that one.

. . . *16*

"THIS IS THE STUPIDEST THING WE'VE EVER DONE," JUNIOR complained. He and Rashad, both wearing khaki maintenance staff uniforms, were strolling down the hall of the third floor of the Monopoly.

"It is not stupid. It's the beginning of our brilliant careers."

"Our brilliant careers in Wharton Youth Correctional. I think I've lost my mind, Rashad. You know that class Miz Rainbolt teaches where you talk about values? Remember that one? I can't believe what I'm doing. Hitting up white ladies on the Boardwalk to impress Rachel Rose, and now I'm robbing the Monopoly with you."

"We are not robbing the Monopoly. We are robbing that cracker's equipment room in order to make the most stunning film that's ever been made on the pageant and Atlantic City."

"You want to explain to me the difference? You want to explain to the ACPD the difference when they're snapping the cuffs on?"

"Cool it, Junior." Rashad rattled the big wad of keys he sometimes carried as an affectation. He'd attached to it the master key Junior had lifted from his mom.

"I don't know why we have to do this, man."

"Junior, your weakened powers of cogitation amaze me. Women don't steal your strength, son, they steal your brains." He tsked. "That naughty Rachel Rose. At least we can put her to work, playing Miss A, 1937. She's pretty enough. And blond and blue-eyed just like her—Bette Cooper. She'll be perfect."

"I agree. But why can't we just use that old camera we've been using?"

"That adjective describes it precisely—old. Old and tired and unprofessional. When you're making a film that's going to be seen by the Master Himself, by My Man, Spike Lee, you use the top of the line. The best."

"You think this is how Spike got started? Stealing video equipment from a surveillance office of a casino hotel? From a man who's *known* to be stark raving crazy? Who'll probably come and slit our throats in our sleep?"

Rashad didn't deign to answer that. Instead, he recited his wish list. A professional camcorder with hi-fi stereo, autofocus, 8:1 zoom. Editing equipment. A topflight VCR. A slew of blank tapes.

"I'm sorry I ever told you about this stuff. I'm sorry my mother told *me*. I'm sorry I was ever born."

"Now, now, Junior. Let's don't get melodramatic. Save it for the movie."

"Furthermore, I can't believe we're doing this in broad daylight."

"You'd rather do it in the dark? Don't be silly. I told you. People never see the obvious. Here we go now. *Maintenance. Accounting. Security Operations.*"

Junior groaned as Rashad tapped on the door.

"Oh, man," Rashad said loudly, for show, though there was nobody to hear except Junior. Wayne had stepped out for just a minute. They'd waited till they saw him go through the door marked Gents, then locked the door from the outside with the master key, locking Wayne in. "I hate it when you tell them you're gonna be here, nobody's home. Can't rely on *nobody* these days. I guess we're gonna have to let ourselves in."

He slipped the master key into the lock and turned it. They didn't have long. Wayne would be hollering.

They stepped inside and closed the door behind them. The room was dim and cold. Racks and rows of state-of-the-art show-and-tell equipment glowed and hummed and whirred.

"Come to daddy, babies," Rashad purred.

. . . 17

HARPO BOUNDED OUT OF THE BEDROOM. THE LITTLE DOG wouldn't stop bouncing around until Sam picked him up and gave him kisses. Then he made the whimpering sound that broke her heart, as if no one had paid any attention to him all day. As if he hadn't had turkey for breakfast, doggie pâté for dinner, and hadn't been walked by herself, by Harry, and certainly at least once by Big Gloria. But still he trotted out his Poor Pitiful Pearl routine. Forget Jewish mothers. There was nothing in the world that could instill guilt in you like a Shih Tzu.

"Okay, little dog. Calm down." She looked over his head while he nuzzled her neck. "Where's Harry? Where's our boyfriend? Is he hiding in a bubble bath?"

Harry never took bubble baths. That was one of *her* favorite pastimes. But Harpo didn't know that. Or did he? Who knew what little dogs knew? He'd know everything if he listened to Sam, who talked to him constantly.

Just yesterday a man on the Boardwalk who thought himself quite a card watched her ask the dog which way he wanted to go. Did the dog speak English? he wondered.

"Nope. He's Chinese. I'm teaching him English as a second language."

"Harry? Harry?" she called now.

He didn't answer. He had to be there. They were meeting Lavert and his mobster friend for dinner in less than an hour.

Then she noticed the message light blinking.

"Oh, no," she said to Harpo.

Oh, yes. Harry said he was already dressed and had met Lavert for a drink. They had to compare notes on the Great Kurt Roberts Scavenger Hunt, and they were closing in on the prize. Would she mind too terribly if they met her at the club for dinner? He'd arranged to have a car pick her up.

"Yes, I would mind very much," she said to Harpo, who gave her his worried look. "He knows how much I hate going places alone."

Now, was that true? If it were, then why didn't she move over to New Orleans and keep Harry permanent company? She didn't mind squiring herself solo all over Atlanta.

"That doesn't matter," she said to Harpo. "When we *are* in the same town, I want him to escort me. Know what I mean, little dog?"

Harpo jumped up into a comfy chair and watched her undress before she stepped into the shower. No time for a bubble bath. She'd been longer than she'd meant to with Rae Ann, who just couldn't stop burbling about how happy she was, winning talent last night, then Fruit of the Loom today: God had surely heard her prayers. Sam wasn't so sure that God cared who won Miss America, but then, how did she know? Maybe beauty pageants *were* what was on His mind when He got overloaded with crack babies, wars, revolutions, AIDS.

Harpo gave her his fishy look. "Okay, okay," she said, toweling off. "That was uncalled for. I know what a pious little dog you are." She reached over and gave him a nuzzle. "And incredibly loyal. I don't see you hanging out with another guy, passing up the opportunity to watch me get dressed." She did a little hootchy-kooch for Harpo, who looked away. "Well, *excuse me.*" She threw on her gold silk dressing gown and continued muttering, "Don't see you passing up the chance to listen to my day.

"Now, let me tell you about my incredibly illuminating interview with Cindy Lou. Boy, talk about your waste of time." She threw open the closet and ran her fingers across her choices. "Help me pick something out here, Harpo. I've got to save the turquoise-blue silk I wore to Carnival for Saturday night. Let's see, no bugle beads, but what do you think about the black velvet evening pants?" She held them up for Harpo's inspection. "That and the red satin smoking jacket, show a hint of black lace camisole under it? You like it? No comment? Well, Harry'll like it. That crud. Do you really think he's found Roberts alive and well?"

She slipped into her clothes, then sat at the dressing table. Her damp curls could dry by themselves with a little fluffing. Now, what jewelry? Maybe her pearls and diamond studs. She picked up the earrings and considered them. They reminded her of June, the woman who'd shown her backstage.

"I must remember to tell Harry about the dressing room and Sleepy Hollow," she said to Harpo, who jolted awake from his nap. She paused while she applied her mascara. She never could talk and do her eye makeup at the same time. She didn't know why. "Can you believe that Cindy Lou? A voice in her room telling her which girl has to win? A voice! Girl needs to get herself into the program, pronto. Poor thing. I'd love to help her—but you know the drill. Got to come to it yourself. Got to bottom out. Isn't that right, Harpo?"

At the mention of his name, the little dog, who'd dozed off again, jumped up and fell off his chair.

Later that evening in Action Central, Wayne Ward would do the same thing when he heard the tape of her conversation with Harpo.

...*18*

SEE, GLORIA, SAID THE VOICE OF HER CONSCIENCE, THAT'S WHAT happens when you start with the gray areas, like you didn't know there was black and white, good and bad, right and wrong. In no time at all it starts to back up on you.

Hush up, she said. I'm trying to watch my game show. Bill Carroll and "The Big One." Though Bill Carroll's not on. Who's that?

You are not. You're just hiding. Don't want to face the truth. Isn't that what you always tell Junior? Boy, God knows what you been doing. No peeping and hiding with Jesus.

It was true. What kind of role model was she for her son, stealing that Kurt Roberts's racehorse money? Taking from a dead man. Just like stealing the silver coins off his eyes.

Now, wait a minute, said her conscience. Even *I* don't know the dude's dead.

Yeah, and we're not gonna know, are we? I sent Clothilde out of that room, cleaned it myself. Removed every trace of him. Every fingerprint. Now there it sits. Empty as a tomb. I opened the door about two hundred times today, hoping the man's back in it. And is he? No.

Did you ask Junior what he'd been up to, since that's what you're so afraid of, Junior did a number on that sucker?

Sure, I asked him. He said he was on the Boardwalk with that little white girl named Rachel Rose. You think I believe that?

Why not? Why don't you go ask her?

Yeah, I'm sure she's gonna tell me the truth.

Well, I think it's come to a sorry pass, you don't believe your own flesh and blood.

I want to. I do want to. And then—

Then?

Then—oh, Lord, I've just about convinced myself everything's cool, Junior did tell me the truth, didn't have the slightest thing to do with that Mr. Roberts, *I'm* the only evildoer in this story, when here comes that Harry—with that huge brother from back home named Lavert. Asking about Kurt Roberts. Asking *me,* seeing as how I'm the head of housekeeping, had there been anything weird happening in his room?

Uh-oh.

That's what I said. That and more. Though I said it to myself, of course. What I said to them—well, I feel just awful. More lies and deception. Exactly like they teach you at Community Baptist, at every church I've ever been to: you start on those lies and deception, they're just gonna keep right on tripping you. And they do. Even with the likes of that Harry who's been so kind to me. *Saved* Junior, and didn't I vow to pay him back? And he keeps giving *me* money like it's Christmas and he's Santa, my ticket to get back home. Get Junior out of this hellhole.

Get *me* out of here, too. Flames about to burn me up. Flames of lying and cheating and creeping and peeping, flames of deception, that's what.

On the TV a skinny blond girl with not enough clothes on, was once a Miss Nevada—is now the one who jumps around like she's got ants in her pants and goes and gets the prizes for the winners on "The Big One"—she's giving some fat redheaded man a video camera.

Oh, my God, he says, over and over. Oh, my God.

Which isn't how you're supposed to talk on the TV.

And then Big Gloria says it herself, Oh, my God.

Because looking at that fat redheaded man cradling that prize, she suddenly sees those security cameras at the Monopoly—clear as day in her mind.

Not just the ones in the hallways, though those too could be incriminating, recording her and Clothilde outside 1803,

Clothilde with that long face telling her there's a hellacious mess inside.

Then there's those secret cameras on top of that. That Wayne doesn't know she knows, but what does he think she is, a stupid fool? Those are *her* rooms. And she's not just some dumb cluck can't tell a dust mop from a head cold. She knows about construction. She knows about sawdust. She knows what Wayne's been doing with those tools.

And that means that Wayne knows what happened in Kurt Roberts's room. Wayne knows about Junior. Or not.

Now the former Miss Nevada is saying to stay tuned for a special announcement about Bill Carroll!

As if Big Gloria cared. What Big Gloria cares about is figuring out what she's going to do. About Wayne. About Junior. About getting herself back on the right side of God—and Harry Zack.

. . . 19

VA BENE WAS A THROWBACK—A SOCIAL CLUB IN A YELLOW-BRICK and brownstone mansion that had once belonged to a mayor of Atlantic City. That was back in the days before a goodly number of the city's elected officials routinely ended up in the slammer.

Harry and Lavert were waiting for Sam on the marble steps when her car arrived, looking, in their evening clothes, like an ad for some hundred-dollar-a-whiff perfume. Well, they were a dashing pair, she'd give them that.

"Miz Adams," said Lavert with a deep bow.

"Wow!" Harry beamed. "Double wow!"

"I'm pissed at you both."

"See what I told you," Harry said to Lavert. "You can always count on my Sammy. I know"—and he gave her a big kiss before she could say another word—"you're going to tell me to hush up. But before I do, I want to tell you we're closing in on Mr. Roberts—and your dough."

They probably were—while she'd been wasting her time with that crazy Cindy Lou. Well, she didn't have to be nice about it. She gave Harry a cool profile as they ankled through a lobby deep in whorled black and red carpet. On the second-floor landing a maître d' in a tuxedo said So pleased to see you this evening and led them into a high-ceilinged room of blinding white linen and dark-suited gents bent over pasta, roasted peppers, mushrooms, and large stogies.

"This way, please. Mr. Amato is expecting you." He slid open a door hidden in the cherrywood paneling.

Sam gave Lavert and Harry the Groucho eyebrows. This wasn't the mob, huh? Secret doorways? Inner sanctum? Was there a story here?

Michelangelo Amato stood up from the sole table in the handsome, green-papered octagonal room. He was almost as tall as Lavert.

Sam had pictured a short, dark gangster with a potbelly, heavy gold chains, shiny gray silk suit. Not this suave movie-star type with serious tailoring and a headful of silver curls.

"How very kind of you to come, Miss Adams." He bowed over Sam's hand, then kissed it.

Puhleeze. But you had to admit it was a charming gesture. Maybe she was going to enjoy this evening, after all. Maybe she'd chat up this ever-so-handsome mobster and see how that sat with her smarty-pants boyfriend and his sidekick.

"I told our friend Mr. Washington here that I always love meeting members of the press. Especially such lovely members." Then he nodded at Harry, paying *him* the compliment. "Shall we be seated?"

The mob welcoming the press, uh-huh. But Sam fluttered her eyelashes.

The small round table was set with creamy china and Baccarat crystal for five. The heavy silver was Italianate. Camellias floated in a Lalique bowl the color of pomegranates. On each plate sat a tiny edible sculpture Cellini would have been proud to claim. A lot fancier than your average pizza parlor. Sam took mental notes.

Michelangelo Amato seated Sam on his right. The spot on his left was empty. Sam snuggled close.

Ma smiled. "My other guest will join us shortly."

"We do indeed appreciate your kind invitation," said Lavert.

"Any friends of Joseph Cangiano's—and besides, we can't have you going away from Atlantic City hungry, can we?" Smiles all around. "Now. I hope you don't mind, but I've taken the liberty of asking our chef to prepare a special menu for us. The fame of your own considerable culinary gifts has preceded you, of course, Mr. Washington, so what Gianni has proposed to do is invite you to indulge him in a little amusement. If you will be so kind as to taste each dish in its turn and identify its ingredients."

"Oh, no!" Lavert laughed.

"Yes, indeed. Since your extrasensory palate discerned, by taste alone, the components of our friend Joseph's mother's prized pasta sauce—even after she'd slipped you a bogus recipe—well, it hit the wire."

I bet, thought Sam. The wire that hooks up all you fancy hoods. The same wire that bullets your bets to Vegas. Yet, who was she to sneer at a good meal—or a charming dinner companion who spoke such pretty copy. She smiled at Ma, then at Harry, who narrowed his eyes. He was onto her.

"Ummm," she moaned over the morsels of the *nuova cucina* pizza. "Ethereal, earthy, yet light on the tongue."

"You sound like Gael Greene," Harry said dryly.

"Do you read her?" Sam turned to Michelangelo. "Her food writing is practically pornographic."

Harry shot her a warning look.

"Potato and truffle with fontina cheese." Lavert stepped into the breach.

"Bingo," smiled Ma. "Now let's get serious." He pressed a buzzer on the floor. A door opened, and a captain and a waiter marched in with a massive green and white tureen. When the captain raised the lid, a heady aroma filled the room.

And a tomato filled the doorway. "I'm *so* sorry," gushed

the luscious young blonde in her little-girl voice. "It took me *forever* to sneak away."

She was as close to a dead ringer for Marilyn as Sam had ever seen. Except her eyes were brown, which also meant the platinum curls weren't for real. But with those curves and that voice, who cared? Now, where had she seen this lovely young thing before? . . .

"Lana DeLucca," Ma said.

The gentlemen stood. Sam nodded and extended a hand. Michelangelo tucked Lana in close at his left side, and Harry smiled at Sam, who held his gaze. Okay, so there went her plan to spend the evening flirting with Michelangelo.

This Lana was a real piece of work, a plum, a peach with a valentine for a face. A tad short in the leg beneath a tight black sequined sheath, but she made up in the chest for any slight deficiency in the gam department. "Miss Adams," Lana nodded back, her smile big and red and bright.

"Please, call me Sam." No need to stand on seniority here, honey chile.

"Lana is the daughter of a cousin of a very good friend of mine."

I bet, thought Sam.

"Michelangelo's been like an uncle to me since I've been in Atlantic City," the young girl gushed. "Oooh, soup. I'm starving. It smells so good. What kind is it?"

"Mr. Washington?" Ma deferred.

Lavert lifted his spoon, breathed in the heady fumes, rolled a sip around his mouth like a fine wine, closed his eyes. "Fennel and celery root. Delicious." He bit into the accompaniment of four kinds of *bruschetta,* whole wheat toast topped with—he identified garlic, green olive pesto, plum tomatoes, and Maryland crab spread.

"Damn!" said Ma. "Gianni's going to slit his wrists."

"Why?" Lana was all big brown eyes.

Ma explained the culinary game. "Oooh," she said. "How cute." Then her forehead wrinkled, for just a moment. "But is there a prize? I don't think I can stand another competition. I'm just about worn out with competition."

Sam got it. She *knew* she'd seen Lana somewhere before. "Are you, by any chance, Miss New Jersey?" The very girl Magic and Connors had wanted her to talk to.

"Why, yes!" Lana dimpled, then the tiny frown reappeared. Ma had said in his introductions that Sam was covering the pageant. "You don't remember me?" Heartbreak of heartbreaks.

"You know, I do, but—wait, were you in evening gown last night?"

"Yes!" Lana clapped her little hands. "How'd I do? I was *so* nervous. I mean, when Phyllis George asks you that question, well, I really do *care* about the environment, those creeps dumping stuff in the ocean you can't even go to the beach, and I've read everything there is to know about waste disposal, but, God, I mean, gee, you're up there in front of all those people, and—"

"You did great," said Harry, smiling into Lana's wide eyes.

Oh, yes, Sam knew that smile. "I had to leave at the beginning of evening gown to file my story," she said evenly, "so I missed you. But I do remember you from the Parade of States."

"The Sierra Club couldn't have given a better answer," Harry said to Lana.

"The what club?"

Ma patted Lana's creamy arm. "I thought it would be nice for you and Samantha to meet one another. It's uncommon for a journalist of Ms. Adams's stature to grace the pageant with her presence—and on the other hand, it's rare for a journalist to have such personal access to an about-to-be Miss America." Ma was all smiles. Lana lowered her eyelashes.

Okay, he was smooth, he was suave. But what was his game?

Was this little evening about extending hospitality to a friend of a friend? Engaging in a good-natured culinary rivalry? Putting together two women who could possibly help one another?

Sam doubted all of the above. But why was she so sure this

evening had something to do with business—and she didn't mean pizza. Had she watched too many parts of *The Godfather?*

"I can't imagine how you sneaked out," she said to Lana. "I thought the pageant's security was tighter than the White House." Saying that, she saw a picture of Marilyn, the real Marilyn, in her spangled dress singing "Happy Birthday, Mr. President" to JFK. Poor, poor Marilyn.

But Lana was too young to have heard the many rumors about how Jack and Bobby both used and abused Norma Jean and then cut her off—her private Justice Department number for Bobby supposedly changed so she had to use the main number like any peon.

"Aren't I awful, sneaking away?" Lana hesitated enough to let you know she'd rather say *ain't.* "I hope you won't tell anybody. I'll get in *huge* trouble."

"Cross my heart and hope to die." Sam made the promise.

"Well, I made real loud noises about going up to Sleepy Hollow to take a nap, and then I rolled up a couple of blankets under the covers on the bed and put a blond wig on the pillow—" She dissolved in giggles. "I just get so tired of being locked up with that chaperone. Do you know they even *sleep* in our rooms? Isn't that silly?"

"It *is* silly. Now tell us something about yourself, Lana. Where are you from?" Harry was all ears.

"Well, I grew up in Newark. But my folks moved us down to Sea Girt a few years ago. I really like it on the ocean. It's not so nice up in Newark anymore—what with one thing and another. There are too many bl—"

And then, just before she finished that word, Ma laid a hand on her wrist and directed his gaze from her brown eyes toward Lavert's—which were very big and very black. Lana gulped.

"Very bad people," she recovered. "There are lots of bad people in Newark these days."

"I bet," smiled Lavert. "I bet there are lots of bad people there who can't tell a citrus vinaigrette from a balsamic vinegar." He flashed Ma a dazzler of a smile. "I'd be right about the citrus, wouldn't I, Mr. Amato, on this *insalata di mare?* It's especially good with the red and yellow peppers and the waxy potatoes. And where *does* Gianni get his seafood? The clams, shrimp, the squid, the sea scallops—incredibly fresh. Not from the Fulton Fish Market?"

Michelangelo didn't miss a beat as they danced together past Lana's faux pas. "That cesspool—? No way. Their fish've been two weeks out of the sea by the time they get to your table. Gianni has sources in Maine. Day boats, we get it in hours. The shrimp are from Louisiana—flown in every morning."

"And you're all from Louisiana, too, aren't you?" Lana burbled.

Sam couldn't wait to see what she stepped in next. "No, Harry and Lavert are. I live in Atlanta."

"Oh. I see. But you grew up there, didn't you, Sam?"

"No." What was she getting at?

"Oh, I guess I'm confused. You and Harry look so much alike. . . ."

They did? Short dark curly hair, but beyond that—?

"I misunderstood. I thought you were Harry's big sister."

Everyone froze, except Sam, who, without missing a beat, turned from Lana to Ma and purred, "So, I understand you're a longtime Miss America buff, Mr. Amato?" She'd even the score later. Had no one never told the little bimbo of the power of the word processor?

"Call me Ma, please. A buff? I don't know I'd say that. I do think Miss America's good for Atlantic City, so I do what I can for the pageant in whatever small way. Also, I know that it's an unpopular stance these days, but I think we've probably come to the end of civilization as we know it when it's wrong to admire beautiful women."

Lana batted her big brown eyes and purred.

"I'll drink to that." Harry raised his glass, and the gentlemen drank to his toast, "To beautiful women." He winked at Sam, and it was a heartfelt wink, full of love. Sam smiled back. That was more like it. Maybe she'd forgive Harry after all for making her come here alone.

Then her gaze landed on another pretty woman. "Lovely painting over the fireplace. *You* paint, don't you, Michelangelo?" She loved saying the line. She'd like writing it, too. Michelangelo Paints Pageant Cuties.

"I dabble." But his smile said the odalisque was his, the nude concubine reclining on a golden chaise draped with blue.

"Lovely," said Lavert.

Harry asked about the model. "A former Miss America hopeful?"

Lana protested. "We do *not* pose like that!"

"Oh, there have been those who did," laughed Sam. Then she told the story. It was in 1935 that the San Diego Fair called *its* beauty contest winner Miss America. The young lady, a curvacious blue-eyed blonde named Florence Cubbitt, was crowned by two promoters who also ran the fair's nudist and midget concessions. They awarded her the privilege of posing in the nude for two years. When Atlantic City finally got around to choosing *its* Miss America, she was Henrietta Leaver, a high-school dropout who was working in a five-and-dime. Henrietta, however, was barely crowned when a Philadelphia sculptor unveiled a nude statue he'd done of her. Henrietta protested that she'd worn her swimsuit the whole time, and had been chaperoned by her grandmother, but the press was having none of it. Henrietta's goose was cooked.

Sam considered adding the one about Janice Hansen, Miss New Jersey 1944, another busty blonde who was found one day in 1958 shot full of holes along with her close personal friend Anthony "Little Augie" Pisano—but she didn't.

Ma laughed at the Henrietta story. Then he turned to Lavert. "Now what do you think about this, Mr. Washington, Gianni's pièce de résistance?"

The main course was duck cakes with sun-dried-tomato butter and arugula and artichoke hearts. Hazelnuts and porcini mushrooms were grace notes in the symphony of flavors. Lavert got it all on the nose. He insisted he be allowed to return the compliment by cooking a Sunday lunch for all assembled, Gianni the chef, and perhaps Michelangelo would like to include his mother, and other friends?

"Artichokes!" Lana exclaimed. "That's how I got involved in pageants!"

"Do tell." Lavert seemed to be amused by Miss New Jersey, a species of dumb blonde you hardly ever saw anymore.

"Should I?" She turned to Ma, her benefactor, sponsor, Big Daddy, who knew?

Ma spread his hands.

"Well, I was in San Francisco visiting my uncle Tony, who's in the wine business, and he does something with shipping and owns a few clubs—anyway, that was five years ago, I was still in high school, and while I was there, there was this Marilyn Monroe look-alike contest, see? The thing was, Marilyn had modeled for the California Artichoke Advisory Board thirty-nine years ago, and the artichoke people had a contest in honor of that. There were thirty-nine contestants, and, well, my uncle Tony had always called me Little Marilyn as a joke—so I entered the contest without telling him as a joke back on *him.* I asked him to meet me the day of the contest down at the Embarcadero Plaza, and there were the thirty-nine of us girls handing out free artichokes. He almost swallowed his cigar when he saw me. You remember that dress Marilyn wore in that famous photograph, the white one, with a pleated full skirt and a halter top with no back?"

"The one in the picture where her dress blew up?" said Lavert.

"That's right! *The Seven Year Itch.* That's the one! Well, that's what we were all wearing, and we paraded across this stage they'd put up, and the crowd that day, it was at lunchtime, voted by applause. And *I* won!"

Sam knew the area from when she'd lived in San Francisco. She could see the crowd: financial district suits, their ties loosened for their thirty-minute lunch break, cheek by jowl with construction workers. She could picture them ogling the thirty-nine contestants with the matching bust measurements. Had that contest taken Lana to Miss California?

"No. I couldn't have qualified, because I didn't live there, but the artichoke thing gave me a taste of it, you know. What it would be like to compete."

Lana liked the competition?

"Oh, yes. It's the greatest thing I've ever done. The girls are really wonderful. You know"—she dropped her voice—"people say that women can be, well, bitchy, when they go after the same thing, but I think most of them are sweet. There *are* exceptions, who I won't name, but most of them help you out. Give you tips. Lend you things."

"Like lipstick?" Lavert was a master of the poker face.

"Lipstick, nail polish, anything you need." Lana paused. "You know, though, even though it's wonderful, I think some of the girls, well, they *try* too hard. Some of them almost have nervous breakdowns, they're so serious about it all. It's just not that hard, you know. All you have to remember is: Don't cry on stage. Never let the judges see you lick your lips. Be prepared. Believe in yourself. And smile a lot—naturally."

"You *sound* serious," said Lavert.

Sam resisted sticking her finger down her throat.

"Oh, I *am*. Don't get me wrong. But"—Lana chewed on her bottom lip—"if I don't win, I'm not going to *die*. You know what I mean? Actually, I don't even *want* to win. Can you imagine, traveling around for a whole year with first one chaperone and then another? Yuk! But, like, for some of these girls, this is the first chance they ever had to dress up in pretty things—and I, well, you know, my uncle Marty runs one of the clubs here in AC, and my uncle Ennio manages a casino in Vegas—so I've spent lots of time dressing up."

Wasn't it interesting that Lana had so many uncles in so many influential positions in so many different cities?

"You haven't seen my talent yet, but—" She drew a deep breath that threw her chest dangerously close to the top of her sequined dress. "I'm a torch singer. That's what *this* is all about, for me." She waggled a hand. "This Miss America thing. Oooooooh!" Lana interrupted herself as the dessert tray arrived.

It included chocolate gelato; hazelnut biscotti with black pepper and lemon and orange zest; and, as a little closing joke, coming full circle with the opening course, a cornmeal "pizza" with figs and raisins, served with Marsala custard. A salute to the pizza king of Atlantic City.

"Sweets for the sweet," said Ma.

"So you're competing, not to win, but for the—exposure." Sam licked custard off her fingers.

"Oh, yes. I want to be discovered. Lots of girls who didn't win pageants have gone on to be stars, you know." She ticked them off. "Delta Burke, Cloris Leachman, Vanna White. Betty Buckley in *Cats*—she placed fourth in Miss Texas. Debbie Reynolds—she's Carrie Fisher's mom—was in Miss California. And Donna Dixon—a Miss Something, I forget—she's married to Dan Akroyd. She does Revlon commercials."

"I see you've certainly done your homework, too," said Sam.

Lana beamed. "Well, I don't read much, but I go to the movies a lot and listen to people. I've watched *tons* of educational TV getting ready for the interviews. And, you know, I watch a tape of *Some Like It Hot* every single day. Because I do one of Marilyn's songs in it for my talent."

"I'd think you'd already have a foot in that door—show biz—through your family connections," Sam said smiling. Like she didn't know what she was saying. But what was Michelangelo going to do? Shoot her at his own dinner table?

"I do," Lana nodded seriously. "But I want to be famous on my own, don't you know? I don't want to be beholden to nobody."

Even Ma had to look away at that one. Espresso appeared at the table along with a cigar humidor and Gianni the chef to take his bows.

"And it's working already, you know," Lana bubbled right along. "Already, people are starting to take notice. You know Bill Carroll, the famous game show host? Well, I met him this week, and you know what he said to me? He said, I would give my right arm if I could make you come on my show."

...20

MICHELANGELO AMATO SAT IN THE BACK OF HIS BLACK LINCOLN Town Car watching three TV monitors.

On one, this new Wednesday Night Football, first of the season, the Forty-niners were slaughtering the Giants. Ma liked that. Not only personally—he'd always hated the New York Giants, a bunch of schmucks, in his opinion—but professionally. The "smart" money had gone to New York. Ma would clean up.

On the second monitor, a filly named Miss America, now wasn't that a great coincidence, was gaining on the outside in a breeders' cup at Santa Anita. That was good for business, too. Big bucks had gone down on last year's Preakness winner, a deep-chested bay called Double Dip.

On the third monitor was the second night of the pageant's preliminary competition from Convention Hall.

"Hey, Willie." Ma tapped on the glass to his driver, twice. Willie was getting a little deaf. "You know I'm the only person in the whole world watching the Miss America play-offs on TV?"

"That's great, boss." Willie would say that to anything, in his mushy way—he wouldn't wear his dentures.

But it *was* great, and it came from having connections. Influence in the right places. Not bad for a kid from MacDougal Street, huh? And, well, okay, in his business there *was* more than a little happening in the electronics field. If it went over the phone lines, computers, modems, munchkins, whatever, it was electric, you name it, Ma had incorporated it into his bookmaking operation.

So it was no big deal to have one of his guys figure out the way to go was to bribe the guy who ran the television equipment van for the pageant in the hall's parking lot. The way it worked, the signal ran from the cameras inside through cables out to the van, then from there it traveled on phone lines to NBC in Rockefeller Center in New York. Tuesday, Wednesday, Thursday nights, they weren't broadcasting the show, just recording and fiddling with it, figuring out the commercial spots, all that stuff. But the man with the van could tap into those phone lines, then, with cellular phone capability, dial it up and bring it to the monitor in the limo. No big deal.

But still, it was a kick in the pants to know this show was his alone. Now he was watching that silly whatsizname, the guy in the black suit, made Ma ashamed to be Italian, doing some faggy dance. The same one he'd seen last night. But on the first monitor, whoa! Way to go, Montana! Pop 'em for another ten-yard gainer. On the second monitor, the filly was now behind by only a nose. And a pretty nose it was. Ma threw the horse a kiss and told Willie to pull over.

He wanted to talk to a man inside Tommy's, and it wasn't about a horse, either. It was about Ma's best girlfriend.

As Ma walked into the bar/pizza parlor, the man, a geezer named Angelo who ran his pizza businesses, did some old-fashioned nonelectronic bookmaking, a little shylocking on the side, was polishing glasses behind the long stretch of mahogany. Forty-niner Ronnie Lott almost ripped the head off a Giant receiver on the TV above the bar.

"Ma! How you doing?"

Michelangelo nodded.

"You want a drink? What can I get for you?"

Michelangelo shook his head. Nothing. After all that fine wine, why did he need the rotgut in Tommy's? And how did he know it was rotgut? He supplied it, that's how.

"Hey, Ma? Cat got your tongue tonight?" Angelo was twisting his head around, getting a little nervous.

Ma knew that. You didn't talk, guys would always blab faster. Guilt abhorred a silence, that was one of the things Ma believed.

When Michelangelo did talk, his speech was an interesting phenomenon. Put him at the dinner table at Va Bene with educated people, he talked like an educated man—which he was, if you counted the school of hard knocks supplemented by a fine library of leather-bound editions, all well thumbed, in his white brick mansion down in Margate. Put him at one end of a table of ebony and purple heartwood surrounded by other members of a legitimate board of directors, he could dazzle you with facts and figures. With a lady, he could quote Romantic poetry like an Oxford don. But put him on the street and he spoke the argot, blasting it out of the corner of his mouth like bursts from a sawed-off shotgun.

"Come here, Ange." He knew Angelo wouldn't want to do it, but he would. The old man limped forward. Come on, Ma gestured with one hand up, four cupped fingers gently goosing Angelo closer.

In a very quiet voice, so soft no one else in the place could have overheard him if they'd tried, not that they were, Ma said, "Ange, now you know I got no patience for arguing. I got a short temper, rather use my hands than talk, so don't get me mad."

"I don't intend to get you mad, Ma." Angelo laughed nervously.

The old man had been around, had paid some dues in various federal establishments, which is where he got his bad leg, and could still break chops with the best of them, but with Ma—well, it paid to pay respect. Besides, he had a personal interest.

"Okay, good. Now here's what I want you to do, no discussion. I want you to stay away from my mother."

"Michelangelo!" Angelo's hands went up, protesting his innocence. "Hey, listen. I mean no disrespect—"

"I know you don't. But I also know you knew my father."

"May he rest in peace."

"May he rot in hell," said Ma. "That son of a bitch was no damned good. But the point here is you knew them when they were married."

"Right, Ma, I did, but—"

"No buts, Ange. You knew them, they were married before God."

"I was best man in their wedding at St. Anthony's in the old neighborhood. Sullivan Street. You know that."

"That's right. You were like my uncle. I brought you to Jersey with me, made sure you had a job, a *good* job, and now how do you repay me?"

"Ma, my intentions are—"

"There *are* no honorable intentions where my mother is concerned."

"I took her to the pictures. I took her flowers. That's all." Angelo sweated when he lied. He wondered, could Ma smell him?

"Don't say that! Don't say that's all! Don't even make me think about other possibilities. I'll go crazy, and you'll go down an elevator shaft."

"No, no. You're right, Ma. You're right. I just thought, you know, your dad's been dead thirteen years, your mother might want a little company."

"My mother don't need company. She has me. I go over to her house for supper. She comes to mine. She wants to see a picture show, she turns on the big-screen TV I brought her. She gets cold on winter nights, I buy her another hot water bottle. You understand, Angelo?"

"I understand, Ma."

Back in the car, Michelangelo lit a cigar and muttered, "Nobody's got no respect anymore."

Willie asked, Where to, boss?

Ventnor, Ma answered, and Willie headed the heavy car toward Michelangelo's main office.

"How'd my filly do?"

"She won, boss. Eighteen to one."

Great. And his boy Joe had pumped another one into the end zone. Forty-niners were ahead by fourteen, three minutes left in the game. Up on the Convention Hall stage some old lady who was Miss America about a hundred years ago was trading jokes with that Gary Collins jerk.

But hey, wait a minute. Ma took a closer look. That wasn't Collins. What the hell—? Was that who he thought it was?

Ma grabbed his remote and punched up the volume.

Oh, Christ, it was. It was Billy Carroll, that little schmuck. He was playing the lounge at the Monopoly, still doing his Sinatra look-alike thing he'd been practicing for twenty years. Now there he was, saying,

"—what a privilege and honor it is to be asked to fill in on this show of shows. Not, of course, that anyone could ever fill the shoes of that grand gentleman, Gary Collins—and we hope you're feeling better, Gary." Carroll gave a big smile and wave out to TV land, out to Collins, wherever he was. Probably home puking his guts out, thought Ma, if he wasn't already, seeing this jerk up there.

Ma had known little Billy Carroll since 1978, when the casinos first opened. Already a regular loser in Vegas, Billy couldn't wait to come and drop a bundle in AC when he was on the East Coast.

That's how guys with the sickness operated. They weren't playing to win.

Little Billy there—looking even more like a midget up on the big stage, barely taller than that Phyllis George—would grab a bundle at baccarat, he couldn't wait to get to a phone and drop it on the ponies. His horse'd come in, he'd be looking for the next race, the next game, the sure thing . . . that'd bust him. Guys like Billy who had the sickness didn't know how to behave unless they were up to their eyebrows in hock—God love 'em.

And Ma was in the business of making it easy for Billy and all his brothers to give him their money.

Gone were the days of the MacDougal Street candy store owner who would leave you waiting while he went to the back of the store to take bets by phone. Kids like Ma who grew up making pocket money running errands, picking up betting slips for barbershop storefront gambling operations, had to look elsewhere.

Bookmaking had gone electronic and mobile. It was run on wheels, over the airways, and by phone mail.

In South Jersey, which was Ma's territory, he operated a dozen "offices" out of vans equipped with cellular phones, laptop computers, digital beepers, printers, and statistical analyses of whatever sporting event was going down. The bets were heaviest within an hour of the event, when the odds had settled down, and as much as could be known about the variables—a quarterback's broken finger, a fighter's latest bout with his girlfriend—were in place.

Then customers, who came to the bookie on a referral basis only—and even then were run through a background check of financial and criminal history just as if they were applying for a major piece of plastic—called in to the vans' cellular phones using their customer codes.

The clerks taking bets handled several lines. Then the clerks faxed the bets to a central office where a bookkeeper punched the information into a computer, in code.

Ma also had another dozen stationary locations, office space or apartments, that housed only telephones on call-forwarding. State-of-the-art electronic security systems alerted the main office if the satellite locations were being raided.

The cellular phone conversations were more difficult for the Feds to monitor. Therefore, the vans were becoming the more preferable form of doing business.

Ma had recently read a newspaper article on the electronic bookmaking business that quoted a federal agent saying what with all the electronic gizmos, organized illegal gambling was not unlike the New York Stock Exchange.

Yeah, that was true. And the thought of it made Ma proud—for a minute. Until he thought about the fact that those stockbroker clowns didn't have to track people down when they got behind. Also, when the suits took money from gamooshes who had made the wrong call on a piece of business—exactly what he did—they didn't stand to go to jail. Unless they were *too* greedy, like that Milken fella.

But hadn't *he* had a grand ride—and when he finished his short time in some country club environs, the man wasn't going to be exactly poor. And nobody was going to be harassing his wife and kids and grandma and grandpa, setting up wires on 'em so the feds knew every time they went to the bathroom.

That's why Ma's children by his ex-wife, the twins, Joey and Jennie, were both at Harvard—taking MBA's, the both of 'em. None of this knocking around for them. They were going to learn to steal legit. Investment bankers. Bond traders. Whatever was going down big time when they were ready to hit the Street.

The Street—only about twenty-five blocks downtown in New York City from where he'd learned to hustle—on the street. Michelangelo leaned back with his cigar and watched Phyllis George and that fool Billy Carroll try to make the swimsuit competition sound like a bodybuilding contest instead of a good old-fashioned peep show and thought about how times had changed.

It was enough to make a fifty-five-year-old man feel *really* old.

Though it made Michelangelo Amato very happy to think he was the only man in the world watching the preliminary competition of the Miss America Pageant on his own private signal, that wasn't exactly the case.

Over at the Monopoly, Wayne Ward was sitting in his Action Central checking out the girls parading—stop, turn, stop, smile—in their shimmery white swimsuits. Copping this show had been a piece of cake for Wayne.

Just like Michelangelo's techie, Wayne knew that the TV equipment van leased by the network was the way to go.

The guy who owned it was a regular joe. Wayne had got to talking with him a couple of days earlier. Busted his butt, this dude named Dean. That's what it said, right over the pocket of his orange jumpsuit. What he did, he owned the van, the whole eighteen-wheeler tractor-trailer. It had a name, too. Said *Mighty Mo* in blue letters on the door. Dean owned all the equipment in the van. He showed it to Wayne, took him on a little tour, introduced him to his utility man. More monitors, cables, decks, recorders, frames, racks, jacks, swing arms, you name it, Dean had it, you needed it to put on a live TV show. That's all Dean did, live. He ran

Mighty Mo out of Easton, PA, the place he called home. He got by there about once a month. The rest of the time, like he was here in Atlantic City for Miss America, then the minute it was over, he'd break down any of his equipment they'd taken inside, load it back into the truck, and hit the road. Drive ten, twelve hours to a hockey game they're broadcasting live out of Toronto. Same drill there, then he's back to Severance Hall in Cleveland, the orchestra's playing. On and on it goes. Drive eight hundred, fifteen hundred miles, set up, do the show, break down, load up, drive. Man gets tired. Man gets bored. Man gets crazy is what he gets, he's not above doing a little number just to break things up. This Dean, he was a big guy with a ponytail, but you wouldn't mistake him for some fruit. It was a righteous truck-driver ponytail, and he knew everything there was to know about each and every piece of equipment in his truck. Wayne could talk with a man like that.

Of course, once he'd heard Dougie say it probably couldn't be done, he'd have copped that signal if it had meant he had to rewire all of Convention Hall lying on his belly up under the Boardwalk. He hadn't had to, though. He'd jawed with Dean, bought him a beer, slipped him a wad of bills—bingo.

Now Wayne leaned back in his chair and munched on a hamburger and smiled, thinking about how much Mr. F was enjoying the show, too, from the privacy of his own office. Wayne had delivered the signal up there to Mr. F's gigantic rear-screen projection TV. It was neat knowing how frosted Dougie must be that Wayne had delivered.

Yep, Dougie. You wanted a job done, you called Wayne Ward. *Wayne delivered.* That was his slogan. In fact, he'd had those words embroidered on his black Monopoly Special Services cap, in red, on the back.

Just wait until Dougie got a load of that.

Willie was driving Michelangelo down Fairmount Avenue on the way to the main office in Ventnor. They were passing through Ducktown, the old Italian neighborhood where Willie still lived. It was getting shabby, yeah, but Willie was comfortable there. He was in a two-story brick, right around the corner from where Nicky Scarfo, who ran all the casino unions, had lived on Georgia before he moved to Philly.

Up ahead was the Albany Avenue Bridge. "They never gonna finish this thing," Willie mumbled to himself. "Waste of the taxpayers' money." Not that Willie had ever paid taxes himself, but still it bugged him.

"What're you saying?" called Ma.

"I said they're never gonna finish this damned bridge. I don't know why they need it anyway. The old one was fine."

"That's how you know *you're* getting old," said Ma. "Hey. Pull over here."

"Where?" They were in the middle of a snarl of traffic. Night and day, this construction mess would drive you nuts.

"There." Ma waved. "Down to the launch. Let's drink a toast to Lana." He'd found the grappa in the liquor cabinet. "Little lady's about to do her swimsuit number."

Willie wheeled the heavy car off to the right side of Albany Avenue, down to a dark dirt driveway that led to the boat launch on the inlet called Inside Thorofare. It was a familiar trip. The thorofare was one of the deepest channels in New Jersey, so deep it was dredged only once a year—by the Atlantic City cops. Always something, someone, they were looking for popped up. Over on the other side was Bader Field, one of the first airports in the country. Ma had a Cessna tied down over there. He hated flying, and especially commercial. If he was going to die, it wasn't going to be with a bunch of people he didn't know puking and screaming and stomping on his feet trying to get to the exit.

"Get back here, Willie. Hurry up. There she is! Wha'dya think? Isn't she something?"

Willie thought she looked exactly like Marilyn Monroe. Exactly. It'd give you chills and thrills up and down your spine. He told Ma so.

"I know," Ma said, after he drank *salute!* to Willie's health and Lana's good fortune. "The hair, the boobs, even that little bit of a belly that Marilyn had. You think that'll lose her swimsuit?"

"Not in my book. But who knows what those judges

think? Look at those other girls." Willie pointed at the TV. "They look awfully skinny to me. I like a girl I can grab ahold of. Something to hold on to. You know what I mean?"

"I know what you mean." He poured them each another shot. "You still grabbing girls, Willie? Good for you."

"I do what I can. Not much." Willie paused, and the two men sipped their drinks silently in the dark. There wasn't a single light down here at the launch. Then Willie said, "She's Big John's niece, ain't she?"

"Lana? Yeah."

"So, you're just looking after her."

"Yeah. John asked me to. That's all I'm doing. Making sure she's comfortable. She's a pain in the butt, though. Too pushy and not so smart. It's not a good combination."

"Uh-huh." Willie sipped for a bit longer.

"You know what she does? She goes around pretending she *is* Marilyn. Marilyn in the movies. The other day, she says to me, I like men who wear glasses. Especially if they get their weak eyes from reading those long tiny columns in the *Wall Street Journal.*"

"That's not so dumb, she's got an eye for the producers."

"It's a line right out of *Some Like It Hot,* Willie. She's memorized Marilyn's lines."

"So? She's not *so* stupid if she can memorize."

"Forget it, okay?"

"Right, boss." Willie poured himself another taste. "So, you're making her comfortable."

"I hear what you're insinuating. Don't go getting any ideas. She's young enough to be my daughter."

"Yeah, well, so are them girls you paint."

"That's right, Willie. They are. And that's all I do with them. Paint."

"I never said different."

"Yeah, but that's what everybody thinks. I know what goes through the filthy minds of gamooshes like you." Ma reached over and clipped the old man on the side of the head with the edge of his hand, but gently. "That's what's wrong with the world today. Nobody has any respect for anybody anymore. The way I look at it, I hire a nude model,

I hire a nude model. I pay a woman to take her clothes off so I can paint her, I didn't pay to screw her. I wanted that, I shoulda hired a hoor. You know what I mean?"

Willie nodded in the big dark car.

"No respect. People throwing garbage in the streets, using language in front of anybody. Women. Children. Mothers."

"I know. It's terrible, boss."

"Breaking in car windows. I tell you what. You show me a man who'll break the windows of a Lincoln Town Car like this, or a Mercedes, a man who has no respect for a beautiful automobile like this, I'll show you a man who'll screw his mother."

"You're right, boss."

"Awh, get out of here. You'd say that if I told you you ought to screw *your* mother. Right, boss. That's what you'd say."

"Right, boss."

"Except that'd be kinda tough, wouldn't it, Willie, considering that your mother, God rest her soul, hasn't been with us for quite some time."

"Right, boss," Willie said, as he climbed back behind the wheel.

"So, we saw all those girls. Wha'dya think of Lana's chances to win swimsuit?"

"I dunno, boss. I told you I thought she looked pretty good."

"You know, Willie," said Michelangelo, leaning back into the soft black leather. "I been thinking, it'd be a nice thing, see what you think, for Big John—who's been so generous to me, granting me permission to run South Jersey as an outsider, taking only a quarter of the proceeds 'stead of a half like the made guys—it'd be nice if his niece Lana, who he's put under my protection for the time she's here in AC, if something nice were to happen to her."

"I think that'd be good, boss."

"You know, you're starting to sound like a parrot, Willie. Starting to get on my nerves."

"I don't mean to, boss."

"You think a man who's as well connected in this town as

me, who's got lots of guys working for him and electronic gizmos coming out his ears, so what he can't tape a movie off his own TV, is capable of making something nice happen for a girl like Lana?"

"I'd think so, boss."

"I'd think so, too. I'd think all it'd take is knowing a little bit more about how this Miss America thing works."

"You mean, like who'd she have to screw?"

"Something like that. But watch your mouth, Willie. Talking disrespectful about Lana is like disrespecting my grandma."

"You don't have a grandma, Ma."

"My mother, then. Same difference."

With his left hand still on the wheel, Willie crossed himself with his right and muttered under his breath. Mary, Jesus, and Joseph. Dealing with Michelangelo, it was hard to keep up. An old man had to be on his toes all the time. It was tough. Very tough. But better than being legit.

"I heard that," Ma chuckled from the back seat. "Keep your hands on the wheel. Your eyes on the road. Your mouth off my business."

Jesus!

...21

WAYNE LEANED BACK IN HIS LEATHER CHAIR—BLACK CALF, cushy—exactly like Mr. F's behind his desk, and watched Mr. F's favorite girl up on that big stage singing her heart out.

She was good! Better than she had to be considering all the trouble that Wayne had gone to to make sure she'd win.

Not that he minded. Planting the subliminals and watching them work, now, that he loved. Those judges didn't have a chance against the messages Wayne was bombarding them with night and day. Though he was worried about how little time he was going to have to program the final judges. They didn't even check in until tomorrow night. Their tapes were done—Mr. F's favorite girl walking down that runway with the crown on, over and over and over, the one from when she'd won her state, but they wouldn't know that. The tape would run, without the sound, mixed into their TV signals. An audiotape he'd dubbed—"and the new Miss America is," with her name—would play on an endless loop while they were sleeping.

But would it be enough?

Wayne gnawed on a fingernail, peeled it off, and chewed it up. He wanted to talk with Mr. F about that. He thought maybe they ought to try some other kind of intervention, though he wasn't sure what. And then there was that business of that bimbo judge telling that woman reporter there was a voice in her room. A woman who drank that much—you wouldn't think she'd notice.

Wayne was more than a little worried. He hoped that he could manage to see Mr. F privately—*without* Dougie—before too long. He'd take him up the tape he'd made of his girl winning, that would be his excuse.

Wayne looked up to the rack where he'd filed the tape.

And then he looked again.

He couldn't believe it.

Oh, no! Christ on a crutch! No!

There was a blank space there. A *big* blank space. The tape for the final judges was gone, along with a couple of others.

Which ones? Oh, God. Wayne's mind was reeling. He searched wildly around the room, flinging over his chair, spilling Coke. Maybe he'd just misplaced them. Maybe he'd taken them down and—but no. Of course he hadn't.

That's what had happened when he was locked in the men's room. He had thought it was just someone playing a practical joke. Then he focused on the equipment rack. Christ Almighty! His best camcorder, a professional deck, a computerized editing controller, and God knows what else! were gone!

Action Central had been robbed!

Wayne reached over and grabbed up the two remaining

cheeseburgers and stuffed them in his mouth. Oh, God. Mr. F was going to be *so* furious. And Dougie, Dougie would be jumping up and down.

Oh, yeah, Dougie would wet his pants over this one, all right.

Or *maybe* it was Dougie who—

"Hello. Hello?" Who was that knocking on the door? "Wayne, it's Gloria. Are you in there? Could I come in and see you a minute? I brought you a little something."

. . . 22

SAM WASN'T THE LEAST BIT SURPRISED MISS NEW JERSEY TOOK swimsuit. You could smell the excitement in the crowd when she'd stepped out on the stage with her platinum curls, big red smile, cleavage that ate Kansas. It made chills run up and down your spine, how much she looked like Marilyn. Even down to the Jell-O-on-springs wiggle.

But she *was* surprised, amazed even, to see Billy Carroll standing in for Gary Collins. He was pretty awful. Phyllis George looked like she wanted to die—or kill him.

She was also surprised that Sally Griffin, the silver-haired beauty strategist from North Carolina, hadn't shown up this evening. In her seat, flashing the badge she said Sally had loaned her, though Sam had to wonder why, was Mary Frances DeLaughter, Ph.D., the tall skinny redhead she'd seen outside Barbara Stein's office whining about being robbed.

She was whining now, too. "These seats aren't *nearly* as good as I thought they'd be. You have to kind of crane your neck—"

Which ought to be pretty easy for someone with a neck like hers. The V-necked tan blouse she was wearing didn't do a thing for her. It was too bad Sally wasn't here to do a little fashion consulting. Up on the stage Miss Minnesota was pounding out an abbreviated version of the *Moonlight*

Sonata. Sam, whispering, introduced herself to Dr. DeLaughter. It never hurt to be polite. You could never tell where your next story might come from.

"Oooooh," said Mary Frances. "I know you. I was in England researching serial murderers, and your name came up."

See? The context wasn't so nice, but Sam was rather an expert. She'd been a young reporter in the Bay Area in the seventies when there was a bumper crop of killers who went for quantity.

"Oh, yes. Everyone knew your name. It was bandied about among the feminist crowd at Oxford."

Well. *That* would give the young whippersnapper from the *Inquirer* something to think about. Definitely a cut above this nonsense. Maybe instead of a true crime book, after she left the paper, she'd think about doing some research—

"And the case you made in your book for the sterilization of men who don't support the children they've already spawned, well, I needn't tell you—"

"I beg your pardon?"

"It was brilliant! Absolutely brilliant. Though I think maybe sterilization is too gentle. Castration would be more the ticket."

"Mary Frances? I think you—"

"Now don't be modest. I *hate* modesty."

So did Miss Kentucky. Up on the stage the girl did a baton-twirling number in a costume that left nothing to the imagination.

"Mary Frances, I didn't write a book. Certainly not *that* book."

"You didn't?"

"You must have me confused with somebody else."

"Really? Oh. Then, you mean you're nobody?"

"Well, I don't know that I'd—" But what was the point? Especially with the *Inquirer* snickering into her root beer. Sam was glad someone had mugged this twit. She hoped her belongings were floating out in the Gulf Stream right now.

"And now, Lucinda Washington, Miss Louisiana, who's gonna show us how to really make a bunny hop! A magic bunny, that is!" Billy Carroll was shouting. He could make the Lord's Prayer sound like a game show promo.

But even he couldn't touch Lucinda. She glided, a black swan in a gown of molten silver, onto center stage to Pachelbel's Canon in D. A large purple velvet cloth edged with gold lay across her right forearm. In her left palm sat a large silver ball.

The music rose, Lucinda smiled, took the ball into her right hand to show you. It wasn't attached.

Then she tucked the silver ball into the crook of her left forearm, about breast height. She pulled the velvet cloth tight with both hands and the ball rolled back and forth across the top of the cloth.

The audience went *oooooh!,* and the ball rolled right over the edge and hid beneath the purple velvet. It bumped around like a child under a sheet looking for a way out.

Ahhhhhhhh! the crowd cooed. Lucinda had them, if not the ball, in the palm of her hand.

Then the silver globe floated out again, and hung in thin air. Lucinda tucked the purple velvet into her right hand, then opened the hand. The cloth was gone.

Good riddance! The ball bobbled up and down.

The audience was delighted. Then the ball snuggled up to Lucinda, as many in the audience would have liked to do, danced up her right arm, kissed the back of her neck, then rolled down her left shoulder. It floated out from her fingertips, out, out, out (an *impossible* distance, said a master magician in the audience to his wife) over the heads of the judges.

And though they were supposed to maintain their cool no matter what, Julian Temple reached for the ball while Eloise Lemon whooped with delight.

The silvery globe twirled around the judges' heads once, twice, while the crowd ooohed and aaahed. Finally it floated back to Lucinda, who made the purple cloth reappear in her right hand and lassoed the ball.

Snared in the purple velvet, the ball struggled, it fought, until Lucinda flung the velvet wide, and, instead of the ball, out poured a cascade of shiny golden ribbons that pooled on the floor.

The silver ball was gone. The purple drape floated down.

Lucinda curtsied and smiled. She'd never said a word. It had been a spectacular performance, as graceful as the most delicate ballet.

The crowd went berserk. *Magic! Magic! Magic!* they called. They clapped their hands and stomped their feet.

The *Inquirer* shouted over the din, "What was that?"

The Zombie was the name of the trick. But *Magic!* was what the crowd shouted. *Magic!* was the one they loved.

. . . 23

"I DON'T MEAN HER ANY DISRESPECT," ANGELO WAS SAYING TO HIS cousin Willie. "Is that what he thinks?"

"You know Ma. He's nuts on the subject of his mother."

"I understand. But Sal's been gone a long time, I thought I'd waited long enough."

Willie reached across Angelo's kitchen table and poured himself another glass. "So wha'dya want?"

"Whad'I want? Whad'I *always* want? To marry Angelina. Same thing I wanted since we were sixteen years old back in the neighborhood."

"Come on. You didn't want to *marry* her when you were sixteen, Ange. You were nothing but a hard-on."

"Yeah, well, I can't hardly remember that, it was so long ago. All I know now is, I've been alone my whole life, and I don't want to die that way. I want to marry Angelina, bring her back to the old country, we'll take my nephew's place in Sicily—"

"You're awfully old for moon/June, Ange."

"A man's too old for romance, he should kill himself."

"Yeah, well, Ma's gonna do that for you, you keep sniffing around his mom."

Angelo smashed his glass down on the tabletop. Red wine sloshed onto the cloth. "I'm not sniffing around. Quit saying that."

"Though—" Willie pulled on his ear.

"Yeah?"

"I got an idea. Listen, you know Ma is baby-sitting that DeLucca girl what's here in the pageant. Big John's niece."

"Yeah?" Ange didn't know it, but that was okay. "And?"

"Ma's got it in his head it would be a nice favor to Big John if the niece won the Miss America thing."

"Yeah?"

"Well, I was thinking, you know that fish we wuz looking for the other day, I was driving you, the one at the Monopoly you said owed you two bones—plus the vig?"

"Yeah?"

"Guess what he's doing here?"

"I know what he's doing here. He's gambling—what any fish is doing here. I done business with him before, he comes down from New York. He come recommended."

"Guess what else?"

"Tell me, Willie. You know I ain't too bright."

"He's a Miss America judge."

"How do you know that?"

"Ma follows the pageant, you know? He's always talking about it. Tonight we wuz watching the show from the Convention Hall on closed circuit, in the car."

"And you seen the fish? I ain't seen him. I went back to the Monopoly, he's split."

"Naw, I didn't see him. I was driving most of the time, anyway. But I seen his picture in one of them programs Ma left in the car."

"That Roberts is a judge? You're sure? Like he could fix this thing for me—I could give it to Ma for a gift he could give to Big John? Then Ma'd owe me a big one."

"I think that's what I'm saying, Ange."

Angelo stood, knocked back the rest of his wine, and slammed the empty glass down on the table like a young man full of piss and vinegar. "Then what am I sitting around here talking to you for?"

. . . 24

"YOU COULD HAVE STAYED LONGER IF YOU WANTED," SAM SAID to Harry as she stepped out of her black velvet pants.

He grinned. "And miss this floor show? Why would I want to do that?"

"Because you were having a good time. Especially when you got into the Randy Newman." Harry played a mean piano.

"Those folks are mostly from New Orleans. They can hear back home sometime."

"Too bad Magic couldn't stay for her own party. Wasn't she great? Good thing she won talent, or I'd really think this thing was rigged."

"Yeah. You know, the delegations have a lot more fun than the girls, but then they don't have to get up at the crack of dawn."

"Whereas we old broads can stay up forever."

"There she goes again," Harry said to Harpo. Then he whistled a few bars of "Silver Threads Among the Gold." "Shall I call room service and ask for a wheelchair?"

"Nope. But some hot chocolate would be nice."

Harry picked up the phone, then belly flopped onto the big pink bed where Sam was now giving Harpo a doggy massage. "So who's going to win?"

"The pageant? Well, let's see. What do we know? So far Rae Ann and Magic have taken talent—which counts a lot. Texas and New Jersey have swimsuit—not as big a percentage, but we know swimsuit winners *win.* We know zip about evening gown."

"I think those four. California looks good. She's smart and she's Asian-American. That's got to count for something."

"Maybe. How about Florida?"

"Florida's strong."

"So that's six. We need ten finalists."

"And your pick for Miss A?"

"Now? Without seeing tomorrow night?"

"You must have an inkling. Sometimes they know from the minute the girls hit town."

"Who's this they?"

"Everybody. The girls—like Debbye Turner, 1990, they say she had it hands down from the getgo."

"Who have *you* been talking to?"

"Guys in the Louisiana delegation."

"Gamblers, more likely, hoping to score on the pageant. Your friends down in the casino."

"Right, Sammy."

"So *some* people probably racked up some bucks with Debbye Turner, huh? Depending on the odds."

"You're not giving up on Michelangelo making book on the pageant, are you? It wouldn't make sense, Sammy. Nothing to base the odds on. Besides, baby-sitting Lana, Ma's probably got all he can handle this week."

"She's a real handful, all right. Ah, sweetheart, the noise you put out about women with smarts—why'd I ever believe any of that for a minute? Ain't nothing changed. Boys still pant after bimbos. That's why we still *have* beauty pageants—the likes of you, Harry."

Harry hadn't meant it that way. But he did think Lana was going to win. "I *like* Texas. I *love* Magic, but she won't take it, though she'll make the top five. But it's definitely Jersey's show. What do you think?"

"No way. Rae Ann. Definitely Rae Ann."

"Oh, Sammy. You're just saying that 'cause Lana's a twit and you're covering Rae Ann."

"Give it up. Lana is *not* taking it. Look, Rae Ann's blond, she's southern, she took talent *and* Fruit of the Loom. The gimp factor that won her Fruit probably gave her mega-points in interview, which carry over, forty percent. A bundle."

"What do you want to bet?"

Sam threw up her hands. She appealed to Harpo. "I ask you—has the man lost his mind?" Then to Harry, "You want to bet on how long it's going to take room service to get here with our hot chocolate?"

"Sucker bet. We know forty-five minutes is the fastest they could deliver a newspaper—and they don't even have to heat that. You want to bet the same grand on Miss A? Then if you lose the Roberts thing and win this, it'll be a wash."

"I'm not losing the Roberts thing, Harry. I'm closing in." She was bluffing, of course.

"No way. *I'm* closing in." Or he might be, if he could get to Big Gloria, who he knew was holding out on him.

Big Gloria, on the other hand, didn't give a hoot about the pageant. What she cared about was her son.

She'd tucked him in, kissed him good night, just like she did when he was a little tyke. And now she stood in the doorway of his room. It was way after midnight, and his bed was empty again. Junior, she cried and wrung her hands. Junior, Junior, Junior, what are you up to? What can I do? I tried sucking up to that crazy Wayne, and that got me nowhere.

Then she fell to her knees. Oh, Lord, just bring back that Kurt Roberts and I'll give him his five thousand—with interest. I promise, dear Lord. Seven-and-a-half percent. No, make it ten. Okay, twelve, that's prime, and my last offer.

. . . 25

THURSDAY MORNING, WAYNE AWAKENED SLOWLY. HE LAY IN HIS narrow cot and floated in and out of a dream filled with the thrum of motors idling. Heavy engines chewing gas, belching smoke among empty buildings, broken glass, starving cats. Baghdad.

He sat straight up with a jolt, grabbed his glasses, and wildly looked about. Then he laughed.

It wasn't Baghdad. It was home—out at the end of the inlet, among the bombed-out, burned-down, dug-up houses across the street from the old Cap't Starn's seafood restaurant. Part of it was a boat, empty and peeling now. Its crumbling parking lot was used by the motor buses after they'd dropped off the day's codgers at the casinos. Bus drivers gathered inside the abandoned building drinking coffee they'd brought in thermoses, eating bagels and Danish, swapping lies.

Beside Wayne on the floor of his third floor bedroom in the turret of the abandoned Victorian he'd homesteaded as if it were another tree house sat the treat Big Gloria had brought him last night—or what was left of it.

A chocolate cake with a frosting of chocolate cream and Cracker Jacks. The prize on top had been a little red plastic camera.

In honor, Big Gloria had said, of his God-given talent for taking pictures.

God-given talent. Innate worth. She sounded a lot like his hero Mr. F.

But she wanted something. He wasn't exactly sure what, but it made him nervous. She kept talking about cameras and pictures, and he realized she knew about the taping in the high-roller suites.

Which he didn't want to think about. Not since he'd realized that the One Very Important Thing Mr. F had asked him to do, the thing he was going to use to Show Up Dougie, was screwed.

Cameras and decks could be replaced, but somehow he had to get his tapes back. Especially the one of Mr. F's girl winning her state, the one he was going to plug into the heads of the final judges. He had to get it back or reproduce it before tomorrow, and he didn't know how he was going to do that because the original tape of that pageant was missing, too. Plus the one he didn't want to think about, the one he hadn't shown Mr. F yet, though it was for Mr. F's eyes only, as James Bond would say. Wayne loved James Bond movies—the glamour, the fireworks, and the hardware were right up his alley.

But James Bond never had somebody like Big Gloria around reminding him of when he'd screwed up. Now what he had to do today was make everything right, or he was going to be in Very Big Trouble. Even worse, Dougie would laugh. Wayne reached down and grabbed a big handful of his chocolate Cracker Jack cake. The sweet crunch made him feel a little better, but not enough.

He closed his eyes and pictured Dougie and knew what would.

...26

SAM HAD THROWN HARRY OUT OF THEIR ROOM ALONG WITH THE morning room-service cart. Fine with him, he'd said. He had a little business to tend to—which is exactly what she was doing.

Someone else from Atlantic City had called about Mr. Roberts. That's what the receptionist in his New York office said to Sam on the phone. And she'd told Mr. Zick that Mr. Roberts was there, at the pageant.

But he wasn't, Sam explained. He'd said he'd returned to this very office on business.

Oh, said the receptionist, popping her gum. Oh. Well, she wouldn't know about that. *She* hadn't seen him.

Well, gee. What do you think that means? Aren't you worried?

Well, I'm not exactly his mother. Or his girlfriend.

She was wearing black, Sam was sure of it. A short black skirt, black pullover, black tights, those huge black shoes with steel toes, tractor-tread soles, and big black grosgrain ribbon ties. Only her hair was a different color—like purple.

Then who is, Sam asked. Who are?

Who are what?

His mother and his girlfriend?

Oh, I couldn't tell you that.

Well, could you have them call me before I file a missing persons report on Mr. Roberts?

With the cops? The girl was incredulous.

That's the usual procedure.

Mr. Roberts wouldn't like that. Her gum popped twice.

Have them call me, okay?

Okay. But I think you're overreacting. He treats *all* his women this way, you know. And *they* don't call the cops. Have you thought about taking a Valium?

I'm not one of his women, I don't take drugs, and I'm definitely calling the cops.

That's pretty radical. Why don't you just hold on? I'll try to reach his mom. Now, if I can figure out how to do this transfer thing—hold on.

"So I went back over there to the Monopoly and did some asking around," said Angelo.

Uh-huh, Willie answered, paying more attention to the cheese Danish in his hand than to Ange. He'd dropped Ma off at the coffeeshop where he always had breakfast and now Willie wanted to enjoy his own.

"Nobody's seen him. Busboys, maids, nobody at the desk. He's still registered, though, ain't that strange?"

Strange, Willie nodded.

"Then I found out he wuzzn't at the show last night. At least that's what a guy told me, Security over at the hall. Said he wuzzn't. Wha'dya think it means, Willie?"

Willie didn't know.

"I think it means I'll go over there myself this evening, see that show. I can't find that Roberts, maybe something else'll occur to me. Some other way of helping out that Big John's niece, Big John, Ma. Myself and Angelina. Wha'dya think?"

What Willie thought was that if Angelo didn't stop saying Ma's mother's name like that, he better get himself over to Sicily, dig a hole and pull it in on top of himself, forget the old broad. He didn't say that, though.

"So, Wayne. What's that on the back of your hat? Let me see."

Wayne just shrugged, kept walking. The last person he wanted to talk to this morning was Dougie. His plan was, he was going to go back into Action Central, now that he'd calmed down, slept on it, and search the whole place *very* carefully. Things had been misfiled before.

"*Wayne delivers.* Hey, that's neat. So, you got yourself another business."

Wayne stopped. "What do you mean another business?"

"Looks like you're into pizzas. *Wayne delivers.* You know what I mean?"

"I am an electronics surveillance, augmentation, and intervention expert. Nothing to do with pizza."

"Sure, sure. But you know what they say, Wayne." Dougie rolled his little shoulders in his little navy-blue blazer, double-breasted, with gold buttons. He looked like one of those airline steward fruits. "Clothes make the man. You don't want to give people the wrong sartorial impression."

Sartorial impression. He'd was gonna sartorially impress Dougie, all right. One more crack like that, just one more.

"Yesssss?" said the throaty voice on the phone. For one delicious moment Sam thought it was Lauren Bacall. "Hold on a minute, darling, my chef just walked in."

Sam was darling, and this was Kurt Roberts's mom.

"Yes, Evan. We're going to make it *very* American. I want barbecued ribs and potato salad and those darling corn bread sticks you did when we had the ambassador. Our guest of honor's French, and you know how they *love* everything American—except us of course. Now, darling, what can I do for you? That hideous girl in Kurt's office said something about you couldn't find Kurt. I don't know why she'd call *me*—but, hold on, darling. It's the man about the flowers. They're atwitter, all the service people out here in Southampton, so happy to have those dreary *summer* people gone, but afraid they won't make another sou until June. It quite throws them off their stride. Now what kind of *American* flowers can we do for this dinner, Lee?"

"Mrs. Roberts? I—"

"I'm not Mrs. Roberts, darling. The Mr. Roberts who was

Kurt's father—that was a *very* long time ago. Call me Glenda. Now where were we? Black-eyed Susans? I don't know. What do *you* think, I'm sorry, what's your name, darling?"

"Sam Adams, and I don't mean to alarm you, but no one seems to know where your son's gotten off to. He's supposed to be down here in Atlantic City judging the Miss America Pageant—"

"Atlantic City? Did you say you're calling from Atlantic City? Isn't that the most *dreadfully* boring place? *I've* never been, of course. But people I know have, and they say, well, that Trump man, what do you expect? And that German wife—"

"I think she was Czech, Mrs.—Glenda. But anyway, your son seems to have called a day or so ago and said he was going back to New York on business and he—"

"If that's what he said he was doing, I'm sure that's what he did. Now, you'll excuse me, I'm sorry. The housekeeper is standing here with the table linens and I have to choose—"

Okay. So Kurt Roberts had a rotten childhood. Sam gave people until thirty to get over being rich, privileged, and underloved. After that, they had to find a better excuse.

"What I think we ought to do is sic Magic on him," said Lavert. He was working on his third cup of McDonald's coffee. "Man, isn't this a shame?" He held out the cardboard cup. He and Harry were sitting on a bench on the Boardwalk. "Sucking down fast food java. For sure, I'm having my stomach pumped the second I get back to New Orleans. Though that sausage biscuit—now, that wasn't too bad . . ."

"Why don't you just hop the cable car out St. Charles to the Camellia Grill and have a couple of chili burgers when you get home? Same difference. Now, getting back, tell me what good would that do us, siccing Magic on Roberts?"

"She's got the same head as G.T., Zack. You didn't know that?"

"She do the voudou?"

"Um-hum. Which is why she's gonna conjure herself up that Miss America title. *If* she really wants it."

"Then, hey, man, call her up. Did she bring a crystal ball along with her, or can she just use that silver one we saw her with last night?"

"Making fun, man."

"Now, wait—*you* tell me this—"

"Mr. Zack, what a fortunate coincidence!"

Harry nudged Lavert. "Kid's named Rashad. Check this out."

Rashad was pushing his wicker rolling chair and wearing his white tie and tails, just like the previous morning. "Have you considered," the young man asked, "what must have been going through the minds of the august fathers of the city of Atlantic City when they placed the very bench upon which you are reposing facing in toward the casinos rather than out toward the ocean? Does that tell you something about the conflict between nature and commerce in this seaside resort? Let's face it, the ocean was here, along with the Native Americans, long before the likes of Mr. Trump, Mr. Scarfo, the Reverend Dunwoodie and the various other dignitaries who—"

"He was talking about bivalve professionals yesterday," said Harry. "Bivalve professionals in New Orleans."

"Shuck and jive?"

"You're quick, man!" Harry threw Lavert a high five.

Rashad didn't miss a beat. "—who have shucked and jived their way into controlling the interests of this city in *their* best interests but hardly in the interest of its true inhabitants. Now, in the film about AC and the pageant my cohorts and I are editing even as we speak, or perhaps that's an overstatement, shooting and editing, I should say, but we'll be finished before you leave, Mr. Zack, you can rest assured—"

"When does he breathe? I've seen lots of young brothers with fancy educations who can do all kinds of numbers—brokering stocks and breaking banks—but they all have to breathe," said Lavert.

"—that the Atlantic City extravaganza courtesy of

Rashad/Sturdivant Productions will be ready for your viewing—"

"Sturdivant? Is Junior Sturdivant your sidekick, Big Gloria's son?" Harry asked.

"He is indeed. He is my codirector, main man, gaffer. Our star, playing an old Miss A, is a young lady named Rachel Rose."

"We got it, Rashad. Listen, did Junior tell you about a man who pushed him in a swimming pool?"

"He did. An unfortunate occurrence. Though I do not think there were any racial—"

"I hadn't thought of this before," Harry said to Lavert. "So you think Junior might have seen the man since?"

"I think Junior would have given the perpetrator of his watery discomfort a wide berth. Junior, like many of our race—"

"Can't swim," Lavert interrupted. "Am I right?"

"He cannot. Now there are many Caucasians who think that that is a genetic defect, but the real—"

"We know the real reason, Rashad. There were no pools for black kids when the likes of me was growing up," said Lavert. "But you guys got pools and the ocean—right here. What's your excuse?"

"*I* swim, sir. It's my friend Junior who seems to have a natural aversion to the briny deep. He says when he jumps in, it feels like somebody smacked him in the face."

"Rashad!" Harry jumped up and did a little victory boogie on the Boardwalk as if he'd made big yardage, scored a touchdown. "You're a genius!"

"Thank you, Mr. Zack. But there's no reason to—"

"Smacked *me* in the face, that son of a gun did, coming out of *Roberts's* room. My mind's been hovering somewhere off the coast, Lavert. This could be it!"

"It's how white people talk," Lavert said to Rashad. "He'll spit it out in a minute when he filters it through his college education and comes up with the exact wording."

Rashad grinned at Lavert as if he might have found himself a new hero.

"That bubba with the stupid hat who popped me in the

mouth Tuesday was coming out of Roberts's room, I'm telling you."

"I've been meaning to ask you about that lip, but I thought you'd come to it in your own good time. I see now that you have." It was difficult, once you'd heard him, not to start talking like Rashad.

"What was he doing in Roberts's room? Don't you think we ought to go ask him?" said Harry.

"What did the bubba's hat look like?" asked Rashad, who was beginning to have a sneaking feeling he didn't want to know the answer. His Miss A spectacular might be hanging in the balance.

"It was black, kind of like a baseball cap. Said *Monopoly Special Services* on the front. And *Wayne Delivers* on the back."

Uh-oh, thought Rashad, who would just as soon have the man whose wonderful video equipment he had lifted left undisturbed.

"Let's go find that sucker and throw the fear of Lavert into him," said the big man.

What a distressing development. Unless, of course, they took him *completely* out of the picture, in which case Rashad would have undisputed title to the camcorder and the editing controller and the . . .

The unfortunate young model who held the title of Kurt Roberts's current girlfriend sounded like a rerun of Cindy Lou Jacklin, only younger. No, she hadn't heard from Kurt. No, she didn't know where he was. But if Sam found him, would she let her know? She really missed him and it had been ages . . .

Neither was Louis, Sam's favorite bellman, the one who had directed her toward Cindy Lou in Rich Uncle Pennybags Lounge, any help when it came to Roberts. He pocketed her ten, which matched the one Harry had given him, though he didn't tell her that. He did tell her the same thing he'd told Harry. No one had seen Roberts since Tuesday afternoon. And yes, he was still registered as a guest. . . .

It was time, she thought, to try Charlie in Atlanta. She stepped into a pay phone in the lobby and pulled out a piece of plastic.

"You what?"

"Want to find this judge who's disappeared."

"Believe me, if a judge's disappeared, they've got more than the Atlantic City PD on it. That's federal, honey."

"A Miss America judge, Charlie."

"Oh." She could hear him chewing on a pencil. "That's different. So, why do you want to find him?"

"Because he's missing."

"You wanta tell me about this from the top?"

So she did.

"And the real reason you want to find him is to win a fifteen-hundred-dollar bet. Am I right on this?"

"No. I want to find him because I think something awful has happened to him, and *no one* can find him, and no one seems to care."

"Sammy, listen, do me a favor. If you call the Atlantic City PD, don't use my name. I have friends there—Captain Kelly, in particular. I'd like to keep it that way."

"Charlie—"

"You've lost it this time, doll. Go work on your suntan, eat some saltwater taffy, fight with your boyfriend."

"He's the one who thinks Roberts is fine."

The tapes and the equipment were nowhere to be found. They were gone for good. Wayne sat in his black calf chair exactly like Mr. F's and tried to think like Mr. F. Now what should he consider here? Who would want to trip him up? Who would want to make a fool of him? Who had been sniffing around?

Well, there was Big Gloria. She'd been sniffing, but that was probably because she wanted his body. She was just acting interested in what he did because that's what women did to show you they had the hots. They didn't like to just come right out and say it. Well, he could solve that little problem.

And who else?

Well, now, Wayne, that was obvious, wasn't it?

The only question was, should he torture the info out of him first, make him give back the tapes and the equipment so Mr. F wouldn't be mad at him, or could he just off him?

No contest, but sometimes it paid to use a little of what Mr. F called discretion.

How discreet did he have to be, though, before he erased Dougie?

"Wait a minute," said Lavert, as he and Harry strode down the long green carpet back to Wayne's office like gunslingers. "Hold up there, Robin."

"What you want, Batman? We don't get back there, the man's going to be gone for lunch."

"Have you thought this thing through? If this Wayne dude, the one who poked you, was sneaking out of Roberts's room, it is highly likely that any info he might give us might be negative rather than positive."

"Meaning?"

"Meaning, Zack, that it might lead us toward a conclusion that would result in our losing our wager."

"You mean, we might find out he did something to *harm* one Kurt Roberts?"

"Exactly."

"In which case, we would *lose* the fifteen hundred."

"My point."

"So what are you suggesting?"

"Only that we realize that if we extract some knowledge—"

"You're still talking like Rashad, my friend."

"—that might lead us to a conclusion that would make us unhappy, we ignore it."

"Don't tell Sammy."

"Don't tell no one."

"Let sleeping dogs lie."

"Dead men doze. Especially *unpleasant* dead men that don't nobody else in the whole wide world except us give a rat's ass about."

"Don't go borrowing trouble."

"Sticking your nose in."

"Gimme five."

Lavert lowered his tall self and the old friends bumped knees, hips, elbows. Wearing big smiles.

...27

"SHE'S THE KIND OF GIRL WHO WOULD WEAR RED HIGH HEELS to a funeral," Lana said to Rae Ann, pointing at Connors McCoy across the dressing room. The girls had just finished rehearsal and were changing back into street clothes.

Rae Ann thought the red heels sounded more like Lana herself. "Honey, why don't you like Connors?"

"Because she's a snot."

"I don't see why."

"*I* do. After she won swimsuit Tuesday night, I went up and congratulated her. Now, did she do the same when I took it last night? Unh-uh. No sirree. She's too busy hugging that colored girl."

When Lana had told Sam that not *all* the girls were sweet, these two were who she was talking about. They'd rubbed her the wrong way from the first night.

"But, Lana, Magic won talent, and she's her best friend. She probably just got carried away."

"All I know is, she better not get it in her head she's gonna win just because she took swimsuit. I took it, too. Besides"—Lana brushed at her platinum curls, watching herself in the mirror—"redheads never win. Blondes do. Of course, the coloreds have been taking it the past few years."

Rae Ann wondered if Lana had forgotten that *she* was a blonde, and a contestant too. *And* she'd won talent, plus Fruit of the Loom. She wasn't real happy with the way Lana talked about Magic, either. Yankees made that mistake a lot, assuming that all white southerners were naturally racist. What would amaze you was how many of *them* were.

"Oh, I just wish the Jersey Devil'd drag them both off. It'd serve them right," said Lana.

"What Jersey Devil?"

Lana turned on her stool. "Right up the road, headed toward Philly." She pointed with her brush out to sea, the wrong direction, but she didn't know that, "there's this huge forest where crazy people live. Pineys, we call them, 'cause the woods are the Pine Barrens."

"What do you mean, crazy?"

"They're like retarded country people living out in the woods."

Rae Ann knew lots of people who'd lived in the country back home in South Georgia—like her family. She wouldn't call them crazy *or* retarded.

"And anyway, nobody in his right mind would drive out there at night. It's bad enough in the daytime, all those little roads, you can get so lost. But at night, that's when the Jersey Devil makes his move."

"Uh-huh."

"No, really! There was an article in the paper not too long ago, the state police found its footprints. *Huge* ones."

"So what did it do?"

"Carried off a bunch of animals. All that was left were little bits and pieces of them. Dogs and cats and ducks."

Rae Ann wasn't very impressed. Wild dogs did the same thing back home all the time.

"And little children."

"Children? Come on, Lana. You don't believe that, do you?"

"I most certainly do. I read about it in the paper. There was this woman a long time ago named Mrs. Leeds who lived in the Pines. Anyway, she had twelve children, and she didn't want any more, and she said if she had another one, she hoped it was the devil. And she had another one, and it was. When it grew up, it flew away on its wings. And it can jump like a kangaroo. Chews up anything living. People in the Pines hang a light to scare it off. At my house, up in Sea Girt, well, it's not all that far away. We leave the porch light on every night."

"Sounds like the loup-garou to me." That was Magic, who, along with Connors, was on her way to get some lunch. "People out in the bayou hang a sieve on their back porch because the loup-garou'll have to stop and count every one of those holes, and in that time, you can sling salt on 'em and that sets them on fire."

"Hi!" smiled Rae Ann. "Why don't ya'll sit down for a minute?"

Lana didn't even look up; she just kept brushing her hair. Magic didn't take it personally. She was getting used to northerners' strange ways, their mamas didn't teach them any better. She went on with what she was saying. "In Louisiana they warn little kids: You better be good or the loup-garou'll get you."

"Like the bogeyman," nodded Rae Ann.

"Yeah, except he's worse than that. He's half wolf, half monster. Actually, he's a werewolf who haunts the bayous."

Lana sniffed. Bayous. Colored girl *would* use some fancy words nobody'd ever heard of.

"So do you become a loup-garou if one bites you?" Rae Ann was up on her werewolves.

"That's one way. The other is sometimes people just make themselves into a loup-garou because they want to do evil."

Lana turned from the mirror and gave Magic a look: Who was she talking about? Magic caught that one and thought, Shoe fits, chile, you wear it.

Rae Ann wanted to know how you turned yourself into a werewolf.

"They rub themselves with voudou grease." Magic laughed. "And they are *bad* looking. Hairy with big ears and sharp nails and bright red eyes. Like that." Magic pointed at Connors's scarlet cowboy boots.

Lana looked at Rae Ann. See? Those red high heels she was talking about?

"They are *hell* to get rid of. Bullets'll go right through them. And they have bats big as helicopters to carry them around. One of their favorite tricks is to drop down your chimney and stand by your bed and yell, Gotcha! Scare you to death, if nothing else. They're thrifty devils, too. Sometimes they turn themselves into mules and work their own land."

"So how *do* you get rid of them?" asked Connors.

"Well, there's the sieve trick, with the salt. The other way is to get yourself a nice frog and throw it at 'em. They'll run off howling."

Lana snorted. "I never heard such a bunch of crap."

"Well, you can say what you want to. But I'm telling you, you think your Jersey Devil's something, you ought to listen up about the loup-garou. Those who don't are sorry."

Was Magic threatening her? Lana narrowed her eyes. You go threatening a DeLucca, you'll eat your words.

"Listen. I'll tell you a true story, about a loup-garou and a beauty queen."

Connors and Rae Ann made themselves comfortable. Lana picked up her mascara.

Magic started, "Over in Cajun country, southwest of New Orleans, which is where lots of loup-garoux live, there was, not so long ago, a beautiful girl named Danielle. She had milk-white skin, a heart-shaped mouth, big brown eyes, and black curls that fell halfway to the ground."

"And she was pure as the driven snow," said Connors.

"Yes, she was, as a matter of fact. Now you get your mouth off my story."

Go, Connors waved a hand. Go.

"Danielle was the most beautiful girl anyone had ever seen. And the sweetest. She grew up in Abbeville in Vermillion Parish, which is mostly swamp, right on the Gulf. Lots of it washed away in Hurricane Audrey about thirty years ago, but that's another story.

"Anyway, when it came time to pick a Miss Vermillion, there was no question but what it was Danielle. All she had to do was smile, and the judges just handed the crown over.

"Now, one of the judges was the mayor of the town of Abbeville, and he was a tiny little Cajun man named Claude, middle-aged, sturdy, not much bigger than a minute. But, of course, in Abbeville, he was a big man. At least, an important man. And he was used to getting what he wanted."

"Which was Danielle," guessed Rae Ann.

"You bet. Right after her coronation, he slipped over to her parents' house and asked for her hand, as soon as the beauty-queening was over. And her father, a simple man who earned what livelihood they had hunting and trapping, knew that Danielle couldn't do any better. Not in Vermillion Parish. And there was no world outside of Vermillion Parish to him, of course."

"Is there a loup-garou in this story?" Lana demanded.

"Lord, lord." Magic shook her head. "You folks are always in such a hurry."

What folks?

Magic just rolled her eyes.

"Don't pay Lana no nevermind." Rae Ann patted Lana on the shoulder as if her friend couldn't help herself. Though, truth was, she wasn't so sure Lana really was her friend, even though she'd *seemed* that way.

"So, here's Danielle, engaged to marry little Claude, whom she doesn't love, barely even knows. And there's nothing she can do about it."

"Except win Miss Louisiana," said Connors, one jump ahead of her.

"That's right. Because then, of course, she'll get to go to Atlantic City, and that'll put it off at least another six months, maybe a year.

"Well, she knows she's not going to have much trouble with the beauty part. And she's got this wonderful Cajun accent and can tell a story like nobody's business. But she doesn't have any talent."

"Then how'd she win her county?" Lana challenged her.

"Parish. She sang a Cajun song and did a two-step. But that wasn't going to get her anywhere up in Monroe at the state judging."

"So what'd she do? Sign herself up with Sally Griffin for some courses?" Connors asked, and they all laughed. Even Lana.

"No. She looked around her house and saw her grandmother's fiddle up on a shelf, and she figured that was the way to go."

"Did she play the fiddle at all?" asked Rae Ann.

"Not a lick. But she remembered her grandmère playing. People said she could outplay the devil. Others said she'd sold her soul to the devil to play like that. Anyway, Danielle thought since she'd inherited her grandmère's looks, maybe she had some of her talent, too, she just hadn't tapped it. So she took that fiddle down and went out in the yard and commenced to playing."

"Like a dream," guessed Connors.

"Like a screech owl. It was the worst sound anybody had ever heard. All the neighbors raced out and started throwing frogs, thinking it was a loup-garou for sure."

"Finally," said Lana.

"Not quite. Hold on. But, of course, it wasn't. It was only Danielle. And, being a determined girl, she didn't give up. She sat out in the yard on a stump and tried and tried while dogs howled and cats ran up trees. Alligators stayed submerged along with the water moccasins. Finally, her mama came out and told her she had to stop, the sound was going to stunt her garden. And just then, Claude drove up in his great big black car, he could hardly see over the steering wheel, and said he wanted to take his sweetheart for a ride.

"Well, Danielle couldn't say no, after all, she was raised to be polite. So she gets in the car with this rich man she hardly knows, he's old enough to be her father almost, and they go driving off. And she thinks, Why not give it a shot? Maybe he's not so bad."

Lana was frowning that tiny frown, the one she allowed herself only a few minutes at a time so it wouldn't stick between her eyebrows. But lookit. What was Magic saying? A short man with money, power, and influence old enough to be a beauty queen's father. Magic was making this whole thing up about her and Billy Carroll. She knew it. She just knew it. Magic was shooting straight at her. Well, she better watch out for ricochets.

"Claude is asking Danielle a million questions about herself, but it's like he's interviewing her. The problem is, the man has no sense of humor. Uh-huh, uh-huh, he says. And no matter how much she throws herself into it, his expression never changes. It's like she's this little ball of energy and cute, and he just sucks it all out of her."

"The Energy Vampire! The Enthusiasm Werewolf! I've been out with a million of them!" Connors had had her share of bad experiences with fix-ups and blind dates. "They're like vacuum cleaners. Bottomless pits of passivity. You could set yourself on fire and sing 'The Star-Spangled Banner,' they'd say, Uh-huh."

"So, anyway, Danielle can see that she's *got* to save herself. Life with this man would be Night of the Living Dead. They're driving and driving, and then they stop at this little clearing, a picnic table beneath a tree dripping with Spanish moss, and it's all very romantic and atmospheric as all get out. There's no conversation going because *she's* stopped talking, though he dribbles out a question now and then. She's trying to figure out how she's going to do something about her talent, get herself out of this fix, when it comes to her! She'll do what they said her grandmère did! She'll sell her soul to the devil!

"But the question is, How? How does she get in touch with him? Is he listed in the Abbeville Yellow Pages? She doesn't have a clue."

"And just then, he drove up in a Lamborghini."

Magic stared at Connors. Go on, she said. You tell it.

She doesn't know it, said Rae Ann, and I wish she'd hush. Hush, Connors, now. Hush.

Oh, all right, said Connors. But she could really use a beer.

I'm going to turn you into a Lone Star in about half a second, Magic warned. Then reached down into her huge purse, pulled out a six-pack, a *cold* six-pack, and said, Who's drinking?

Now *that* was magic, even Lana would grant her that one. She took her brew and even said thank-you. They wrapped tissues around them, being as they ought to maintain some proprieties, being in the Miss America dressing room.

Now, can I go on?

Do it, girl, said Connors.

"The most handsome young man Danielle had ever seen rode up on a palomino. You laugh, Connors, your ass is grass."

Connors didn't even peep.

"And he leaned down to the picnic table and said, 'Danielle, my sweetie patootie, I'm going to marry you and take you away from this miserable little toad.'

"Needless to say, Claude was pissed. What the handsome young man had forgotten, if he'd ever known it, was you shouldn't insult a little man, because he'll kill you."

Lana sipped her beer, considering. There was that little man stuff again.

"And then the handsome young man, whose name is Jean-Paul, hands Danielle a fiddle. He says, Take this, my darling dear heart, and fiddle your way to freedom. She stands up to thank him, and he leans over to kiss her. Claude, super offended, jumps up and swats him one, which causes Jean-Paul to bump Danielle's lip so he sort of takes a little nip out of her."

Dunh-dunh-dunh-dunh. Connors was making the *Jaws* sound. Sort of a combination *Jaws* and loup-garou.

Magic ignored her. "Now, Claude is not your total fool. He realizes that if Danielle can really play the fiddle, she has a good chance of winning Miss Louisiana and then going on to Atlantic City, and if she wins there, which she very well might with a magic fiddle, well, he's looking at another year by his lonesome. Plus, what's this guy on the horse *really* got in mind?

"'Please, take me home, Claude,' Danielle is saying, fluffing up her curls and wiping the blood off her mouth. Jean-Paul has ridden off into the swamp. She's holding the fiddle very carefully, on the other side of her *away* from Claude, her mother not having raised any idiots.

"'Fine,' says Claude. 'But promise you'll come with me to the Courir de Mardi Gras tomorrow night.'

"'Oh, sure,' said Danielle. Anything to get home and see if her magic fiddle really worked.

"Now, the Courir de Mardi Gras, because I know you're

about to ask, is this tradition that Cajun people celebrate out in the country at Carnival time. Men set out on horseback and ride from house to house collecting all the ingredients for a gumbo big enough for the whole community—a chicken here, sausage there, okra, tomatoes, onions, hot peppers, and so on—and then they bring it all to the square in the center of the town where men cook it up. Then they have a big dance.

"So Danielle agrees to go to the Courir de Mardi Gras and Claude takes her home.

"Once she's there, she sits out on the stump and picks up the fiddle, expecting to hear the most wonderful sound, but nothing happens. She bows again. Nothing. The fiddle is absolutely mute, no matter if she plucks it or bows it—which is a kind of miracle in itself, though not the one she was hoping for.

"So now Danielle is really distraught. Here she thought she'd gone and sold her soul to the devil, and it turned out to be a dud. A fake. Just the handsomest young man she'd ever seen on horseback, but what good did that do her? She was still engaged to Claude, and she didn't have a pageant talent worth spit.

"She moped around the house the whole next day, plucking the fiddle now and then, but still zip. Her mama kept asking her what was wrong. Nothing, Danielle answered. Nothing, nothing, nothing. Girl, you've got yourself such a negative attitude all of a sudden, you've not only put a hex on my garden, but the Courir de Mardi Gras didn't even stop here. Probably thought my tomatoes was poison. And her mama was right. No one had come by.

"And nobody did until about six o'clock, when Claude drove up in his big black car. He had his black curls all oiled down. And he was wearing a black suit and a black string tie. Danielle thought he looked like the devil, and she didn't mean that nicely, either. He hadn't cleaned beneath his fingernails and he smelled like hair oil. She found him truly disgusting. She didn't think she'd be able to eat any gumbo, much less do any dancing.

"'Aren't you going to bring your fiddle along?' Claude

asked slyly. Like he had something up his sleeve. Which he did.

"Oh, okay, she would. What difference did it make? What difference did anything make? Life with Night of the Living Dead, she'd probably commit suicide on her wedding day anyway, have it over with. She certainly wasn't going to *sleep* with this creature with dirty fingernails.

"So they drove to the square, and Claude was squiring her about. Danielle was such a favorite, and, after all, Claude was the mayor, even if he was a creep, everyone's paying their respects. But behind their hands, the little old ladies were saying Danielle was looking peaked."

"What is peaked?" asked Lana, who was redoing her hair with a curling iron now.

"Pale. Wormy. Tired. Anemic."

Connors hooted at that last word, and Magic handed her another beer. Suck on that, girl, and shut up.

"Everybody's eating gumbo and drinking beer and dancing to beat the band and having a *good* time, except Danielle, of course, who's searching the crowd for Jean-Paul. But he's not there. Claude pulls her by the hand to dance a Cajun two-step, and Danielle, who's a wonderful dancer, finds she can barely keep up with the *chank-a-chank* beat. She's *so* tired and depressed. Claude says maybe she ought to eat some gumbo. But she says no, she just couldn't. No, no beer, either. She sits herself down on a bench, and Claude says to wait right there, he's going to get her some gumbo anyway. Oh, okay, she says. And she watches all the people she's grown up with and loved her whole life having a wonderful time, and wondering how *her* life came to such a pass. One minute she was a carefree girl enjoying life and good looks and the next thing she knows she's a beauty queen and her life has turned to shit."

Rae Ann and Connors and Lana *all* howled. They could identify with *that* one, all right.

"She reaches in her bag and pulls out the velvet sack her grandmère had made for *her* fiddle, and in it is the fiddle Jean-Paul gave her. The silent fiddle. She sits staring at it with a miserable look, and suddenly into the square rides

Jean-Paul on his palomino. He's carrying a bag of mushrooms that he's gathered in the woods, and he throws them in the gumbo.

"The pot bubbles up and the most wonderful smell fills the air and everybody wants seconds.

"Then he pulls to a halt in front of Danielle and says, 'Play for me, most beautiful lady.'

"Forget the compliments. 'I can't,' she pouts. 'This fiddle you gave me is no damned good.'

" 'Play.' This time he said it like a command. So Danielle stood, tucked the fiddle under her chin, and pulled back her bow. She'd show him. She'd show him what cheap goods he'd given her as a gift, making her promises. Men!

"She laid the bow on the strings, pulled, and the sound that poured out of the violin was pure honey. It was filled with such radiant sweetness that all the people first laughed, and then wept. The tone was centered and vibrant as a bell. The tone was golden, the absolute essence of Danielle's soul. And the tune she played was one no one had ever heard. It was an air full of light and angel wings and tinkling bells and sugarplum fairies and wonder. It told of all the beauty in the world. It spoke of walks through forests filled with delight. It sang of magic.

"And everyone danced to Danielle's Air, as it was thereafter known, though no one could even hum it, but they *knew* they'd heard it. Grandmas danced with Grandpas who danced with their sons and daughters and small children and babes-in-arms and dogs and cats and raccoons and twittering birds. Oh, it was a grand waltz and two-step and gavotte and get-down boogie and tango and cha-cha-cha. For part of the magic of it was, every time the rhythm changed, the people followed it like flowing water. Everyone was Fred Astaire and Ginger Rogers.

"Except Claude. Claude stood on the sidelines with a frown on his face and his arms crossed. And then, in a particularly magic moment, Jean-Paul leaned over to Danielle and told her to let go of the fiddle and let go of the bow, and she did, and they went right on playing without her! Jean-Paul, the most handsome young man in the world, took the beautiful Danielle in his strong arms and he hugged her and swung her and they do-si-doed.

"At that, Claude, the little man whom Jean-Paul should not have crossed, reached up his sleeve and pulled out a pistol. When Danielle and Jean-Paul whirled past, breast to breast, he fired, one, two, three, four, five, six, and all six bullets found their targets. They entered Jean-Paul's back, passed through their two hearts beating as one, and out of Danielle."

"Oh, no!" cried Rae Ann.

"And on they danced, on they whirled, out of the square and into the swamp. All the people cried and raced after them, hoping to save them, this most handsome of men and the most beautiful of girls. Behind them, the fiddle still played Danielle's Air, though the song grew slower and softer and sadder with each note.

"The people searched and searched, but they couldn't find them. They couldn't even find the traces of their blood. Until finally one little boy cried, Look! And they all looked, and there were the tracks of two wolves on the muddy bayou bank. The tracks led to a live oak, and there it looked as if the wolves had stood on their hind legs and had done a little jig. And then they disappeared."

"The bullets went right through them," breathed Rae Ann.

"That's right," said Magic. "When Jean-Paul, who was a loup-garou, bit Danielle, he turned her into one, too. And they ran off into the swamp to be loup-garoux together and forever."

"And what about Claude?" Lana demanded.

"Oh, Claude. He took himself back to his office and sat in his great big chair until he felt important again and commenced to waiting for next year's Miss Abbeville Pageant. You know those beauty queens. They're like streetcars. You wait long enough, another one'll come along."

"That is *not* how that story ends," Rae Ann protested.

"Naw, you're right. It's not. It ends when they go off together to be the most gorgeous loup-garoux in the bayou. I made that last part up for Lana."

Lana just kept looking at herself in the mirror. See? See what Magic said?

It wasn't bad enough that the two of them (girlfriends!) came butting into her story about the Jersey Devil and made it seem like *nothing*.

And that Connors had taken swimsuit too and thought she was hot stuff.

But on top of all that, both of them were making fun of her. Making fun of her and Billy Carroll.

She'd seen them watching her and Billy when they were dancing Monday night at that club, *perfectly* innocent. But that's what this story was all about. Dancing and a beauty queen and a short man in a powerful position.

You didn't have to be a rocket scientist to figure that out.

...28

THE PRESSROOM WAS PANDEMONIUM, FORMER MISS AMERICAS everywhere, reporters milling about: Who's she? Is she somebody? Who's that?

As far as Sam could tell, the former Miss A's looked like any bunch of overdressed doctors' or lawyers' wives. Not a bit prettier. In fact, if you were going by looks alone, she had better-looking friends—though they didn't wear as much makeup. And, all the former beauty queens sported huge rocks—stand-ins, perhaps, for that rhinestone tiara that just wouldn't do for street wear.

But it *was* fun to see, up-close-and-personal, faces that she remembered from pageants of her girlhood.

Mary Ann Mobley, Gary Collins's wife, Miss A 1959, was a tad hollow-eyed but still pretty, if you liked them on the real thin side. Donna Axum, 1964, had blossomed out. Now what was that about her husband, or was it ex, the Texas legislator who had run into some trouble . . .

"That's Yolande Betbeze." The *Inquirer* was pointing at a short brunette with a wide sensuous mouth, deep into her fifties. In a white blouse and navy slacks, she was the only former Miss A who wasn't dressed for a cocktail party. She was the one Malachy had talked about, his favorite from Alabama who'd told the pageant to take a hike because they didn't like her liberal politics. Sam dug for Malachy's autograph book.

She'd almost reached Yolande when she ran smack into Dr. Mary Frances DeLaughter and her tape recorder.

Mary Frances's color was high, her red halo atremble. "Isn't this exciting, all these artifacts in one room?"

"I don't think I'd say that aloud, Mary Frances."

"Well, they *are!* You just hardly ever see so many American icons simultaneously! I don't know where to begin."

Sam backed off, not wanting to be anywhere close to Mary Frances when she did.

"And by the way"—Mary Frances whirled just before Sam escaped—"last night I checked a bibliography, and you're right, you didn't write that book I was thinking of."

"Gee, Mary Frances. You know, I didn't think I did."

"But I did find that series you did on the serial murderers in San Francisco. The one you won a prize for."

"Yes?"

"I didn't like it one bit."

"Hey, thanks, Mary Frances. Thanks a whole bunch."

But Mary Frances was gone, hot on the trail of Marian Bergeron, Miss A 1933. Marian was the one who at sixteen almost punched out the backstage director who tried to remove her swimsuit in his rush to get her into an evening gown. Maybe she'd punch out Mary Frances.

"Is Dr. DeLaughter your new best friend?" The *Inquirer* laughed.

"My latest candidate for burning at the stake. Except she'd love it. I'm sure the woman's into pain."

"Come on over here." The *Inquirer* grabbed Sam's arm. "You *don't* want to miss the Cheryl Prewitt Salem Show."

She certainly didn't. She'd been hoping for a peek at Miss America 1980 and Rae Ann's idol. And there she was, holding court at a table against the wall. Four reporters were already hunkered in, bug-eyed.

It was easy to see why. For starters, there were the diamonds. Rocks sparkled at her ears, her neck, her shoulder, her wrists, and, most of all, her fingers. Sam looked over the shoulder of one young blond reporter who wore jeans and not a smidge of makeup to see that she had sketched into her notes the had-to-be-ten-carat marquise-cut hunk of ice on Cheryl's left hand, surrounded by smaller diamond paving stones.

Cheryl was explaining about her work with the Oral Roberts ministry. She'd always sung for the Lord, ever since she was a little girl. She was already doing that when she was in the car wreck, she and some neighbor kids, that threw her right through the windshield and cut up her left leg so bad it was two inches shorter than the right.

A girl with a limp, she kept right on singing and witnessing for the Lord. Then when she was a teenager and decided she wanted to enter beauty contests back home in Mississippi, it occurred to her one evening to ask the Lord, in a prayer meeting, to heal her leg.

And He did. Cheryl can prove it, can show you the medical reports, because she had just been for a checkup a little while before the healing—reports showing that left leg, two inches shy of the right.

But even with both feet firmly on the ground, the way had not been easy for Cheryl. No, sir, she'd started out trying to win Miss Choctaw County, and try as hard as she might, she never did. But she kept on and eventually won Miss Starkville. Then there was no stopping her. She streaked right on through to Miss Mississippi and the Atlantic City crown.

Sam could see why Cheryl was Rae Ann's heroine. They had a lot in common.

Except whereas Rae Ann had decided that she wanted to repay the pageant system, which had done so much for her, by designing evening gowns for other pageant girls, with Cheryl it was swimsuits.

This very minute Cheryl was explaining the suit designed by Ada Duckett, which was worn by four swimsuit winners in a row at Miss America—and two of them, Debbie

Maffett and Cheryl herself, actually won in that very suit. The Supersuit, they called it.

And when Cheryl went into the swimsuit business herself, not only did Ada Duckett (who offered a two-hour seminar on how to put on a suit) come to work for her, but she gave Cheryl the Supersuit—now one of her very proudest possessions.

Did Cheryl do anything else with her time? Other than take care of her two children, her husband—who was also with the Oral Roberts Ministry—write inspirational books, make inspirational tapes, cut inspirational recordings in Nashville? Why, yes, she did. She also produced a line of pageant shoes—the clear acrylic ones girls wear with swimsuits. There's a pump, a sandal, and a sandal with rhinestones.

Cheryl said to come on by the trade show, if you wanted to see them. "If they give you any trouble at the door, you just mention my name."

Sam vowed she'd do that very thing, tomorrow maybe. But right then, though she doubted that any of them could be as much fun as Cheryl, she scanned the room for other favorites, like Bess Myerson.

Now, there was a woman with a swimsuit story. The one and only Jewish Miss America, and a tall, leggy one at that, had been too long for the suit the pageant gave her. It rode up. Bare cheeks were not the fashion in 1945, and Firm-Grip hadn't been invented yet. So Bess and her sister stretched and stretched the thing, and ended up sleeping in it.

But poor Bess, her life had become a nightmare involving a younger lover and her reputed attempt to lower his alimony by bribing a judge with a job for her wacko daughter, who then testified against her mother the judge. Bess wasn't going out much these days.

But here was another opportunity, little Barbara Stein, plowing through the mob full steam ahead. Sam stepped into her path. "Barb, I was wondering if you could tell me who took Kurt Roberts's message when he called to say he had to leave town?"

To Barb, Kurt Roberts was day-before-yesterday's catastrophe. Today she was worried about Dexter Dunwoodie and his Shame Girls, who were still picketing outside. They were threatening to block the Boardwalk Saturday night, in an effort to gain national TV coverage. "What's Roberts to you?"

"I'm doing a story on judges, and can't believe someone would forfeit this opportunity."

The little redhead's mouth twitched for a moment, then she spit, "Lois Eberhardt. She's never gotten a message wrong in fifteen years. Call her in my office. Tell her I said peanut butter."

"Peanut butter?"

"Today's code. It'll clear you. But don't try it tomorrow." She marched off, a little general scanning the horizon for gunfire.

Peanut butter. Sam hadn't heard one she liked as much as that since Richard Nixon's plumbers.

Then she spotted another familiar face. It was Kay Lani Rae Rafko, the nurse/Miss A who'd been interviewed in the movie *Roger and Me.* Sam was dying to ask her how she *really* felt about the autoworkers in Michigan, but before she could make her way through the crush, Cindy Lou loomed over her.

The former Miss Ohio looked like something the cats drug in. Cindy's chrome-yellow silk jumpsuit played hell with her complexion, though it probably matched the bruises behind those shades she was still wearing.

Cindy Lou stood right in her face. Hands on her hips. Feet wide. Sam stepped back.

"Keep him away from me," Cindy Lou spit.

"Whoa! Keep who? What are we talking about?"

"Keep your boyfriend and that huge friend of his away from me or I'm going to have the whole bunch of you charged with harassment."

Uh-oh. What were Harry and Lavert up to now?

"And don't give me those big innocent eyes. I *know* what you're doing. I *know* the rumors you're spreading around. I *know* you're telling people I had something to do with

Kurt's leaving town so they're starting to look at me funny, when the truth is, I don't have a clue where he is. And I don't *care* either. But I know what my rights are, and I know that your editor is going to be very interested to know that you're making up stories when you can't find one, spreading rumors and lies. I hope your paper has good insurance, honey!"

"Well, does it?" asked the *Inquirer* from behind Sam as Cindy Lou stomped off.

"It has Hoke Tolliver," Sam grinned. "My managing editor would love to get his hands on old Cindy Lou. Literally. Which reminds me, I ought to give him a call and his daily report on his honey Rae Ann."

But inside, Sam wasn't so flip. For just a hunch (and a bet), she and the guys were nosing around pretty hard. It wasn't as if Cindy Lou didn't have her own problems. They ought to call off the game, kick back, chill out and forget about Kurt Roberts. Everybody else had. She'd file her silly stories. They'd all have a good time.

That was her plan. Right after she'd checked out the peanut butter.

. . . 29

OKAY, THE WAY WAYNE SAW IT, THINGS HAD GONE TO HELL IN A handbasket. He had to consult with Mr. F, and quick.

Here it was. Cindy Lou, the tall drunk in Roberts's room, was onto the subliminals in her room, ratting out to the woman reporter in 1801 about 'em. Big Gloria was sniffing around his bod, which was good, but jawing all the while about cameras, which wasn't. There was the missing equipment—plus that tape of Mr. F's favorite girl waltzing down the runway. *That* was the biggie. Plus that other special tape he'd made for Mr. F's own personal viewing pleasure. And Little Dougie was busting his chops from jump street, never easing up. Never giving him any breathing room. Pushing pushing pushing like those little dudes always—no, he couldn't say that, Mr. F wasn't so tall himself. And now, now, this was the last straw, that reporter woman's boyfriend and this gigantico jigaboo come sniffing around about Kurt Roberts. Leaning on him *real* heavy, like they really knew something.

They'd snuck up on him in Action Central, tapping on the door politely, pretending they were cops.

"Detective Leonard, Major Crime Squad, Northfield Barracks," the big jig said, flashing a badge that looked like he'd bought it in a FrankFair toy department.

Wayne was close. Actually, the badge was part of one of Lavert's Carnival costumes, the one where he dressed up as Black Bart, who used to recite poetry while he was robbing stagecoaches out West. Bart wasn't really black, but nobody in New Orleans knew that. Or cared.

"Detective Dutch." That was the curly-headed reporter's boyfriend, saying that was his name. Which it wasn't.

Wayne called him on it. He said, "You think I don't know who you are? You're staying in 1801, asshole."

"Which means?" The boyfriend bit down on his words real hard and narrowed his eyes like smoke was curling into them. Like Robert Mitchum in that detective movie Wayne had rented a couple of months ago. Like he thought he was cool.

"Which means you ain't no cop."

"Why does the fact that I am staying in this hotel mean I'm not a cop?"

Well, Wayne wasn't exactly sure. But it didn't *seem* like a cop would be staying in a suite with a reporter.

"We have reason to believe that you have some information about the disappearance of one Kurt Roberts," the big jig said, holding out a notebook.

In it, Lavert had started scribbling possible menus for the lunch he was going to cook for Michelangelo et al. on Sunday. He was thinking about quail and polenta. He was thinking about a veal stew. He was also thinking about surprising Ma completely and doing an old-fashioned red sauce Italian that would beat the socks off Ma's mom's cooking, and he'd heard Angelina Amato was no slouch in that department.

"Yeah?" said Wayne. "I don't even know no Kurt Roberts."

"The gentleman staying in 1803? I myself saw you coming out of his room Tuesday afternoon." That was the boyfriend —who either was or wasn't a cop. Who was choosing not to mention that was also the afternoon Wayne had laid into him pretty good.

Wayne said, "Yeah? Well, you know, security's my job."

"Indeed," said the jig. "Could you explain to us exactly what it was you were doing, securitywise that is, in Mr. Roberts's room?"

"Securitywise, I was checking on the locks."

"Really? That's part of your duties, here in operations, to check on guests' locks?" The jig looked like he didn't believe him.

"Yeah. He said he was having trouble with 'em."

"And you fixed the problem," said the boyfriend.

"Yeah."

"Did you notice anything *unusual* at the time?"

"What do you mean, unusual?"

"Oh, you know—" said the boyfriend.

And then the jig finished for him. "Puddles of blood where you did him when he surprised you lifting his room."

"Fuck you, Jack."

Lavert didn't even think about it. He just pulled back his right fist, then laid it across Wayne's jaw. That was roughly the equivalent of getting smacked by one of the cinder blocks that held up the boards that supported Lavert's considerable library back home in the French Quarter.

If Lavert had thought about it, he would have *broken* Wayne's jaw. As it was, Wayne was sprawled on the floor, out cold.

"That one's for you, bro," he said to Harry as they let themselves out.

"You shouldn't have."

"Think nothing of it."

"No, I mean, I wanted to do it myself."

At that, Lavert stopped dead in the hall. "We can go back. You can stomp on his ribs for a while."

"Naw. I'll take a rain check."

Wayne didn't know any of that last part, of course. He didn't know anything past when he said *Jack.*

What he did know, now, was that ice helped the pain. He was using equal parts on his jaw and in his Scotch.

And what he thought was that this business was getting to him—even if they *weren't* cops. Making him think he ought to ask Mr. F if it wouldn't be the best thing if maybe he walked away, which he'd always been so good at doing, till this thing was over, till after Sunday anyway. Then they'd all be pulling out faster than the Miss America Special, and things would quiet down again. He could just go back to maintaining surveillance on the high rollers in their rooms. Wayne knocked back the last of the Scotch.

Yep, he was going to tell Mr. F everything, Take it to the Lord in prayer, as his friend Thelma Thirty used to say when she had a snootful. Lay out to Mr. F his failings and transgressions and fears, the ones that woke Wayne up, night sweats in the small hours, ask for his forgiveness and his advice. Hoping he'd say something in that way he had, like, Look on the bright side. Everything's coming up roses. No use crying in your beer. Mr. F had the most original way of talking. It gave you a whole new perspective on life.

If only he could get past Mr. F's assistant—and he didn't mean Dougie this time.

There was this new girl who'd popped up at the executive reception desk. Young and juicy but prissy, too—kind of like one of those Miss America girls. Like I'm the cutest little thing you've ever seen and I've got tatas out to East Jesus, but if you touch me I'll scream and sic the cops on you.

Her name was Crystal.

Wayne had walked over to Mr. F's office while he worked all this out, and now there was Crystal sitting at reception. With hair so black it looked like it'd leave a mark on your hand if you touched it twisted up on top of her head. She was wearing a black dress with a collar that came up to the very tippytip of her chin, but the bottom of the dress, well, if it was any shorter, you'd see France.

"Mr. Franken's in a meeting," she said.

"So, tell him I'm here and it's an emergency." It really hurt his mouth to talk.

"Your name?"

Like he hadn't told her at least a dozen times. Was she stupid, or had she been taking lessons from Dougie? Maybe she was Dougie's girlfriend. She was about the right size, and she'd popped in right after he did.

So he asked her. He said, You Dougie's squeeze?

She looked at him like he'd asked her if she picked her nose or chewed her toenails. But she didn't answer his question. Instead, she said, "Mr. Franken is not to be disturbed."

"Says who?"

"Says he. And I say I can smell booze on you, and you know that is strictly against the rules—drinking on duty. The Gambling Commission is very strict about these matters."

What he'd like to do right now was pop her one across the mouth. Instead he said, "And I guess you're going to narc on me to Mr. F."

"I didn't say that. Excuse me." She turned to a buzzer that she seemed to think was calling her name. Ummm-humh. Ummmm-humh. Then she said to Wayne, "Mr. Franken is going to be busy for the rest of the day. *Top*-level meeting. You can wait if you want to, but you'll be wasting your time."

Oh.

So there Wayne was now, stomping around out on the sidewalk that ran back from the Boardwalk between the Monopoly and the Convention Hall. Some fresh air might help him figure out his next move. Maybe he ought to just walk anyway, call Mr. F from a Motel 6 somewhere, tell him things were *too* weird—

"Hey, Wayne. Man, you know, that number we did? Funny thing, I got another guy's interested in it, too."

What? It was Dean, the guy from the equipment van. The one who'd tapped into the Miss America show for Mr. F. But he wasn't supposed to *tell* anybody else about it. Wasn't that why Wayne gave him the three hundred dollars?

He said that to Dean, but Dean said, Hey, it was cool. This other guy was *connected.* Didn't talk to nobody. Dean gave Wayne a big wink.

Connected to what, Wayne asked.

Like, connected, man. Hey, what happened to your face? Somebody pop you?

Wayne looked all around, then said the words out of the corner of his mouth, what he thought Dean meant. Connected to the—you know?

Shhhhhhh. Never say that aloud.

So, the guy paid you a lot?

Dean nodded.

So why? So what did he want the show for? So maybe he had some special interest, like Mr. F. Wouldn't that be something? So, so, so, he was starting to sound like Dougie.

Dean put a finger to his lips. You never ask, he said.

Well, like, would he, huh? There might be something in this. Like something Wayne could offer up to Mr. F that would make him be not so mad at him about losing the equipment and the tapes. Not that *he* lost them, but they were in Action Central, which was *his* responsibility.

Dean said he didn't know. It'd be tricky to ask any questions, considering.

Wayne reached in his pocket and found a Franklin. That was one thing about working for Mr. F. No problem with cash flow.

Dean said it'd be a reach, but he'd see what he could do.

. . . 30

YOU COULD SAY PEANUT BUTTER ALL YOU WANTED TO, BUT THAT didn't mean somebody was going to hand you a sandwich—or any information.

The woman who had taken Kurt Roberts's message at the pageant switchboard had nothing to give Sam. No, she'd never talked with Mr. Roberts before, so she had no reason to think it was really him on the phone, but then she didn't have any reason to think it wasn't either. Sam could tell from her tone that the woman thought Sam was inordinately suspicious. The way big-city people are. And she found it unattractive.

From the top, she said, in response to Sam's prodding, and no, she most certainly did not tape-record calls, why on earth would she do that, she wrote them down on pink message slips and that was good enough for anybody around here, Mr. Roberts called and said he had received a call from New York and he had to return on business. He didn't sound strange. No, he didn't. But then, she didn't know what would be strange—for him. He sounded regretful, as would anybody in his right mind who had to leave the pageant and was letting people down. Maybe a little like he had a cold. That was all she remembered. You know, this was their very busiest time of year, it was like working the switchboard at Grand Central Station and Christmas at Macy's rolled into one, she imagined, and she couldn't be expected to remember every detail of every call.

But Sam knew the phone company's records of the Monopoly's calls would show that call from New York. Except there was no way to access them unless the police were investigating a missing person, and no one seemed to care enough to file the report. Not his office, his mom, his girlfriend, certainly not Cindy Lou, not the pageant.

Okay. The handwriting was on the wall. She was giving

this thing up, just like Cindy Lou had suggested—right after she talked with Big Gloria.

Harry already asked all that, said Gloria, when Sam found her sipping on a diet cola in her little office, taking a break from her supervising duties. Gloria kept on flipping the pages of her magazine, the one that gave detailed plans for turning garages into family rooms, thinking maybe if she was rude, since Sam was southern and could tell the difference, she'd go away.

The more folks came poking around in her business, asking questions about that Kurt Roberts, the more Gloria was thinking maybe she'd take the stash she had—what Harry had won her, plus the five thousand stuffed under her mattress—and head for New Orleans. She'd call Aunt Beautiful, who lived in the Faubourg Marigny, tell her to pull out the guest sheets and start making her some gumbo, she was coming home.

That way, no matter what had happened to Roberts, even if it was nothing, she'd have Junior back home where things were real. Where there was family and a *real* city, been there since the Spanish and the French, with *real* traditions and customs and beliefs, not a make-believe place like Atlantic City with a false front on it, the Boardwalk and the casinos, like one of those movie sets.

Which got Big Gloria to thinking, who made them—movie sets? Who built those things? And how real did they make them, or was it like she'd read about the food you saw in magazines, it looked good but you couldn't eat it? Maybe she'd ask Junior's friend Rashad, who knew a lot about movies.

But what was this Samantha Adams asking her now? Big Gloria pulled back from Hollywood and heard this: Had anybody else come around looking for Kurt Roberts?

And then Big Gloria said yes. Yes, there was. Somebody she'd completely forgotten about till Sam asked the question just like that. There was that old man with the limp who had come around, when was that, Tuesday, she thought. Yes, it must have been Tuesday, because now she remembered thinking about it when she saw that woman who reminded her of a Kewpie doll who said she was looking for Miss New Jersey, Big Gloria wasn't ever sure *what* she was up to, and then there was Wayne busting Harry in the lip. That was all on the same day.

That, and Junior getting pushed in the pool by Kurt Roberts, but she wasn't bringing *that* up, for sure.

What? said Sam. What? A Kewpie doll and Miss New Jersey and *who* busted Harry in the lip? *What* man with a limp?

Yeah, said Gloria, seizing on that last and hoping she'd give Sam enough that she'd just trot her curious self away. The man with the limp was old. Wearing a white shirt and black pants and one of those beige windbreakers like old guys always do.

And what else?

Well, he gave me some money to call him if I saw that Mr. Roberts, said Gloria.

He did? Samantha was looking really excited. Good. Gloria could tell she was on the right track here, feeding her something that would lead her far, far away from Junior. Because she didn't think Junior knew Angelo.

She did, of course, know him, that is. She'd bought pizza in his place plenty of times on her way home when she was too tired to cook. His place, Tommy's, on the edge of Ducktown made really good pizza pie, lots better than those chains, your Dominos. Angelo didn't recognize *her,* of course. A man like him would never pay any attention to just another nigger maid.

Yeah, said Gloria. Ange gave me, I think it was twenty dollars.

Ange? Ange? You mean you *know* this man?

Gloria couldn't see that it would do any harm to tell her, so she did. She also told her that people said there was gambling went on in Tommy's, the name of the place the old man Angelo ran. So maybe Sam might want to be careful if she went over there to talk to him.

. . . 31

IT WASN'T FIFTEEN MINUTES AFTER SAM HAD GATHERED UP HER notebook and her bag and scooted out like a scalded cat that Big Gloria crossed her arms across her ample chest and narrowed her eyes at another woman tripping down the hall. Well, lookahere. At least Miss Kewpie Doll had the right floor this time if she was going to drag out that tired story about being a hostess looking for Miss New Jersey.

"May I help you, ma'am?" Big Gloria put on her southern accent like it was a Sunday-go-to-meeting frock. She wasn't above camping it up to keep herself amused.

Miss Kewpie Doll opened her mouth. She was wearing the same pale lipstick as before, outlined dark, and a flowing purple silk shirt above skintight black pants and black catch-me do-me pumps. All of a sudden she recognized Gloria from their earlier encounter on the eighteenth floor, and her mouth fell shut.

It crumpled at the corners, and big tears filled her eyes.

Big Gloria had seen that look more than once. This woman's heart was broken. Oh, shoot. As if Big Gloria didn't have enough on her plate. But she found herself reaching out for Kewpie. "Sugar pie, what's wrong with you? What has that old booger gone and done?"

That was all it took. Miss Kewpie Doll, who actually was and always had been Darleen Carroll, dissolved in Big Gloria's arms.

"Every time I turn around, he's gone, and when he's there, he's whispering on the phone," Darleen sobbed. "It makes me feel like dog doo-doo. He's screwed around before, but never right in my face. He doesn't even have the common decency to hide it anymore. And I'm embarrassed that I even care."

Darleen's black mascara tracked lava flows down her

cheeks. She reminded Big Gloria of Tammy Faye Bakker when she really got revved up.

Big Gloria took Darleen by the arm and led her into a maid's room, plopped her down on a big trolley of clean white cotton sheets, and said, looking at Darleen closely, "Didn't I see you that day at the pool?"

"What day?" Darleen wailed.

"Tuesday, when my Junior almost drowned." Darleen's tears had made Gloria forget she was never going to remind anyone of that incident again.

"Oh." Darleen stopped her sobbing and gave Big Gloria her full attention. "That was *your* son?"

Gloria handed her a clean washcloth with *Monopoly* embroidered on it, white on white. "Junior. Uh-huh. He's a good boy really, but half the time I want to kill him. Be glad you got yourself a girl. Girls are easier."

"That's what *you* think. That was *your* son at the pool? Rachel Rose can't stop talking about him."

"No, don't tell me. The pretty little blond girl who was at the pool?" The one who Junior said he'd been with Tuesday night. This woman's daughter was Junior's alibi.

"That's the one," said Darleen, and the two women sat and stared at one another for a long moment.

"My son and your daughter," Big Gloria said finally. "Oh, Lord."

"Oh, Lord, is right." Darleen, smiling a little now, reached over and gave Big Gloria's arm a squeeze. "I think Rachel Rose is showing her mom's good taste, but her daddy—"

Big Gloria still didn't have a clue who Darleen's husband was, had no idea that he was the emcee of her favorite game show. "He's gonna kill her, right?"

"Right."

"And *you* want to kill *him?*"

Darleen ran her cat-pink tongue along her teeth as if to test their sharp edges. "I want to cut his liver out and eat it for breakfast."

"Over this Miss New Jersey? Is that really who you're looking for, honey?"

"Over lots of Miss New Jerseys. She's just the latest in a long line."

"God, I hate that. My husband, Junior's father, was famous for his tomcatting."

"And you married him anyway?"

"Well, you know how it is. You don't think he's gonna be slipping around on *you.*"

"Isn't that the truth?"

They both stared off into the distance for a few minutes. Then Big Gloria reached into the pocket of her uniform and pulled out a pack of Kools. She offered one to Darleen.

"No, thank you. I stopped a long time ago."

"Me, too," said Big Gloria, lighting up.

"Give me one of those things."

Gloria lit one, handed it to her, and they smoked and thought about the men in their lives. Then Big Gloria blew a series of three perfect smoke rings.

"Neat trick."

"I know lots of neat tricks."

"Oh, yeah? Like what?"

"Oh—I'm real handy." Big Gloria held her cigarette out at arm's length and studied its tip, considering—"I'm good at painting, plumbing, plastering. I do dry wall, a little electrical. What I really love is fine cabinetry." Just saying the words brought the feel of the smooth wood to her hands. That's what she was going to do, the first thing, when she got to New Orleans. Buy herself some wood and build Aunt Beautiful something. Then see about setting herself up in some kind of building business. Not have to ever talk to crazy people again. Just saw and hammer and glue and plane, that clean smell of wood filling her head, get Junior in some kind of program, teach him a skill, too, he'd have something to fall back on, help him get himself through college. Now *that* was an idea.

"Dear God," said Darleen. "Do you really?"

"Really what, honey?"

"Do you really know how to do all those things?"

"Sure do. I don't get much of a chance around her, except at my own house."

"I'm an interior designer," Darleen said brightly. "In Newport Beach."

Big Gloria nodded. She didn't have a clue where Newport Beach was or that it was inhabited by thousands of Republicans with more money than good sense whose second or third wives had lots of time on their hands for things like nail wrapping, body sculpting, and—when they finished with their bods—redoing their houses.

"I have a terrible time finding good people to help me," said Darleen carefully.

"Really?" Big Gloria lowered her chin and exhaled through her nose.

"The weather's nice in southern California all year long," said Darleen. "So there's hardly ever a day a person—a person who wants to work—can't."

"You don't say?" It was beginning to sound to Gloria like all of a sudden there was more than one option in this world for a person who was handy.

"Especially a talented person."

"What about an especially talented person who has the keys to Miss New Jersey's room?"

...32

WHEW! THERE WAS MORE TO THIS MISS AMERICA SHOW THAN YOU might think. The singing, the dancing, the moves, a hundred boobs bouncing around the stage at one time. The two hours went by just like that! Afterward, Billy Carroll was higher than a kite, sitting at the counter in Monopoly's coffeeshop, trying to get himself around a couple orders of waffles.

"Hi, Mr. Carroll." A breathy young brunette touched his left elbow.

"Well, *hello*, little lady." He gave her his big smile and was about to move in closer when he saw Mama on her other side. Mean as a linebacker and a body to match in a red, white, and navy polyester pants suit. Billy reeled his smile back in. "How you doing?"

"We're doing just fine. We liked your show tonight. Didn't we, Mama? I told Mama I thought you were every bit as good as Gary Collins. Didn't I, Mama?"

Mama gave him a semi-weak smile and narrowed her eyes as if Billy were going to throw her cute little daughter to the floor and molest her right there if he had half a chance, which wasn't all that far from the truth.

"So you're here for the pageant?" he said to the daughter. "Thank you, honey," to the waitress who stopped by with the imitation maple syrup.

"I'm Jennifer. Jennifer Lynn Karlsen. I'm into pageants," the little girl said, smiling around her gum, cute, like she had a secret she was dying for you to find out.

"Really?" He was trying to pay attention to what she was saying, girls hated it if you didn't, but he was also checking himself out. Patting, to make sure his hair was in place. Sniffing, he'd run up to the room right after the show, thank God Darleen hadn't been there, he didn't need *that* kind of downer, grabbed a quick shower and a change of clothes. He'd been soaking wet from the TV lights, but he couldn't remember if he used his deodorant. He hoped so. As soon as he finished with these waffles, he was going to step into Rich Uncle Pennybags, have himself a couple or four Brandy Alexanders to settle his stomach, and then see if he couldn't find himself some action. A tender young redhead, maybe, to hang on his arm for luck while he played himself some baccarat.

"Into pageants, huh? You don't say. Here, let me light that for you."

The girl laughed. "You're going to light my gum?"

Billy looked down. Juicy Fruit, it sure was, the girl had taken out of her purse. She was chewing gum and drinking a glass of milk.

"*You're* not one of the contestants, are you?" He smiled at Mama to let her know he wasn't about to pounce on her darling.

"Go on." She gave his arm a shove. "You think I'd be

sitting here? I'd be headed for my room to take off that makeup and get myself some Zs. Anyway, haven't you met all the girls?"

Why, yes, he had. Though not for any length of time, of course. And some of them, well, he knew better than maybe he wanted to, all things considered.

Like Miss New Jersey, for example. He had wanted to know Lana DeLucca *very* well, but once you were in his position as an emcee, things changed. There were other priorities.

Back before he'd stepped into the emcee slot, like on Tuesday, well, he'd thought it would be something if he'd offer Lana a teensy little spot on his show, and she'd tumble for "The Big One"—in a manner of speaking.

But, now. You could never tell, those Big Guys at NBC would be watching. See how he did. Who knew when they might decide Collins had gone the distance and they'd be ready for a new stud? One who had already proved himself. And who hadn't gotten himself into any tights with the girlies. A man in his position needed to think about things like that.

So, he wasn't exactly thrilled tonight when right before the show, one of those hostesses came up to him saying Lana wanted him to come backstage, up to the dressing area. It was an emergency. The woman was actually wringing her hands.

He didn't want it to look like he knew Lana *personally,* not that he did, really, at least not *that* way, but what was he going to do? He couldn't just say no. Not with Phyllis George standing there giving him that fishy look.

Which reminded him, if and when he did get the show, Phyllis was history. Let her go take care of By George, her fried chicken company. He didn't like women who were that savvy. He was *married* to one of those.

Anyway, upstairs he went, and there, bouncing up and down out in the hall, right outside the dressing room, was Lana in a long T-shirt, screaming at the top of her lungs that her dress was gone! Somebody had stolen the gown she was wearing for her talent tonight, her lucky gown, the one that was an exact copy, except longer, of Marilyn's when she sang "I Want to Be Loved By You" in *Some Like It Hot!* It was in her bag she carried over from her room! What do you mean did she look? That's where she left it! And then she opened the bag and what was there? A chenille bathrobe! A pink chenille bathrobe like her Nana used to wear! She couldn't sing in a bathrobe!

Well, no, she couldn't. Billy would certainly agree to that. But he didn't know what he was supposed to do about it.

Call somebody! she'd screamed at Billy. Don't you have juice? Don't you know people? Aren't you on TV?

Well, yeah. But, gee.

Then, just like that, Lana said, Fuck you very much, turned to the hostess, and demanded a phone, in her hand, this instant, pronto.

Well, see. That sort of thing couldn't be good for a man in his position. No favorites, that was the rule, and he'd even learn to be nice to their mothers. Like Mama here, in her patriotic polyester, sitting on the other side of Jennifer.

"Mrs. Karlsen," he said, practicing, "where are you two pretty ladies from?"

"Michigan. A suburb of Detroit. We're Norwegian."

"Oh, really?"

"Yes," Jennifer beamed. "And this year I made ten in my state pageant. Next year I'll take it, for sure. So my pageant committee told me I ought to come along with the state delegation and see it all firsthand. So I'd know exactly what to expect, you know."

"Well, that's great, you think you're going to be Miss Michigan next year. You'll sure be a pretty one."

"Not think. I *know*. I'm completely focused on it."

"Oh, yeah?"

"Completely. You know, in 1988 Gretchen Carlson won. That's C-A-R-L-S-O-N. I'm K-A-R-L-S-E-N. But we're both from the Midwest, and both Scandinavian, and have that kind of drive and determination that Scandinavians have, and I'm following her program."

"Uh-huh." Billy signaled to the waitress for the check.

"Do you know what she did? I'll tell you what she did.

First of all, we both had this very serious talent that we've been working on since we were little girls. She played the violin. I play the harp. She graduated from Stanford in Organizational Behavior, and I'm following right in her footsteps. Organizational Behavior is a very handy major to have if you're dealing with people all the time. That's what the pageant world is—people, people, people.

"But, anyway, just like Gretchen, I came in first runner-up in Miss TEEN—that's Teens Encouraging Excellence Nationally—a couple of years ago. That gave me a taste for pageants and made me realize that I had the basics: the talent, communication skills, discipline—"

"Excuse me. I'm going to have to—" There was only so much a man could listen to. Especially if there was no reward.

"So I went on to Stanford, and every year I've tried for state. I made ten each year, and next year's mine."

"That's—"

"For interview, I'll start six months ahead this time, and do about seventy-five mock seven-minute interviews. I'll get people from all walks of life to be on my interview panels—you'd be surprised how much people are willing to help—because Miss America needs to be able to reach out to everyone. We'll videotape every last one of those interviews and I'll study them."

"Do you—"

"I'm practicing how to walk and stand and sit for my interview. If your hands are fidgeting, you can forget what your mouth is saying, because they'll just be staring at your hands. For the content part, I study current events about two hours a day. And I'll work out about three hours a day with a body trainer, starting in January. Right now, I do about two hours."

She'd gotten his attention now. Four hours? Five? Six? When did these girls live?

"Oh," Jennifer laughed. "That's just for starters, isn't it, Mama?"

Mama nodded.

"After I win state, I'll go down to Texas and have Chuck

Weisbeck put me on an Olympic athletes training program. I do other stuff too."

"Like what?"

"Well, every single day I watch videotapes of Miss America and other pageants. I watch everything they do. Like right now I'm concentrating on the way the girls react when their names are called for the top ten. When they're walking across the stage, they always say thank you to the judges, and do this little motion of extending their hands out to them."

"I've always said to thank people," said Mama. "They may not always remember it if you do, but they sure do if you don't. You don't ever want anybody to think you're rude."

That was a pretty long speech for Mama, whose mouth clamped right back into a tight line. Billy examined her face to see if, yes, maybe, way back there in the distance she'd looked a tiny bit like Jennifer. Maybe twenty-five years and a hundred pounds ago. It was frightening.

"I'll use the same exact preparation immediately before the pageant that I do for performing the harp. I read that Gretchen Carlson had a ritual, too. What I do is pray that God will be with me. Then I visualize myself going through the performance. Every single moment of it. I take myself through every step."

"Including walking down the runway with the crown?" Billy had done something like that, imagined himself on "The Big One," right up to giving out the prizes, before he got the job.

Jennifer's eyes shone. "Especially walking down that runway. But only after I've gone through every other step. It takes enormous discipline, you know. The main thing is to give them *exactly* what they want. It doesn't matter what *you* want. But each pageant is different, so you have to figure out what they're looking for, and that's exactly what you give them. You make yourself over in their ideal image."

"It takes sacrifice," said Mama, nodding. "Discipline and sacrifice are what's important in life."

Billy bet Mama *loved* Michigan winters, trudging five or six miles through the snow, lugging a stranded cow over her shoulders. And then building a fire. No, building a house and then building a fire. Jesus, these pageant people were weird.

Then you had your girls like Lana. He bet Miss Wiggles didn't know the meaning of the word discipline. In fact, he'd bet a hundred Lana had never even broken a sweat—hey, wait a minute. Who was he betting this hundred with?

"We've got to be going." Mama was pushing off, pulling Jennifer along with her. "Got to get to bed. Get up early. Do our calisthenics."

"Hey, I wish you luck. Hope to see you here next year. Here, let me get your check. Be my pleasure."

Mama was a little flustered, as if their twelve-dollar tab was going to compromise Jennifer somehow.

"I insist. Go on. Get out of here. Go get your beauty sleep. Both of you." He gave them the wink. He'd learned how to say smooth things like that doing "The Big One."

Waiting for his change Billy thought, well, it took all kinds. Darleen would love these two. He'd have to tell her about them, if she was ever speaking to him again. If she ever got over her change-of-life pout. Of course, when he told her, he'd have to say he talked to them backstage or something. Coffeeshop, late at night, Darleen would think he was hitting on the little broad. Darleen had a very suspicious mind.

"Very nice, very nice." The gravelly voice was right behind him. "You want to buy my coffee, too? Or maybe I ain't cute enough."

Billy turned, but he didn't have to. He'd know Angelo's voice anywhere. It played in some of his worst nightmares.

Angelo Pizza leaning on him. Angelo holding a gun to his head. Angelo taking his Rachel Rose, saying, We're just going to borrow her for a little party. You don't mind, do you, Billy boy, let her work off a little of what you owe us?

But this time, he was *glad* to see the man. "I was gonna call you." He slapped Ange on the back, carefully.

"Uh-huh."

"No, really. You know, I'm doing this gig, this Miss America thing, emceeing it, that Gary Collins got sick—"

"I know," Ange said.

"You do? Really!" Billy was amazed. It didn't seem like the kind of info Ange would keep up with. Except, these guineas, you'd owed 'em money, they knew every time you went to the bathroom.

"Yeah, I sawr you this evening." Ange had that kind of New York accent that put an *r* at the end of the word.

"You did? You were at the Miss America show?"

"Yeah. Miss California won talent. Miss Florida won swimsuit. Nice rack on that girl. What else you want to know?"

"I'm just surprised you were there, that's all."

"You think I never leave Tommy's?"

"Hey, I'm not saying that, Ange. Actually, I was going to call you because I got good news. This gig is paying me a bundle. I'm gonna be able to pay you off—"

"When?"

"When I get my check."

"The vig don't wait for checks, Billy. You know that."

"No, man, really. I'll give you the whole thing."

"I'll means I *will,* Bill. In the future. Vig don't want to know about no *will.* Vig keeps ticking till money is *now.* Vig plus the loan."

"So that's why you're here? To bust my chops?"

Billy could feel himself getting wet under his armpits. He *hadn't* used the deodorant. He could smell himself. He hated that. He'd have to go take another shower before he checked Uncle Pennybags. He couldn't go in there stinking. *If* he went in there. *If* Angelo didn't decide to give him two in the caps right now. You could never tell with these guys. They'd as soon cripple you as look at you. Christ.

"I'll tell you, Billy." Angelo had walked him out into the lobby now. He wouldn't blow him away in the lobby, would he? In the middle of old folks looking to make a quarter, a dime. Big spenders, thought they were having a great time, dentures smiling. Oh, Jesus. Please, let him live that long. Collect on his Social Security. Angelo saying, "Reason I went to the Miss America thing tonight, I was looking for another guy who owes me. I thought maybe he could do me a favor, but he wasn't around. Kind of missing in action, you know what I mean?"

Billy laughed nervously.

"But then I saw you up on that stage, doing your singing and dancing—"

"Yeah? How was I?"

"You stink. But, anyway, I said to myself, you know, Ange, there's more than one way to skin a cat."

Billy really wished Ange wouldn't say things like that. He could just see himself, like Saint Whatsit, flayed, walking around with no epidermis to speak of. Guys like Ange knew people who did things like that.

"I watched you real close up there, and I said to myself, Billy, who owes you, would be more than happy to do you a little favor."

"You're right about that, Ange. You are sure as hell right about that."

"So, Billy—"

...33

MICHELANGELO DIDN'T KNOW WHAT THE HELL WAS GOING ON.

First, he gets a call from his mother saying she has a bone to pick.

"Ma," he said, "what's the matter with you? Is your arthritis acting up again? Call the doctor."

"I don't need a doctor for what ails me, Mikey. I want you to come over here."

"I will, darling. But later, if you're not sick. If you're sick, *butta la pasta,* I'm on my way."

"I'm not sick. Well, not that kind of sick. What I'm sick and tired of is your butting in my business."

"Mama! What's got into you?"

"Nothing, that's what. Nothing for a very very very long time, and now that something's about to, you're standing in the way."

"What are you talking about?" She couldn't mean what he thought. His mama didn't talk like that. Didn't *think* like that.

"He didn't say nothing to me, but I know this is your fault. You said something to Ange, didn't you?"

"Ma, I—"

"Don't lie to me, Mikey. I always know when you're lying. I didn't live with your father for thirty-five years not to know lying. Where have you been, Sal? Out. Out I know. Out where? Out with the guys. Out with the guys named Malzina the Whore. But that's water under the bridge, and now it's my turn."

"Your turn to what, Ma?" He knew he shouldn't have asked that.

"My time to have a good time. To kick up my heels. To go dancing."

"I'll take you dancing, Mama. Just last month you danced at Cappy's wedding."

"Cappy's wedding. I don't want to sit around with all the other old ladies in black lace down to my ankles. I dance, the kids all say, Isn't that cute, Gramma is dancing? Forget that. I wanta do the hootchy-kooch."

"Mama!"

"I'm not talking about getting married. I'm too old to get married. But I'm not too old to have fun. Isn't that what that Madonna said, Girls just wanta have fun?"

No, it wasn't Madonna, but what difference did it make, details, when his mama had gone *pazza?*

"Everybody talks about what a shame it is, a nice Italian girl like her running around in her underwear. I say, Have all the fun you can while you're young. I never did. I did what every girl in the neighborhood did—got married, got pregnant. Not that I would trade you for anything, Mikey, but, enough already. I read, you know. I read those magazines, I watch the TV. The world has changed. Girls have fun."

"Mama, you're not a girl."

"Don't talk back to your ma, son."

* * *

Then Eddie from Tommy's is on the phone.

"This better be good, Ed. I'm not in the mood."

"I don't know if it's good or bad. Probably bad."

"Then make it quick."

"This long tall brunette broad comes into the place a little while ago. Good-looking. Wearing a short black skirt, them black stockings, and a red—"

"This is quick?"

"Sorry, Ma. She's looking for Angelo. I ain't never seen this broad before, you know, so I tell her he ain't in."

"Was he?"

"Naw."

"Great, Eddie. What if he had been?"

"What?"

"Never mind. So, you tell her he's not in."

"Yeah. And she starts asking all these questions, like I think the twist is wearing a wire. She's dropping stuff about what a good gambling town AC is, how she's bored with the casinos, understands Ange can turn her on to some other action. She don't know what's she's talking about, you know what I mean, Ma?"

"Like she's humming it?"

"Huh?"

"Never mind. So you think she's a cop?"

"I think so. Except she didn't have a cop's eyes."

"Tell me, Eddie, she have short dark curly hair?"

"Yeah, and a short black skirt. I mean, she ain't no spring chicken, Ma, but for an older broad, she's like—"

"An accent?"

"Yeah. Now that you mention it. A little. Kind of like—did you see that movie *Steel Magnolias,* boss?"

"A southern accent, Eddie?"

"Yeah. How'd you know that?"

"She ain't a cop, Ed."

"No? You know her?"

"She's a newspaper reporter."

"Same thing."

* * *

That's not enough, Lana DeLucca's on the phone scream ing bloody murder.

"Lana, calm down. Are you hurt, sweetheart? Can you te me where you are?"

"I'm standing backstage at Convention Hall in my under wear. And somebody stole my pink Marilyn number! One o these bitches stole it, Ma."

He didn't have a clue what she was talking about.

"Your pink Marilyn number?"

"My dress! Somebody lifted my dress!"

Oh, Jesus. Girls. "We'll get you another dress, darling."

"You *don't* understand." Wow, the girl could cut cold stee with that voice. She ought to register it. "In twenty minutes half an hour tops, I'm supposed to be onstage singing ' Want to Be Loved By You' exactly like Marilyn in *Som Like It Hot* wearing my custom-made eight-thousand-dolla nude-colored organza sequined gown, high in front, th back V-cut to my butt. As it stands now, I'm wearing th pink chenille bathrobe some bitch left in my garment ba when she lifted my dress."

"Start with your bust measurement and calm dow before you give yourself a heart attack."

It was Mama again. "Mikey, I been thinking, what yo said."

Thank God. She'd probably forgotten to take her medica tion and now she had and she was back on keel.

"I've been thinking maybe you're right about Ange Maybe I'll wait and look for a younger man. Knows som things I don't know. Can teach this old bitch some new tricks."

"Mama, stay right there. I'm on my way."

"Better bring your key. I'm out of here."

Not an hour later, Lana's on the phone again.

"Wow! Where did you *get* this dress? It's not the same but—wow!"

"I know a guy."

"You're fabulous! And I just wanted you to know, I mean

I was really spazzed there for a while, but I'm gonna be fine."

"That makes me happy, sweetheart. I want you to be happy. Big John wants you to be happy, too."

"And, Ma?"

"Yes, sweetheart?"

"Listen." The cut-through-cold-steel voice was back again, though this time she'd wrapped a little velvet around it. "I'm sure it was Miss Louisiana and Miss Texas. Those girls are farting around all the time, acting Miss Goody-Two-Shoes. The next thing I know they're sucking up to me like they're my friends. *They* took my dress, Ma."

"Are you sure?"

"I'm positive." She paused for a count of three. Oh, this girl was good. The real Marilyn had nothing on her when it came to timing. "And I think Big John would like for you to do something about that. Don't you?"

. . . 34

WHO WAS THAT KNOCKING AT HER DOOR? THE BIG BAD WOLF? Gloria hoped so. If it wasn't him, it had to be the cops. And what was she going to tell them about Junior?

Mama, they'd say, it's after ten o'clock. Do you know where your child is?

Well, it was a whole lot easier to ask that question on a bumper sticker than to answer it in real life, especially if you had a teenage son. Gloria'd tell 'em that, if she let 'em in, now peeping through her peephole.

"Gloria? I hope I'm not disturbing you."

"Lavert? Lavert Washington, is that you?"

"Me and my cousin Lucinda."

What was Gloria gonna do? Let 'em stand out there in the dark? Homefolks? Even if she was in her tatty old robe?

"Ya'll come on in." But wait a minute. This wasn't just

any Cousin Lucinda. This was Miss Louisiana. Big Glori recognized her from her picture. She pulled her robe tighte feeling fat, saying how she wasn't dressed for company.

"We're the ones who ought to be apologizing," sai Lucinda. "Sorry to be disturbing you so late, dropping i like this."

"Don't be silly. Come on, ya'll sit yourselves down. Wha can I get you? You want some coffee?"

"Not a thing, Gloria. We know you're tired. We jus wanted to come over and talk with you for a little spel about some things seemed important," Lavert said.

Wasn't it amazing, a man big as that could speak s gently? Just listening to the sound of his voice made Gloria' mind feel easier. She thought Lavert had missed his calling He should have been a preacher man.

She told him that, and Lavert laughed. "I don't know a how the Lord would hold with a man spreading His wor who'd served time in Angola."

"The Lord knows what's in your heart now," said Gloria "He ain't studying what's over and done."

"But that's what you've been doing," said Lucinda.

Now, Gloria knew that Lucinda's nickname was Magic She'd heard Magic could work it, too. Ladies from he church, proud to have a sister in the pageant, had bee saying, You seen that Louisiana girl, she gone conjure herse up that Miss America crown, you just see if she don't. The were Christians, those church ladies, but, like Gloria, the held onto the old back-home ways, too. It's all mixed u together, Gloria had tried to explain to Junior more tha once, if you be from the South. 'Course, that's what voudo was in the first place, the way of Africans practicing thei religion, hiding it from Massa and Miss Ann.

"What do you mean?" Gloria asked Magic. "What do yo mean I been studying what's over and done?"

"What Junior did bad is over and done. And it's not wha you think he did, in the first place."

"Oh, Lord!" Gloria covered her face with her hands an rocked back and forth in her chair like she used to whe

Junior was a baby. Before he got all big and bad. "Oh, Lord! I knew that boy was in trouble."

"He is and he ain't," said Magic, dropping back into the language of home, comfortable as Gloria's bathrobe, which she wished she was wearing instead of this tight black dress, pantyhose, and underwire bra she couldn't wait to get back to her hotel room and take off. "What you think he did, he didn't. But he did something else bad. I see two things. I dreamed them last night, why I wanted to come over here and talk to you, this is the first chance I had.

"Now I can't exactly describe them for you. But they're not like what you think. They're silver, not red, and silver you can always put back. It's not spilled, like the blood, that once it's gone and made its stain—well, we women know, don't we, blood never comes out?"

"We do, we do." Still Gloria was rocking. "What's my Junior done? What's he? What's he?"

"Shhhhh," said Lavert, laying his big sweet hand on her shoulder. "We ain't here to tattle on the boy, and truth is, Magic don't exactly know. Do you, cuz?"

"I don't have a clear picture," Miss Louisiana said. "But when Lavert came and was telling me about how he and Harry Zack are looking for that Kurt Roberts and he's telling me this long-drawn-out story, and then he gets to the part this afternoon about running into that young boy Rashad, Junior's friend, and how something Rashad said reminded Harry of Wayne, another *bad* white man, and they went off to see him, and that didn't lead anywhere, I said to Lavert, You missed something important there, Big L."

"How did you know?" asked Gloria.

"Because when he said your name and your son's, I remembered my dream, I didn't know what it meant before that, and a knife turned in my heart. I could feel your pain. So, I did some water-gazing on it. Like I said, Junior did bad, but it's silver, gold, or green. We're talking about money, here, Gloria, not murder. Though—" And then she hesitated.

What? said Gloria.

What? said Lavert.

"—Junior *could* be in danger. He and Rashad and somebody else. A blonde. Little blonde. I see pictures that could do them harm. I don't think they know it, though."

"What do you mean, pictures?" asked Gloria.

"Photos. Or maybe a movie. I'm not sure. I do think they ought to watch where they step, and who they step on."

After they left, Big Gloria sat up for a long time, reading her Bible, praying, meditating—and when none of that worked, she went back to old-fashioned worrying.

Evil *would* out. And how did she know that the silver Magic saw wasn't *her* silver, the money *she'd* stolen from that Kurt Roberts? And the pictures? Rashad made movies. Maybe that's what Junior was doing, out late every night. Making a movie with Rashad. *Dirty,* probably, boys being boys. And a blonde? That *could* be little Rachel Rose. But then, Miss New Jersey was a blonde, too, and look at the evil she'd helped Darleen do to that girl. Oh, Lord, chickens *would* come home to roost.

...35

THE MISS AMERICA PAGEANT BEGAN AS A SCHEME CONCOCTED BY Atlantic City hoteliers to extend the summer season. By 1921, bathing beauty contests at the shore had been around for some time, but that particular year the city fathers decided to ask regional newspapers to choose contestants from submitted photographs. The hopefuls were brought together *after* Labor Day, the traditional end of the commercial season, where one among their number was ceremoniously crowned.

Margaret Gorman (sixteen years of age, 5′1″, 108 lbs., 30-25-32) who was to become the first Miss America, has been quoted as saying she does not remember who sent her photo to the Washington *Herald.* But when reporters came to her home to tell her she was Miss Washington, they found her with other kids in a nearby park shooting marbles. Miss America 1921 won a trophy worth fifty dollars and then went back to high school.

But for Atlantic City, the show had been a hit. The next summer, the production budget was doubled to fifty-one thousand dollars, and the city fathers got down to some serious planning. Contestants, who this second year arrived from as far away as Los Angeles, paraded down the Boardwalk in elaborately decorated rolling chairs. Girls competed in both evening gowns and swimsuits. In fact, everyone paraded in bathing costumes—city commissioners, firemen, policemen, lifeguards, and the entire pageant committee.

In those days the Miss America pageant included neither talent competitions nor scholarships. But there was controversy aplenty. When newspapers were still choosing the contestants, an occasional lady with a "professional" reputation showed up. In the 1923 pageant, Miss Alaska turned out never even to have been close to the Great White North, *and* she was married—which at the time was frowned upon but not yet a disqualifier.

Today, Miss America must meet residence requirements from her qualifying state and be a U.S. citizen between the ages of seventeen and twenty-six. She must never have been married or have had a marriage annulled. She must never have been pregnant or convicted of the slightest misdemeanor.

The 1926 winner, Norma Smallwood, married an oilman who later divorced her in proceedings involving adultery charges. She was also alleged to have served alcohol to her underage daughter, Des Cygnes L'Amour—which translates, "Of the Swans the Love." Swan's mother, Norma, refused to return to Atlantic City to crown the 1927 queen because the pageant refused to cough up her requested fee.

By this time, the pageant was under fire from a growing number of hoteliers who felt that, hang the money it brought in, the hoopla was tainting a family resort with a tawdry show girl image. From 1928 to 1933, the contest was mothballed.

Even after its revival, scandal continued to dog the pageant. In 1936, there were cries that the pageant was fixed when Miss Philadelphia—who lived only a hop, skip, and a jump up the road from AC—won. No one, however, has ever proved that any Miss America pageant was anything but on the up-and-up—though the hue and cry has resounded every time a Miss Philadelphia (and later Miss Pennsylvania) takes the title.

But nothing, before or since, has quite equaled the scandal of 1937—except perhaps the Vanessa Williams debacle. This was the year Bette Cooper, Miss Bertrand Island, New Jersey, won the crown.

Bette, sixteen, blond, blue-eyed, and so innocent she hadn't even had a first love, had visited an amusement park located on Bertrand Island in Lake Hopatcong, near her home in Hackettstown, NJ, earlier that fateful summer of 1937. Posted about the park were advertisements for a beauty contest, and Bette, challenged by her friends, entered it.

Much to her astonishment, she won. The next surprise was that Miss Bertrand Island was franchised to the Miss America Pageant, and she was expected to participate.

Bette and her parents, unsophisticated folks, were chagrined. Bette attended a private day school where she was captain of the track team. She was a regular suppliant at the Presbyterian Church. Beauty contests were about the last thing on her mind.

However, the Coopers decided, what the heck. A week in Atlantic City might be a nice way to end the summer. So they packed up and moved to the beach the first week in September. Bette, however, as did many girls before and after her, exposed to the damp nights and cold ocean air, caught a cold. She was miserable.

Nonetheless, Bette made a good showing, though—modest to a fault—she certainly had no thought of winning. She did well in the optional talent competition singing "When the Poppies Bloom Again." Then she was named winner in the evening gown competition, and things became serious.

"What if you were to win?" asked Lou Off, the very handsome, urbane and sophisticated twenty-one-year-old from one of Atlantic City's best families who had volunteered to be Bette's chauffeur for the week. "What if you were?" he asked the sniffling Bette, who had become sicker throughout the week with her miserable head cold. (And more in love with Lou, said some.)

Others said that Lou's family had reservations about the pageant, and Lou shared those views.

In any case, when Lou took Bette for a long drive Saturday afternoon before the final judging, he told her that if she won, she could forget about him, because he wanted nothing to do with publicity.

And when she did indeed win, Lou didn't show at the ball following her coronation.

Bette's father thought she ought to forget the whole thing and go back to school.

Now let us not forget she was only seventeen years old and still had that terrible head cold.

In any case, in the middle of the night, Bette called Lou Off and said she wanted out.

He said he'd be right over.

She didn't want to go to the Steel Pier in the morning to greet the press, she sobbed. She didn't want to stand beneath a huge electric sign that said COME SEE MISS AMERICA 1937. She didn't want anything to do with any of it, and her family didn't either, and they'd come to rely on the sophisticated Mr. Off who could even find his way around New York City, sixty miles away from their home in Hackettstown, as if it weren't Sodom and Gomorrah.

Lou Off said, in that case, he'd help.

Rashad, who was still filming his movie about Bette and Lou, said to Rachel Rose, "Now, what we're going to do next is you're going to climb down the fire escape there and jump into the waiting car. That's how Bette made her getaway with Lou."

"I'm going to break my neck in these heels. Do you really think Bette wore her evening gown when she split?"

"No," Rashad said patiently, "I do not. But we are not dealing wholly in fact, Rachel Rose. We are dealing in fantasy. That's what movies are. And I have neither the time nor the money to lay the whole thing out exactly as it happened. So by having you, as Bette, wear the gown and the tiara, you get the picture that she's Miss America escaping, running away, *forget* the pageant. Do *you* get the picture, Rachel Rose?"

"I get it, Rashad." Then she whispered, "God, he's so touchy," to Junior, who was playing Lou Off, which would have been a racial incongruity considering the politics of 1937, except that after all, this little ditty was for Spike Lee, right?

"That's because he's afraid the cops are on our tail," said Junior. That's what Junior was afraid of. That and Big Gloria skinning him alive for sneaking out of the house every night to practice the art of filmmaking. Practice, your *butt,* Mama would say, she got hold of him.

"I am not," Rashad insisted. "And I wish you'd stop with that racket and help me get this show on the road. You know, Harry's not gonna be here forever, man. It's Thursday night and counting. I only have till Saturday, Sunday morning at the latest, you know they're gonna blow."

"You could mail him the videotape, Rashad," said Junior. "There's no law that says you have to put it in his very hand. Besides, you don't even know that he can get it to Spike, and even if he does, what's to say Spike—"

"Stop!" Rashad commanded. "Just because you choose to operate with limited ambition in this sinkhole called Atlantic City which is hardly, believe me, *hardly* representative of the larger world outside, because you choose to be pessimistic and small-minded, because you choose not to look up at the stars—"

"He's about to launch into his I Have a Dream routine any second," Junior said to Rachel Rose.

"I most certainly am not," said Rashad. "I am about to roll this camera, and Rachel Rose is about to skinny down that fire escape and land her sweet little booty in that convertible, and you're about to lean over and give her a big hug and a discreet kiss and a thumbs-up that she flew in the face of convention and abandoned all the Miss America folderol—"

"We got it, Rashad," said Rachel Rose. "Now can we do it? I've got to get home. If my parents catch me out again with my dad's rental car, they'll start with the tar and feather routine."

"Your folks are *so* charming," said Rashad. "I keep meaning to invite them to an NAACP meeting. Or maybe we could introduce them to the Reverend Dunwoodie. You think we ought to include the rev in our video for local color, as it were, Junior? Nawh. That would be an anachronism. They didn't have crazy marching niggers back then. No marching niggers of any description, for that—"

"My mother really is okay, in her crazy kind of way," said Rachel Rose, who'd learned you just butted in if you wanted to talk around Rashad. "It's my father who's the jackass."

"Rachel Rose!" said Junior who might be very confused about his values these days, what with one thing and another, but he knew they did not include calling your father names like that. Of course, Junior never called his anything, since he hadn't seen the man since he was two.

"Rolling!" said Rashad.

. . . 36

MR. F HADN'T ANSWERED ANY OF HIS CALLS. WAYNE DIDN'T know *what* to think. Unless, of course, that Crystal, in cahoots with Dougie, had never put them through.

Which is more than likely what happened. Which is why Wayne had parked himself on the floor outside Mr. F's office at the crack of dawn. He'd just catch Mr. F on his way in. Show *them* who was stupid.

But that was two hours ago, and Wayne had dozed off. Which is why he was now being subjected to the ignominy, a word he'd heard Mr. F use before and had asked him what it meant, of Dougie and Crystal staring at him like he was a bug.

"Absolutely *disgusting,*" Crystal said. Well, his shirt *was* wet, but sleeping people weren't responsible for drool.

"Was there something you wanted to see Uncle Tru about?" Dougie grinned, as if he didn't know.

Wayne didn't know exactly how to answer. He didn't want to give Dougie the satisfaction of saying yes. So he scrambled up and pretended he hadn't heard the question.

Crystal gave him a little smirk as if she knew anyway, thank you very much. She unlocked the door to the executive offices and slipped in, closing it sharply behind her.

Wayne wanted to slap her.

He wanted to slap them both.

No, slapping was too good for Dougie. He'd stick with his original plan of taking Dougie with him when he walked. One way or another. Any time now.

"So, Wayne. I was telling Crystal about your collection of sexy videos, and she said she'd like to see some. You know what I mean?" He gave Wayne a big wink like they'd gone out scouting tail together, which they most certainly hadn't. "I told her you had some pretty exciting stuff, and I was wondering—"

Wayne couldn't believe it. Dougie was going to ask *him* for a favor? That must be what getting an MBA from the Wharton School did, made your head first big and then crazy.

"I was thinking about it, and I know she'd really like something like the one we saw in Uncle Tru's office. Little old Crystal likes a little salt with her sugar, you know what I mean?" Dougie licked his lips in a way that made Wayne want to throw up. "You know the one of that big old girl whaling away on that guy? They were doing it, and then she's giving it back to him as good as she got? You have anything else like that—maybe with two women? Too bad that's the one Uncle Tru told you to erase."

Wayne shook his head. "Don't have it."

"I know! That's what I'm saying, it's too bad you erased that one, but what about something else?"

What the hell was Dougie talking about? He hadn't erased the tape.

That was one of the tapes that was stolen. That *Dougie* had stolen. Dougie knew that. Or maybe that's *why* he was doing this song and dance. Maybe after he'd nabbed the stuff, he'd screwed up that tape somehow and now he was nosing around for another copy. Well, he could just go whistle Dixie for that. Not that Wayne had a copy anyway.

"I didn't erase the tape, Dougie. What are you talking about?"

Dougie looked puzzled. "Of course you did. I was standing right there in the room when Uncle Tru saw what he was looking for, that judge said what he did about Uncle Tru's girl, and he said Okay, you can erase it now. Didn't you do what he said?"

Erase *it?*

Wayne had erased *him.*

. . . 37

"I HEAR YOU'RE LOOKING FOR A FRIEND OF MINE."

"Angelo's your friend?"

"Crippled guy?"

"Uh-huh."

"*Old* crippled guy?"

"Yes, Ma."

"Runs a pizza parlor?"

"Right again."

"Never heard of him." And then Michelangelo laughed like a man who knows the world and his place in it and sleeps like a baby. "Samantha, why don't you just tell me what you want, and I'll pass it along. Angelo doesn't like to talk with strangers."

"He likes to talk with hotel maids."

"Explain."

So Sam told him about Angelo visiting Big Gloria, not just once, but twice, looking for Kurt Roberts.

"And what's your interest?"

"I'm looking for him, too."

"Because—?"

"Because he disappeared."

"Sounds like a job for the ACPD."

"It would be, if anybody reported him missing."

"So he's not missing?"

"Nobody seems to think so except me."

"Who's nobody?"

"The pageant staff, his office, his mother, his girlfriend in New York. His girlfriend here thought it strange he was here one minute, gone the next, but then—she hears voices, too. After enough vodka."

"Not a reliable witness?"

"Not exactly."

"What did the voices tell her?"

"You really want to know?"

"I'm waiting."

"She said there were voices in her room that told her she'd be hurt if she—she's a preliminary judge for the pageant—if she didn't vote for Miss X to make the final ten. She thinks something happened to Roberts because he didn't like Miss X. Or at least that's what she thought a couple of days ago. Yesterday she seemed to be considering suing me for slander."

"You're kidding. So, who's Miss X?"

"She wouldn't tell me."

"That's pretty funny. Sounds like a great gimmick for a bookie, he could get voices to speak to quarterbacks, jockeys, pitchers."

"Uh-huh." Then she paused, trying to frame the next question.

"*I'm* not making book on the pageant, if that's what you want to know. There's no percentage in it. Wouldn't be good business."

"It had occurred to me."

"Now why'd I tell you that? You going to ask me that next?"

"Right."

"I hate to see a nice woman like you wasting her time. You think there's betting on Miss America, I'm telling you there's not. Sports, that's another story. But you don't want to go around asking questions about that."

"Okay. Got it. But let's just say, speaking hypothetically, if someone *were* making book on Miss A, would the odds come from Vegas?"

"Sure. Hypothetically. That's where they all come from. On anything. Who'll be in the Super Bowl. Which unions'll go on strike this year. Which Latin dictators are going to fall down boom boom and hurt themselves."

"How would they be made—on the girls? Hypothetically?"

"Well, the closest thing would be racehorses. You'd look at the stats. Which states have won a lot?"

"California, Michigan, Pennsylvania, Mississippi, Texas, Oklahoma."

Then Michelangelo started to noodle around with the idea. "Being a fan of the pageant, I'd say your minorities stand a good chance. After that, blondes over brunettes."

"Redheads aren't big winners. Freckles don't photograph well."

"I'd spot tall over short."

"What do you think about talent?"

"Piano or singing over some oddball thing. Then, once the prelims begin, you've got your swimsuit and talent scores. You know swimsuit's the biggie. Of course, *if* you were doing it, any money that went down before midnight Thursday is sucker money. After that, things get serious."

"After the preliminaries are over?"

"Sure. They're like the play-offs. After those, you've got your ten."

"But we don't know who the ten are until Saturday night."

"*You* don't know."

"You do?"

"Sammy, Sammy. It's a small town."

"Uh-huh. And you're still telling me nobody's making book?"

Michelangelo laughed. "Right. But you sound like somebody dying to put down some money."

"I don't think so. I'm already overextended."

"Look. My advice to you would be this: take what I just gave you if you want to play around with what-ifs in a story. I'll be your 'informed source.'"

"I appreciate that."

"And forget nosing around. I'm serious."

"I understand. But can you tell me one more thing?"

Michelangelo sighed. "I can try."

"Has anybody ever fixed the pageant?"

"Not that I know of. Naaah. It'd be too hard. What're you gonna do? Buy off both sets of judges? It might've been easier when there was one. Now there are two—too many variables, too many pockets, too many mouths. Naaah. I'd say it can't be done."

And that was indeed the truth—as Michelangelo saw it. He'd done a little asking around since his conversation with Willie, and the pageant did seem to be bribe-proof.

"So *that* wouldn't be why your friend Angelo was looking for Kurt Roberts?"

"Usually, I'd say, if Ange was looking for somebody, it's because the somebody owed him money."

"Ange is in the habit of lending people money?"

"Ange can be a very generous man."

"I see. And how do you think he might feel about someone who took advantage of his generosity?"

"I think he'd take a dim view of it."

"Uh-huh. So, you think it might be possible for *you* to ask Ange if he found Mr. Roberts?"

"I think it would. But I want to get back to your interest in this Roberts. I fancy myself a student of human psychology, and what I'm hearing you say is that you're going to a lot of trouble to track down a guy simply because you *think* he's missing—even though nobody else does? And nobody else cares?"

"Well, I have these intuitions. Feelings."

"Hunches. Yeah, I know a lot about hunches. Lot of people in AC have hunches. They can be very expensive—you know what I mean?"

"Yeah, well, mine could, too. If I'm wrong, I stand to lose a bundle."

"This is a bet? The Kurt Roberts thing is a bet?" Michelangelo's laughter this time was richer than Angelina's chocolate gelato.

...38

LANA DELUCCA SAT AT HER DRESSING TABLE TEASING HER HAIR, which didn't seem to want to behave this morning. It was a crying shame, she thought, knowing that you couldn't trust anybody anymore. Oh, the girls acted like they were the sweetest. They'd do anything for you. Lend you lipstick, nail polish, you name it.

And steal your custom-made evening gown.

Well, Michelangelo had certainly come through in a pinch on that one. The dress he'd had delivered to the dressing room wasn't the same, of course, but it was close. The thing was, once she'd realized these girls were like anybody else, it had made her uneasy. That meant the pageant was like real life. Disaster could strike again at any time. From any place.

Lana narrowed her eyes—she was more than a little nearsighted—and peered across the room. Naked girls were everywhere, changing into swimsuits and wraps for the beach number rehearsal. That was one thing about this pageant business. You couldn't afford to be modest, that was for sure. Every time you turned around, somebody was stripping you down, zipping you up, measuring your butt, your boobs, your body fat, your muscle tone, taping, spraying, teasing, combing, currying you. Now she knew how her uncle Jimmy's racehorses felt.

Well, it was almost over. Rehearsals the rest of today and the parade this evening. More rehearsals tomorrow, and then the finals, and they could all go home and fall down. And pork up. Lose those diets, like now.

Except Miss America, who would hit the road.

And Misses Louisiana and Texas, who would be swimming with the fishes if she had her way.

Look at them over there, giggling together. She bet they were lovers. She just bet. She'd never liked southern girls. She couldn't hardly understand a word they were saying. And these two thought they were *so* smart. Taking the wind out of her Jersey Devil story. That big redheaded Connors giving girls financial advice like she was some kind of stockbroker, for chrissakes. The other one, Magic, reading palms, telling fortunes, making everybody laugh with her tricks. Pulling coins out of ears, rabbits out of makeup kits. She bet that's what they'd done with her dress—just made it disappear.

She knew it was them. All sweetness and light like they were just here having a good time, didn't give a hoot about winning.

That was a joke. Any girl here would sell her first kid to win, and anybody who said different was full of it.

Well, they weren't getting to her again. She had her dresses and her costumes hidden away in a place in her hotel so safe they'd never think of it.

So there!

"Hi, Lana, how y'doing?" It was Rae Ann, Miss Georgia. Now she was different. She really *was* sweet. And, like real. "Have you been doing your visualizations?" Rae Ann asked.

Lana didn't know what she was talking about.

"You know, what I told you the other day. I do this every time before I step on a stage. You draw an imaginary circle on the floor, and in that circle is what you want. You stand outside that circle and you think about what you want. You really concentrate on it. And then you concentrate on what it's going to feel like when you have it. When you can really feel that, feel it in your bones, then you step inside the circle, and it's like a glow comes all over you. Then you *know.* You *have* it."

Lana frowned, and that little wrinkle appeared between her eyes. She'd felt tingly glows before, sure, but they didn't have anything to do with imagining. They were real. Rae Ann was so religious, though, she probably didn't want to hear about them. But speaking of religion. "That may work for *you,* Rae Ann, but I wonder the same thing about it that I wonder about guys praying before, like, a football game."

"Huh?"

"Well, you know. If the Giants pray to win, and then let's say the Redskins pray to win, how does God decide?"

"Well, gosh, Lana, I don't know. I never thought about it like that before."

"This is the same thing. If we *all* imagine stepping in that circle and winning, what's gonna happen? Does God flip a coin like the umpire at the beginning of the game, or what? Or is it like little kids asking for things from Santa Claus? Is it whether you've been naughty or nice?"

Rae Ann just stared at Lana. Lana could tell Rae Ann was super-impressed with all this philosophical stuff.

Just about then, wouldn't you just know, Miss Louisiana waltzed over and leaned down to her and said, "I've been thinking about you a lot, and there's something I've got to tell you. In fact, I dreamed about you last night."

Uh-huh. Right. Dreamed what? An apology for snitching her gown? Well, it was too late. Lana had already taken care of her and her buddy. Sometimes you couldn't just say I'm sorry and walk away. Not if you crossed a DeLucca.

"Yesssss?" she smiled up at Magic.

"There's good news and bad news. I'm going to give you the bad news first."

Oh boy. She was really full of it, wasn't she? Like all this mumbo jumbo magic bit *meant* something.

"Look at me, Lana," Magic was saying. "Look into my eyes."

Lana rolled her big browns at Rae Ann, who was standing there with her baby blues looking like saucers, her mouth open, gaping at Magic. Then Lana slowly, like she was bored to spit, met Magic's. In that instant, a thrill shot straight through her. It was like brushing up against a live wire.

Magic said, "You need to be careful. Very careful. I think there's someone trying to hurt you."

Right. You, that's who!

"So you stay on your toes. I heard about your dress last night, but that's not the whole bad thing. That may be part of it—"

"Well, you ought to know," Lana blurted.

"Why, Lana!" Rae Ann, who was still standing there, wasn't used to people being so rude.

"You get away from me, Magic Washington! Get away and stay away! I'm warning you!" Heads snapped all over the dressing room.

Magic said, "You don't understand."

"I understand all I want to." Lana picked up her hairbrush and waved it in front of her. "You back off. Do you hear me? Out of my face!"

Magic turned tail and strolled off, trying to look casual, but Lana knew she'd rattled her. Good! "There, there," Rae Ann soothed. She took the brush out of Lana's hand. "You're just going to upset yourself. Shuh. Shuh." She ran the brush through Lana's hair like she was soothing a baby. "This is no time to get yourself all upset. You've got to keep your concentration. Keep focused on winning."

"Well, I know she's the one who took my dress. She and that Connors. And then she comes sucking around, trying to freak me out with that mumbo jumbo."

"I know that's what you think, but that's just nerves. Nobody's trying to hurt you. Hush, now. Hush." Rae Ann brushed and brushed. She hummed a little lullabye under her breath. And then she stopped.

"What?" said Lana.

"Nothing."

"What?"

"I was just wondering what the good news was. You know, the good news Magic mentioned." And then Rae Ann looked down at the brush she was holding in her hand. "Oh, my God! Blessed Jesus!"

Rae Ann *never* took the Lord's name in vain. *"What?"* Lana screamed and wheeled around.

Rae Ann, open-mouthed, held out the brush. It was filled with a handful of Lana's long blond hair—snapped right off at the roots.

. . . 39

WAYNE DAYDREAMED A LOT. HE IMAGINED ALL KINDS OF things. But never in his wildest had he painted this picture.

He was sitting in Action Central thinking about the conversation he'd had with the equipment van man, wondering if there was somebody else trying to fix the pageant and why, when all of a sudden, like the voice of God coming out of the wall, Mr. F says, "Wayne, I'd like to see you in my office right now."

It was amazing. Wayne had never been on the receiving end of this voice thing. It really did feel like God talking to you. And, in this case, of course, it was, sort of—Mr. F being his daddy and his mama and his teacher and the Baby Jesus all rolled into one.

So he dropped his cola, stopped mid-bite of a cheeseburger, and hustled his butt over to the executive offices faster than a speeding bullet—that's what Mr. F would say.

"He's expecting you." That's what Crystal *had* to say. You could tell it really burned her.

"Come in, Wayne. Pull that door to behind you." Mr. F was sitting in his black calf executive chair, the very one that Wayne had copied, wiping his little round rimless glasses with his left (and only) hand and a handkerchief monogrammed TUF in one corner. T-U-F. Wasn't that something? Wayne had never known Mr. F's middle name. On the top of Mr. F's specially built desk, his trains were going. Sante Fe.

Southern Pacific. B&O. Rolling stock. They were really something.

"Could I offer you some orange pop?" asked Mr. F.

"Why, yes. That'd be nice." Wayne settled back in the chair Mr. F had waved him into, across the desk. It was black leather too, but with chrome. By Vanderow, he'd heard Mr. F tell somebody once. "I'd like some, thanks." Wayne sneaked a peek around the room to make sure Dougie wasn't hiding in a corner. He didn't seem to be. Well, that was good. It was about time he and Mr. F had a heart-to-heart. There were lots of things he wanted to tell him, and Dougie's double-dealing, sneaking and hiding and stealing were right up there at the top of the list.

"You know, Wayne, I've been thinking it's about time we had a heart-to-heart. Laid a few cards on the table."

Wayne was absolutely amazed. No wonder the man was a billionaire. He was also a mind-reading genius.

"Wayne, one of the things you learn if you hang around this gambling business very long is when to hold and when to fold. And when to pull in your horns."

Wayne nodded. He wasn't sure what Mr. F was getting at, but he knew he'd figure it out. As long as Mr. F hadn't started out yelling at him about those tapes, well, Wayne was happy.

"They've always said that this business is recession-proof, but it looks like that may not be the case. We've got shallow pockets all over the place."

Shallow pockets. Wayne tried to picture them.

"What we've got here is a trickle down."

Wayne saw a leaky faucet.

"It all snowballs."

That was easy.

"We all took it in the shorts from Trump, just for starters."

Wayne winced and crossed his legs.

"You know, the man overdeveloped. Already had two casinos, he opened the Taj, just a monument to his dick. It didn't bring any more business into the city. All it did was divide it up, take from the rest of us. And we're not going to get the business back till he folds one."

Wayne saw the Donald standing in a corner. Holding his dick. Everybody pointing at him.

"On top of that, we got this oil business. Crazy Arabs, oil prices go up, gasoline goes up, we don't get the drivers."

Wayne saw cars full of gamblers turning around on the Garden State, heading back home.

"Your high rollers, they gamble discretionary income."

Wayne got a blank screen on that one.

"Person owns his own business, he's cutting back, because he's not bringing in as much."

Okay, Wayne could see that guy, frown on his face, staring at his cash register.

"You'd be surprised, the variables. Bad weather, they stay home. Flu season, they stay home. War. Football play-offs. Super Bowl. Then freaks like this Reverend Dunwoodie, that's very bad for business, Wayne. Man shut the expressway down two hours yesterday, cost us a million. *Us!* And that kind of stuff spills over. People don't want to be around trouble, especially with the coloreds."

Wayne could see the solution to that. Just get an eighteen-wheeler, run that sucker over.

"The players who keep coming, high or low, are the retirees on a fixed income who pop over every other week for entertainment. They're still coming in droves."

Wayne could sure see that. Those AARPs on the buses with their coupons in their spotty old hands.

"We're cutting back on the buses, cutting back on the free chips and meal vouchers. Lots of those grandmas just play those freebies, gobble the meals and get back on the bus."

Shame on them. *No free lunch.* Everybody knew that one.

"So here's what we got. We don't want to cut back too much on marketing because we don't want to lose market share. But we've got to trim expenses where we can. And back-of-the-house is the most sensible place to start."

Wayne saw a big pair of scissors. He nodded at Mr. F who was looking right at him through his little rimless glasses.

"Well, I really do appreciate your taking this so well, Wayne. I knew if I explained it to you, you'd understand."

Understand? Understand what?

Mr. F was around the desk now, handing him an envelope and shaking his hand. Which was always kind of awkward, because you had to remember to give him your left.

"We're going to miss you, Wayne. You've been a real integral part of FrankFair Enterprises, and believe it or not, this hurts me a lot more than it hurts you."

That's exactly what his mama used to say when she beat him bloody with a belt, the one she said had belonged to his daddy. Exactly.

...40

So, Scoop, Sam said to herself staring out the windows of her hotel room at the surf. What are you going to write today for the folks back home about The Miss America Pageant: A Scholarship Program?

Tuesday Rae Ann had won talent. Wednesday she became Miss Fruit of the Loom. Last night's story Sam had recapped, interviewing all the preliminary winners: Rae Ann again, Magic, Connors and Lana, Florida and California. She'd re-explained the judging system. She'd done a sidebar on Cheryl Prewitt Salem, the gospel-singing Miss America 1980, swimsuit manufacturer, and Rae Ann's favorite role model.

Rae Ann had held forth about how serious she felt about being a role model herself. How she had to be on her toes all the time. She couldn't ever curse, not that she ever did anyway, but you could never tell when the devil might put a bad word in your mouth. You had to have good values and handle yourself well. You had to be an angel.

Sam had debated whether or not to quote her. But what was the alternative? She could leave it out, but she couldn't make it up.

What the hell? So Rae Ann wasn't a brain surgeon. Neither were most of the *Constitution*'s readers.

But today was the tough one. There was no competition, only the parade at five. She could cover the trade show. Michelangelo had convinced her there was no book on Miss A. How about the psychology of losing? A quarter of a million girls each year participating in pageants, aiming at the Big Tiara, all of them losing except one.

Meanwhile, she could answer the phone.

It was Harry, probably, checking in from his morning adventures with Lavert. Twisting her tail about Kurt Roberts. Or maybe Michelangelo calling to say, yes, Ange found Roberts and he killed him and now you can go collect the grand and a half from your cute boyfriend and his big buddy. Harpo stood at her feet, indignation curling his little black lips. He hated loud noises.

"Hello?"

Son of a gun, it was Cindy Lou Jacklin. Talk about your losers.

"Listen," Cindy Lou said, "I wanted to apologize for being so rude to you yesterday. I was having a bad—"

"Hey, that's okay."

"—day and I was so worried about Kurt, and I thought that you thought that I had *done* something to him. And I feel so silly, telling you that stupid story about voices. I think it must have been a bad dream, but that's all okay now."

"What do you mean?"

"I feel so much better now that Kurt called. You know, it had been over two days, and—"

"He *what?*"

"He called. You know, he can be *so* sweet, and he said he was *so* sorry he—"

"Where *is* he?"

"I'm *trying* to tell you!"

"I'm sorry. Is he okay?"

"Of *course* he is. He said he had no idea anybody would be worried about him. But then, nobody was, really, except me. And you."

"Where *is* he, Cindy Lou?"

"In the Bahamas. He got a last-minute call that a story he had done down there, well, all the film got destroyed in some kind of accident at *Vogue,* and it was for a cover story on deadline. So he had to get everybody together again and go down and redo it."

So. So why wasn't she thrilled? Because she hated to admit she was wrong? Boy, did that suck. Get herself to a meeting and talk about *that* one.

"I'm flying down Sunday morning to join him. Isn't that great?"

"Sure is."

Way to go, Cindy Lou. Fly right down into the arms of that sucker, see if he'll break one of yours.

I'm a dreadful loser, Harpo, she said to the little dog after Cindy Lou hung up. A spoilsport who cannot stand to be wrong. And Harry's never ever going to let me forget this one.

Harpo pounced on his squeeze toy, a rubber hamburger. He dropped it on her foot and barked.

Good idea, she said, tossing the toy across the room for the little dog, who rarely spoke. *You* tell Harry. I'm not.

. . . 41

"THIS IS CRAZY, YOU KNOW THAT?" SAID ANGELINA AMATO, strolling down the Boardwalk. "In broad daylight."

"You love it," said her lover.

"Love it? I'm scared to death. I wish we could just stay home. If only Mikey didn't have the house watched."

"What are you scared of, honey?"

"Him, Mikey."

"Afraid of your son? I don't believe that."

"Not for me. It's what he's going to do to you I'm worried about."

Angelo Carlo smiled. Ma wasn't going to do nothing to him—except reward him when Ange delivered the Miss America crown to his girl, Miss New Jersey, compliments of Billy Carroll. He reached over and took Angelina's hand. "That's why we play our little games, so he won't catch us. Besides, they're fun. Didn't you love the one when we put me in the wheelchair with the dark glasses and cane, you in the nurse's uniform? I think it really turned you on."

"Ange!" she warned.

"Relax, hon. Why are you so nervous today?"

"This is sacrilege. Besides, we can't walk hand in hand. People are staring."

She had a point. He let her hand go.

They were almost there anyway, the Centurion, a casino hotel way down past Convention Hall toward Ventnor. It was an older place that was licensed in the name of someone named Phillips with the New Jersey Gambling Commission but was owned by a close personal friend of Angelo's.

"I can't wait." He gave her a big wink.

"Don't start, you."

"I already have." He brushed himself against her as they made their way through the crowds. The Convention-Hall drones were already setting up the bleachers for the parade. The Boardwalk was jammed. And Angelo was hard.

"You're a dirty old man," she snapped. But he saw the twinkle in her eye.

"Not bad, huh, for a guy of seventy-one."

Beside him, Angelina came to a dead stop. Alarmed, Angelo turned. "You okay, hon? Did you trip? I know, that thing's too long. I'm sorry, it was the best I could do—"

"Seventy-two," she said.

"What?"

"You're seventy-two."

"Angelina, I know how old I am. I'm seventy-one this past Fourth of July."

"Seventy-two."

"You're right. I'm seventy-two." Angelo was exasperated. Here he was feeling like a colt, like a sixteen-year-old walking down the Boardwalk with his girl, sea breeze on his boner up under the black robe, and she'd made him lose it. "Jesus Christ!"

A passing couple stared at Angelo, shocked.

"Forgive me," he mumbled. They were right. He shouldn't be taking the Lord's name in vain. Not in this getup.

"*You're* right," Angelina was saying now. "Seventy-one."

"What difference does it make, hon? Seventy-one, seventy-two? We ought to be glad we're still around. And have each other." And I can get it up, he added to himself, wondering if he could again when they got upstairs.

A black kid dressed in evening clothes pushing a rolling chair gave them the high sign. "Beautiful day, beautiful day." Then a gaggle of old ladies stopped. "Hello, hello. Great day for a stroll." He turned to Angelina. "This is fun. Let's do it again tomorrow."

"No way. You come up with something else."

"Oh, hell. I *love* this robe. Gives me a lot of room. You know what I mean?" He did a little bump and grind.

"Fifty Hail Marys, Ange. *I'm* going to do fifty, at least."

"Honey, you do fifty every time we kiss. Don't you think this number is gonna be a little more expensive? Especially when I get you in that Sinatra suite, the one they decorated special with the mirrors on the ceiling?" Then he leaned over and whispered in her ear. Or as close as he could get to it with the wimple.

"Angelo, stop it!" But she couldn't help blushing.

"I told Ricky to put the full spread on for this friend of mine who was coming. I already picked up the key." He pulled it from his pocket and showed her. "We've got the champagne, the fruit, the canapés, the hot and cold running dancing girls—just teasing. The tub for two, bubble bath. Nothing but Sinatra on the stereo."

"Nothing but me and you," Angelina said, getting in the mood.

"Nothing between us."

"Nothing now except this outfit," she said, running her

fingers lightly across the black gabardine that draped down her full bosom.

Angelo's eyes lit up.

"Not a stitch under this." Then she smiled demurely as Sister Mary Catherine at St. Anthony's.

"Oh, Angelina," he breathed.

Thank God, they were finally there. Naked statues struck poses all around the entryway. Angelo couldn't wait to get like that. Not that he had the body he once had, but—

"Father, Sister," the doorman threw the doors wide. "Welcome to the Centurion."

"Bless you, my son," Angelo said. "Bless you."

"You're laying it on pretty thick," Angelina said as they crossed the wide lobby.

"So I'll do a thousand Hail Marys. Two thousand. It's gonna be worth every one of them." And then he patted her rear end as they turned face-front in the elevator behind the operator. "Penthouse, please."

"Certainly, Father."

"And, Angie," he leaned into her wimple again, "I always knew you took a couple years off your age. But it's okay. Older broads turn me on."

. . . 42

"HEY, MAN, I WAS JUST GONNA CALL YOU."

Why didn't Wayne believe that? Dean, the equipment van man, was standing outside the loading dock with a bunch of other guys. Now he was looking around, kind of nervous like. Maybe he wasn't supposed to talk to civilians on his lunch break, but Wayne was still wearing his Monopoly Special Services cap, which ought to count for something. Besides, even the uptight Convention Hall Center geeks weren't *that* security crazy, were they?

"Hey, man, let's take a walk." Dean took Wayne by the

arm, pulling him past a bunch of grunts setting up parade bleachers on the Boardwalk. Dean was holding a pepperoni sub in the hand that was free.

"What's the matter?" Wayne asked.

"You know, we're going to talk business, I don't want any of those other guys listening in."

Hey, hey. That must mean he had something good. He knew who else was willing to cough up some bucks for the Miss A signal. Maybe even why.

"So what's the word?" Wayne asked, trying to imitate Dean's low-slung walk. The dude strolled like he was sitting in a Maserati, which Wayne thought was supercool.

"Word is"—if Dean lowered his voice any more, Wayne was going to have to borrow a hearing aid from one of the geezers passing by—"listen, man, I could get in a *lot* of trouble telling you this."

Wayne knew what that meant. He palmed Dean a hundred like Dean was the maître d' in Park Place, the Monopoly's exclusive high-roller club.

Dean's eyebrows wiggled, but his mouth didn't move.

Well, Wayne had another one where that came from. The petty cash fund for Action Central was pretty big, and then there was all the equipment he'd bought at Ace Electronics —he had a deal with the guy—that had never found its way to the Monopoly's back door. That was cash in his pocket.

Plus, of course, just for the hell of it, on his way out, he'd grabbed Crystal, Mr. F's little bitch of a receptionist, knocked her out, dragged her into a maid's room where he'd dumped her into a laundry cart and wheeled her up in the service elevator to 1803. Nobody was going to be using that room for a while.

He'd tied her spread-eagled to the bed and said, "Honey, don't you worry. You're not going to be lonely for long. Those busboys and porters love a bargain, and at ten bucks a pop, you're gonna get lots of takers. I posted a sign, CHEAP TWAT, in the men's room of the employees cafeteria."

He hadn't, but he was thinking about it. If he made it twenty-five—figure she could handle six, seven an hour—count it up.

Dean was staring at the three hundred in his hand like he was trying to figure if that was as high as he could push it. The answer must have been yes. "Okay," he said, twisting his head around to see if anybody was watching. If Wayne was a cop, he'd have arrested him on the spot and figured out the beef later. "It's Michelangelo Amato and it's Miss New Jersey."

"No."

"Yes."

"No."

"We gonna stand around arguing about it all day, or what?" Then Dean strolled off.

He did have a point there. And Wayne had to get moving. Now that he knew who to approach, he had to figure out a plan and execute it, and he didn't have much time. How much? He checked his Rolex, exactly like Mr. F's. Then he stopped dead in the middle of the Boardwalk.

"Yo! Dude!" he yelled at Dean's back, but Dean just waved him off. Okay. So he didn't want a solid gold Rolex that left a bad taste in Wayne's mouth now that Mr. F had disowned him. Thrown him out like garbage. All that trouble, didn't even *care* anymore about the Miss America thing. Who could figure? But he bet this black kid knew which way was up, rolling down the Boardwalk here with his wicker chair.

Wayne was right.

Rashad took the watch and said, "Thank you for your munificence, oh kindly gentleman."

Which Wayne thought was bullshit.

Rashad knew it for what it was, shuck and jive.

But he also knew who Wayne was, the electronics bubba he and Junior had ripped off. The man finding him and making him a *gift,* now that had to be a sign of good things to come.

. . . 43

IT HADN'T TAKEN LAVERT LONG TO SWEET-TALK THE SECURITY guard named Tiffany at the door of Atlantic City High School down at the traffic circle where Atlantic met Albany. He told her she looked a lot like the statue of the pretty woman in the monument outside, Liberty in Distress was her name, a memorial to WW I. He told her if *she* was ever in distress, he'd be happy to help her out. Tiffany giggled and sent a runner to the office to look up Junior Sturdivant's schedule and deliver him down here, pronto.

Who's this? Junior had said, walking the cool dude stroll. But there was fear in his heart. He *knew* it was all going to catch up to him. The shoplifting, the wallet-snatching, the video equipment. He figured he was looking at hard time in Wharton Correctional up in the Pine Barrens. He'd be eighteen, a Piney for sure, and God knew what else by the time he got out. He knew who this huge brother was. He was the law. He was justice. He was dues.

So he wasn't surprised when the huge brother took him outside and threw him up against a wall with the flick of one hand like he was nothing and said, "Junior, I know you think you're bad."

He was surprised to see the white guy who'd saved his butt from the swimming pool, though. Guy looked like he hadn't shaved in three or four days. He came ambling up with a little smile and stuck out his hand. "Harry Zack. I think we've met."

Uh-oh. Junior knew this routine. The big black dude was playing the bad cop. The white one, the good. Junior hadn't grown up watching "Hill Street Blues" for nothing.

"So, Junior," Harry said. "We think you've got a few things you'd like to tell us."

"Unh-uh." Junior drew a circle on the sidewalk with one of his hightops.

The big brother slapped him up against the head. "That's no way to talk, son. Stand up straight and speak English."

"No, sir, there's nothing I have to tell you, sir." Junior slid an eye over toward Lavert. The pretty talk seemed to satisfy him for the moment. Which was good, because his brain felt like scrambled eggs inside his skull.

"What did your mama tell you last night when you got in?" the brother snapped.

What? *Mama* had sicced the cops on him?

"Speak up, son," Harry said.

"She—uh, she said that I had better watch my butt, stay home. That I was in big trouble and that people knew it."

"Do you know what she's talking about?" That was Harry.

"No, sir."

"Sheee-it." That was the brother. "We gonna have to jack you up, son?"

"No, sir."

"What'd you do to that white dude that tossed you in the pool? You track him back to his room, let yourself in with your mama's key, beat him up pretty good, didn't you, Junior?"

Holy shit. *That's* what they thought?

"No, sir. Absolutely not, sir. I never did."

"So what did you do to him?"

"Nothing! I've never seen the dude again."

"You're sure?" The big brother had his face down right in Junior's. It was a fearsome sight. Junior was afraid for a minute the brother was going to lean right over and bite off his nose.

"I'm sure. Sure as shooting. Scout's honor. Sir." Junior held up two fingers. Then three. Then four. He never could remember how that one went.

"We understand you're in the filmmaking business," said Harry quick like, like he was trying to confuse him.

Oh, God. They knew that too, the video equipment.

"I help a friend out when I can. *He's* the one who knows the business." Oh, shit! He'd just pointed the finger at Rashad. Now he was a rat, on top of everything else.

"It seems to me that that's the kind of thing a young dude like you ought to be pursuing, instead of shoplifting, hitting little old ladies upside the head," said the brother.

Lavert knew about the shoplifting from Gloria, but the other part, he got lucky, making it up as he went along. But Magic said money, it made sense.

Junior thought, would he say that, about the filmmaking, if he knew they'd lifted the equipment? Who knew? But he feinted in the other direction. "No, sir. I never. I never hit any little old lady—"

"Shut up! Stop your lying!" Then the brother was back in his face again. His breath was hot and smelled like coffee. "You ever been in jail, little dude?"

"No, sir."

"Cute little thing like you, you know how long you'd last before a bunch of dudes big as me'd have you in the shower playing pick-up-the-soap?"

"No, sir. Yes, sir." It wasn't something Junior wanted to think about.

"You know what you'd have to do every night to make sure somebody didn't kill you in your sleep?"

"Yes, sir. No, sir."

"Well, whatever you think it might be, smart little dude, double it and then triple it, and then kiss your ass good-bye."

"Yes, sir."

"Now, we want you to watch your step, Junior. Do you understand what we're saying?" That was Harry.

"Yes, sir."

"Are you sure?" The brother bellowed in his ear like a drill sergeant.

"Yes, sir!"

"Then get your ass back in school and straighten up and fly right and watch your p's and q's!" The brother whacked him one more upside the head just to make sure.

After Junior had marched smartly back up the steps as if he'd made straight As in Basic at West Point, Lavert said, "How'd we do?"

"I think maybe that last set of orders you gave him was a little confusing."

"In about a New York second I'm gonna confuse you," Lavert growled, then leaned his head back and laughed. They were slapping hands before they were through.

"He didn't know nothing about Roberts," said Lavert.

Harry agreed, then asked, "You think we did it? You think Junior's gonna mind his mama and watch his butt? You think I can stop worrying about him? I just hated it when Sammy told me I was responsible for him since I dragged him out of that pool."

Darleen looked around the lobby at the crowd waiting for the elevators. Everyone else was wearing pageant badges, big hairdos, and polyester blouses. Darleen hadn't figured out exactly how she was going to get into this trade show, but she knew that if she didn't do some serious shopping soon she was going to go into withdrawal—or kill her husband. She thought maybe if she spent several thousand dollars of *his* money on a little beaded number, Billy Carroll might live a few more hours. Waiting for the elevator, she rooted around in her bag, wondering if her California resale license would get her in.

"Oh, I wish we didn't have to go home," said Rachel Rose, whom she'd dragged along.

Darleen stared at her daughter, who was dressed head to toe in tattered black. She looked like a refugee from some Eastern European country. "A week ago you were kicking and screaming you wanted to stay home and hang out with your friends, the last week before school starts."

"I know. That seems like a lifetime ago."

Oh, Jesus. To be fifteen again and in love. To be thirty-six and in love, for that matter.

"Now, you're being—prudent—with this boy, aren't you?"

"Oh, Mom." Rachel Rose rolled her eyes. "Not so loud. And please, not in public."

Her daughter was right. She apologized.

"It's okay."

God, how *nice* her kid was. And they were still able to talk. It was amazing, Rachel Rose hadn't gone completely mute when she hit puberty.

Darleen gazed fondly over the top of her daughter's head—and there he was again. The old man with the white shirt, the dark pants, the windbreaker, and the limp.

This wasn't the first time she'd noticed him.

She wasn't exactly sure when that was, but it was like every time she turned around today, he was in the corner of the picture. At breakfast, on the Boardwalk, and now—

"Do you know that man?" Darleen pointed.

"Who?"

"Him."

"I don't see who you're talking about."

He was gone. It was nothing, she said. No need to frighten Rachel Rose. That would make her feel *more* guilty.

And God knows she felt guilty enough. Darleen had lain awake all night thinking about the terrible things she'd done to Lana DeLucca—wondering why she'd put the blame on *her.*

Billy was the one she ought to be trashing. Little sucker didn't even wear his wedding band, said it was too tight. Yes, indeed, the real culprit had been lying there right next to her while she was staring at the ceiling. She could have reached over and picked up that big lamp and crushed his skull. That would have been doing things right. Except, given his hair helmet, the damned lamp would've probably bounced back in her face and broken her nose.

Darleen smiled at the thought. At least she hadn't lost her sense of humor. *Anyway,* she knew what she was going to do today, right after she bought herself and Rachel Rose some *very* expensive little numbers.

She was going to find Lana and 'fess up. She was going to apologize to her and return her gown and see what they could do about her hair. Darleen knew this Hollywood hairdresser who had the most fabulous wigs—he could air-express one.

It was times like these Darleen wished she were Catholic.

She could go to church, confess, light a few candles, it'd be over and done with. Jews, no way, they had to stare their transgressions in the face, apologize, make restitution, and *still* feel guilty the rest of their lives.

"Hi!"

Darleen jumped.

"Sorry, I didn't mean to startle you. Aren't you Billy Carroll's wife?"

Darleen looked up at the tall brunette. She was vaguely familiar.

"I'm Sam Adams, Atlanta *Constitution.* I saw you out at the pool with Billy a few days ago."

Not exactly an afternoon she wanted to remember. Billy being a horse's ass with the waiter. Embarrassing her like she'd just embarrassed her daughter.

"You two going up to the trade show?"

"Yes," Darleen smiled brightly, then introduced herself and Rachel Rose. "I don't know if we can get in."

Sam said come along with her. She was sure she could help them.

So they'd be a while. Angelo, hidden behind a tall redheaded woman who was Dr. Mary Frances DeLaughter, would stay on the elevator, then go back down to the lobby and loiter behind a palm. Angelo had a lot of patience, as long as this thing didn't run over into his date with Angelina.

But seeing as how he was so close to the prize, it wouldn't hurt to take out a little insurance. Dealing with a flake like Billy Carroll, you could never be too careful. Marks like him never did what they said they were gonna do—unless you had 'em by the short ones. The way Ange figured it, Billy's short ones had just stepped off the elevator.

Patience was not, however, one of the virtues belonging to Dr. Mary Frances DeLaughter. She nabbed Sam the minute she'd pointed Darleen and Rachel Rose in the direction of Jeannie Carpenter and her beaded gowns.

"I'm finding it very difficult," she said, all atremble with seriousness, "to identify a contestant who epitomizes the transcending qualities of American womanhood. Someone who could serve as an icon for feminism, who understand the game that is being played here and is using it to her own advantage."

"Someone very clever?" Sam smiled.

"Yes."

"A young woman who *really* has her priorities in order?"

"That's the ticket."

"Someone who can verbalize all the dreams for powe that American women have tucked away in their bras?"

Mary Frances looked at her a bit oddly. Okay, so she'd pushed too far. But she had the girl to twist Mary Frances's brain all right. And vice versa.

"Miss New Jersey, M. F., is going to be your star. Now, if you have trouble reaching her," Sam leaned forward, "don't tell anyone I told you, but she's staying at my hotel, the Monopoly. Room 1505."

That done, a smiling Sam sailed toward the jewelry counter, where she would buy Miss America key chains for Malachy and Uncle George. It was a great day to be alive and in full possession of your faculties as well as a couple of major credit cards.

. . . 44

"JUNIOR, MY MAN, IT'S GOING TO BE SPECTACULAR," SAID Rashad. "I really love this shot of you zooming down the beach road with Rachel Rose. I mean Bette."

"It's going to be spectacular when they put our butts in jail, all right. You think you can get your friend Spike to come and make a movie of us in stir? *Fools on the Pea Farm* I can just see it on the marquee."

"Would you please *stop* being so melodramatic. You don't even know they were cops."

"They were cops."

"Then why didn't they arrest you?"

"They're toying with us. That's what cops do."

"We don't have time for this, Junior. I've got to finish editing this stuff today if we're going to screen it tomorrow. Harry'll understand that this is rough cut. But I want to see what he thinks. Now hand me that footage of you and Rachel Rose driving around the Pine Barrens, you're talking her out of being Miss A."

"I have a terrible feeling about this. That big brother, man, he looked in my eyes and he could *see* me stealing these cameras."

"Tape, please. Thank you."

"He's about the size of a freight train, and he's telling me all about how I'm gonna be somebody's girlfriend in jail. He scared the bejesus out of me."

"Huge dude? Junior, you are *so* dense. I met that—" Junior looked up at the monitor. "Awh, man. This is the wrong tape."

"The label says Pine Barrens. That's it."

"It's the Barrens, all right. But we didn't shoot this stuff. Hey, that's the guy who gave me his Rol—"

"Jesus. I don't know. Wait a minute. That one." Junior pointed to the other man. "That's the hard-on who pushed me in the pool. But—oh, God! Rashad! What's he doing? What the hell?"

"Don't get so excited. Obviously they're just goofing. And it's free! Murder in the Pines. What a great subplot!"

...45

HARRY AND LAVERT HAD DECIDED TO TRY THEIR LUCK DOWN AT the Centurion before the big parade. "Spread some of it around," Lavert had said, smiling his big smile. But that was a joke, because both of them had been on a winning streak since they hit town. Harry still hadn't shaved, *his* special magic trick, and his luck had held. They were standing in line now to cash in, their hands full of chips.

"Big Gloria's going to have a smile on her face tonight," said Harry.

Lavert laughed. "You've turned into a one-man social welfare department here, my man."

"Naw. You know, it kind of started as a joke, but I really would like to see the woman take Junior and get back to God's country. This place'll rot your soul. Hanging around inside casinos, eternal night."

"Be night in the ghetto, too, all the time. You know, I been thinking."

"Uh-huh?"

"We've done this whole thing wrong."

"Which one?" asked Harry, noticing that the short man with the big hair over in the credit line was Billy Carroll.

"This Roberts thing. I don't know why we went asking questions, chasing our butts all around. We didn't have to do jack."

"What are you saying?"

"It was a negative proposition, my man. All we had to do was wait for your sweet girl to prove us wrong. We didn't have to prove ourselves right."

"Are you sure?"

"What do you mean, am I sure? Seems to me, she can't come up with the dude with some holes in him or something, we get the scatch."

"You don't think she's going to hold us to a note from his mama or something? Saying she's sorry he couldn't come to Atlantic City no more, but—"

"No! That's what I'm telling you. *She* said something's happened to him. So *she* has to prove it."

"I don't know, Lavert. Sammy's tougher than that. I don't think she's gonna roll over on this one."

It was Harry's turn at the window now. He shoved his pile of chips through and the cashier counted out eleven hundred dollars. "Just a moment, sir," he said. He pushed a form through the window for Harry to sign.

"Boy, I hope you pick up a bunch of losing tickets at the track before the end of this year. The IRS is gonna eat up your behind," said Lavert.

"Yeah, well, I never have any problems dropping it at the Fairgrounds—"

But before he could finish, he was interrupted by Billy Carroll's yowling. "What d'ya mean, no more? Do you know who I am?"

Lavert looked down at Harry, gestured with a finger to one eye. "Breakfast's what he is. About two bites."

"Billy Carroll. Host of 'The Big One' and emcee of this year's Miss America Pageant!" Carroll was bouncing up and down on his lifts so hard he looked like he was about to take flight.

"I guess the guy didn't know," said Harry.

"And furthermore, I have played in this town for twenty-five years!"

"Casinos ain't been open that long, fool," Lavert said softly, stepping up to the cashier. It was his turn now.

"I earn more in one week than you do in a whole year, and you're telling me my credit's no good? So what if I've drawn twenty-five? I'm good for that and more. Do you speak English? Can we get somebody over here who can?"

Lavert was signing his receipt. "I fairly do hate people who say things like that. I tell you, Harry, the assumptions made by middle-class white people in this country are enough to give you heart failure."

"I couldn't agree more."

"And I hope a whole bunch of them come and make those assumptions in our restaurant, don't you? Labor under the delusion that the world's their playpen and the toys don't stop. Their pockets full of gold plastic."

"I do, my man."

"How are you boys doing today?" It was a little old black lady in a bright red polyester pantsuit and comfortable shoes who was in line behind them.

Her husband, who was carrying her bag, couldn't help but brag. "We hit the dollar slot for five thousand dollars."

"That's great, dad," Lavert beamed at them. Then leaned

down to take a closer look, glanced back at Harry with a question on his face.

The little old lady turned to her husband and whispered, "We can't cash this in, Ange. You have to show ID."

"You're right. I forgot. Well, hell, let's go upstairs. We'll take a little lie down."

"Okay," she said brightly. And off they trotted.

"I don't know what's wrong with you people," Billy Carroll was screaming.

"What's the matter, man?" Harry asked Lavert.

"Those people—they weren't black."

"They looked black to me."

"I know. But did you listen to them?"

"They're Yankee colored folks, Lavert. They talk different."

"Shut up, fool. Those were your folks wearing makeup, I'm telling you."

"Yeah, and I guess that ID business they were talking about doesn't mean they left their drivers' licenses upstairs, it means they're gonna go up, get their guns, and rob the bank, right?"

Just then a white man in a navy blazer, almost as big as Lavert, pulled up under his own steam, though Harry wouldn't have been surprised if there'd been a bulldozer behind him, he had that kind of momentum. "Sir?" he said to Billy Carroll, cutting him out of the line with his body like Billy was a bad little calf. "Sir, could you come over here with me just a moment?"

Shift manager if not assistant casino manager, Harry thought. Hell, maybe it was the casino manager himself leaning on Billy Carroll, whose face was starting to pucker like he might have himself a good cry.

"I don't know what you're talking about!" Carroll was right in the man's face as Harry and Lavert strolled off.

Later, Billy Carroll would be ashamed of himself. Ashamed of losing control with a nobody like that. He should have insisted on seeing the vice president in charge of casino operations when the big lug hustled him out.

But, on the other hand, Billy thought—taking another shower, getting ready for his ride on the float with that bossy Phyllis George who'd probably try to tell him how to wave—maybe it was just as well.

He had already dropped another bundle, all in credit, since he'd gotten the call from Barbara Stein about doing the emcee number.

Only because he was nervous. Which was understandable, prime-time exposure like that.

Plus, there was Angelo leaning on him.

He'd told the man he'd do what he asked. But, God almighty, it wasn't going to be but half a second if he did that before the shit would hit the fan, and his career in broadcasting would be history.

Billy had been in some tights before, but never one like this.

The way he figured it, he'd just keep leading Angelo on, saying yes sir, boss to everything he asked. Then he'd do the right thing, and, once he paid Angelo the cash he owed him, plus a little bonus, hell, what difference would it make?

This wasn't *GoodFellas,* for Christ's sake. And the pageant was just a bunch of silly little twists. Who'd care day after tomorrow? It wasn't important. It wasn't the Super Bowl. It wasn't like Angelo was going to fit him for a pair of concrete overshoes, size eight, hold the lifts 'cause the little man won't be standing in them.

Was it?

...46

THERE WAS NOTHING TO CLEAR A MAN'S HEAD LIKE A DRIVE IN the country.

About five o'clock, just as everybody else was settling into the Miss America Parade and all that silly shit on the Boardwalk, Wayne headed out of town in his red 1968 Mustang, a car he dearly loved. He'd thought for a few minutes about taking a rental car, the Mustang being such a standout, but then, nobody in Atlantic City ever noticed anything anyway, and the people where he was headed, well, there weren't many of them in the first place, and in the second place, they never talked.

Besides, he didn't want to waste the money. Now that he was out of a job—well, it might not be long before Michelangelo Amato took him on, probably wouldn't be, but you could never tell. All that talk Mr. F had done about bad times—who knew how far that might go? Maybe even the mob had more than it could handle, had fallen on lean days. Though he didn't think so.

Anyway, Dean said Michelangelo wasn't mob. Michelangelo was *connected,* he kept saying, like he thought he was hot stuff, talking the lingo.

And anyway, even if *everybody* had to suck it in, including connected dudes, whatever that meant, Wayne knew he had plenty of resources when it came to hard times. In fact, with this little trip, he was hoping to kill two birds with one stone.

First, he had the business in the trunk to take care of. Second, he was scouting for where he might set up a homesite, push came to shove. Wayne was good at living off the land. Hadn't that been exactly what he was doing when Mr. F found him?

Wayne looked out the window at a church sign. *Drive in and drop off all your suffering with us. We'll wash it clean.* Well, that was a sign, all right. A sign he needed to stop thinking about Mr. F. That was over. Dead. Done and gone.

Back to his plan, that *was* what he'd been doing—at that stage of his life, when Mr. You Know Who found him. Living in that tree house. Living off the fat of the land and what he could lift from the FrankFair, Grand Union, and Radio Shack. Depending on his innate skills and his innate worth. He had learned even more skills since then. And he had a lot more cash. Yeah, Wayne figured, looking to be careful he didn't miss the turnoff in Egg Harbor City from White Horse Pike onto the Egg Harbor–Green Bank Road, he'd be just fine, thank you very much, Mr. You Know Who.

He knew his way around. Especially this area. One of the things Wayne loved about it was how, thirty minutes from Atlantic City, headed inland like you were going to Philly, you could hang a right and be in wilderness in no time flat.

The Pine Barrens were one of the last true wildernesses in this country. Six hundred and fifty thousand acres, the size of Grand Canyon National Park, with a population density of fifteen people per square mile. In one area of the Barrens, over a hundred thousand acres, there were only twenty-one people. Wayne had not only visited, he'd read up.

He could tell you that the eastern part of the Barrens—which he was driving his Mustang in now, along a dirt road that was two tracks in the sand with brush growing up between them—was covered with dwarf forests as far as a man could see, looking up over the tops of the trees. Over to the west and north stood oaks and pines and tall white cedars. It was tannins and other organic waste from the cedars that gave the dark color to the water that flowed so freely here. In summer, the water, while uncontaminated as pure rainwater or melted glacial ice, was so cedar-dark with those tannins you couldn't see the bottom of the riverbeds.

Wayne was driving toward one of those rivers, Bass River, right now.

The car was bouncing against scrub-oak boughs and blueberry bushes. Running over rattlesnakes. There were lots of rattlers in the Pines. Probably lots more snakes than people, but they all made out.

In the old days, it used to be that Pineys, that's what the folks who lived here called themselves, lived completely off the land—the way Wayne liked to do. They didn't have FrankFairs, Grand Unions, and Radio Shacks, but they had the sphagnum moss to sell to florists, wild blueberries, cranberries, cordwood, and they made charcoal. They sold holly, mistletoe, pine, and greenbrier for Christmas decorations. They gathered wildflowers in the spring, made birdhouses out of cedar slabs, sent box turtles to Philadelphia to keep the snails out of the cellars.

Some of those things remain. Pine Barrens cranberries,

commercially grown, furnish a third of the country's supply. Charcoal's gone. Wild game has declined. Many Pineys now have jobs outside.

But they come back and stay home, given the choice. They love their wild land. And they love to be left alone. Like Wayne.

Yes, Wayne thought, maybe he wouldn't even call on Michelangelo Amato with his Grand Plan.

Maybe he'd just tuck in here and become a Piney with the rest of them. Build him a shack. Or reclaim one that was falling down. There were plenty of them. Nobody would care.

He'd met some Pineys. They were good people. Quiet. Shy. Though once he'd sat with some old men and shared their food, and boy, could they tell some tales.

There were those who said Pineys were all touched in the head because of inbreeding, but those people didn't know what they were talking about. Pineys just liked to mind their own business.

There was a lot to be said for that, minding your own business.

Now if Dougie had learned to do that, instead of telling tales on him to Mr. F all the time, he wouldn't be in the pickle he was in now.

Wayne kept bumping along till there was Bass River, just up ahead. Wayne pulled the Mustang right up to the edge of it. Dark as ink, the water was. You couldn't see a thing through it.

He turned off the ignition, opened the door, stepped outside. Wayne lifted his arms to the sky. Christ, the air smelled so sweet. It was great to be away from that stinking city. You wouldn't think that a town that was right up on the Atlantic Ocean could smell bad, but AC did. It smelled of rot, sweat from the gamblers, the stink of unwashed kids.

Dougie was going to start to smell, too. He'd smell up the Mustang if Wayne didn't get him out of there.

Wayne whirled in a circle, took a look around. Miles and miles of deep forest. Nobody in sight but just us critters. He opened the trunk, and, holding his breath, dragged Dougie's blanket-wrapped body out. Then it didn't take but a minute to roll him over and over. *Kerplop.* Dougie dropped beneath the surface of the cedar-dark water.

Just like Kurt Roberts, somewhere around here. Up a few miles, maybe. Wayne had taken a different road that time.

He felt bad about contaminating the water, but, hell. There was *lots* of water. It wouldn't take long before it ran clean again.

Wayne dug in his shirt pocket, lit a cigarette, and took a deep drag. He'd stopped smoking a long time ago, but every once in a while, times like this, a job well done, an unfiltered smoke was just the ticket.

It had been simpler this time. With Kurt, well, he'd wanted to *show* Mr. F the job well done. So there'd been the video camera he'd had to set up. It was hard to find the right height to get everything he wanted in the picture. He'd wasted a lot of time fooling with the tripod. And, somehow, the camera, all that high tech stuff, well, it just didn't feel right, here in the Barrens.

But this time, this time Wayne had done good. He'd done perfect.

...47

SAM WOKE UP LAUGHING.

"What?" Harry croaked.

"Wasn't it one of the ten best things you've ever seen?"

Harry sat up, reached for the phone, and ordered a carafe of coffee. At the end of the bed, Harpo stretched and glared at him, then rolled over.

"You think the little dog would have loved the parade?" He called to Sam who was in the bathroom brushing her teeth.

"Oh yeah. He'd have braved the crowds and noise to have

seen the Reverend. Harpo's crazy about folks walking o water."

Sam had always loved a parade. Ever since she was a littl girl, she'd delighted in parking herself curbside, hip to hi with other strangers who couldn't wait for the first wail o the motorcycle escort.

Atlantic City's Finest had done the honors for Mis America. They wore shiny black leather boots and knife pleated gabardine and made lots of noise revving up thei bikes.

Sam had a prime spot at a press table right outsid Convention Hall. The *Inquirer* had saved her a seat. On he other side was *USA Today.* The parade rolled right pas them down the Boardwalk.

The New Jersey Air National Guard, all spit and polish marched close behind the motorcycles. Then the 389t Army Band from Fort Monmouth just up the shore playe "Stars and Stripes Forever." Half the crowd waved littl flags.

Phyllis George and Billy Carroll rolled by in a vintag Cadillac convertible with superlative tail fins. Phyllis was i a red velvet suit with matching hat. Billy Carroll looked lik a candy cane in red and white stripes.

"They all wear stupid clothes for the parade," said th *Inquirer.* "Next to the Old South Ball tomorrow night, it' the best chance for major dress-up."

The whole flock of former Miss A's was next, each in he own convertible, each more gaudily dressed in feather boa and ruffles and flowers than the one before.

"No limits on *their* Frederick's of Hollywood charg cards," cracked *USA Today.*

"Wouldn't those rad-fems from Santa Cruz die? Too bad *they* weren't invited to this parade." The *Inquirer* explained. "When the Miss California Pageant used to be held in Santa Cruz, the local feminists protested by marching bare-breasted. They'd kind of lost track of the real world, and were *outraged* when guys lined up with the whistles and the lewd comments."

Oh, boy. Sometimes Sam sorely missed California.

But here at hand were more marching bands, the mayor of Atlantic City, more spit-and-polish police, then the outgoing Miss A in what looked like a Carmen Miranda outfit. Another band, Atlantic City's first fire engine, and then the Girls.

Miss Alabama was sitting atop a cotton bale in a ballgown of metallic red and white gingham. Her hair was in braids. Daisy Mae in tall cotton.

Miss Alaska was swathed head to toe in white furs, surrounded by a pack of huskies.

Miss Arizona was a vision in green with a pink flowered headdress perched in a tan convertible, a human imitation of a saguaro cactus.

And so it went. Five girls in convertibles, then a band, a powerboat racing team float, Ernie the Elf, Mrs. Wheelchair America, Elvira's Finishing School, the Lions Club, then five more girls in costume.

Rae Ann was number twenty-eight. She was Scarlett robed in peach satin complete with hoops and pantaloons. Louisiana was forty-three, and Magic was done up as a Tchopitoulas Indian, one of the black Carnival organizations who wore elaborate headdresses, war paint, and spangles. She threw a doubloon at Sam, who tossed her a big kiss, and it was just then that all hell broke loose.

The Reverend Dexter Dunwoodie and his Shame Girls had been released on bail after their arrest for obstructing traffic. They'd met with the mayor and the city council, who had agreed to consider their grievances in return for the reverend's promise to leave off messing with the pageant. But there was nothing to keep them from showing up as spectators.

The rev was sitting right across the Boardwalk from Sam.

He stood now, dressed in a robe of white streaked with scarlet. Ketchup, thought Sam. His girls were in their usual burlap robes with the aluminum foil crosses, carrying their tambourines. They were a pitiful band, thought Sam. An afternoon with Elizabeth Arden would do them a world of good. Suddenly they stood, too, shaking their tambourines at Magic and shouting. "Shame!" they chorused. "Whore Woman of Babylon. Traitor to your race! Oreo!" But wait these were *white* girls.

Magic shot them a look, and when that didn't work, she yelled, "Shut up, fools."

The rev and his girls grimly unfurled a banner that read MISS AMERICA IS THE WHITE MAN'S PLAYTHING. MISS LOUISIANA GO HOME.

At that, Lucinda leaned over and said something to her driver. He shook his head no, so she reached down and pulled the emergency brake. Tires screeched for a mile and a half behind them.

But there were no rear enders. Before the parade had started Barbara Stein had given the drivers a pep talk. *"One* of my girls ever has even a suspicion of a whiplash, you can just deliver up your firstborn to be drawn and quartered on nationwide TV."

Magic looked down on the Reverend Dexter Dunwoodie from her perch atop the convertible. There was cold fire in her eyes. The crowd grew still.

"You have embarrassed me." She threw the words like ice cubes. "You have indeed *shamed* me, for your own self-interest."

"You have brought the shame upon yourself!" The reverend bellowed in his best fire and brimstone voice. "You have ignored the voice of the Lord. You have sought to glorify yourself at the expense of our children. You don't *care,"* and he dragged that word out so long you could almost see it "about the poor underprivileged black children of Atlantic City."

"And I guess you think your acting the horse's ass proves that you do!"

At that Magic's arms slowly rose toward the reverend. Light from the late afternoon sun danced off her red and silver sequins, blinding those nearby.

But others could see the reverend's eyes focus on the huge imitation diamond in the middle of Magic's bosom. "Watch the diamond, rev," she said softly. "Watch it now. Watch it. Let everything else float on by."

The reverend resisted only a moment. Then his head began to loll. His eyelids fluttered.

"Just let all your worries go. Put 'em down. Set 'em aside. Let your mind go. Relax. Relax. Relax."

The rev's ankles above his scuffed Murphy and Johnsons turned to rubber. His head lolled.

No, no, no . . . He was gibbering.

"Don't resist. Let it slide."

Shame, shame, shame . . . the girls chanted.

(Chain, chain, chain, Harry echoed in the bleachers, sitting beside Lavert.)

"Now come walk with me. Talk with me. Let's fly out into this cool early evening light."

The rev's ketchup-streaked robe flowed about him as he followed the trajectory of her hand. He climbed up to the top of the bleachers through the parting crowd, some of *them* hypnotized, too. He was high above the Boardwalk—and right at its very edge, overlooking the broad beach below.

Magic waved her hands and the rev did the Boardwalk Boogie on the narrow bleacher seat. She snapped her fingers, and his body wriggled.

Yes, the crowd said. They nodded their heads, yes, yes. Do it, Sister Magic, do it to it. Yesssssss.

Then Magic brought her hands together, her fingertips touched. Some later swore they saw blue lightning flash. She flung her hands *open* and *out* and *up* till her arms were raised above her head in celebration, jubilation. *Yes!* the crowd roared. Yes, yes, yes.

And the Reverend Dexter Dunwoodie—who never in his shucking and jiving life had ever witnessed magic, much less a miracle—jumped high up up up off the top step of the bleachers, over the edge, and flew out out out, landing on the wide sandy beach. He rolled like a ball. Magic waved her hands out out out and he got up and ran, his Johnson and Murphys barely touching the sand. He ran with his eyes closed straight into the Atlantic. There were those who thought he'd walk right on.

But a wave with his name on it caught him in its arms and

carried him out. In seconds he was beyond where the lan dropped off and the deep dark water began.

Then Magic dropped her arms to her sides. The rev san like a rock.

He didn't even fight. He just bobbed up a couple of time one, two, three, actually, and disappeared.

"Now *that,*" Lavert had said to Harry, "is a loud nigge who can't swim."

"It's a crying shame the shore patrol was so Johnny-on the-spot, don't you think?" said Harry after he climbed ou of bed to open the door for room service.

"Oh, I don't know." Sam was always much more generou when she was within reach of a cup of French roast. She' bribed the kitchen with ten dollars and a bag of the goo stuff so they didn't have to drink the hotel's usual swill. " don't think Magic wanted to kill him. She just wanted t show him."

"Well, she did that all right." Harry paused and stared a Sam over the top of his coffeecup. "What *did* she dc anyhoo? Was that just hypnosis?"

"Magic."

"No, no. What did Magic do?"

"I just told you. *Your* folks, Harry. Big Easy voudou."

"What do you mean, my folks? Magic's black, did yo notice?"

Sammy whistled the opening bars to "Old Black Magic' before Harry tackled her and wrestled her down to the bed

"You're awfully chipper this morning," he said. "Wha does this mean?"

"Happy. Means I'm happy."

"Hey! Me, too! You want to come back home and be m lady?"

"Maybe."

"Really? Really!"

"Well, you know, I've been thinking about it, and I'd lov to—except." She made a long face.

"Except what?"

"Except I can't afford it."

Harry's steel-gray eyes narrowed, the left one, which drooped just a tad, having less far to go. He smelled chicanery in the air. "You, Miss Got Rocks?"

"Well," Sam drawled, "since I have to pay you and Lavert that damned grand and a half—"

"We won! We won!" Harry stood and jumped up and down on the bed, his arms raised above his curly head like Stallone.

"You look really stupid," said Sam looking up at him. Actually he looked like a little kid in his blue-and-white striped pajama bottoms.

"We won! Oh, I can't wait to tell the big man." Then he flopped down full length, his face in hers. "I want every delicious little detail."

Sam jumped out of bed, marched into the bathroom, slammed the door, and turned on the tub. She yelled, "No way. Not a damned word. You get the money, but that's it."

Harry threw the door open. To the blue-and-white stripes he had added one of her long black stockings tied around his head pirate-fashion. Between his teeth he clenched the single red rose from their breakfast cart. "Zee lady is vairy pretty and pink in her bubble bath."

"Zee lady insists on being left alone with her sorrows. Out!" Bubbles dripped off her arm onto the bath mat.

"Zee lady is in zee company of her beloved who has nothing to do and nowhaire to go zeez morning now zat zee mystery eez solved and he eez a rich man." He dropped the rose onto her bubble-covered breast. His mouth followed the rose.

...48

WAYNE WAS BOUNCING UP AND DOWN ON THE SOLES OF HIS OLD Reeboks. He wasn't exactly thrilled about the idea of coming back to the Monopoly since he'd had to give up his security badge. A hard case in a rent-a-cop suit could go to grab ahold of him, and then who knew?

The doors opened on fifteen. Wayne looked both ways. Nobody in the hallway. Good. He headed down toward 1505.

KISS. Keep it simple, stupid. That was one of the mottos he learned from You Know Who, Mr. Big Deal Tru Franken.

Here it was, Wayne's Plan to win the friendship and influence of Michelangelo Amato. He had his palm-sized top-of-the-line Jap digital camcorder with hi-fi stereo 10x power zoom with macro and a flying erase head in the canvas bag thrown over his shoulder. He'd tell Miss New Jersey, Michelangelo's favorite girl, that what they had to do was make a tape of her walking down a runway in her gown with a crown. They could fake the runway on the Boardwalk down toward Ventnor.

In his bag he had a crown with only a few rhinestones missing he'd picked up at a pawn shop. He'd dazzle New Jersey's chaperone with his phony NBC badge and explain that the tape was for a promo for Japanese TV. It'd be beamed by satellite. It was your international beauty coverage. The Japanese were crazy for blondes, it could change New Jersey's life.

Did that sound good? Wayne liked it. Besides, these girls were all tits and no brains, so she'd believe anything. All you had to do was wind 'em up and point 'em in a direction and they'd smile and pose and walk and wave and smile.

Then, once he had the tape, he'd take it over to Michelangelo at his club. He'd paid Dean another hundred to find out where The Man hung. He'd show him the tape, explain about how he could plant the picture in the judges' brains. The Final Judges. Then Michelangelo would take him on.

Miss New Jersey would win. Wayne would be Michelangelo's right-hand man. And that would be that. Actually, Wayne could help Michelangelo in lots of ways. He'd realized, after talking with Dean, he knew a lot about The Man's business.

He'd thought, last night, about whether he really wanted that, after he came back in from the Pines, and he'd decided, why not go for it? If it didn't work out, well, the Pines were still there. But one more shot at the bright lights and the big time. Why not?

Wayne was rehearsing his speech in his head.

"Hi, I'm Wayne Ward from NBC, and I'm here this morning to—"

Christ! What was that?

Up ahead, the fire door had opened, nobody was supposed to be using that. And this tall, tall as him, skinny redheaded woman was creeping down the hall in her flats, not looking behind her. Not seeing Wayne.

She had a tape recorder in her hand! She was from some radio station probably, about to horn in on Wayne's show. He didn't have time for this. He had a lot to do today.

Or maybe the old broad had been hired by one of those other state delegations to poison Miss New Jersey!

Now, there was a possibility. Whatever she was up to, no good, that was for sure, she was creeping along, creeping, creeping, then stopping with her ear to the door.

See? If she were legit, would she be doing that? She reared back, about to do God knows what, when Wayne pounced.

The phone was ringing up in 1801.

"No," Harry murmured. "Unnmmh-unh."

"Harry."

"No!" He smothered her mouth with his.

But she slid away from him and felt for the receiver. "I can't let it ring. It could be—"

"Christ!" Harry rolled over and joined Harpo staring up at the ceiling. "It *better* be Him and not that damned Hoke!"

It was Win Kelly, Captain Win Kelly from the Atlantic County Major Crime Squad in Northfield, inland on the mainland from Atlantic City, he said, as if maybe she wanted a geography lesson. Which she didn't. Not right now.

"I hate to disturb you like this," Kelly said, letting her know he could hear another agenda in her voice, "but our mutual friend Charlie from Atlanta let me know you were in town—"

He did, did he? He had told her to stay away from the local cops.

"Charlie said you'd been sort of nosing around a fellow you thought was missing?"

"Kurt Roberts. Well, he's not. If that's what this is about, you should talk—"

"I told him we didn't know anything about any missing pageant judge, but we do have a couple of other situations here in your hotel, and I just wondered, seeing as how you'd been asking questions—" Kelly sounded like Chuck Yeager. But then, so did Charlie. It was probably something they taught ace detectives when they took those special seminars with the FBI at Quantico.

"So what's up?" Sam was motioning to Harry for her pen and notebook.

"Well, first of all there's this fellow Douglas Franken who's been reported missing by his uncle—Tru Franken. You know who he is?"

"The discount mogul who owns this hotel."

"Right. He seems pretty upset that nobody can find his nephew Dougie."

"Don't know either one of them."

"Well, the thing is, we found somebody else who'd been missing, though nobody had reported *her*, a little receptionist to Franken named Crystal. Seems to have been a special friend of Dougie's."

"Nope."

"We found her in Kurt Roberts's room, right next to yours, about an hour ago."

"Really?" Sam sat up and stared at the wall between the two suites as if she ought to be able to see right through it. "In Roberts's room? I didn't hear a thing."

A testament to the soundproofing in the Monopoly, *or,* what with the bubble bath, the rose . . .

"A maid found her this morning. Head of housekeeping called security, who called us. They should have found her last night, when they were doing turndown, but since nobody'd been in Roberts's room for a few days, I guess they were letting it slide—"

"Is she dead?"

"Crystal? Nah. She's a real good nose breather, though. She'd been tied naked to the bed with her panties in her mouth. She was pretty hungry, probably'll have a head cold, and was mad as hell. Said a fellow employee, actually *former* fellow employee, Franken just let him go, named Wayne Ward, tied her up. Said he was going to send her up some company, though nobody ever showed. We wondered if this same Ward might have something to do with Dougie's being scarce, and it's interesting Crystal was in Roberts's room. You know anything about this, by any chance?"

Wayne. Wayne Ward. She put her hand over the receiver. "Harry? What was the name of that guy who popped you in the lip?"

"Who wants to know?"

"Detective Win Kelly, Major Crime Squad."

"Oh."

"Babe, is there any chance he knew Kurt Roberts?"

"Well, it was Roberts's room he was coming out of when I ran into him that morning."

"We'll meet you downstairs in the coffeeshop in about half an hour," Sam said into the phone.

. . . 49

PEOPLE LOITERING OUTSIDE IN THE HALLWAY, IT DIDN'T MAKE AN difference. Lana wasn't in her room. She'd given her chaper one the slip.

She'd started out her morning trying on the dozen blon wigs her chaperone had found for her—that and trying t calm down.

It didn't help that her chaperone kept saying that Che wore wigs. Dolly Parton wore wigs. She didn't give a damn who wore wigs. She wanted to get her hands on the bitche who had hidden the little tiny razor blades in her brush tha had zipped handfuls of her hair right off at the roots.

She'd called Michelangelo and given him an earful abou it. No one could do this to a DeLucca. He'd said he couldn' agree more, but she thought it sounded like he was readin the paper at the same time.

Never mind. Just wait till this was all over. Her uncle John knew plenty of people all over. Those two bitches could run but they couldn't hide.

Then she tried to read some Carl Sandburg, because he was one of Marilyn's favorite writers. She thought maybe that'd help her calm down. He wrote about Lincoln, one of Marilyn's heroes. Well, Lana tried. She'd tried and tried, but she just didn't get it. All those big words didn't make her feel any better. They made her feel stupid.

Next she sent her chaperone out to get her a turkey sandwich, no, she didn't want the one from room service, and a big glass of milk.

With her gone Lana could tuck into the bottle of champagne in her minibar. She *knew* champagne calmed her down, and just like Marilyn, she drank it from a special glass with her name engraved on it.

She was sitting, just like Marilyn, wearing a bra and nothing else—she never wore panties—sipping champagne and bleaching her upper lip when suddenly she had an idea. Maybe she'd go get her evening dress from its hiding place downstairs in the wine cellar, safe from those bitches. Run through her Sugar Cane routine one more time.

So she drained her glass, found the key, threw on a pink sweater, a pair of white slacks, and her fluffiest wig. She'd take the stairs and call it exercise.

Darleen Carroll stepped off the elevator on fifteen just in time to see Lana slip through the stair door marked Exit in green lights. She called Lana's name, but Miss New Jersey kept going.

Damn! Here she'd just gotten up her nerve to apologize, and she was going to have to chase the silly twit all over the hotel.

But there was no other way around it. The elevators were too slow, and she didn't know what floor to go to. Lana could be headed anywhere.

So Darleen pounded down the stairs after her. If she'd known this was going to be a foot race, she wouldn't have worn her gold mules. "Lana! Lana!" she called. "Wait up."

Below, Lana walked faster, then picked up speed, holding on to the stair rail and almost sliding. Her heart was in her mouth. Had those bitches sent someone else after her? Well, nobody was going to catch Lana. Nobody. Nobody.

"Could you come back later?" Harry called to the maid at the door. "We'll be out in about five."

It wasn't the maid. It was Rashad. "Mr. Zack? Junior and I are here with the video we'd like to screen for you."

"Yours." Sam pointed at the door, pulling on a bright yellow sweater and black and white checked trousers. "Captain Kelly is waiting."

Harry threw open the door. "You guys don't know about calling?"

"I know that this is a heinously inappropriate intrusion upon your privacy and your time," Rashad began. Behind him Junior stood on one foot and then the other. When he saw Harry, he almost bolted.

Harry held up a hand like a traffic cop. Junior still thought he was a detective. "Stop. Junior, I'm—listen, we've got to get downstairs. I'll explain later."

Junior still didn't look too sure.

"Cool it," said Rashad. "Chill, man. The dude's not lying."

Harry said, "We'll meet you back here in an hour, but we've got to go."

"Great!" Rashad's smile was blinding. "We'll wait right here in the hall."

"Hi, Rashad. Junior." Sam smiled, bustling out past them. "So much for our leisurely morning in bed," she hissed in Harry's ear as they headed for the elevator.

"Hey! Who answered the phone? Did I answer the phone?"

"Listen, why *did* Wayne Ward slug you in the mouth? And why does Junior think you're a cop?"

Harry gave her his professional insurance investigator shrug.

By God, Darleen said to herself, panting, seriously out of breath, she was going to catch this bimbo and apologize to her if it was the last thing she ever did.

And it might be. Even the workouts with Guido, her personal trainer in Newport Beach, hadn't prepared her to run down fifteen flights of stairs in her high heels, which is why she'd kicked them off on fourteen.

Lana made it through the stairway door on the ground floor about thirty seconds ahead of her. It was a good thing the girl had all that shiny platinum hair—which Darleen spied at the end of the hall up ahead flashing past a sign that said Employees Only.

...50

This was even better than he'd planned. Wayne pulled his red Mustang right up to the front door of Va Bene. *This* was super.

The doorman was trying to wave him away, but Wayne just ignored his signal, stepping out of his car, right up in the man's face.

"I'm here to see Mr. Amato."

The doorman took in Wayne's cap, on backward so it read *Wayne Delivers,* his T-shirt, tattered jeans, and Reeboks. Wayne knew that look. Guy cleared four-fifty an hour, trying to make him feel like dirt. Like salesclerks in fancy department stores. Now that was one thing about the help in FrankFairs. Mr. You Know Who insisted that they treat *everyone* as if they were absolutely bursting with innate worth. Which they were, of course—except this bozo, who was about to be full of something else in about half a second.

"No way," the doorman said.

"No way what? No way Mr. Amato's here or no way you're going to let me see him?"

"Neither. Beat it."

So Wayne slammed the butt of his .38 into the side of the guy's head and stepped over him.

Win Kelly was a big man with a thick shock of prematurely white hair who spent a lot of time tucking his shirttail back into his gray slacks.

He asked questions in that dry Chuck Yeager voice, and, like Charlie, still had some humor in his blue eyes. That was a wonderment, Sam thought, after all they'd seen. Kelly had mentioned that he used to be with New York City Vice until he grew up and realized he didn't need to beat up on himself that bad every day just to think he'd done some good.

It was a philosophy Sam found interesting.

"So, I guess we don't need to go borrowing trouble, worrying about this Roberts, too, if this," he looked at his notebook, "Cindy Lou Jacklin can vouch for his being safe and sound in the Bahamas."

"Well," said Harry, as much as he hated to, "you know, nobody ever did exactly follow up on that."

What was he getting at? Well, they'd just taken old Cindy's word for it, hadn't they? No one had seriously considered that Cindy Lou might be lying.

Damn! Damn and double damn!

Win Kelly shrugged. Well, anyhow, they'd put out an APB on this Wayne Ward, who, by the way, had a very interesting sheet and shouldn't have been employed in a casino hotel anyway, the Gambling Commission being very strict about employees' priors, even if they weren't handling money.

What exactly did Wayne do here? Sam was curious.

It was funny about that, said Kelly. Tru Franken, and an odd bird *he* was, didn't want to get very specific, but Kelly had asked to see his setup. Ward did surveillance, which all the casinos did to some degree, watching the action on the gambling floors—which was perfectly kosher. But Ward took it a few steps further. Kelly was talking about video cameras, taping, esoteric high tech stuff. Voice-overs.

Voices? Did he say voices?

Who *was* that woman? Lana was running as fast as she could through the back-of-the-house. Maybe she ought to stop and ask one of the busboys for help.

But she was almost to Mr. Franken's private wine cellar where her dress was hanging. Though she'd have to say when she'd tucked her dress in there yesterday with the man who was a friend of Michelangelo's, it looked to her like most of the stuff on the floor wasn't wine, but orange pop.

Now she only had to make it behind the big green door up ahead and then turn to the right, unlock the wine cellar with the key on the chain around her neck, and she was home free. Then she'd grab her dress and wait inside for the crazy lady to get lost.

* * *

"I'm so sorry," said Vic, the captain who always took care of Michelangelo. "I hate to disturb you, but there is this man outside who insists that he has an appointment. I'm sure he doesn't, Mr. Amato." Vic rolled his eyes. "But before we send him away, I thought you ought to know—"

Ma was dining alone today. He'd just finished a plate of spedini, one of his favorites. Italian bread with melted mozzarella smothered in a light anchovy sauce. It wasn't good for his arteries, but it was good for his soul. That, with a glass of dolcetto, slightly chilled. Then a green salad with a small bottle of San Pellegrino. A little espresso.

The good food took his mind off his problems. Sometimes Michelangelo felt that the weight of the whole world rested on his shoulders. Well, *his* world, anyway.

The boys who worked lookout said his mom was out of the house every day. He knew there was something going on they were afraid to tell him. And he wasn't sure he wanted to know.

Then there was Lana, a real pain in the butt if there ever was one. Who'd she think she was, Vito Corleone, ordering hits left and right? *Those girls took my dress; do 'em.* On the other hand, she was Big John's niece, and under Ma's protection. It was hard to know where the boundaries might lie in Big John's eyes.

One thing he'd decided, Miss DeLucca getting on his nerves, the hell with a fix. There was no money changing hands on the pageant anyway, so it wasn't like he was going to make anything except some goodwill with Big John. For that there were other avenues that were less complicated.

But the next thing he knows, Angelo Pizza calls him up and says not to worry, he's heard Ma wants the girl to win, he's got it wired.

What the hell did that mean? Angelo was a good man, but Ma would rather he didn't branch out on his own. Ange hadn't served all that time in Danbury for having New Jersey's most creative criminal mind, even when he was young. And what with Ma's recently expanded bookmaking business, the heavy investments in IBM equipment and several telecommunications concerns, he wasn't interested in bringing any unnecessary attention to himself. Where there was smoke there was fire, in the feds' eyes, and Ma had no intention of getting burned.

And now, *now,* there's strangers tracking him to his club. A man couldn't enjoy a quiet meal without some jerkoff interrupting him.

"Bring him in," said Ma. Maybe this was the time to make an example. Show what respect demanded. Word would get out on the street, and at least he could eat a lunch in peace.

Lana was standing right in front of the wine cellar door. The little woman, whoever she was, with the multicolored hair piled up on top of her head, was breathing right down her neck.

"Lana!" she screamed, practically in her ear. "Lana, wait!"

Wait, her ass. Lana leaned over, pressed her chest right up against the lock, fiddled with the key—the chain she was wearing it on around her neck was just long enough—click, got it, great, jerked open the door.

"Wait! Wait! There's something I've got to tell you!"

Lana put one foot in the door, turned, and grabbed at what was closest, anything to get this broad off her tail, reached up and snatched off her long blond wig and tossed it at the woman's face.

"Ouch!" Darleen yelped. For Lana had grabbed the key too. The chain broke and the key popped Darleen right in the mouth.

Lana slammed the door shut. Whew! Safe at last. Maybe there *was* a point to the chaperones after all. At least they kept the crazies off.

"So you see," Wayne had settled himself down at the table in Ma's private dining room as if he'd been invited, "I'll make the tape of your girl like she's taking her victory walk down the runway, and then I'll implant it in the judges' heads, and your Miss New Jersey will win."

"Really?" Ma used his warm voice. He wanted to keep this bugger talking until Willie, who was out in the car, ould answer the beeper. Besides, this was pretty interesting ıfo—from a nut case.

"Yeah, and it works, all this stuff works. It's just like, well, ou know, you use a lot of electronic stuff in your business. sn't it great what you can do these days?"

That stopped Ma cold. What did this freak show know bout *his* business?

"Yeah, you know, I was talking with a guy one day who aid all the bookmaking in town was high tech. I didn't elieve him, so I tried to tap into it, and I have to give it to ou, man. That call-forwarding from the dummy offices to our central office, wow! And the volume you handle on that nainframe is terrific."

"You don't say."

"Hey, I'm impressed. And listen, I brought you something hat just popped up. Kind of a surprise, you know. This hing I stumbled into, it's like this pageant business could be spy novel, you know what I mean? They've got people all ver the place doing tricks, planting stuff, I don't know what ll they're up to. And, of course, it's hard to get 'em to talk, ut I thought that might be more up your alley."

"What do you mean?"

Wayne rubbed his hands together. He was standing off and watching himself, in a way. It was just like in the movies. "You're gonna love this! I caught this broad trying to sneak into your Miss New Jersey's room, so I nabbed her. I've got her outside."

"Where outside?"

"In the trunk of my Mustang. You want to come out and see?"

Well, screw it, Darleen Carroll thought, fingering her cut lip. It wasn't worth a cracked front tooth to apologize to a silly little whore who was doing your husband.

She hoped *all* Miss New Jersey's hair fell out and her boobs sagged and her butt dropped. Overnight.

Shoeless and sweaty in her turquoise silk big shirt and black capri pants, Darleen retraced her steps back into the Monopoly's lobby.

Or almost.

Just before that last turn of the hallway, there was a bi Phoenix palm in a blue ceramic Chinese pot decorated wit white golden-eyed swans. Darleen the decorator was wor dering if the pot had come from mainland China and ho much it would cost her in volume, when a hand reached ou from behind the palm and grabbed her.

Inside the wine cellar, Lana stripped off her pink sweate white slacks, and bra and slipped into her evening gow There were those who would say that her dress was too rac for Miss America, but Lana wasn't one of them. The fron didn't show a thing. It was cut high, and there were *lots* c beads and sequins over her boobs. Of course, in this col cellar, her nipples were a problem, but tonight she'd do th old Band-Aid number. The back of the dress was something dipping to below those two cute little dimples just above he butt.

But the point was, it was almost an exact copy of the dres Marilyn had worn when she sang the same song in *Som Like It Hot*. Lana was *doing* Marilyn, so it was okay. Right What was really super was how close this dress was to th original. Her lucky original. The one that was ripped off.

Just thinking about that made Lana mad all over again that someone would have the nerve! Her eyes went out o focus, seeing the faces of Magic and Connors. She'd ge them for this. Oh, yes, she'd get them. But then she saw wha she'd been staring at. Stacked in the mahogany shelve above the orange pop were cases of nothing but the best. Sh ran her fingers across a few bottles, then pulled out a Veuv Cliquot. No glasses, but what the heck? One of the nic things about champagne was you didn't need a corkscrew.

"Tell you what," Ma said, folding his napkin. "Your car's out front? Why don't you drive it through the alleyway to the side of the club around to the back? There's a private parking lot behind the back door. I'll meet you there."

"Fine and dandy." Wayne was feeling good, sounding

more like Mr. You Know Who all the time. Letting those slick phrases he'd learned from him just roll right off his tongue. "Speaking of alleys, this'll be right up yours. You're gonna love it, I guarandamntee you."

"I'm sure." Ma nodded at Willie, who'd just stepped to the dining room door.

Rashad was all over the place in the living room of Sam and Harry's suite, arranging chairs, plumping pillows, slipping the tape into the VCR. "Hey, did you bring any popcorn?" Harry asked.

"Oh, my God." Rashad slapped himself in the forehead. "I forgot it. I can call room service."

"He's teasing," said Sam. "Calm down, Rashad. Now tell us what this is about." Then she leaned over and whispered to Harry, "This better not take long. I want to get moving on this Wayne Ward thing."

"Well. Harrumph." Rashad cleared his throat and looked over at Junior, who gave him the high sign. Rashad was wearing full formal dress this morning, down to the gray spats. Junior was more informally attired, but cool.

Whatever they lacked in filmmaking skills they more than compensated for in style, thought Harry. These two would land buttered side up.

Rashad began to explain about the film's subject, Bette Cooper, Miss Bertram Island, New Jersey, who'd decided in the middle of the night, after being crowned Miss America 1937, that she'd just as soon pass. And Lou Off, the Atlantic City socialite, who'd helped her make her grand escape.

Junior added, "That part's true. What we've done, though, is tie it in with a fictional gangster story that takes place in the Pine Barrens. You know, kind of a film noir. The beautiful versus the bad. Innocence played against evil."

Rashad stared at his normally silent partner, then said, "Why don't we just roll it for you?"

And so they did.

On the TV screen Rachel Rose shimmied down a fire escape

and landed in a convertible. Junior, playing Lou Off, dro her, as Bette, still sniveling with a terrible head cold, dow along a beach road. He was telling her how he was sure she wa doing the right thing. The Miss America business was just tc gauche. He headed toward Margate and a fishing boat he ha docked there. As the sun rose on Sunday morning and th Steel Pier where the Miss America festivities were about to b thrown into turmoil by the disappearance of its Cinderell the fishing boat headed north toward that same pier, where would dock.

"Neat!" Harry exclaimed. "Did this really happen?"

"Every jot," Rashad replied.

Darleen awoke to total darkness. At first, she thougl she'd gone blind.

Then she realized that she was in a storeroom of som kind. It smelled of cheese.

"Let me out of here," she shouted and kicked the doc with her bare foot.

"Hold your horses!"

The door opened slowly, and Darleen blinked. At first sh couldn't make out a thing in the bright light. But then sh focused. It was the old guy with the windbreaker and th limp who'd been following her.

"So, how much," he said in a gravelly voice, "do yo think your husband Billy loves you, Mrs. Carroll?"

Oh shit. If *that* was the scam, she was a goner.

. . . 51

INSIDE THE WINE CELLAR, LANA HAD FINISHED PRACTICING TH boop-boop-a-doop routine she'd perform tonight. She wa good. She was *sure* she'd be one of the ten finalists. The she'd changed back into her pink sweater and white pant and taken a little nap.

Now she was rested and relaxed and ready to go back upstairs and face her chaperone, who would be mad as hell, but so what?

Lana stood and stretched like a kitty, grabbed her dress, and reached for the door.

But it was locked.

She tried turning the knob to the right, to the left. Nothing.

That was because the dead bolt had to be unlocked from the inside, and Lana didn't have the key.

She'd smacked Darleen Carroll in the mouth with it and then slammed the door.

"Okay, open it up," said Michelangelo. Willie was looking over his shoulder, though there was no one else in Va Bene's parking lot. The Lincoln was pulled up right beside the red Mustang.

Wayne licked his lips. Oh, this was going to be so good. Michelangelo was going to be so pleased. He could just tell by the look in the man's eyes. He wanted to make this last as long as possible.

"Now," said Michelangelo.

Okay, okay. For an Italian, the man sure didn't have much of a sense of drama. Wayne unlocked the trunk and paused with the lid still down. "She says she doesn't know anything."

"Open it!" Michelangelo growled.

And his manners weren't nearly as good as Mr. You Know Who's. But Wayne could adjust. Wayne could get used to his style. It was just a matter of time.

Wayne flipped up the lid. There was the tall redheaded woman, bound and gagged. But she wasn't moving at all.

"This is great stuff!" Harry exclaimed at the video. "You guys are really good!"

Junior and Rashad beamed with pride in the darkened hotel room. The show was on hold.

"So that's what they really did?" asked Sam. "They

docked right there beside the pier where the Miss America festivities were supposed to be held? While people were looking for Bette Cooper everywhere else? It's like 'The Purloined Letter.' "

"Exactly," Rashad grinned. "Now, do you want to see the rest?" He punched the remote button again. "This is the second intercut of the subplot. You saw the red Mustang earlier driving into the Pines. Now here's the action."

"Get me out of here!" Lana screamed. She had great lungs from her singing lessons. "Help! Help!"

But no one heard her. The walls of the wine cellar were two feet thick with heavy insulation.

Lana plopped down on a case of orange pop and buried her face in her hands. This couldn't be happening to her. She was Lana DeLucca of the Sea Girt DeLuccas. Her daddy was an underboss. She'd won swimsuit. She was going to make ten. She had an excellent shot at taking the crown. Shit like this didn't happen to Miss America finalists.

"I'm going to smell like a pizza," Darleen said, "if you don't get me out of here."

"You're awfully cool for a lady who's being held for ransom." Angelo pulled up a chair beside her and handed her a little glass of Chianti.

"If you think Billy's got any money, you might as well shoot me now."

"I know Billy ain't got no money. He owes *me* money."

"So *you're* the loan shark. That's what this is all about?"

"Sort of."

"Look. How much is he into you for? I run my own business. I have some funds."

Angelo reached over and patted her hand. "Nice thought, but it don't work that way. Listen, you hungry? You can have some pizza. Or we'll make you some noodles. See, the way this happens, Billy's gonna do me a little favor, we're gonna let you go."

Darleen sighed. "I wouldn't count on it."

* * *

"She's dead," said Michelangelo, staring into the trunk.

"Oh, well, listen. These things happen. This was just a little added extra attraction. But, what do you think? I'll go get Miss New Jersey, make the tape, plant it in the judges' rooms. Though"—Wayne pushed his Monopoly Special Services hat further back on his head. His aviator glasses were fogged. And suddenly he realized that he'd lost it somewhere in a little blip, like the shock treatments. His plan didn't make sense. There was *no time* for subliminals to kick in—"maybe we ought to do something else, too. You got any ideas?"

"Yes, as a matter of fact I do," said Michelangelo, turning and giving Willie a small nod. "I tell you what. Willie here is going to drive you in my car over to the Ventnor office. I'll stay here for a few minutes and make arrangements to have this," he gestured at the Mustang's trunk, "taken care of, and then I'll join you over there. Your car will be fine." He placed a heavy hand on Wayne's shoulder. "Don't worry about it."

"Great! Great!" Wayne was really excited. Things were going even better than he'd hoped.

"Oh, my God!" said Sam.

Rashad flipped Junior a look. This was going really swell. Both Harry and Sam loved the video. Especially this scary part they'd spliced in with the guys out in the Pines. Like the old Miss America footage they'd used—no need to reinvent the wheel when the stuff was at hand. Especially when you were under the gun of a deadline.

"Do you *know* who that is?" Sam asked.

"Yeah," said Rashad. "That's the dude who pushed Junior in the swimming pool, the one who's playing dead. He's a photographer—not a bad actor, either, huh? The other one is this spaced-out nerd who works in the Monopoly. Junior's mom knows him, right, Junior?"

"Yeah," Junior nodded. But he was getting a little nervous. Sam and Harry were acting weird. He bet they knew something about the equipment being lifted. He was beginning to wonder if Harry wasn't lying about the cop business.

"It's Wayne Ward, isn't it, Harry?" said Sam.

Harry nodded, mesmerized by the sight of Wayne rolling Kurt Roberts's body over and over through pine needles, then down a bank and into a river of dark water. "That's Wayne, all right." Then he turned to the two young men. "Hey, guys, where'd you get this footage?"

Damn, thought Junior.

. . . 52

AT NINE O'CLOCK, AN HOUR BEFORE THE BROADCAST OF THE MISS America Pageant live from Atlantic City, Michelangelo and Willie were driving through Ducktown in the Lincoln. Michelangelo picked up the phone.

"Ma?" It was Petey from the Ventnor office. "Listen, a call came in from Vince over at the club. There's this woman, Stein or something, from Convention Hall trying to reach you. She practically called the cops, trying to track you down. I thought you'd want to know."

"What's it about?"

"Something about Miss New Jersey? Missing in action? I don't know what the hell they're talking about, boss. You want the woman's number?"

Goddamnit! Ma slammed the receiver so hard Willie jumped in the front seat.

"That little bimbo! Now she's missing. Pageant's looking for her, looking for me. Remind me never to get mixed up in this kind of business again, Willie."

So where did Ma want Willie to take him? Did he want to forget going by Tommy's?

No. It was only a block. They'd go see what Angelo Pizza wanted first.

Billy Carroll tripped over his own words introducing the governor of New Jersey in the preshow up on the big stage.

"Stuttering. God, he's worse than ever," Sam said to the *Inquirer* from their vantage point rampside. "And his color's bad." Had he caught Gary Collins's stomach flu? Was he going to faint halfway through the show?

The *Inquirer* predicted a rocky evening. Then, looking over Sam's shoulder, her eyes widened. "Uh-oh. Uh-oh."

Sam turned. No. Please, no. She didn't have the strength.

Sam was already running on pure adrenaline. This beauty business had turned out to be so much more exhausting than she'd ever dreamed.

Not to mention that she and Harry had spent a good part of the day with Rashad and Junior and Captain Kelly who wanted to hear *everything* they knew, from the top. Meanwhile, he said, the APB on Wayne Ward hadn't turned up a thing. Wayne had probably split.

Later, Kelly got back to her. He was a nice man. Cindy Lou had copped to making it up about Roberts in the Bahamas. "Said she did it to get you off her butt." Sam could hear his wry grin. Not funny. Not funny at all, she'd been fifteen years in the business and had taken the woman's word just like that. Kelly had sent a man up to Cindy Lou's room to see what the hell this voice business was she kept yapping about. And they'd sent a crime scene team off to the Pine Barrens. Nothing there yet.

Then Rae Ann called. She wanted to know if Sam was still interested in a last interview before the big show.

It had been worth the time.

Rae Ann met her in the pressroom in Convention Hall. She'd brought along the field director for the Georgia state pageant. Ron Templeton was tall, dark, handsome—and a flight attendant who lived in Dallas. But he grew up in Valdosta, and his heart lay with the Peach State and its pageant, and flying back was no big deal. He was responsible for coordinating the efforts of twelve local pageants. Pageants were his hobby, his passion, his religion, his life. All his best friends were into pageants. "We all love each other," said Ron. "It's just like when I used to do local theater. Romance, the spectacle, the magic of fairy tales come true. Don't you love fairy tales?"

Sam left them visualizing victory and raced over to the trade show to pick up a package from Jeannie Carpenter, the bugle bead lady, before the sales floor shut down for good at five.

Back in the hotel room, she'd sprawled on her bed to catch her breath when Big Gloria pounded on the door. The cops were still holding Junior! And Rashad!

It took Sam half an hour to calm her down, explain that Kelly had promised to get the wallet-snatching and burglary, which had come out as the boys had told their tale, reduced to probation. All Gloria and Rashad's folks had to do was go sign for them.

In the end, Harry had poured Gloria a couple of shots of Jack Daniel's, which worked better than the explanations, then called Lavert to drive her over to Northfield Barracks.

Seven-thirty and counting, Sam had already blown off the Old South Ball. She grabbed a ham sandwich, a quick shower, and tossed on her turquoise Carnival gown.

"Gorgeous as the first time I laid eyes on you," said Harry, buttoning the studs on his tuxedo shirt. "Sazerac Bar of the Roosevelt."

"The first time was out at the airport, and I was wearing a skirt and sweater. Black, as I remember."

She had to be tired, she was being so picky. Harry snuggled up behind her and gave her a hug.

"I'm sorry I'm being such a grump. I'm wrung out. I can't *wait* to get out of this town."

"You're going to let Captain Kelly catch Wayne Ward on his own? Not going to stay and tell him how?"

Sam ignored the sarcasm. "I've told him all I know. Now all I want is to go home and lie down. Not look at any beauty queens for maybe the rest of my life."

Given that, Sam was in no mood for Mary Frances DeLaughter, Ph.D., heading down the Convention Hall aisle straight at her.

"Samantha Adams!" The woman screamed at the top of her lungs. "I have such a scoop for you!"

Scoop. Right.

"You *what?*" Michelangelo shouted.

"It's gonna work like a charm, Ma. Trust me."

He'd kidnapped the emcee's wife? Unbelievable.

"I didn't hurt her. She's a nice woman. Real cooperative. She's right here."

Angelo opened Tommy's pantry door and a tousled Darleen Carroll stepped out in her bare feet.

She was the cutest thing Michelangelo Amato had ever laid eyes on. She was an angel. She was perfect. His heart soared. He'd do anything to win her. Anything. Just name it.

"*Who* grabbed you?" Sam was writing as fast as she could while glaring at the *Inquirer* and *USA Today* over her shoulder. It was *her* story. "You pick up that phone," she said to the *Inquirer,* "before I can file this, your ass is grass."

"That's what I'm telling you," said Mary Frances. "I don't know. I was standing in front of Miss New Jersey's door, about to knock, when he grabbed me."

"And the next thing you remember?"

"I was tied up in this dark place. I realized later, of course, it was a car trunk."

"How much later?"

"I don't know exactly. It was around ten this morning, I guess, when I was in the hotel—and then—gee, I guess it must have been about two or so when they pulled me out."

"Who's they?"

"I never saw them. Two men, I was still blindfolded. They said I would be all right, they would help me, but they didn't want to get involved. They carried me inside in a chair. I couldn't walk at first."

"Inside where?"

"They didn't take off the blindfold. I don't know."

"Jesus Christ, Mary Frances!"

"Well, *you* should have been there. You wouldn't quibble

about a little thing like a blindfold if somebody pulled you out of a car trunk, I can tell you that!"

She had a point. But what kind of story was this, Mary Frances a witness to her own kidnapping, and she didn't know jack. Though it didn't help to snap at her. Sam apologized. Then what?

"They untied me. Somebody with big soft hands massaged my wrists and ankles. Then they gave me some wine. After a while, they loaded me into a car and drove me somewhere. Then they put me in another car, then in a taxi that brought me back to the hotel."

"You were in two cars and a taxi?"

"Yes. It was in the taxi that the driver said to me, 'Lady, you can take your blindfold off now.' So I did."

"What kind of taxi?"

"A white one. I was about six blocks from the Monopoly on Atlantic Avenue."

Sam sighed, "Mary Frances, why do you think you were kidnapped?"

"I have no earthly idea." She shrugged. It wasn't *her* fault.

"And did you hear any names at all during this whole thing?"

Mary Frances paused for a minute. Up on the big stage, Billy Carroll was in the middle of a bad rendition of "Mack the Knife" when he forgot the words. Sam had never seen a professional entertainer so nervous. Then Mary Frances said yes.

"Yes, I heard one name. The man who spoke first, who had a very nice voice, a *warm* voice, do you know what I mean, once he said to somebody else, 'Don't worry. That Ward's ticket is punched.' I think Ward was someone's name, don't you?"

"Yes, I do." Sam was holding her breath. This was connected to Wayne somehow. How? "What did the police say when you told them that, Mary Frances?"

"Police?"

It wasn't possible. "You just came from the police, didn't you?"

"I did not. When I was mugged they didn't do a damned

thing except waste my time. I helped this policeman fill out a dozen reports, and he never even had the courtesy to call me back. They didn't find my wallet or my tape recorder, so I was set back in my research. So this time, I said to myself, forget it, Mary Frances. You're not hurt. And you're not missing the finals. I'm seeing Miss America crowned if it kills me!"

Sam and the *Inquirer* and *USA Today* stared at one another over Mary Frances's head. Then Sam excused herself. She had to make a couple of phone calls.

Back in the dressing room, all hell had broken loose. "You mean we won't go on?" Miss Alaska was practically hysterical. "If they can't find her, we won't go on? But what will we do?" Then the young lady from the frozen North got down on her hands and knees and searched under the dressing table as if Miss New Jersey might be hiding there. Just out of spite.

"I think we should pray," said Rae Ann.

"Better yet, let's form a posse and go round her up," said Connors. "She's probably just shacked up somewhere and lost track of time."

"No," said Magic with *that* look on her face. "She's not shacked up. I think she's *locked* up somewhere. Somewhere close by." She took a deep breath. "I smell grapes."

"This was a terrible misunderstanding," said Michelangelo, handing Darleen into the back seat of the Lincoln. "Angelo will pay for this."

"Oh, well," Darleen said, smiling from up under her eyelashes at the darkly handsome semi-mobster who made her heart race like she was sixteen again. "People make mistakes. I don't think you should be too hard on him. You do know why he did it, don't you?"

Ma directed Willie to take them to Convention Hall. Then, he answered Darleen, "No, I don't, and I don't care. He could have *hurt* you. The man's dangerous."

"Well, he treated me like a newborn babe, except, of course, when he grabbed me. But what he said was, he thought if he could fix it so Miss New Jersey would win, you'd be happy and wouldn't mind if he wooed your mother."

Ma slammed his fist down on the seat between them. Darleen jumped, and he was embarrassed. Not a good start at turning over a new leaf, but this was blood. "He can forget my mother."

"Now," Darleen soothed, "you shouldn't be like that. He told me all about how he's loved her since he was sixteen years old. Don't you think it's time you let him have his chance? Besides, he *said* she loves him, too."

Michelangelo shrugged. She might be an angel, but she wasn't Italian. She didn't understand.

"I think it's awful," Darleen went on like she was talking about the weather, "when people are close-minded. When they don't grow. Never change." Then she looked down at her feet and wiggled her bare toes. Could he drop her by the Monopoly? She needed to get some shoes before she went to the show. Then, she added under her breath, first thing in the morning, she was going to call her lawyer, start her divorce.

Divorce. What a beautiful word. "Willie," he tapped on the glass. "The Monopoly."

"Sure, boss. But, you forgot about Lana?"

Oh, shit! Oh, shoot! He had. Not that he much cared—not now. "Miss New Jersey," he explained to his dear heart, "she's missing in action."

"I beg your pardon?"

"Disappeared. No one can find her. Barbara Stein with the pageant called me because I'm—sort of Lana's sponsor. You'll excuse me, I've got to get in touch with that Barbara Stein." Ma reached for the phone, but stopped when Darleen grabbed his arm.

"Oh, my God, Michelangelo! My God!"

Melanie, who weighed three hundred pounds, put down the joint she was smoking and turned to Sylvester, the Monopoly's other switchboard operator. "I've got a woman here, says she's Miss Louisiana and says we've got Miss New Jersey locked in the wine cellar. Is that like the one about Prince Albert in the can?"

"I don't know." Sylvester, who worked another job as a bartender and had heard it all, shrugged. "I've got one too, on my line, says the same thing. Must be *some* party. *He* says she's in Franken's personal cellar. *Real* pushy. I hate that type. Wants me to call the g.m. and says I better do it now. What do you think, Mel?"

"We'll flip. Heads, we get her out. Tails, let the bitch rot. I think this pageant stuff is so stupid anyway. I mean, you ever see any *fat* girls up there?"

Billy Carroll was sweating bullets. It wasn't bad enough he had the Angelo thing to worry about. And Darleen, they'd nabbed her. Christ! His kneecaps were one thing, but Angelo was threatening to off his wife if he didn't do him the favor he'd promised.

And now, they're telling him backstage that the show might be delayed for a few minutes because one of the girls is missing. But it can't be delayed! It's live! He'd have to improvise! Jesus, Mary, and Joseph! That time a couple of years ago, the judges couldn't decide who the winner was, and Gary Collins had to fill in like ten minutes. Talk about your twisting in the wind. It was one of the worst things he'd ever seen in his life. Even Collins's wife, that Mary Ann Mobley, was making fun of him. And if Collins couldn't do it—Christ! Was Phyllis George going to help him out? *That'd* be a cold day in hell. A *few* minutes of live airtime would be the end of his career. The end of his professional life. He'd never work again. He'd die. Once he paid off all his gambling debts, he wouldn't have a cent. He'd starve to death. What would he do?

Of course, there *was* Darleen's money. Which he'd inherit. If she died.

Outside Convention Hall, fireworks exploded and lighted the summer sky. Inside, at the stroke of ten (Thank you,

God, Billy Carroll breathed) Eastern Standard Time, the music rose. Klieg lights raked an audience glittering with diamonds and cubic zircons.

In his plummiest tones an unseen announcer proclaimed: "The *Miss America* Pageant! Ladies and gentlemen! Something *fabulous* is happening here tonight!"

The big gold curtain parted on the Miss America dancers, who soft-shoed and sang their way through the now-familiar routine to strains of Leonard Bernstein's "Tonight." The back curtain lifted, and there they were. The Miss America finalists, *all* fifty of them.

Over at the Monopoly the flip of the coin had turned up heads, and Lana DeLucca had been rescued from Tru Franken's private wine cellar in time to slap on a wig, her makeup, and a short sheath of blue and off-white, and there she was parading down the runway singing, smiling, waving —no one the wiser.

The energy in the auditorium was high and hot. The *Inquirer* turned to Sam. "Okay, scout's honor, the truth. Now aren't you among the converted?"

Sam shook her head. "Afraid not."

"But you tear up every night. I've watched you!"

Sam waved at Rae Ann. Magic. Lana. Connors. "And I told you, I cry at telephone commercials on TV, too. When they reach out and touch someone, I go to pieces. This?" She gestured up at the girls on the ramp. "It's the same thing. Pretty girls, sincere as hell, breaking their butts, it pushes a button. But still, it's silly. And there's more downside than up, I think, coaching them to make themselves over into a mold."

"But they're *themselves.* They're told to be themselves."

"Oh, honey. Just *look.*"

There they were. Fifty Barbies, 5′7″, 117 pounds, 35-22-35, in different flavors. Sincere and earnest as all get out.

"You lose the bet. *However—*" and then Sam pulled a gift-wrapped package from beneath her chair. "I can't tell you how much I appreciate your coaching, and I couldn't have written my stories without you."

Inside the box was a satin baseball jacket covered in red, white, and blue sequins. Emblazoned across the back were the words *Miss America Pageant.*

"The best Jeannie Carpenter's elves could provide on such short notice." Sam smiled. "I hope it fits."

Michelangelo was surprised. When Darleen returned from her hotel room to the Lincoln where he and Willie were waiting, she'd changed into gray sweats and little red running shoes. She leaned her head in. "I've decided I don't want to go to the pageant. I'd rather go for a long walk than sit in the audience waiting to see what my husband decides about saving my life." Angelo had explained the entire scam to her—and the possible consequences.

"I can get a message to Billy, it's all off," said Ma.

"No," Darleen shook her head. "Let it go."

"Then come on, get in. You don't want to walk by yourself this late at night. It's not safe."

Nope. She was going to walk.

Michelangelo sighed and heaved himself out of the heavy car. He hated walking on the Boardwalk. The sea air was bad for his sinuses.

"You ought to try the West Coast," Darleen smiled. "It's a lot nicer."

Up on the big stage, the former Miss Americas had paraded up and down. The about-to-be-former Miss A had taken a turn. The preliminary judges had stood for bows. So now the second-biggest moment of the evening had arrived, the announcement of the ten semifinalists.

The girls, still dressed in their short dresses of fuchsia, blue, and off-white, filled the stage. Lynn Anderson, the about-to-be-former Miss America, handed the envelope containing ten names to Phyllis and Billy.

"You don't know how it feels until you're standing up there." Phyllis was bouncing with excitement. "You can't wait to hear those names, so read them, Billy!"

Pushy bitch. Had to get those last two cents in. But oh,

Jesus, what if Miss New Jersey hadn't made ten? *Then* what would he do? Would Angelo hold him responsible? He scanned the list quickly, but not fast enough. Phyllis gave him a little nudge. "Billy?"

"Now, they're *not* in alphabetical order, folks," he said. "Here we go!"

"Let's swap ballots," the *Inquirer* commanded Sam and *USA Today*. "Whoever picked the most wins fifty."

The girl never stopped. She was as bad as Harry.

"Miss California!" Billy shouted. The crowd of girls on three risers parted and a tall blonde, tearful and beaming, made her way out of the pack. "Thank you," she mouthed to the preliminary judges, her hands out, fingertips toward them as she passed.

"Dr. DeLaughter?" A tall young man in a navy blazer and gray pants was leaning over the back of the press section. "Which one of you is Dr. DeLaughter?"

"Miss Florida!" The short blonde shook her fists in victory and pranced across the stage to join Miss California.

Mary Frances looked straight ahead, ignoring the plainclothes detective. Sam pointed at the back of the professor's head.

"Miss Texas!" Connors had made the cut! Sam felt her mouth go dry. She *did* care.

"Ma'am? I'm afraid I'm going to have to ask you to come with me. We need to ask you some questions."

"Miss Louisiana!"

Behind her Sam could hear Lavert's "All right, Magic!" even over the thundering applause. Big Gloria and Junior and Rachel Rose were on their feet—this being Junior's last Atlantic City hurrah before Gloria hauled him off to New Orleans. Forget Newport Beach, Big Gloria had said to Rachel Rose's tears. They were headed home. But there were always letters. Phones. Planes.

Over on the other side of the ramp, Rashad, who'd talked his way into the photographers' section, was filming like crazy. His next feature was on black magic. Or Black Magic. He hadn't decided.

"Miss Georgia!" Sam was on her feet screaming, Way to

go! Tears poured down Rae Ann's face as she joined the other four semifinalists.

Sam was crying too. She was excited! Oh, it was too bad Hoke wasn't watching. He'd said he couldn't stand it. Sam was to call him when it was all over.

"I'm not leaving until this is over!" Mary Frances never turned her head to look at the young man.

"Miss New Jersey!"

As Lana wiggled across the stage in a new version of the Jersey Bounce, the crowd lost it. Home state girl makes ten!!!! Cowbells rang and streamers filled the air.

"I'm afraid Captain Kelly really needs to speak with you right now about what happened to you this afternoon." The young man was trying to keep his voice low, but firm.

"Later," Mary Frances snapped.

"Ma'am, if you don't come with me now, I may have to arrest you."

"Miss Hawaii!" Orchid leis flew.

"Arrest me?!"

"Miss South Carolina!"

"Mary Frances, I think you ought to go with him. This is serious business," said Sam.

"Miss Colorado!"

"You! You would! You told on me. You told them about the kidnapping! I know you did!"

"What do you mean?" Sam smiled her most innocent smile. It was interesting, what a pleasure it was watching the woman who'd insulted her, called her a nobody, get hauled out for questioning by this nice young cop. But after all. This *was* serious business. This was about Wayne Ward.

"And Miss Ohio!"

"I hate you! I hate your guts!" Mary Frances shouted at Sam as the young cop took her arm.

Sam waved bye-bye. Then she found Harry and Lavert in the crowd and gave them the high sign. Rae Ann and Magic and Connors. Not to mention Lana. This was *great.*

"You won!" the *Inquirer* was shouting in Sam's ear. "You picked eight of the ten!"

Hot damn! So what if it was silly? It was thrilling too!

Then Sam settled back in her rampside orange plastic kitchen chair to enjoy, at last, thank God, the very final end of the Miss America Pageant.

Out on the Boardwalk—while the ten semifinalists paraded in swimsuits, sang and danced their hearts out, answered one last socially relevant question before a television audience, 20 rating, 44 share—Darleen and Michelangelo strolled.

They talked about the things people talk about when they first meet: where they grew up, went to school, families. They also talked about their kids. Darleen explained about her decorating business. Michelangelo talked about pizza parlors. They both liked Italian food, hot jazz, great hotels, remote islands with nothing to do but lie in the sun and order silly drinks.

Then Michelangelo asked, "What were you doing when Angelo grabbed you?"

"I was going back to my room to find some shoes. I threw mine off when I started chasing Lana down fifteen flights of stairs."

"Uh-huh. You mind if I light this cigar?"

"No, go ahead. You want to know why I was chasing her? I'll tell you. I was chasing her because I wanted to apologize for stealing her dress and planting razor blades in her hairbrush."

Michelangelo was impressed. Acts of vengeance. Then he laughed. Lana, that silly twit.

"I was mad at her because I thought she was fooling around with Billy. Then it dawned on me *he* was the one I ought to be after."

"Your vendetta was aimed at the wrong person."

"Something like that."

They walked for a while in silence. They were long past the glitz of the hotels, down toward the end of the seven miles of wooden strand, when toward them strolled, arm in arm, a couple of little clowns. One of them was dressed as a hobo, the other was in a polka-dot clown suit. Both of them wore whiteface. The hobo waved his cane as they passed. The other one croaked Good evening.

"Atlantic City." Darleen smiled. "It's not *all* bad."

Michelangelo turned and stared at the clowns' backs. There was something awfully familiar about that voice, that walk. But it couldn't be. Naw. He patted Darleen's hand. "So what are you going to do if Billy does the right thing?"

"There is no right thing for Billy anymore. It's too late."

Just like it was too late for Kurt Roberts and Dougie Franken. Kurt had been in the cedar-dark river longer, but both of them had slammed into logs and rocks, been cut by shells deposited by the ocean eons ago in the sandy soil, nibbled on by fish. Kurt had lost his nose. Dougie, his ears. Neither of them was very pretty.

It would be into October, a month after Miss America was crowned and all the beauties had gone home, before a two-day rain would wash the cedar water clear. Then a young man named Fordy, rowing his canoe, would sight first Kurt and then Dougie, far, far downriver from where they'd been dumped. The crystalline-pure water would reveal every blade of grass on the river bottom, every strand of Kurt's hair, styled once upon a time on Madison Avenue, the insignia on Dougie's gold ring from the Wharton School. But Fordy, whose family had been Pineys for four generations, knew that soon the water would flow cedar-dark again, and just because these outsiders had found their watery grave in the Pines, that was no reason to bring in more.

Up on the big stage, the ten girls had gone through all their paces, Miss America had paraded one last time to the strains of "There She Is" and waved farewell, then handed Billy and Phyllis the envelope that the man from Price Waterhouse had handed her. There was no delaying the moment of truth any longer. Billy Carroll had to make some hard decisions. Now.

Five names were printed on the card in big, black capital

letters. The first was the fourth runner-up. The next two were third and second runners-up. Then he would read the last two names. The first was almost-won, first runner-up, who would become Miss America if anything, God forbid, happened to the young lady whose name was fifth on the card. She, number five, was the one who would take the long tearful stroll, an orchid-bedecked scepter in her hand, a rhinestone crown atop her curls, while Billy sang "There She Is."

Now, if that was Miss New Jersey, Billy would be safe from Angelo. His kneecaps would be rescued as well as his wife.

However, that wasn't what the card said. Miss New Jersey was not the fifth name.

But Billy was the one holding the card. He was the only one who knew what it said. Not even the judges, who'd turned in their scores to the men from Price Waterhouse, knew the final tabulations. Only the Price Waterhouse guys knew, and the way the show worked, quickly cranking toward midnight, the director right there giving him the "hurry up" roll of the finger, he'd call the first four names, they'd each pretend they were thrilled to death to come in also-rans, then the new Miss America would burst into tears, kneel to receive her crown, do the parade number, and the credits would roll. In the closing shot, *if* they had the time, she'd be on the stage surrounded by her joyous court of forty-nine losers. There simply wouldn't be time for the Price Waterhouse guys to figure it out, come from upstairs, from out of the little room where they did the tabulations, and say, Wait just a damned minute here.

Of course, they would afterward, and Billy's career would be blown to smithereens. He'd be known forever as the fool who'd tried to fix the pageant.

If he didn't do it, Angelo would kill Darleen—and he'd inherit her money.

Goddamnit to hell! Why couldn't the Jersey bitch have just won?

* * *

Out on the Boardwalk, Michelangelo checked his watch. Midnight was five minutes away.

Darleen smiled. "Does that mean one of us is going to turn into a pumpkin?"

"I hope not." He turned her face toward his for their first kiss, nervous as a schoolboy.

"I can't stand it another minute," Sam cried, her fingers crossed. "I really do hope Rae Ann wins."

"A hundred on Texas," said the *Inquirer.*

"Oh, shut up!" But Sam shook on it.

"The fourth runner-up, and the winner of an eight-thousand-dollar scholarship, is Holly Shannon MacNeill, Miss California!"

Thank you, thank you, Ms. MacNeill mouthed to the judges as she crossed the stage and hugged Lynn Anderson, but Sam didn't think she looked very grateful.

"The third runner-up, and the winner of an eleven-thousand-dollar scholarship, is Rae Ann Bridges, Miss Georgia!"

Well, so much for the lucky rabbit's foot and Rae Ann, but she truly did look thrilled. Hoke would be crushed.

"The second runner-up, and the winner of a fourteen-thousand-dollar scholarship, is Lucinda Washington, Miss Louisiana!"

Magic would get her wish. Her performance tonight had been the most wonderful yet. The crowd had gone nuts. Magic was on her way to the big time.

"And now, ladies and gentlemen, that leaves seven finalists," Billy Carroll announced, and the camera panned the seven, holding hands, all smiling as if their lives depended on it.

Sam inspected the field. It wasn't a tough choice. She'd be happy to pay the *Inquirer* a hundred bucks for Miss Texas to win. Go, Connors, go.

Wayne Ward might have felt the same way—if he'd been feeling anything, which he wasn't. At least he'd have been torn between Connors and Lana. For it was Miss Texas, a homegirl from Tru Franken's native state, whom Franken had met a few months earlier when she was breaking a bottle of champagne over the front door of a FrankFair down in South Texas. It had been obsession at first sight that had led to that fiddling and fixing, those tapes and cameras, the subliminal implants. Connors McCoy was Tru Franken's favorite girl, or she had been before he'd gotten back on track with interest rates, falling attendance in the casino, loans due, long-range losses, shortfall. His FrankFairs weren't doing so hot either in the recession. And money was his Big Mama. His main mistress.

But Wayne had done all he could to make sure Miss Texas won, before he'd switched his allegiance to Miss New Jersey at the last minute. Not that it really mattered now. For with a little assistance, he'd driven his red Mustang off the old wooden pier down below the Albany Avenue Bridge into the Inside Thorofare, the deep channel that was dredged once a year—and that dredging had been last week.

By the time the cops found him fifty-one weeks from now it would be impossible for the coroner to tell that Wayne had been unconscious when the red Mustang took the long roll off the short pier—or anything much at all.

Captain Win Kelly would tell the Atlantic City *Press* that it was a cold trail and a frustrating case. There'd be some muttering in a three-paragraph story in the *Press,* some young reporter remembering a connection between Wayne and the disappearances of Douglas Franken and Kurt Roberts, whose bodies had never been found and whom nobody really missed, except a few ladies with a taste for short men and/or abuse. By that time, Win Kelly would have figured it all out. He'd even give Sam a jingle late one night to run what-ifs by her. But the proof—that was an entirely more elusive matter.

Billy Carroll took a deep breath. "Now, ladies and gentlemen, I'm going to read two names. The first will be the name of the first runner-up, who will receive a twenty-thousand-dollar scholarship. And that is—" Billy paused.

His future, his fortune, his wife, and her life hung in the balance. And then he read exactly what it said on the paper. "—Lana DeLucca, Miss New Jersey!"

Lana shook her head like she couldn't believe it. She hadn't won. She'd come in second! What the hell!

"And now, the winner, the new holder of the title American women have aspired to for over seventy years, Miss America, Connors McCoy, Miss Texas, come and greet your subjects!"

There. It was done. Billy braced himself for the submachine-gun fire from the audience, but it didn't come.

Instead, while the crowd roared, Connors McCoy, the new Miss America, turned toward Billy. She was supposed to walk over to Lynn Anderson to be crowned, but she didn't. She took the microphone from Billy's hand while he stared at her with his mouth open.

"Ladies and gentlemen, judges, Miss America Pageant, I'm so sorry," Connors said. "I never thought in a million years it would come to this, but I can't accept the crown."

Over in the booth, the director was going crazy. Billy and Phyllis were dumbfounded. The orchestra was waiting to play "There She Is." Television time, which cost hundreds of thousands per second, was running out.

"You see, I just thought it would be a wonderful experience—"

You most certainly did not, Sam said aloud. You started the whole beauty queen business as a joke on your mother and you know it.

"—but I never in my wildest dreams thought I'd win, so it wouldn't matter. But you see, the Miss America Pageant has very strict rules." The Convention Hall audience rubbed its hands, licked its lips, and sucked in its collective breath. Here came the dirt. Another Vanessa Williams scandal. "The rules say that Miss America can never have been married or convicted of even the tiniest misdemeanor—and, well, I've been both."

The *Inquirer* had already reached for her phone. She was talking to an editor in Philadelphia and listening at the same time.

"When I was eighteen I ran off and was married for two days till my daddy had it annulled. *And* I was arrested for smoking marijuana at a Texas Aggies–LSU game."

What the hell? Who hadn't been? Awwwwww. No dirty pictures? No real smut?

"So"—Connors smiled her big smile, lifting that little beauty mark on her top lip that Kurt Roberts hadn't liked—"I'm afraid, as much as I'd love to wear this crown, I'm not going to tarnish it with my transgressions."

She bit down on that last phrase just a little too hard for you not to get the sarcasm if you had half a brain. Sam shook her head. Too much! The *Inquirer* was shouting into the phone over the roar.

Connors turned and grabbed the crown away from Lynn Anderson, then held it out to the Marilyn look-alike. "Lana DeLucca, Miss New Jersey! Girl, *you're* Miss America! Come get this baby!"

The crowd, half of whom were from New Jersey, was standing on chairs, screaming, throwing programs and soft drink cups. This was as good as the Giants taking the Super Bowl in the last minutes with a field goal! This was excellent! This was stupendous! This was Jersey justice!

Billy Carroll fell headfirst to the stage in a dead faint.

Lana bent her knees and dipped down while Connors crowned her. Now that was more like it! And the faceless NBC announcer who'd begun the evening with *Something fabulous is happening here tonight!* got his big chance, Billy being unconscious. He belted "There She Is" so loudly his mama, out there in TV land, almost had a stroke while Lana DeLucca wiggled down the runway, her bosoms bouncing in her flesh-colored gown—Miss America, by God, and don't you forget it!

Harry fought his way through the crowd. He swooped Sam up in a big hug, then laid a long, slow kiss on her. "It's over. I love you, pretty lady. Now, you ready to go home?"

"And give Malachy Champion his autograph book? You bet. Right after Lavert's lunch tomorrow, you put me on that plane, Music Man."

"To New Orleans."

"Unh-uh. Atlanta. I love you, too, Harry, but I've got to go home." Oh, he looked *so* sad. "At least long enough to give Hoke my resignation." On second thought . . .

Harry leaped three feet. "And *then* New Orleans?"

"We'll talk about it later. But right now, sweet Harry, I've got to get to a phone."

She almost got away, but Lavert leaped over the top of a row of chairs to join them. "You believe that jive? You believe that Connors? Girl cost me a bundle."

"Who'd you bet on?" Sam laughed.

"Connors. Who you think? Magic said she was going to win."

Maybe she did, said Sam. Maybe she got what she wanted.

Lavert shook his head. Women. Next time, he'd get it in writing. Spell it out. He punched Harry in the arm. "And you? What'd you lose, that mini-Marilyn won it with her hootchy-kooch?"

"The farm. Lost the farm. I bet on Connors, too."

"But, guys! She won," said Sam. "Connors really won."

"I don't know if that's what the man's gonna say, comes to pay-up day."

"What man?" Sam gave Harry her fishy look.

"Man who wrote the book."

"Book? Book? Who'd you bet with, Harry?"

"I bet with my man here, Lavert."

"Lavert didn't write any book. And he just said he bet on Connors, too. So how could he have bet with you?"

"Cookbook. I'm writing a cookbook, sugar." Lavert gave her the big grin.

"I hate you both. I hate you when you do me like this."

"Do you like what?" Harry reached over, but she slipped away. She really did have to file her story and talk to Hoke.

Harry turned to Lavert, both of them following her to the phones. "Man, what do you think? How does that work? Could we have still won the bet with the pizza man?"

"Unh-uh. It's like a replay. We lost. New Jersey won."

"New Jersey. The lovely Miss DeLucca." Harry whistled

a couple of bars of "I Want to Be Loved By You," her song, and did a passable soft-shoe. But *nobody* could do Lana's wiggle.

Lavert was thinking about it. "Naw, Texas, man. Texas *really* won. The girl folded, but she *was* Miss America, man. She was perfect."

"Hey!" Sam yelled from the phone. "Give it up. *Nobody's* perfect." Then she smiled a Miss America smile, warm and winning, into the receiver, just like the magazine said she should. "Hoke, I've got some bad news and some worse news. Which do you want first?"

WHEN HARRY ZACK ASKED SAM ADAMS IF SHE WAS SURE SHE DIDN'T want to drive up to Tupelo Days and the Third Annual International Barbecue Cookoff, she'd said, "Are you nuts?"

Harry had pushed Sam's porch swing back and forth a couple of times and stared off south across Lake Pontchartrain toward New Orleans where he lived. "Does that mean no?"

"Means much as I would love to cheer you on at the cookoff, since you and Lavert opened the Rib Shack it's been 'cue, 'cue, nothing but barbecue—which the little dog doesn't eat, and I'm counting fat grams. Besides," she hefted a notebook, "I'm working."

Sam called her book-in-progress *American Weird* and was enjoying the research, talking with folks like the Civil War Bungee-Jumpers who planned to rubber-band off into the Mississippi River at Vicksburg right across from where Grant's flotilla had parked.

The work was a relief from her years as a crime reporter—first for the *San Francisco Chronicle* and then back home to Atlanta and the *Constitution*, from which she'd taken a leave, probably permanently. She'd about had her fill of people whose notion of good times was inflicting serious damage on one another with guns, knives, sticks, stones, flame throwers, cyanide, ropes, high-pressure hoses and weed cutters.

But Harry hadn't given up. "You could take your laptop with you. I'm staying with Red Holcomb, that man I told you wants to talk to me and Lavert about 'cue franchising. We met him when we were over there visiting one of Lavert's cousins. He has a big old house, you could work. Maybe even pick up an idea or two. Town ought to be lousy with weird."

"I don't need any more material right now. I just need to hack this proposal out."

Harry took a long slug of his Dixie beer, then held out the bottle and started at it for a minute. "Cookoff's honoring Japan this year. Samurai hog smokers versus folks like the Chickasaw County Chip Chunkers with the promise of a Mississippi Toyota plant a major factor. Can't you see them big ole bubbas trying to out-bow the Japanese? Might come down to an arm-wrestling contest to see who's the most polite first. Might mean *I* have a chance to win."

"Ummm." Sam wasn't paying much attention. She ran a hand through her short dark curls, much like Harry's, and lifted another pile of notes from the porch floor.

"I'd sure love to have your company. Most folks have a whole team, and Lavert's gonna have to stay home and mind the store." Harry paused as a jet flew over, just about the same size as a heron in the near distance. "I bet there'll be some good music, too."

Harry Zack was a musician himself, a thirty-year-old uptown New Orleans society bad boy who, after he'd run out of song-writing luck in Nashville had tried process-serving, oil-rigging and insurance-investigating before he'd opened a BBQ place with his best friend Lavert, an ex-con whom Harry had known since their days at Grambling State where Lavert played football and Harry was The Only White Boy.

"Well, it's too bad about Lavert. Long drive'd give ya'll the chance for some superior male-bonding."

"Okay. Okay." Harry stood and strolled the length of the porch with Harpo, Sam's little white Shih Tzu, in tow. "I guess you're just going to force me into spoiling the surprise."

At that Sam looked up at his back, at the dark curls just brushing the neck of the gray T-shirt—he needed a haircut again—the hard slim waist, the faded jeans, the right leg pped where he'd caught it on a snag. They'd gone catfishing ie night before, a balmy very-end-of-March evening, had iade love in the boat pulled up against some tall grass. Got aten alive by mosquitos. It'd been worth it. Everything had een worth it so far with Harry, her boy toy, ten years her unior, turned lover for real. So real she'd left Atlanta a few ionths ago, rented—on a look-see basis, you understand—his house on the north shore of Lake Pontchartrain to see ow it felt to be closer to him. Last night they'd been real lose.

"We driving up in a pink Cadillac?"

"Oh, shoot." Harry had a great grin. "You guessed."

"And Elvis really is alive, come home to his birthplace to isit, and you've arranged us a blind date. You tagging along as haperone."

"Now you've gone and taken *all* the fun out of it."

Harry's Aunt Suzanne's 1963 Cadillac *was* pink, and it ported tail fins, a rag top, and wrap-around sound. Hitched to he rear was a trailer carrying a fifty-five-gallon crude oil drum n wheels—Harry's smoker. The Caddy's trunk was stacked vith oak and ice chests full of pork, including a 125-pound vhole piglet especially raised for the cookoff. And handed lown from Lavert's grandmother, the ingredients for Rib hack secret sauce.

Friday morning, Harry was leaning on the horn with one and, trying to comb his curls into a D.A. with the other. He'd een pressed to choose between his *BBQ is My Life* and his *Elvis Lives* T-shirts. He'd gone with the King.

Wow! Sam said when she stepped out on her front porch nd saw him. A tall pretty woman of forty with high cheek-ones, a bright red mouth, and an aristocratic nose, Sam was vearing a plain white cotton sweater that advertised nothing ut her curves, a pair of old khakis cinched with a brown voven leather belt, loafers, and a bright scarf twisted through ier short dark curls. Wow! yourself, he answered.

"Get over here, bubba, let's start this weekend off with a big iss."

Harpo rolled his eyes. It was going to be a long ride for a

small dog who didn't care for kissing or loud or road 'cue. An didn't know from Elvis, though they shared the same birth day.

"Little darlin'" Harry sang at the top of his lungs, doing h Jack to the King routine on the interstate all the way t Jackson. No time for Delta backroads, Harry wanted to g there before dark and set up his rig, but at Jackson they turne onto the Natchez Trace, the parkway following the path o Indians, hunters, and boatmen who'd sold their boats as we as their goods in old New Orleans. The two-lane ran a lon diagonal through nothing but green—pasture land, forest fields, and swamps from Natchez to Nashville—without word of advertising.

"Bandits." Sam was reading from the Trace brochure they' picked up at a rest stop.

"Wild Indians," said Harry who'd driven the Trace befor

"Oprah Winfrey."

"I beg your pardon."

"Didn't we just pass by Kosciusko? That's where Oprah wa born."

"You know the weirdest things."

"That's what I do for a living, sweetheart. Now fill me in o little old Tupelo." Sam imagined it to be a village, a wide plac in a dirt road peopled with Faulkner's Snopeses—chew spitting white trash living in houses with no doors who'd jus as soon shoot you as walk around. After all, Faulkner' Yoknapatawpha County was only seventy miles west, an Philadelphia, Mississippi, was sixty miles south, where they' buried the murdered civil rights workers Chaney, Goodman and Schwerner in a dirt dam.

"And a quarter of a century ago," said Harry. She could tel he was irritated. "God, you sound like a Yankee. You lived in San Francisco too long, think anybody outside of Atlanta o New Orleans is going to bite your head off, suck your bloo like iced tea. You been watching double-feature reruns o *Deliverance* and *Easy Rider?*"

"So you're saying Tupelo's like everyplace else in the U.S. o A.? Main Street dead, lousy with Jack-in-the-Boxes, satellit dishes, and shopping malls?"

"Actually, it's a pretty little place, prosperous, set in rolling armland and forests, and downtown's still alive around the ourthouse. They're doing some gentrification, lawyers fixing p old houses after everybody up and built new ones on the utskirts. But mostly it's your average twenty-five thousand niddle-class New South consumers, a van and a Honda in the arport. Even Massas in the Big Old Homes are mostly oncerned with paying off their Gold Cards, don't have time o hate nobody else no more than any other God-fearing Amuricans."

"Shucks," said Sam. "Here I'd been hoping for some real rash to sink my teeth into," Then she went back to reading loud from a pile of books about Elvis to put them in a Tupelo nood.

The land was beginning to roll as Sam and Harry left the Delta behind and headed toward Appalachia's toes. But nough already, said Sam of the pristene Natchez Trace Parkway. Enough green, enough scenery. I want to see a Burma-Shave sign. A McDonald's. Give me Rock City.

Finally there was the Tupelo exit and they clover-leafed onto West Main Street on the outskirts of town. To the north stood open fields and a little airport. To the south they'd cut down the trees, poured concrete in cul-de-sacs with names like General Hood, Breckenridge, Stonewall Court, Rebel Drive. Never let it be said that the glory of the Old South ever died: it lives on in expensive tract housing.

Warehouses loomed in an industrial park. There was a lot of furniture manufacturing around Tupelo said Harry, the expert, who'd visited once before. They passed a spanking new mall, two barbecue pits, crummy and authentic-looking, another older mall which had seen better days.

Six minutes off the Trace they were in the old Tupelo amidst a covey of Protestant churches, three blocks of quaint two-story buildings still bustling with hardware stores, ladies' clothiers, a stationer's, a cleaners, an art museum, antique shops on Main Street. Sam could see the copper dome of the old courthouse a block away. Then they rumbled east across the railroad tracks toward what looked like the poorer side of town. A forgotten shopping center foundered in acres of a weedy parking lot. They made a right into the fairgroun under a banner that welcomed them in brilliant blue to Tupel Days and the Third Annual International Barbecue Cookof

This was the very place, Harry announced, that Elvis ma his professional debut.

"Go 'way," said Sam. Not this shabby fenced field scattere with trucks, tents, campers and few outbuildings, though t dusty old grandstand looked like it might seat a coup thousand.

"Hey, he was only ten. He stood on a chair to reach th microphone and sang 'Old Shep.' Won second prize in th talent contest, five dollars, and free admission to all the rides.

Sam threw her mind back to county fairs of her childhoo The thrill of it, the Ferris wheel, the merry-go-round, th Tilt-A-Whirl, bumper cars. That would have been somethin a kid not having to beg for just one more time. Especially poor kid.

"Howdy, howdy. Can we help ya'll?" A large blond friend looking man in a red-and-white checked shirt, overalls, and straw hat that proclaimed him to be a Holy Smoker leane down to the Caddy. "I'm Cooter Williams, your official," an then he stopped, put his hands to his mouth and yodele "Sooie, sooie pig," then resumed his normal drawl, "greet and I have to tell ya'll this is one fine-looking pink Cadilla Ya'll here to sip some whiskey, get down with the hogs, smok and wallow?"

Sam shot Harry a look as he stuck his hand out the windo and grinned. "Cooter, I'm Harry Zack, this is Sam Adam and we sure are." Five minutes later Cooter had them signe up, backed in, and unhitched. Harry's plot was a staked-o area about twenty by twenty—one of a hundred-and-twent five in four double rows.

"Not many folks here," said Harry looking around at th sprinkling of cooking rigs already set up. He pulled a diet sod out of the cooler for Sam along with two cold Dixie beers.

"Don't mind if I do, thank you kindly," said Coote "Nawh, most of 'em'll come in tomorrow. Be ready to part hearty by sundown. Don't take all day to do the ribs, yo know. Get them done, then the shoulder, Sunday's the whol hog and the final judging. There'll be more folks than you can shake a stick at by then."

"Well, I'm looking forward to it. Is Red Holcomb around?" Harry asked. "He said he might meet us here."

"Nawh. He was here earlier. I reckon he slithered off somewhere."

Harry winked at Sam, then said to Cooter, "Guess Red's not your best friend."

"Well, you could say that." Then Cooter seemed to remember his manners, tipped his beer at Harry. "Hope I didn't mash your toes."

"Actually, I don't know him very well, but we're talking about the possibility of doing a little business. Sam and I are staying with him for the weekend."

Cooter took a long pull on his beer and killed it, belched, begged their pardon, then squashed the can flat with one huge hand. "Well, you know what the lady said. Diamonds are a girl's best friend. Red ain't no girl, but he's got plenty of diamonds and gold and silver and cars and buildings and land and you name it, he's got it, or he's about to buy it or trade it, but the one thing he don't have in this town is a single friend."

"Great." Sam punched Harry. "Bubba, you've done it again. I can't tell you how happy I am I left my work and my front porch to spend the weekend with Mississippi's Hitler." It had been a long time since her last meal, fat-free at that, and she was more than a little cranky.

"Well, ma'am, I wouldn't go that far," said Cooter, nodding thanks as Harry handed him another beer. "Though there are those who've said him and Saddam Hussein, you couldn't tell 'em apart in the dark."

Harry nodded. "That's real interesting. Listen, Cooter, what kind of wood you using in your smoker?"

Right, Harry. Change the subject before your girlfriend goes and turns this car around and/or registers you both in the nearest Ramada, Hyatt, or Holiday Inn. Sam let the guys debate the virtues of hickory versus oak versus mesquite while Harpo lapped up his second bowl of water. Then she leashed the little dog and was about to take him for a stroll when something caught her eye. "Excuse me, Cooter? What is that?"

She was pointing at an object under a blue tent that looked like an old Coca-Cola machine lying on its side with a stove pipe sticking out one end. Smoke was blowing out of the pipe. It smelled good.

Cooter scratched his head under his hat and asked, "Ma'am, is this your first Q-off?"

Sam nodded. Obviously she'd committed a gaffe of the first order.

"Well, that is a smoker." Then Cooter pointed at an old butane tank in the next space. "And that is a smoker." Across the way was an aluminum beer keg that was also a smoker, as was something that she had taken to be a mobile home. Cooter shook his head as he pointed out the latter. "Now we discourage those big guys," he said. "For a rig like that, you need some kind of sponsor, and you do that, next thing you know, you'll be like the contest up in Memphis. I don't mean to criticize anybody, they produce some mighty fine smoked meats up there, but it got to where your ordinary feller felt like a pine tree in the middle of a bunch of redwoods, you know what I mean? The bankers and the lawyers and the Pepto-Bismol and Wonder Bread folks, they have the kind of funds behind them, put on such a show, bands, parades, costumes, crystal chandeliers hanging over million-dollar rigs, well, that's why we started this 'un in Tupelo, try to keep it to just folks."

Then from somewhere behind them, there was a clanging and a couple of shouts. "What the hell was that?" asked Cooter, who had wheeled and was headed toward the sound when his portable phone, hidden by his stomach and his overalls, started ringing.

"Earl? What? Son, slow down, I can't make out what—well, did you call 911? Then hang up and I will!" Cooter's fat face was grim as he punched in the three numbers. "Hello? This is Cooter Williams over at the fairgrounds. We've got a man just turned on his rotisserie and it blasted him halfway to East Jesus. No, no. I don't know. Yes, I'll do that." Then Cooter stuffed the phone back in his overalls and, still holding his beer, took off running toward the back of the lot faster than you would think a fat man could.

Sam threw Harpo in the Caddy, yelled Stay, then she and Harry took off after Cooter.

Mary Ann was sitting in her room in the Tupelo Ramada Inn on North Gloster touching up her Fire and Ice manicure and evaluating her afternoon.

She had found a wide variety of things to hold her interest in that truck stop she and Dewey had pulled into. She'd fingered Jockey shorts and undershirts, cowboy boots, motivational tapes that would teach you how to become a salesman if you wanted to drop off the long haul. Tacky lace undies to take home to your lady, let her know you'd been thinking about her on the interstate. Hundreds of dirty cards, only a few of which were funny, all of which were sexist, lots of Preparation H, Campbell's soup in little plastic tubs, beef jerky, potato chips and other not-so-good-for-you foods. No fresh fruit. But the most surprising thing was the area marked Truckers Only.

After you, ma'am, Dewey had smiled, opening the door for her with a little bow like she was a lady. Like he didn't intend to take her into the white-tiled shower, lock the door, strip her of her black French lace teddy from her own lingerie line, one heck of a lot nicer than the $19.95 jobbie for sale outside, soap her up six ways to Sunday, then take her likewise.

"You've got a great body." She'd said that afterward when she grew tired of waiting for him to. But she meant it. Nicer than a lot of younger men.

"Karate," he'd said staring at himself in the mirror right next to the machine that dispensed rubbers, razor blades, shaving cream, deodorant. "Keeps me in shape." Sliding his comb just so through a heavy coat of brilliantine.

"Is that where you learned those moves?"

"Country boy like me sure don't know what you're talking about, ma'am."

Then he'd kissed her and they'd done it again nice and easy, like they'd done it lots of times before, would do it even more before they were through.

Uh-oh, she'd said to herself, back on the road. That's what happens to women, Mary Ann. A little good loving and their brains turn to mush. Men, they just look at it for what it is.

Sex. Plain and simple. Girl, she lectured herself, keep your eye on the goal.

"Hey!" Dewey had grabbed the wheel, back on the road "Watch what you're doing."

It had turned out to be a lot harder than she'd thought wrestling that monster down the blacktop. There was absolutely no leeway. Not an inch on either side. Ten forward gears, five high, five low. One reverse, not that she had any intention of going backward.

Then Dewey had said, "You never told me why you're going to Tupelo. To visit Elvis's birthplace?"

"Uh-huh. That and see a girlfriend."

He'd laughed.

"Well, I am." He couldn't prove she wasn't. And she wasn't so sure she wanted anything else to do with Dewey, other than what she'd already done. A little burst of passion like that, it cleared your sinuses, helped you focus. Now she had business to do.

"Tell the truth," he said.

It was so weird. It was like he could make his voice suck the real story right out of you. And the next thing she knew, she was telling Dewey about how right before Carlin died, he was up on that big rock . . .

"And he starts talking this trash about how would I feel if I found out I wasn't the only woman in his life? And I say it wouldn't surprise me one bit. Nothing he would do would surprise me one bit. And he says, well, what if it was more than seeing? And I say, You mean like kissing? Being silly, you know. Like he wouldn't be screwing her. Like he hadn't screwed jillions of women, for all I knew. After all, he was a traveling salesman. I just assumed, given what a generally rotten human being he was, he did that too, and I must say it made me nervous, once this AIDS business started. He says, More than kissing, more than screwing? I say, You mean like loving? Carlin, you never loved anybody in your whole life except your own selfish self.

"And then—" Mary Ann had stopped. They'd listened to the bumping of the truck and the whooshing of the wind for a couple more miles.

Finally Dewey'd said, "So that's the woman you're going to see, the one he was talking about?"

It was so strange, that he knew that. "Uh-huh," she said.

"Why do you care now, if he's dead?"

"You want to know why I care? I'll tell you. Because this Lawyer Rakestraw who called, he said to my friend Luci that his client, this woman in Tupelo, was married to Carlin not only *first,* but *still was,* and therefore, we had not even been legally married and *furthermore,* I could go whistle you-know-what if I thought I was entitled to a penny of his one hundred fifty thousand dollars worth of pharmaceutical company accidental-death life insurance."

Now Mary Ann screwed the top back on her Fire and Ice and said aloud, practicing, in the empty motel room: Well, we'll just have to see what we can work out about that, won't we, Ms. Dixie McClanahan? Mary Ann narrowing her eyes, looking real tough.

Dead people was exactly what Dewey Travis was thinking about. He'd made a flying trip up to Holly Springs after he'd dropped Mary Ann at her motel, and now he was sitting out in the Elvis McDonald's parking lot thinking about people who were dead—and well-done hamburgers.

The first thing he always did when he drove down to Tupelo was come here and have himself a Big Mac, large order of fries, ketchup please, king-sized Co-Cola. The Big Mac would be well-done of course, the way Elvis liked them, the only way you could get a burger at McDonald's.

This was the starting point of his Elvis pilgrimage. He did it the same way every time. He started here to fuel up, both on the burgers and on the museum. He thought it was fitting that the Tupelo Elvis Museum—which was how he thought of it, the collection of framed pictures, albums, citations, awards—should be in a burger palace.

Then he'd go over to The Birthplace, where the twins Elvis Aron and Jesse Garon were born that frosty morn, just like it said in that song about the ghetto. He'd sit outside for a while, studying the little two-room shack Vernon Presley had built, borrowing one hundred eighty dollars to do it, then lost the house when he couldn't make the payments on the loan.

Once a Birthplace tour lady had told Dewey that Vernon never had had a head for money, even though Elvis let him manage his affairs, which maybe hadn't been such a good idea, but that just went to show you how much Elvis loved his daddy.

But, she'd said, waving her hand around the tiny house, Vernon was good at building. The Birthplace was a sturdy little thing that stood up to the winds of that awful tornado of 1936. The lady showed Dewey a story about the tornado in a book, it killed over two hundred people in Tupelo—no Presleys among them, praise the Lord. They'd gathered in Uncle Noah Presley's house, the tour lady said, the men lining up against the south wall to try to hold it up against the winds—which they did. Gladys and Elvis, who was just a babe, huddled in a corner.

To think that Elvis could have died right then! It was enough to make you puke. But there was a lot about young Elvis's dirt-poor life here in Tupelo that turned Dewey's stomach. He hated to think about little Elvis, from the wrong side of the tracks, teased to pieces by the kids at Milam School. That's where he had to go when his family was kicked out of their house in East Tupelo. They moved into a shack on Mulberry Alley inside the city limits, the neighborhood called Milltown right next to the fairgrounds, near the dump, across from colored quarters. The Milam kids teased Elvis because he was a hick, because he didn't have the right clothes and precious few of the wrong ones, and because he liked to sing and show off like he knew he was good—even then.

Yes, those memories hurt Dewey, but he bore the pain willingly, though sometimes, like now, he popped a few Valium to smooth it out. That constant aching in his gut, he thought of it as his Elvis stigmata. It was part of the process of becoming Elvis, feeling his anguish, thinking his thoughts, walking in his shoes. Take a walk in my shoes, Elvis said that a lot. Sang it, too. Dewey looked down at his blue suede boots.

Then he stared in through the big plate glass windows. There was a lot of Elvis, *strong* Elvis, inside. He took a few deep breaths. And a lot of Red Holcomb. He'd been coming down to Tupelo to look at Holcomb, and the others, for the past few weeks. Refining The Plan.

Dewey hadn't picked Red to go first. He wasn't sure about the timing of Red's Big Date. He was working on that. He might save the biggest and best for last, like eating chocolate-covered cherries, biting a little hole, slowly sucking out the creamy sweet until the walls collapsed, then closing down on the round red prize, ka-chunk.

He'd thought about that, the proper order of things, adding up Red's numbers. The number of his big old fancy house up off Highland Circle with the garage full of fancy cars. Their license tags. The street numbers of Red's warehouses, his pawn shop, his office on the courthouse square, Dewey wasn't sure what it was for. Dewey followed Red right to the door of the Coffee Pot and Orleans Deli off the square where Red grabbed a cup of joe to go. There were two groups of men—bankers, lawyers, bondsmen, pharmacists, funeral directors, stock brokers—who met every weekday morning to drink coffee and jawbone, but Red wasn't part of either one so Dewey didn't add the street number of the coffeeshop to his total. Dewey knew numerology just like Elvis. Elvis's magic number was eight.

Dewey also knew this trip was very important. The signs were right. The numbers and the planets were lined up. If he did things right, in their proper order and at the proper time, his life would change forever.

SARAH SHANKMAN is also the author of *Now Let's Talk of Graves* and *She Walks in Beauty.*